THE LION OF THE NORTH
A MEDIEVAL ROMANCE

BY
KATHRYN LE VEQUE

Copyright © 2015 by Kathryn Le Veque Novels
Print Edition

Text by Kathryn Le Veque
Cover by Kathryn Le Veque

Reproduction of any kind except where it pertains to short quotes in relation to advertising or promotion is strictly prohibited.

All Rights Reserved.

Library of Congress Control Number 2015-055

KATHRYN LE VEQUE LIST OF NOVELS

Medieval Romance:

The White Lord of Wellesbourne
The Dark One: Dark Knight

While Angels Slept
Rise of the Defender
Spectre of the Sword
Unending Love
Archangel
Lord of the Shadows

Great Protector
To the Lady Born

The Falls of Erith
Lord of War: Black Angel (also related to The Dark One: Dark Knight)

The Darkland
Black Sword

The Wolfe
Serpent
Scorpion (Also related to THE QUESTING)
The Lion of the North

The Whispering Night
Netherworld

The Dark Lord
Devil's Dominion

Unrelated characters or family groups:

The Gorgon (Also related to Lords of Thunder)
The Warrior Poet
Guardian of Darkness (related to The Fallen One)
Tender is the Knight
The Legend
Lespada (Also related to Lords of Thunder)
Lord of Light

The Questing (related to The Dark Lord, Scorpion)
Beast (related to Great Protector, The Dark One: Dark Knight)

The Dragonblade Trilogy:

Dragonblade
Island of Glass
The Savage Curtain
The Fallen One
Fragments of Grace

Lords of Thunder: The de Shera Brotherhood Trilogy

The Thunder Lord
The Thunder Warrior
The Thunder Knight

Novella, Time Travel Romance:

Echoes of Ancient Dreams.

Contemporary Romance:

Kathlyn Trent/Marcus Burton Series:

Valley of the Shadow
The Eden Factor
Canyon of the Sphinx

The American Heroes Series:

Resurrection
Fires of Autumn
Evenshade
Sea of Dreams
Purgatory

Other Contemporary Romance:

Lady of Heaven
Darkling, I Listen

Time Travel Romance:

The Crusader
Kingdom Come

Note: All Kathryn's novels are designed to be read as stand-alones, although many have cross-over characters or cross-over family groups.

Novels that are grouped together have related characters or family groups.

Series are clearly marked. All series contain the same characters or family groups except the American Heroes Series, which is an anthology with unrelated characters.

There is NO particular chronological order for any of the novels because they can all be read as stand-alones, even the series.

For more information, find it on Amazon in **A Reader's Guide to the Medieval World of Le Veque.**

AUTHOR'S NOTE

Welcome to Atticus' story. We have some interesting names in this tale, so I want to make sure we're all on the same page with pronunciations (the emphasis is on the capitalized syllable):

Isobeau – Eees-uh-BO
Tertius – TER-shiss
Titus – TIE-tus
Warenne – war-EN (if you recall, de Warenne was the family name of Davyss de Winter's mother, Lady Katharine, in LESPADA)

"A Day of Much Slaying"
That's what the Battle of Towton was called, which is a major battle in the War of the Roses. It was also a battle that was fought in late spring in a blizzard and is one of the more terrible historical battles ever fought in England. If the men weren't freezing, then they were drowning in the river north of the battlefield as they tried to flee. It's said that so many men drowned in the river that they created a human bridge for the remaining armies to flee across. Over 70,000 men faced off on the field that day; 42,000 Lancastrian alone, so this was an absolutely massive battle. Towton is to England what Antietam is to the American Civil War. The total dead at Towton were estimated at 1% of England's population, or about 20,000 men. Towton plays a small but pivotal role in this novel.

Also, let's clarify the family ties here of the secondary characters because there are a lot. It's probably best to do it this way rather than a diagram:

- Warenne de Winter – descendent of Davyss de Winter (LESPADA)
- Maxim de Russe – son of Sir Bastian de Russe (BEAST) and his wife, Lady Gisella le Bec. Gisella is the youngest daughter of Sir Richmond le Bec (GREAT PROTECTOR).
- Alec le Bec – son of Gannon le Bec (second son of Sir Richmond le Bec) and his wife, Lady Sparrow Summerlin. Alec is named for his ancestor, the great Alec Summerlin (THE LEGEND).
- Adam Wellesbourne – Married to Audrey Wellesbourne, Maxim's sister and the daughter of Sir Bastian de Russe and his wife, Lady Gisella. Adam and Audrey are the parents of Matthew Wellesbourne (THE WHITE LORD OF WELLESBOURNE). This means that Matthew Wellesbourne has the blood of Richmond le Bec and Bastian de Russe in him, among others.
- Kenton le Bec – son of Stefan le Bec, who is the eldest son of Richmond le Bec (GREAT PROTECTOR), and his wife, Lady Arissa (who is the bastard daughter of Henry VI). Kenton is Richmond's eldest grandchild.
- Tertius de Shera – a descendant of Maximus de Shera (THE THUNDER WARRIOR) and Lady Isobeau's brother.

It's all very complicated, but suffice it to say that all of the le Bec knights, as well as Maxim de Russe, are related to Henry VI through their grandmother, who is the bastard daughter of Henry IV (read GREAT PROTECTOR for this background if you haven't yet already), so fighting for Henry's cause for these knights is a given. Warenne de Winter, Earl of Thetford, fights for Henry's cause because the de Winters always fight for the crown, no matter who it is (or how poor a king he is!).

And there are so many connections in this book! Isobeau de

Shera, as mentioned, is descended from Maximus de Shera, so if you haven't read the LORDS OF THUNDER trilogy, then it's a must-read. It will give you a ton of insight into Isobeau's ancestors, the great Thunder Lords. Also, as mentioned, is the Wellesbourne clan (THE WHITE LORD OF WELLESBOURNE). We meet Matthew Wellesbourne's grandfather and see his father, Adam, as a young man. Matthew's grandfather, Andrew, is a badass. Enough said.

Lastly, Kenton le Bec, a secondary character, will have his own novel coming out shortly after this one called WALLS OF BABYLON. Don't miss it. I'm particularly fond of Kenton.

This "author's note" is a little long, so I'll conclude by saying I truly hope you enjoy Atticus and Isobeau's story. If ever two people deserved a happily ever after, these two do.

Hugs,
Kathryn

PROLOGUE

March 29, 1461 A.D.
Battle of Towton, Yorkshire
Ascension of Edward IV

"THERE HE IS," a knight in snow-covered armor hissed. "Do you see him?"

His companion, with a bushy red beard and dirty blond hair, was focused on a copse of white-encrusted trees off to the south. It was early morning and snow was falling so heavily that it was as if a thick blanket of the stuff had been tossed onto them. Breath hung in the air from both man and beast alike, and the sun, though risen, was shielded by heavy clouds.

"I see him," the knight with the bushy beard said. "He has already deployed all of the men, including his brother. He will not be alone much longer."

"Are you sure Atticus is away?"

"I am sure. I saw him ride off."

"Then we must move quickly. We promised Mowbray we would

start with Titus."

"He really wants Atticus."

"I know. But if we can sway Titus, Atticus should follow."

Spurring their horses forward, the pair charged down a small and snow-covered incline, heading towards the right flank of the massive Lancastrian army that was poised on the rise, waiting for the Yorkist opposition to move into place. This day had been weeks and months in the making, years even, as the largest army England had ever seen upon her own soil was moving into position to decide the fate of the country. Would Henry VI remain on the throne, or would his young cousin, Edward, wrest the royal reins of command? Well over seventy thousand men would soon decide upon an answer. Hell was coming and it was coming very soon. With that in mind, the two knights made haste towards their target in the distance.

Sir Titus de Wolfe was standing next to his big, brown charger, a mean horse with a fierce temper. He was rather fond of the beast, though, and had been feeding him small green apples and handfuls of oats throughout the morning, an incentive for the horse to obey him. He needed persuasion. As Titus muttered a last few encouraging words to the horse, he had no idea he was being stalked.

The end, for him, was nearer than he knew.

"De Wolfe!"

Titus turned towards the sound of his name, seeing two Northumberland knights riding up to him. These were men under his command, men he had fought with for a few years. He knew and trusted them. He put the apples for his horse back in his saddlebags.

"What are you two doing away from your posts?" he asked. "I told you two to cover the far end of the right flank. Why have you returned?"

The knight with the bushy beard dismounted. "Something very serious, de Wolfe," he said. "We must speak with you."

Titus looked up from his saddlebags. "Now?" he asked, perturbed. "The earl wants you in your position, de la Londe. Get to it. We can speak afterwards if there is still a need."

Simon de la Londe shook his head, ice crystals from his beard raining onto his chest. "I am afraid it is too important to wait," he said. "I will only take a moment. I come with a message for you."

Titus scowled. "A message?" he repeated. "From whom?"

"Norfolk."

Titus' scowl faded and genuine bewilderment took hold. "De Mowbray?" he asked. "How is that possible? He is not even here yet."

De la Londe nodded patiently. "He is a few hours out," he said. "We received his messenger with a message for you."

Titus' confusion only deepened. "What in the world would the Duke of Norfolk have to say to me?" he asked. "And how does he even know me? I am one knight among thousands here today."

De la Londe looked over the battlefield, at the lines being drawn and the thousands of men preparing to risk their lives for two men who would be king. He glanced at his companion, Declan de Troiu, and noted de Troiu's serious expression. The man nodded, firmly, as if to give de la Londe the push he needed to speak. De la Londe returned his attention to Titus.

"The Duke of Norfolk wishes to deliver this message," he said. "Wield your sword for him, swear fealty to him, and he shall provide you with a manse and lands in Westwick. The lands are rich, as are the taxes. Convince your brother to join you and he will grant Atticus a baronetcy. Do this and you shall be well rewarded. Refuse and you shall die."

Titus was staring at de la Londe. There was no discernible reaction in his features but his gaze implied that he was both confused and shocked with de la Londe's message.

"You cannot possibly be serious," he hissed. "Did Norfolk's messenger tell you that? Where is the bastard?"

De la Londe drew in a long, deep breath. "He is out of range," he said vaguely. "The messenger came to remind us of what Norfolk himself told us this last night when we met with him. He has granted Declan and me lands for swearing fealty to him. Titus, don't you see what is happening here? We fight for a madman, a king that is daft and unstable. We fight for a lost cause. Edward has the support of the major barons and he also has the support of France. He has Warwick with him, for God's sake. Warwick is nearly impossible to beat."

A warning bell went off in Titus' head; it was clear that Simon and Declan were not here as a neutral party or even an allied party to relay a message from the enemy. From what de la Londe had just said, *they* were now the enemy. Shocking as it was, it was the truth.

Titus thought quickly; his broadsword was sheathed in his saddle behind him. He couldn't get to it undetected. He had an assortment of daggers on him, but de la Londe probably did too. So did de Troiu. It would be two against one but Titus was confident he could prevail. But he had to get the upper hand and strike first, eliminating de la Londe before de Troiu came down on him. He could already sense a battle coming and he was disgusted; enraged and disgusted.

"Am I to assume you have accepted Norfolk's bribe?" he asked steadily.

De la Londe nodded. "We have," he said, sounding almost regretful about it. "Titus, come with us. Fight with us. This is a fight that Henry cannot win."

"We outnumber the York supporters."

De la Londe sighed heavily. "For now," he said. "Norfolk is four hours away and he brings ten thousand men. When he comes, he will turn the tide. Lord Fauconberg, fighting with Warwick, has hundreds of archers and he has the wind at his back. You will be killed, Titus; everyone here will be killed. I, for one, do not want to die."

Titus' jaw ticked. "So you climb into bed with Norfolk," he growled. "I never thought I would see the day, Simon. You disappoint me."

Simon shrugged, having difficulty maintaining eye contact. "Better a disappointment than a dead man," he muttered. "Will you join us, Titus? Will you join us and speak to Atticus about joining us as well?"

Titus shook his head. "I will not," he replied. "My fealty is to Henry Percy. I am sorry your fealty was not as honorable, Simon. If you are quite certain that is what you wish to do."

"It is."

He seemed as determined to turn as Titus was determined not to turn. "I am having difficulty believing your loyalty can be bought," Titus said, trying to insult de la Londe into letting his guard down or even walking away from him. "You are no better than a common mercenary. Where is your honor, man?"

De la Londe would not waver but Titus' insults struck a chord in him. He had always admired Titus, his commander and his friend, up until a few moments ago. "My honor wants to survive just like the rest of me," he replied, pointing to the armies in the distance. "This is a fight that Henry cannot win, Titus. And I am not ready to die this day."

Titus took a step back, in the direction of his horse and his broadsword. "I suppose each man must follow his own path in life," he said. "But this is where our paths diverge, Simon. If you are truly serious about serving Norfolk, I will give you a few minutes to ride out of my sight. If you do not, I will kill you."

De la Londe scratched his beard, looking at de Troiu. "There are two of us," he said. "Two against one, no matter how good you are. Unfortunately, I have a task to perform and you are now standing in the way of it. If I cannot recruit you, then I have orders to kill you so you will not warn the others. I have been asked to speak to every man in Northumberland's knight ranks. Norfolk has offers of wealth and lands for all of them."

Titus looked at the man as if he had completely lost his mind. "You cannot be *serious*?"

"I am, indeed."

Titus sighed sharply, shaking his head in a gesture that implied he was truly disgusted with the situation. But his thoughts were really calculating just how fast he could get to his broadsword before de la Londe, who was closer to him, could unsheathe his broadsword and impale him. The odds weren't good and Titus knew it. Pretending to ponder the situation, he swaggered casually in the direction of his horse, moving closer and closer.

"Then I should re-think this," he lied. "I have a wife now. Lands of my own would be most beneficial for her. She would like to be the lady of her own manse, I think."

De la Londe wasn't an idiot; he had served with Titus de Wolfe for five years and knew the man was sly and cunning. He also knew why he was moving near his horse and he panicked, putting his hand on the hilt of his broadsword. The moment he did so, Titus snatched his broadsword, unsheathing it from the side of his saddle and slashing it in de la Londe's direction.

De la Londe was slower than Titus by a fraction of a second but it was enough time for Titus to slash Simon across the face and neck with the tip of his broadsword. Simon screamed and fell back as de Troiu, too far away to engage with his broadsword, withdrew a massive dirk from a sheath on his saddle and hurled it at Titus, catching the man in the torso just beneath his right armpit.

Impaled, Titus staggered back, falling to one knee as the very large blade pierced his body, carving through both lungs and nicking a major artery. As de la Londe struggled with a massive gash to his face and neck, de Troiu flew off his horse, broadsword in hand, and rushed Titus, who lifted his sword just in time to fend off a blow that would have cut his head off. But the force of the blow was enough to send him backwards in his weakened state and when he fell back, de Troiu lifted his broadsword again and gored Titus straight through the gut.

It was a mortal wound, one that cut through more vital organs. Titus was down, unable to defend himself, as de Troiu lifted his sword again to finish him off but de la Londe stopped him.

"Go," he bellowed. "He is as good as dead anyway. Get on your horse and go. We must leave this place."

De Troiu turned to de la Londe, seeing the blood pouring from his face and neck. "Christ," he hissed. "Look at you. You are bleeding to death."

De la Londe was fumbling in his saddle for something to stop the bleeding but he couldn't find anything suitable. Titus' horse was several feet away and he saw something that looked clean and white peeking out from a saddlebag. He snatched Titus' clean tunic from his saddlebags and held it tightly to the wound to stop the torrents of blood. He staggered back over to his horse.

"Get mounted," he gestured to de Troiu. "We must get out of here and return to Norfolk."

De Troiu leapt onto his horse, snatching at the reins. "But the others –?"

"Nay!" de la Londe bellowed, blood in his mouth from the gash Titus had inflicted. "There is no time. Let us return to Norfolk and tell him that we were nearly killed by Northumberland's knights when we attempted to recruit them. With the gash on my face de Mowbray will believe me."

De Troiu didn't have much more to say to that. He simply tightened his reins and charged off to the south, followed by de la Londe as the man struggled to control the bleeding on his face. It was a wild ride across snowy fields as they raced southward, towards Norfolk, leaving the battle to commence on the great, snowing fields behind them. The battle that would later be called "A Day of Much Slaying".

The Battle of Towton had begun.

CHAPTER ONE
~ THE LONG FAREWELL ~

> A Day of Much Slaying
>
> There was a day, not long ago, beneath a sky of graying,
> Where men were called to battle.
> This day, so bold, of heroics untold,
> Was known as the Much Slaying.
>
> —Unknown poet, 15th c. following the Battle of Towton

March 30, 1461 A.D.
The Towton battlefield aftermath

THE BATTLE, MORE than most, had been brutal to a fault. Even though it was March, there had been a heavy snowfall most of the day, adding to the misery of a battle that had seen seventy thousand participants fighting for the houses of Lancaster and York, in the culmination of battles upon battles with seemingly no end. Yet this battle had an end. It was almost over; decisively over. The smell of victory was almost as heavy as the smell of death.

The big knight plowed his way through the slushy, bloody snow, mingled with mud that gave it a brick-red appearance. There were bodies everywhere of the dead and dying, and he found himself stumbling over men who were breathing their last and calling to gods or wives or mothers. Still, he ignored them, singularly focused at the moment. He had been summoned.

A bone-weary foot soldier had called him to Northumberland's tent. His liege, the Earl of Northumberland, was part of the contingent of the defeated in a battle that had virtually wiped out the House of Lancaster. The Yorkists were now in control and Edward IV had taken the throne from Henry. It was almost too surreal to believe, in any case. But the big knight with the worn, dented armor and circled, dark eyes that hadn't seen sleep in two days didn't care about any of that at the moment. If what the foot soldier had told him was true, he would soon be facing his own particular brand of grief.

His charger had fallen in the first few hours of the battle so he crossed the snowy, bloody field on foot. As he mounted a small rise and struggled not to slip in the bloody sludge, a wounded knight in heavy armor suddenly rose from the dead, emitting a strangled growl as he charged with his broadsword leveled. The big knight lifted his weapon, a massive blade forged in Rouen with the de Wolfe family crest on the hilt, and engaged the wounded knight in a nasty sword flight that, when the blade was knocked from his weary and frozen hand, turned into a fist fight.

It was a short and brutal fight as the big knight threw several punches to the head of the wounded knight, driving the man to his knees and finally back to the ground. Even then, the big knight didn't stop; he took the wounded knight's own weapon from him and shoved it through his neck.

Grunting with effort, exhaustion, and perhaps despair, the big knight collected his fallen sword and continued across the frozen moor, slipping in the coagulated blood, heading for the collection of tents on the southwest side of the field where Northumberland's encampment was lodged. By the time he reached the tents, his breath was coming in big, great, foggy puffs. Against the sunset and the snow, he looked like a primal beast making its way through the mists of time. It was a surreal and mystic vision.

It was a sad and defeated encampment. Where there had been hope only yesterday, now there was the start of trappings of defeat.

The snow had attached to the fabric of the tents, soaking them and causing them to sag, much like the sagging spirits of the men they sheltered. The big knight headed straight for the largest tent, half of it collapsed under the weight of the melting snow.

The tent belonged to his liege, the Earl of Northumberland, who had been killed along with thousands of others that day. Now, Henry Percy's advisors were in charge because there was no one else. Northumberland still had over a thousand men that were still mobile; that was only a guess because the death rate was so high that no one could even guess how many men Northumberland had really lost that day. The big knight ignored the beaten, defeated soldiers standing around the entrance, men who looked at him with sorrow and perhaps some fear. Eyes watched the knight as he disappeared into the sagging tent.

It was warm and stale inside in spite of the condition of the tent, smelling of shite. A brazier was glowing –hot with burning dung and peat, offering a small measure of warmth against the freezing temperatures. But it was dark inside the tent and all the big knight could see were silhouettes of men, phantoms in the darkness, and his eyes sought out those he recognized. As he struggled to adjust to the dim light, a man suddenly appeared in front of him, blocking his path.

"Atticus," the man said, relief in his voice. "Thank God you have come. What have you been told?"

Sir Atticus de Wolfe was trying very hard to keep his composure. "My brother has been injured," he said. "Where is he?"

Warenne de Winter, Earl of Thetford and one of the defeated of the Battle of Towton, gazed steadily at the knight known as The Lion of the North. Atticus had been given that name for very good reason; Atticus was a de Wolfe and all of the de Wolfe knights were legendary in Northumbria. It all began with The Wolfe himself, William de Wolfe, and now that male line had culminated in perhaps the fiercest and most cunning knight of all. Much like his ancestor, Atticus was the stuff legends were made of. Men both revered and feared him.

But he also had a fierce temper and had been known to tear men apart with his bare hands. Warenne had seen confirmation of that particular talent himself. It was therefore imperative that he keep Atticus calm in the face of what was to come. If he didn't, there was no telling what de Wolfe would do. Warenne dreaded that specific thought.

"He is resting," Warenne said softly, putting his hands on Atticus' broad chest to prevent the man from moving forward for the moment. "I must speak with you before you talk to him, Atticus. You must listen to me. Will you do this?"

Atticus was looking around the tent, spying his brother's legs about ten feet away from him. Titus was lying down and there were men around him, enough so that Atticus couldn't see his brother from the knees up. Seeing his brother in a prone position did nothing to ease his anxiety and he looked at Warenne imploringly.

"What happened to him?" Atticus asked. *Begged.* "I was told he was injured."

Warenne sighed heavily; a younger man bearing the great de Winter name, he was muscular and handsome with dark hair and dark eyes. He was a respected commander and ally of Northumberland, and a close friend of the de Wolfe brothers. He knew how hard Titus' mortal injury would be on Atticus and with that in mind, thought carefully on his reply.

"You will listen to me carefully, Atticus," he said quietly. "I will tell you what I know but you must vow to remain calm. Your fury will not help your brother. Is that clear?"

Atticus' eyes narrowed, briefly, as if struggling to process what the earl was telling him. "Fury?" he repeated, bewildered. "What in the hell happened?"

"Your vow, Atticus. You will remain calm."

Now he was frustrated. Atticus nodded impatiently. "You have it," he said. "What happened to my brother? Tell me now."

Warenne drew in a deep, pensive breath. "Titus tells me that he was summoned by de la Londe and de Troiu," he said, keeping his voice low. "This was just after sunrise. He was approached by these two Northumberland knights, men you have fought with time and time again. He did not think anything strange of it. Atticus, did you see your brother at all today?"

Atticus thought a moment. "I did not," he confessed. "But I saw him before sunrise and he said nothing about de la Londe and de Troiu. I did, however, see those knights after sunrise in the heat of battle. De la Londe looked to have a serious wound to his face. Why? What do they have to do with this?"

Warenne's jaw ticked faintly, so very sorry for what he was about to say. "They are traitors," he said simply. "Although they are Northumberland knights, and men well paid with a history of service to Northumberland, they have evidently been in negotiations with John de Mowbray, Duke of Norfolk. De Mowbray promised them money and lands if they would swear fealty to him and help turn the tides of this battle. Evidently, de Mowbray asked them to recruit men from Northumberland's stable of knights. They did not approach you with this offer, then?"

Atticus was stunned. He had served with de la Londe and de Troiu for four years. They were good knights and he trusted them, so this news was quite shocking.

"They did not," he said, clearly surprised. "Are you sure of this?"

"I am."

Atticus shook his head, baffled. "I would not believe them capable of treason."

Warenne rubbed his eyes wearily. "Neither did Titus," he said.

"De la Londe and de Troiu approached your brother with de Mowbray's proposition. When Titus refused, they tried to kill him to silence him so he could not tell others what they had offered him. That is the story your brother told me. I cannot find de la Londe or de Troiu to confirm this, but there is no reason why your brother would lie. He is mortally wounded, Atticus. He will not survive the night. Sit with him and tell him of your love for him. This will be your last chance to speak with him in this life."

Atticus stared at the earl. For several long, painful moments, he simply stared, as if unsure how to react. Disbelief swept his features followed closely by anguish in its most raw form. Atticus' face, usually so expressionless, was now flooding with emotions he could not control. *Titus... dying.* Dear God, was it possible? Was the man he admired most in this life soon to leave him? He finally hung his head, reaching out to grasp Warenne as if struggling to hold on to something, anything, to keep him from falling to the ground. Warenne, in turn, held the man's arms tightly.

"It is not true, Ren," Atticus hissed. "This cannot be true."

Warenne could feel the man's anguish as it flowed through his body, entering Warenne's at the point of contact and flooding him with grief. His heart hurt so badly that he could hardly stand it.

"It is true," Warenne murmured. "I am so very sorry, Atticus. I love your brother very much. I feel as if I am losing my own brother."

Atticus was holding Warenne with a death grip, staring at the ground. He realized that tears were finding their way to the surface and he blinked rapidly, chasing them away. Nay, he could not show emotion now, not when the Northumberland advisors were standing about, watching him for his reaction. They had already lost their liege today and were brittle enough without watching Atticus de Wolfe lose his composure. The Lion of the North was beyond the pull of emotion, always in control of himself. He was a rock when all else around him was crumbling.

Except now; Titus, his beloved older brother, was dying. *Dying*. Dear God, was it even possible?

Atticus let go of Warenne and turned in the direction of Titus. He pushed through a pair of advisors, men he knew, but said nothing to them. He was focused on his brother, intensely focused on fighting off an emotional breakdown. As he came upon the man, supine on Warenne's personal cot, he could see that Titus' naked torso was wrapped tightly with bloodied bandages as the earl's personal surgeon bent over him, inspecting something on Titus' chest.

Reality hit him, causing his knees to weaken. Titus was pale and pasty, the look of a man who was standing in the shadow of death. Atticus stared at the bloodied wrappings a moment, feeling his heart shatter. A million pieces of pain exploded into his body, causing his limbs to ache and his knees to weaken further. Physical pain manifested. When he managed to tear his eyes away from the bloody linen and look at Titus' face, he could see that Titus was looking at him with those hazel eyes he knew so well. When their gazes met, Titus smiled grimly.

"You are here," he sighed weakly. "Praise the saints that you are alive. I had feared otherwise."

The surgeon moved away and Atticus' knees gave way as he knelt down next to his brother, taking the man's hand and holding it tightly. The moment he gripped the man's warm flesh, the tears very nearly returned. Titus was warm and alive in his hand. According to Warenne, that was not to be for much longer. He could hardly grasp the concept.

"There is no Yorkist in England that can topple me," he said, his voice tight. He was trying to make the moment light but failing. His smile faded. "What happened, Titus? Ren said something about de la Londe and de Troiu trying to kill you."

Titus de Wolfe gazed steadily at his younger brother by two years, a man he had helped raise when their mother had died those years ago. They were so very close, the two of them, and he knew his passing would be very hard on Atticus. It had been just the two of them for so long that he could only imagine how he would feel if the situation were reversed and he was the one about to lose his brother. He knew he would feel incredibly alone. But even that description couldn't begin to scratch the surface of the true loneliness and abandonment he would feel. He would be lost. With that in mind, he squeezed his brother's hand as tightly as he could, feeling his flesh one last time, something to be remembered in the afterlife.

"They have turned," Titus said softly. "Norfolk has promised them riches if they would serve him and recruit others to serve for him. They approached me and I refused, so they tried to kill me so I could not warn others. Do not trust them, Atticus. De Mowbray will want you most of all. You must not let them approach you and you must not trust them. Do you understand me?"

Atticus nodded in agreement, with deep regret, as Titus confirmed the information he'd been told. He sighed heavily. "I still cannot believe it," he said. "But the fact remains that they tried to kill you for refusing their offer. This I cannot abide. I will seek them out and I will punish them, Titus. Make no mistake; this will not go unanswered."

Titus shook his head. "Not now," he rasped, swallowing hard because he was beginning to have trouble breathing. His legs were strangely numb as well and he knew that his time was very limited. There was much he had to say before the veil of eternal darkness claimed him. "I have something much more important for you to do now, Atticus. You must take care of my wife. That is the only thing of import."

Atticus wouldn't be easily swayed from thoughts of vengeance. "You do not have to even ask," he said. "You know I will take care of her regardless. But de la Londe and de Troiu…."

"Listen to me," Titus cut him off as forcefully as he could. "Isobeau… I realize we have not been married very long, but in that time… in that time I have grown quite fond of her. She is a warm and wonderful and beautiful woman, Atticus. It is imperative that she remarry a man who is worthy of her."

Atticus was still lingering on de la Londe and de Troiu. "Of course I will select a man worthy of her," he assured him. "You do not even have to ask, Brother. I will make sure she is well taken care of by someone who will treat her with respect and kindness."

"I meant you, Atticus."

Atticus' eyebrows lifted in surprise and astonishment. "*Me?*" he repeated. "You want me to marry your wife?"

Titus squeezed his hand, although the gesture was weaker than it had been only moments earlier. It was clear his life was fading. "You are the only man I trust," he whispered. "Atticus, she is all to me. These past two months that she has been my wife have been the two most wonderful months of my life. I know you will be kind to her and that you will respect her. It is most important that you marry her, Atticus. I… I could not bear it if another man were to have her."

Atticus tried to keep the look of horror off his face. "Titus, I… I cannot marry," he said. "Not her, not anyone. You know this. You know my mind and future is not focused on a wife. There is the battle in support of Henry, now more important than ever as Edward takes the throne."

Titus would not be put off. "You *must* marry her."

"And you would have her widowed twice if anything happens?" Atticus hissed. "I will not stop fighting if I marry her, Titus. She will be secondary to my vocation."

Titus looked at him; *really* looked at him. Tears began to stream from his eyes and down his temples. "Please," he begged, a tight whisper. "Isobeau is the most important thing in the world to me. Please marry her and be kind to her. I will trust you, Atticus. You must do this for me."

Titus' tears poked holes in Atticus' resistance. In fact, it destroyed his resistance altogether. He was shocked to see the tears, the emotion, coming from Titus, who had perhaps been one of the strongest and most emotionless people he knew. But in this brief conversation, he could see one thing clearly; Titus' new wife was much more entrenched in her husband's heart than Atticus could have ever guessed. He was, frankly, astonished. He never suspected Titus capable of such emotion. Squeezing his brother's fingers again, he placed a big hand on the man's forehead.

"As you wish," he said, giving in without another word of argument. "I will... marry her and take care of her. You needn't worry. Isobeau will be well tended."

Titus closed his eyes, emitting a sigh of relief. "Thank you," he whispered sincerely. "I can die in peace knowing she is taken care of. Bless you, Atticus. And for the years of being my brother and sharing a bond with me that few men know, I thank you. I love you very much."

Now, the tears were returning to Atticus' eyes, but this time he could not stop them. *Is this really the end?* He thought. *Is this really the last time I will ever speak with my brother?*

"And I love you," he whispered tightly for the lump in his throat. "You are my older brother, Titus. I have always worshiped you. I am not sure how I am going to go on without your guidance and your wisdom."

Titus opened his eyes, although it was a struggle. The peculiar numbness in his legs had now reached his chest. It was difficult to breathe.

"But you will," he ordered. "You will go on and you will do great things. You are The Lion of the North, a man so fierce that your reputation borders on myth. You are the greatest de Wolfe of all. Know that I am proud, Atticus... so very proud that you are my brother. It... it has been an honor...."

He faded off. Atticus didn't try to stop the tears now; they streamed down his cheeks as he bent over his brother. "Titus?" he asked hoarsely. "Titus, can you hear me?"

There was no response. Northumberland's personal surgeon, who had been standing behind Atticus during the exchange, moved around Atticus and put his fingers on Titus' neck. After a moment, he lifted both eyelids and peered into the glazed eyes. Then, he looked at Atticus and shook his head.

"He is gone, my lord," he said quietly.

Atticus released his grip on Titus, his hands flying to his head as if to hold back the explosion of grief that was building.

"Nay," he breathed. "He is not gone. Not yet."

The surgeon nodded his head again, glancing over at Warenne, who had also been watching the exchange. There was great concern on Warenne's features as Atticus went into denial.

"I am afraid he is," the surgeon said, putting himself between Atticus and his dead brother. "I will make sure your brother is properly cleaned and prepared for the return home. I will take care of him, my lord, I swear it. Mayhap you should go with Thetford now. Go with him, Sir Atticus. There is nothing more you can do for your brother."

Atticus stared at the man, his hands still on his head, as if hardly understanding what he was being told. His gaze moved back to Titus, who was pale and still upon the pallet. In fact, he seemed rather peaceful. Atticus pushed the surgeon aside and put his hands on his brother.

"But he is still warm," he insisted.

He knew it was a stupid thing to say even as he said it. The surgeon shook his head again, motioning to Warenne, who quickly came forward.

"He is dead, my lord," the surgeon said again, removing Atticus' hand and gently pushing the knight towards Warenne. "Please go with the earl now. I will take good care of your brother."

Atticus' first instinct was to resist, to deny what he had been told, but he knew deep in his heart that the surgeon was correct. Titus was truly dead. Atticus had seen far too much death in his lifetime and should have been conditioned to it, but he found when it came to Titus that he was not. He wasn't conditioned at all. Still, he had to maintain control. He couldn't let others see him in an emotional state. With every ounce of willpower he possessed, he steeled himself against the reality of Titus' demise. The truth was that he was numb.

Quickly, he wiped any remaining tears from his face and stood up even as the earl came to him and tried to help him. Atticus shook the man off, though not unkindly.

"I will take him back to the Lair," he said, sounding hollow and matter-of-fact. Greif had him reeling. "He will be buried there with our mother."

Warenne was watching Atticus closely, with great regret. He could see that the man was off-balance, stunned. "Of course, Atticus," he agreed softly. "Shall I send a messenger to Wolfe's Lair to inform Solomon de Wolfe of his son's passing?"

Atticus didn't respond for a moment, seemingly lost in his own world of grief and turmoil. He was trying very hard to think clearly, to plan what needed to be done. Anything to stave off the sorrow of Titus' death. At the moment, he was pretending it never happened. He was ignoring it, hoping the anguish of it would leave him alone, at least for a while. *Stay strong!*

"Nay," he said. "I will inform my father personally when I deliver Titus home. For now, my first task will be to return to Alnwick Castle to inform my brother's wife, Lady de Wolfe, of her husband's passing. I can make it to Alnwick in four or five days, but I will need a good mount. I lost my horse in battle this morning."

Warenne put a hand on him, stopping him from charging right out of the tent and jumping on the nearest horse to ride to Alnwick Castle. "Wait, Atticus," he said. "With our defeat, Northumberland's army must all return to Alnwick immediately and reinforce her against an onslaught by Edward's forces. I realize you want to return at this moment, but look around you; with Henry Percy dead, Northumberland is in need of leadership. With Titus gone, that unfortunately falls to you. You need to secure the men and organize them for their return to Alnwick where you may then inform Lady de Wolfe of her husband's passing."

Atticus looked at Warenne, his expression torn between Titus' death and the immediate plans for Northumberland's survival. With their defeat at Towton, everything was in question now. That is, everything but one particular point.

"There are other Northumberland knights to assist with that," he said, his jaw flexing. "There is le Bec, Wellesbourne, and both de Russe knights. There is even Lady de Wolfe's brother. There are at least five excellent knights to organize the men to return home, but for me, there are things I must do."

Warenne didn't like the rather deadly look in the man's eye. "I have not seen Lady de Wolfe's brother for hours," he said. "Le Bec, Wellesbourne, and both de Russe knights are already out assessing the damage. You are needed very badly, Atticus. You must organize the breakdown of Northumberland's encampment and make sure the wounded are separated for the return home. You must also ensure that the earl himself makes it back to Alnwick and to his family. We have a new Earl of Northumberland now, you know. A twelve-year-old lad must now helm a mighty empire."

Atticus' hazel eyes were riveted to Warenne, the deadly gleam evident. He didn't seem swayed by the fact that a child was now his liege. "I cannot help, Ren," he said. "You will forgive me, but there are things I must now do that do not include Northumberland's future."

Atticus had never disobeyed an order in his life so his answer surprised Warenne. Technically, he wasn't Atticus' liege but he was his superior. Atticus was bound to obey him. But, then again, men suffering the pangs of grief could behave oddly.

"Atticus, please," Warenne begged quietly. "You will have all the time you need to tend to the things you must do but for the next few hours, will you please take charge of Northumberland's troops and move them away from this place? You cannot walk away when you are needed most."

Atticus' expression hardened. "I must find de la Londe and de Troiu," he said, his tone a growl. "There is no negotiation on this. I must find these men and I must kill them."

Warenne knew that; he'd known the moment Atticus had entered his tent and had been told of the treachery against his brother that Atticus would seek out those who had betrayed Titus. He also knew there was no way he could stop him; more than love or passion, vengeance was perhaps the strongest emotion of all. It could move mountains or dam rivers. Once it was in a man's veins, it was not easily removed until the vengeance itself was sated. That was the only antidote. Warenne sighed faintly.

"Atticus, you must listen to me or your father will lose two sons," he said, his voice low. "You must return to Alnwick so that you may inform Lady de Wolfe of her husband's passing. You must also inform all of Alnwick that there is a new earl. In fact, I will go with you to accomplish this. Henry was my friend, you know. I will then send men with you to escort Titus back to Wolfe's Lair for burial.

Those are the things that must be done first. After that, you will be free to seek out de Troiu and de la Londe to do what must be done. All I ask is that you not act rashly or without great consideration to the situation. A man who acts without thought in a hazardous situation is as good as dead and right now, you are prepared to run off and get yourself killed. Do you think de Troiu and de la Londe will simply throw aside their swords and allow you to kill them? Of course they will not. They are seasoned men, just as you are. They will defend themselves against you and if they have the chance, they will kill you. I cannot bear to lose yet another friend. Please, Atticus... *think*."

Atticus was glaring at Warenne by the time the man finished but Warenne also realized that it wasn't so much of a glare as it was an expression of extreme grief and disappointment. There was great pain reflecting in Atticus' eyes because he knew Warenne, a wise and just man even at his young age of thirty-three years, was correct. Atticus had to be smarter than those he sought to kill, which meant he had to be methodical in their extermination. Running off blindly to challenge them would more than likely not work. His sense of revenge, that age-old hatred that was filling his heart, would have to wait for the moment.

But its time would come.

"I will not stop," Atticus finally said. "I will never stop until de Troiu and de la Londe are dead."

"I know."

"Then understand this has nothing to do with Norfolk seeking to turn Northumberland knights into traitors and everything to do with justice for my brother."

"Killing them will not bring Titus back."

"Mayhap not. But they will be punished for what they did. I cannot let their deed go unanswered."

Warenne was coming to think that he'd already lost Atticus; the man was singularly focused on revenge. Not that he blamed him. There were shadows of revenge in his heart, too, cast there by a day of defeat and sorrow. He'd seen his mighty army humbled, his men killed, friends killed, and his cause badly damaged. The battle at Towton had been a disaster all the way around. He cleared his throat softly.

"When you do kill them," he whispered, "twist the sword just a bit more for my sake, so that I may fulfill my sense of vengeance as well. Titus did not deserve what they did to him."

For the first time, Atticus could see that Warenne, too, held the same sense of punishment that he did. It was as close to revenge as the even-tempered earl could come and Atticus finally felt as if the man understood somewhat. That moment of clarity helped Atticus a great deal. It made him much more willing to obey Warenne's immediate commands.

"Nay, he did not," Atticus finally said, hanging his head because he could no longer look the man in the eye. His sense of grief was now threatening to overwhelm his sense of rage. *Stay strong!* God help him, he was trying. "That being said, I will pull the men together. I will ride to Alnwick with the army. I will return Titus home. But after that, I go on the hunt for de Troiu and de la Londe."

"I know."

Atticus drew in a long, deep breath, struggling to focus on the tasks that lay ahead. He struggled to push aside his grief for the moment, clearing his mind. "You say that you have seen le Bec, Wellesbourne, and both de Russe knights," he said. "I must go in search of Tertius. Let us pray that Lady de Wolfe has not lost her brother in addition to her husband this day."

Vastly relieved that Atticus seemed to be calming, Warenne nodded his head. "Find de Shera," he said. "As I said, I have not seen him in hours. The last I saw of the man, he was to the north near Cock Burn. You may want to start there."

Atticus nodded, thinking of Tertius de Shera, a knight who was also his friend. In fact, he was close with all of Northumberland's knights. Three of them were cousins, all grandsons of the great Richmond le Bec – Sir Kenton le Bec was the son of Richmond's eldest son, while Sir Adam Wellesbourne had married Kenton's cousin, Audrey, the daughter of Richmond's youngest daughter and the mighty Bastian de Russe. Lastly, Sir Alec le Bec was the son of Richmond's second son, Gannon. All three of these knights were related, as were the de Wolfe brothers and Tertius de Shera because Titus had married Tertius' sister. Warenne had a close-knit stable of knights because of these family ties and he liked it that way. Men who were linked by blood were sometimes more loyal and bonded than others.

But it was a bond that had been shattered this day between Atticus and Titus. Already, Atticus felt lost and alone because he'd never been without his brother. Finally acknowledging Warenne's command, he couldn't help but glance at his brother as he prepared to quit the tent. He shouldn't have done it because one glance at Titus' ashen face fractured the weak composure. He broke away from Warenne and returned to his brother's corpse, dropping to his knees beside the man and pulling him into his arms.

No one had expected that sudden move; one moment, Atticus was speaking with Warenne and the next, he was on his knees, clutching Titus against him. The surgeon, who had been cleaning the man up, was very nearly pushed out of the way as Atticus held his brother for the very last time. It was a deeply poignant and sorrowful moment, one of finality.

Atticus couldn't leave without bidding his farewell to Titus in his own way. He loved his brother deeply and holding the man's cooling body against him somehow made everything more real; life and death and the sense of vengeance that was starting to eat away at Atticus' soul. Already, it was like a cancer, threatening to consume him. Hugging Titus against him, he whispered in the man's ear.

"I swear that you shall be avenged," he pledged. "As I live and breathe, I shall punish those who have done this to you. It will be my all for living, the force that drives me. I swear your death shall not be in vain. You will be well remembered, Titus. But those who did this to you will pay."

With a final kiss to Titus' cooling cheek, he lay his brother back down and very nearly ran from the tent. Only outside, in the freezing weather and the blanket of white across the ground, did he let the tears fall unashamedly.

For Titus, he finally wept.

CHAPTER TWO

> Ionian scale in C – Lyrics to My Heart Awakens
>
> As the sun will rise, my heart awakens.
> Your voice is beauty to my ear, my soul cannot be contained.
> As I watch the sun rise, it reflects my longing,
> 'Tis only you I dream of, the hope for love is restored.
>
> —Isobeau de Shera de Wolfe, 15th c.

Alnwick Castle
April 04, 1461 A.D.

T HE WEATHER HAD been fickle, petulant, and quite mad. At least, that is how she looked at it, but at the moment it was behaving itself. From the snows that had fallen at the end of March to the very spring-like weather they were currently experiencing, it was enough to make one's head swim. The earth, now warmed by the weak sun that had decided to emerge from behind the veil of winter, was becoming alive with blooms and blossoms and little creatures that liked to dart about the fields. Even the bugs were celebrating, swarming and dancing upon the newly green earth. It was, in truth, delightful.

Lady de Wolfe, know personally as Isobeau de Shera de Wolfe, was experiencing the first real freedom from heavy winter cloaks and scratchy woolen garments in months. The day was a bit cool but certainly nothing like it had been. She was dressed in a gown of linen, lavender in color, with long sleeves and a snug bodice. The shift underneath was the softest wool possible, giving her some warmth against the cool breezes, but for the most part she relished in the weak sunlight as she stood in a field northeast of Alnwick's walls close to the River Aln, running her horse in circles with a lead and giving the big mare some exercise. Having been cooped up in a stall for weeks on end, the big, white mare was nearly as stir-crazy as her mistress was. As Isobeau held on to the lead and let the horse run in circles around her, she laughed as the animal literally kicked up her heels. The horse was happy, too. For the moment, all was well in the world.

Her husband had given her the horse as a wedding gift. She smiled as she thought of Titus, perhaps the most handsome and powerful knight in all the realm. He was very kind and very funny at times, and she was quite fond of him even though theirs had been a contract marriage.

Isobeau's father, Calpurnius de Shera, had contracted with his friend Solomon de Wolfe many years ago when Titus had been fifteen years of age and Isobeau had been two. At the time, it had seemed like quite an age difference but when they were finally married when Isobeau turned twenty-one years (because her father could not stand to part with her any sooner), their difference in ages was nothing at all. Titus, who had been initially reluctant to the marriage, had forgotten any resistance when he'd set eyes upon his stunningly beautiful bride. He took back every nasty thing he'd ever said about his father, her father, and the union in general. He had been smitten with her from the start.

With pale blond hair and green eyes, Isobeau was all shades of lovely. He had also discovered that his new bride was also very sweet and rather animated, with a wicked sense of humor, but she was also very quick to temper. She didn't have much of a calm demeanor, something blamed on her ancestor, the great Thunder Warrior Maximus de Shera. Family legend had it that he was quick to temper as well. But along with the ancestral temper, Isobeau also had the brilliant de Shera mind. She never forgot anything and she could read, write, and do math sums in her head. Those particular traits that would have shocked some men impressed him greatly.

Titus and Isobeau had spent the two weeks following their wedding coming to know one another, spending nearly every waking moment together, until the Earl of Northumberland mobilized his army and took it south, into Yorkshire, to intercept troops loyal to Edward. Isobeau didn't pay much attention to war although, as a de Shera, she should have. She was much more interested in her horses, her cats, and in the songs she wrote. She loved music and would play her harp to accompany herself as she sang, a talent that had seriously enraptured Titus. But her husband's departure with the earl's army made her more aware of the battle for the English throne than she wanted to be. She hated to see him go.

So she focused on the things she loved in his absence and mostly on the music she liked to write. Since Isobeau had been a child, she had a great love of music and having been taught to write at a young age, she was able to put the words and music in her head down to parchment. Her father's solar had been covered with pieces of parchment or vellum that she had scribbled songs upon. There was more of Isobeau's writing in Calpurnius' chamber than there was of his, but Calpurnius had loved it. His wife had died when his children, Tertius and Isobeau, were very young, so for a very long time it had only been the three of them. His children were his life until Isobeau's marriage to Titus de Wolfe had changed that.

But not too terribly much. She was still her father's daughter, now with a husband she had grown quite fond of. Her song writing had increased with the event of a new husband who had soon departed after their wedding, and she learned to pass the days of his absence by creating music for Titus. They were sweet songs, perhaps a bit naïve and adoring, alluding to their life together and a future she was looking forward to. She was particularly fond of one called

The Heart Awakens because it said everything that she was feeling. She couldn't wait to sing her songs for Titus, accompanying herself on the harp her father had brought all the way from Italy, and she hoped that Titus would understand what had transpired in her heart during his absence. She hoped he felt the same. She also couldn't wait to tell him of the child she was carrying.

Smiling at the thought of her baby, she put a hand to her still-flat belly. She was fairly certain of the pregnancy, as her menses had stopped, and Lady Percy's personal physician had confirmed it. *A son.* She was positive that she was carrying a de Wolfe son, one who would be a great knight just as his father and his uncle, the man who was called The Lion of the North, were. Thoughts briefly shifted to Atticus de Wolfe, a new brother she's barely said just a few words to because he was always so busy with Northumberland's business, but she hoped the great knight would take the time to help train his new nephew. She was certain that with Titus' request that he would. Therefore, her son would be trained by the finest.

Somewhere in her daydreams of Titus and their child, Isobeau had lain down upon the cool grass, gazing up at the bright blue sky as her mind wandered. Her horse's lead was still in her hand but the horse had stopped running circles and was now grazing next to her. She finally sat up and looked around, wondering how she had ended up on the ground. Thoughts of her husband often did that. On days like this, with peace across the bucolic countryside, it was hard to believe there was a war going on. She was anxious for Titus' safety and anxious for him to return so that they could get on with the rest of their lives.

"Isobeau!"

Isobeau turned in the direction of her shouted name, shading her eyes from the sun. She could see three girls approaching; the older girl carried a toddler in her arms while the third girl, her age somewhere between the other two, waved her arms wildly and ran in Isobeau's direction.

"Is-o-*BEAU!*" the child shouted.

Isobeau grinned at the three Percy women, daughters of the earl and his wife, Eleanor. Margaret, the eldest at fifteen, had taken to Isobeau right away because she had recently lost her older sister to marriage. The next daughter, Eleanor, or Ella as they called her, was the blond six-year-old with a wild streak in her, whilst the baby, Elizabeth, was sweet and affectionate. How Isobeau loved tending Elizabeth; she hoped for a daughter such as her someday. After her mighty son, of course.

"Greetings, Ella!" she waved at the small child as the girl ran to her. Eleanor plopped in her lap and Isobeau hugged the child. "Where have you been?"

Eleanor wrapped her small arms around Isobeau's neck and squeezed enthusiastically. "With Mam," she said. "Mam says you must come inside, Is. She says to hurry."

Eleanor always called her "Is", but it came out of the child's mouth sounding like "Eees". By this time, Margaret was upon her, rocking baby Elizabeth on her hip. Isobeau looked to the older Percy girl curiously. "What is the matter?" she asked Margaret. "Why must I come inside the gates?"

Margaret was a rather morose girl without a lick of personality. She seemed perpetually depressed, perpetually bored. "You cannot see the road from here," she said. "A rider came about a half hour ago and told my mother than my father's army was returning home. That is why Mother says you must come inside now."

Isobeau set Eleanor on her feet and quickly stood up, brushing off her dress of dirt and grass. "How exciting," she said happily. "I have just been sitting here wondering when they would come home and now they are finally here!"

Isobeau's heart was racing as she thought of Titus returning and she wanted to make herself presentable before he saw her. Her long hair was a mess and there was grass all over her skirt. She began scurrying back to the great, walled fortress of Alnwick, pulling her horse along as the three young women ran along behind her.

"My mother says the army is just north of Felton and should be here within the hour," Margaret said. She always called Lady Percy "My mother", even when she was addressing her directly. It wasn't simply "Mother"; it was "My mother" in all things. "My mother said that the messenger told her that the most recent battle was a terrible loss."

Isobeau looked at Margaret with concern. "What does that mean?"

Margaret caught up to her, rushing along beside her with little Elizabeth bouncing vigorously with every step Margaret took.

"I am not sure," she said. "My mother sent my brother and two soldiers out to meet the incoming army and see to my father's return. Papa will be here soon and all will be well then."

Margaret seemed confident but Isobeau wasn't so sure. She couldn't shake the sense of concern she felt. *The battle was a terrible loss.* Loss of what? Territory? Men? Knights? Suddenly, her apprehension for Titus' safety took on a new dimension. She was very anxious to see him. Something inside her, a little voice in her head, told her to get back to the castle quickly. There was no time to waste.

Picking up the pace, she made haste for the hulking fortress of Alnwick Castle.

"She knows, Atticus." Sir Kenton le Bec, part of the advance party that reached Alnwick before the bulk of the army, met Atticus at the great gatehouse of Alnwick. "She was with Lady Percy when we told the woman of the earl's demise. Lady de Wolfe asked me a direct question about Titus' health and I could not lie to her. I hope you understand that."

Atticus looked at his very tall, muscular friend. Kenton le Bec was perhaps the best knight he'd ever known next to Titus and he trusted the man implicitly. Still, he felt some frustration at the admission even though he did, in fact, understand. As the remains of Northumberland's army trickled in through the open gates, Atticus removed his helm and wiped at his sweating forehead with the back of his hand.

"I understand," he grunted. Then, he shook his head as if exasperated. "I should have ridden ahead to tell her. I should have gone with you."

Kenton put a big hand on Atticus' shoulder. "You were where you were most needed," he said quietly. "You rode next to Titus' body the entire way home. I do not blame you for not wanting to leave his side. There is no shame in that."

Atticus eyed Kenton. "Except that I left you to inform Lady Percy of her husband's passing," he said, "and my brother's wife along with her. That should have come from me."

Kenton could see that Atticus was angry at himself for things beyond his control. The man had spent the past six days in almost complete silence, riding beside his brother's body as it was transported along with the earl on the same wagon bed. The men lay side by side, wrapped tightly in canvas from a small tent the men had cut in half to use as burial shrouds for them. Northumberland's surgeon had cut bushels of fresh rosemary to pack around the bodies to cover the stench, but on the sixth day after their deaths, nothing could adequately cover the smell of decay.

Even now, as the wagon bearing their bodies entered the inner ward of Alnwick, they could smell that sweet-pungent stench of death. Unfortunately, there were several other wagons bearing the dead that they had been able to gather from the slaughter at Towton, so the very air around them smelled of putrefaction. It was as if they were bringing death back to Alnwick as it followed them home from Towton.

Kenton, the most stoic and professional of all knights, watched Atticus' expression as the wagon bearing his brother's body moved past him. He could see the grief in the man's eyes even if his weary face remained expressionless. Kenton was hurting, too; they all were. And they were all equally furious with the news that two of their own had turned on Titus. Though it was not their right, all of Northumberland's remaining knights had that same sense of vengeance that Atticus had. Treacherous knights, men they had trusted, were an insult and a danger to them all.

But that was something they could not focus on at the moment; they had an earl to bury, friends to bury, and a castle to secure. Vengeance would have to come at another time, as Warenne had stressed the entire ride back to Alnwick. Since de Winter's base was in Norfolk and not far from the Duke of Norfolk's seat, de Winter and his thrashed army had returned to Alnwick with the Northumberland army in the hopes of healing the injured and recuperating somewhat before making the long trek home. Moreover, it was clear that de Winter was very concerned for Atticus. They all were.

With that in mind, Kenton moved to take over Atticus' duties and let the man deal with his brother's wife. He addressed Atticus' last statement.

"Then go to Lady de Wolfe now," Kenton said quietly. "She was quite broken up the last time I saw her."

Atticus didn't look particularly enthusiastic about it as he glanced at the big, brown-stoned keep of Alnwick that had been there since the days of William the Conqueror. It was old and solid, the seat of Northumberland for centuries. It had been home to him for years but now all he felt was emptiness when he looked at it; too many memories of Titus within those old walls. He took a deep, sorrowful breath.

"I will go," he said. "Did you tell her about Tertius also?"

Kenton nodded. "She asked," he replied. "I told her that her brother is well."

Atticus lifted his eyebrows to that statement, sorrow in his action. Her brother was alive, yet his was not. He realized that there was some bitterness towards her because of it. "I have not seen Tertius since we entered Alnwick," he said, looking around. "If you see the man, tell him to go to his sister. Mayhap he can bring her some comfort."

Kenton merely nodded. As Atticus put his helm on the saddle of the young, big-boned warhorse that had belonged to the earl, de Winter rode up in to their midst, bringing up the rear of the army astride his vibrant, red rouncey. As the horse threw its head around, spraying foam from its mouth, Warenne flipped up the visor on his helm and looked at Atticus and Kenton.

"That is the last of the army," he said. "Thank you again for letting us seek shelter here while we tend the wounded, Atticus. We shall try not to be terrible guests."

Atticus smiled weakly. "I would put you to work mucking the stables to pay for your keep," he teased his friend. "But since you are allergic to horse shite, I suppose I will spare you."

Kenton had a lazy half-grin on his face at the young earl's expense as Warenne laughed outright. "Put me in the kitchens, then," he said. "See if you do not find horse shite in your stew someday. That will teach you to make a slave out of me."

Kenton chuckled and even Atticus snorted. "Unfortunately, I believe you," he said. Then, he glanced at the gates of Alnwick as the chains tightened up as men began to close it. "Kenton will show you where your men will bed down. I will put you in the keep, however. You will enjoy all of the hospitality that Alnwick has to offer, but for now, I must see to my brother's wife. I will seek you out later."

The smile faded from Warenne's face. "Do not worry over me," he said. "Le Bec and I will do what needs to be done. Your most important task is to tend Lady de Wolfe. She will need your comfort."

Atticus closed his eyes, briefly, as if dreading what was to come. "Did I tell you that Titus asked me to marry the woman?" he said, looking to the shocked faces around him. "On his deathbed, he told me he could not bear it if his wife married another man. He made me promise to marry her and take care of her. I am not entirely sure how the woman will react to such a thing. I am not entirely sure how to tell her."

Warenne, with a young wife of his own, wasn't unsympathetic to the sensitivity of women, especially in a situation such as this.

"Be honest," he told him quietly. "This is a trying situation and anything you tell the woman is bound to shake her under the circumstances, so it is best if you are simply honest with her. Tell her everything and allow her to become accustomed to her new future. You may as well get it all over with at once."

Atticus nodded with some resignation, knowing that de Winter was more than likely correct. There was no use in delaying the inevitable. As he opened his mouth to reply, he was cut short by a great wailing coming from the big, brown-stoned keep of Alnwick.

All three knights turned to see Lady Percy, her women, and her children exiting from the keep, being directed towards the wagon that contained the earl's body. The wailing was coming from Lady Percy's women as they wept over the death of the earl. Atticus watched the group as they made their way over to the wagon, now positioned against the inner wall along with several other wagons bearing bodies.

"Kenton," he said, his jaw flexing unhappily. "Make sure they do not disturb my brother's body in their grief. Take Titus somewhere quiet and safe. I am sure Lady de Wolfe will want to view her husband without an audience of Lady Percy's foolish women about."

Kenton nodded. He was already on the move. As Warenne directed his horse over to the left side of the ward, towards the stables where his men were gathering, Atticus headed for the keep in search of Lady de Wolfe.

The wailing in the courtyard irritated him greatly. Truth be told, it grated on his already brittle composure and he tried to block it out as he mounted the retractable steps to the keep. Alnwick was an enormous complex of walls, two baileys, outbuildings, stables, and a keep that was more a series of buildings than one solid structure. Atticus entered through the main entry, emerging into the cool and dark entry that smelled heavily of smoke.

From the chaos of the bailey, it was oddly still in the keep. There was a hall directly in front of him, one that serviced the family at meal time when they weren't feasting with guests, and Atticus could see servants milling about in the dim expanse of the hall. He entered the two-storied room, stopped the first servant he came to and asked where Lady de Wolfe was. The servant couldn't tell him but he found someone who could. According to a kitchen servant, she had just come from Lady de Wolfe, who was huddled in her chambers.

With heavy steps, Atticus made his way to the third floor of the building, heading down a corridor that took him to the north side of the complex. This was where visitors were usually housed, where he intended to put de Winter, and he headed for the door at the end of the corridor that had belonged to his brother. *Had.* Atticus braced himself as he approached the big, oak panel set within a dogtooth arched doorway.

He lifted a fist, hesitating a moment, before knocking softly on the door. Receiving no immediate response, he knocked again, louder. This time, a woman on the other side shouted at him.

"Go away," she bellowed.

Atticus cleared his throat softly. "It is Atticus, Lady de Wolfe," he said. "Will you please admit me?"

There was no answer at first, but then the door flew open and Isobeau was standing in front of him, her lovely face pale and her cheeks wet with tears. Atticus gazed back at her, feeling the physical impact of her expression as strongly as if she had slapped him. There was terrific sadness there. Before Atticus could speak, however, Isobeau broke down.

"What happened?" she demanded, half-sobbing and half-yelling. "What happened to my husband?"

Atticus thought he had been braced well enough against the onslaught of her grief but evidently he wasn't. He could feel himself starting to crack in the face of her crying.

Crying for Titus.

"He was killed, Lady de Wolfe," he said as evenly as he could. "I am sorry you had to hear it from le Bec. I have come to speak of the circumstances if you wish to hear them."

She looked at him, open-mouthed, as if he had just said something outrageous. "Circumstances?" she repeated. "I suppose that it does not matter what the circumstances are. He is dead, is he not? You were there; why did you not protect him?"

Now she was delivering verbal punches to his gut, firing the same questions he had been asking himself for six days. He struggled not to match her emotion and he certainly struggled not to show it. He felt as if he were defending himself to his brother's new wife, a woman he barely knew. She barely knew him as well, otherwise, how else could she accuse him of neglect when it came to Titus? Anyone who knew him, and knew of his bond with Titus, would not have asked such a thing.

"We were separated at the time his death came about," he told her as calmly as he could, hoping an explanation might ease her. "My lady, I loved my brother deeply. I hope you know that if I had been given any control or knowledge of what was happening to him, I would have most certainly done everything I could to help him. I would have died if it meant saving him. Do not think for one moment you are the only one feeling pain over his death because, for certain, you are not."

There was a reprimand in his words, something bitter lashing out of him unexpectedly to push her back, just a bit. She had hurt him, accused him, and now he was striking back. Surely the woman could not accuse him of not being willing to help his brother; damn her for suggesting it.

His rebuke worked. Feeling the verbal slap of his words, Isobeau's anger eased but her sense of sorrow did not. She fixed on Atticus, her hand to her chest as if to keep her heart from shattering into a million slivers of anguish.

"But he is dead," she whispered, her gaze upon him imploring. "How could such a thing happen? You were there… other men were there… surely someone could have saved him?"

Atticus' expression tightened. "Had someone loyal been there, I'm sure they would have."

There was great regret in that statement but Isobeau was ignorant to it. She was only focused on her own pain and sorrow. But she labored to push aside her grief, coming to realize that she was all but accusing Titus' brother of failing to prevent the man's death. She was so muddled with distress that she didn't know what she was saying. It all seemed jumbled up in her heart and mind, for she was unable to make any sense of it.

"I…I am sorry," she said after a moment, moving away from the door so the man could enter. "I know you would not have… I should not have said such a thing. Forgive me."

Atticus came into the room, hesitantly, as she moved away from the door and went to sit next to the hearth. She had a small, damp kerchief clutched in her fingers, holding it to her nose as she sniffled. Although Atticus closed the door behind him, he didn't make any attempt to move further into the room. He simply stood by the door, eyeing his brother's grieving wife and wondering what to say to her. She was displaying every emotion he was feeling but was too composed to let himself go. He almost envied her lack of restraint where her grief was concerned. He wished he could let himself go, too.

"There is nothing to forgive," he told her evenly. "You have every right to feel sad and angry. I feel sad and angry, too. It is I who must ask your forgiveness. I should have been the one to tell you about Titus. I am sorry it had to be le Bec."

Sniffling into her wadded kerchief, Isobeau shook her head. "It does not matter who told me," she said, sobbing quietly. "The end result is the same. I have been informed of my husband's death."

Atticus watched her a moment; his guard had been up upon entering the room but he could feel himself easing as he came to understand that Isobeau was mourning Titus just as he was. Whether or not he was openly sobbing like she was, they still had that grief in common. That horrific bond of anguish connected them. At the moment, he wasn't even sure what to say to her so he just started talking. Unfortunately, he gave forth all of the warmth one would when discussing the weather or planning a battle. He came across as unfeeling, cold, and without tact.

"I was with Titus before he died," he told her. "His last words were of you, my lady. He asked that I marry you because he said he could not stand it if another man became your husband, so I agreed to his request. We will be taking Titus back to Wolfe's Lair for burial next to my mother and as soon as he is buried, I will marry you because I do not feel comfortable doing it whilst he is still above ground. There is something inherently disrespectful about that."

By this time, Isobeau was looking at him with shock. She had stopped sobbing, now staring open-mouthed at Atticus.

"He... he asked you to marry me?" she repeated, aghast. "But... this is of no offense towards you, Sir Atticus, but I do not wish to marry you. I have just lost my husband and already I must consider remarriage? I will not!"

Atticus was actually offended although he tried not to be. He should have been relieved, for it would have made an easy excuse not to marry the woman. She didn't want him and he didn't want her. In truth, he wasn't sure what he had expected from her, but a straight denial hadn't been a possibility. A man of considerable pride, her refusal was enough to put a nick in the wall of his composure, enough of a nick to weaken him. His jaw ticked as his stinging reply was formed.

"What you want is of no concern," he said, his voice hard. "You will do as Titus asked and so will I, regardless of my personal feelings. My brother asked me to take care of you and I promised him I would. Why should this bother you so much? You act as if you have been married to my brother for years rather than months. Two months ago, you did not even know the man so I find your tears at his passing insulting to say the very least. I have been with my brother for all thirty-three years of my life and if anyone has a right to tears, it is I, so spare me your fabricated grief. You did not know my brother as I did and therefore have no right to act as if your grief is stronger than mine."

He spouted nasty words, words that shocked and upset Isobeau so much that she visibly flinched when he was finished. Still seated in the chair by the hearth, she could see that he was truly serious. He meant what he said. Isobeau had barely had a few words with the man prior to this moment so to see his bitterness, his pure hardness, was truly something to behold. But in that bitterness she saw the depths of his grief; something flickering in the green eyes told her that he was feeling much more than his stiff demeanor let on. But that feeling did not excuse his rudeness.

"Mayhap I only knew him for a few weeks at most, but in those weeks, I became quite fond of him," she said, her voice trembling from anger and hurt. "He was kind and he was affectionate. I mourn for a wonderful life cut short with a man I was quite fond of and I will not let you take that away from me. How dare you even try, Atticus de Wolfe! How dare you try to diminish what I am feeling! How would you even know? You do not know me at all!"

Atticus remained cool. "I am not attempting to take anything away from you," he said. "I am stating quite clearly that you have no right to mourn someone you only knew a matter of days before he left for war."

Isobeau couldn't believe what she was hearing from the man's mouth. Was it possible he was so cold? His words were devastating. But was it even possible that he was correct? Did she even have a right to mourn a man she had barely known before he left her to go to war? Not only had he upset her, but now he confused her. Agitated, overwhelmed, she growled at him.

"Get out of this room and leave me alone," she said.

With that, she turned her back on him, facing the hearth that was smoldering gently. She didn't want to speak with him anymore, nasty man that he was. She wanted him away from her so that she could clear her mind and mourn her husband in private. She was trying not to hate Titus' brother at the moment and found his presence agitating. She kept waiting for him to leave, hoping he would, but he simply stood there and didn't make a sound. Now, his refusal to leave was coming to infuriate her.

"I said get out," she told him. "I will not tell you again."

She heard his joints pop as he shifted position on those big, muscular legs. "And if I do not?"

"If you linger any longer, you will find out."

Isobeau heard him snort and she jerked her head around, startled at the sound, to see that he was smiling. It was a thin and ironic smile, but he was smiling nonetheless. Her eyes narrowed dangerously but before she could explode at him, Atticus turned and put his hand on the door latch.

"I believe you," he said, lifting the latch. "But know this; this will be the one and only time I will allow you to give me orders. This is your chamber, therefore, I will obey. But I will be back so you had better prepare yourself for that event."

Isobeau glared him for a long, tense moment before turning away. "I am not sure why you would," she said. "I do not want to see you."

Atticus lifted a dark eyebrow. "Be that as it may, you have no choice," he said. "I would assume you want to see your husband and I would assume you want to accompany him back to Wolfe's Lair for burial. Unfortunately for both of us, we will be seeing a good deal of each other. You may as well resign yourself to it."

Isobeau didn't want to resign herself to anything that had to do with this man. "I would assume my husband's body is here at Alnwick," she said, her tone cold. "Where is he?"

"He is safe."

"That was not the question."

Atticus' piercing eyes lingered on the woman who was not afraid of his manner, his attitude, or of him in general. *She is strong, this one.* He sensed strength in her. Odd he'd never noticed before but, then again, he'd spent little time around her. "It is the only answer I can give you, as I do not know where my men have put him."

"You will take me to him when you know."

Atticus nodded slowly. "I will."

Isobeau didn't answer him, mostly because there was nothing more to say. Their encounter had been harsh and painful, making a bad situation worse. Without replying, she returned her attention to the hearth, hoping he would take the hint and simply leave. This time, he did.

When she was positive he had left, the tears returned with a vengeance.

CHAPTER THREE

> Ionian scale in Bb – Lyrics to The Sorrow Within
>
> *The colors of darkness shadow my world,*
> *The memory of you now blurred with sorrow.*
> *Would that I could hold you again I my arms,*
> *But such things are shades of a ghostly past.*
>
> —Iseobeau de Shera de Wolfe, 15th c.

TERTIUS WASN'T SURPRISED to find his sister's chamber dark but for a fire in the hearth and a small taper upon the table where she sat. As he entered the chamber, for the door was not locked, he could see pieces of parchment scattered all over the table and some pieces on the floor. Scraps of discarded writings were everywhere.

Tertius remembered that before they had left for Towton, Titus had indulged his new wife's passion for writing music and he had purchased quite a bit of expensive parchment from the parchmenter in the village outside of the castle walls. The man, who was quite skilled at transforming animal skin into a writing surface, had given Titus a deal on imperfect parchment that was difficult for him to sell. Therefore, Isobeau had more parchment than she probably knew what to do with but, knowing his sister, she would find a way to use it. Isobeau was industrious and busy that way.

"Izzy?" Tertius asked hesitantly as he came into the room. "Duckling, what are you doing?"

Isobeau didn't even look up from what she was doing. She was furiously scribbling something on an uneven piece of parchment by the dim light of the taper and her fingertips were stained black.

"I am glad you have returned safe, Tertius," she said, sounding oddly detached. "Titus is dead, you know."

Tertius paused next to her table, gazing down at his sister's blond head. He sensed something very strange about her and it concerned him. "I know," he said, his tone dull with grief. "What are you doing, Isobeau?"

She dipped her quill into the inkwell, tapped off the excess ink, and continued writing. Tertius could see that she was scribbling chords as well as words.

"I am writing a song," she said. "I will sing it for Titus' funeral. He loved my singing, you know. I think he would like it if I sang at his burial."

Tertius understood a bit more now. He knew his sister well enough to know that she was a strong woman and, at the moment, she was trying to be very strong. She was also expressing her grief perhaps the best way she knew how and that was to put it into song. Since she had been a little girl, she had put everything into song. Reaching out, he picked up a piece of parchment that was next to her hand, one that had evidently been tossed aside. He held it up to the light to see what words were contained upon the carefully treated hide.

"*The colors of darkness shadow my world,*" he murmured, reading the dark and smeared letters. "*The memory of you now blurred with sorrow.* Iz, are you certain this is something you want to sing at your husband's funeral mass? I am not entirely sure this is appropriate."

Isobeau came to a halt, looking up at him with confusion and some unhappiness. "It is what I am feeling, Tertius," she said. "Why is it not appropriate?"

Tertius was a bit more restrained than his passionate and young sister. He had seen much in life as a warring knight whereas she had led a relatively sheltered one as a fine lady in an excellent house. Although the de Sheras were still great battle lords, their home of Isenhall Castle had been spared anything major for the past twenty years. Therefore, all Isobeau had known was peace.

With a sigh, he reached out to take an ink-stained hand and pulled her off her stool, away from the table and towards the hearth. Isobeau went with him, reluctantly, and he set her down in a cushioned chair while he took the other, sitting wearily against the silk pillows. His pale, shadowed face studied her against the firelight from the hearth.

"I am so sorry about Titus," he said softly. "I know you were very fond of him as he was of you. Any mention of your name would set him to grinning, you know. He was anxious to return home to you. I am so very sorry he was not able to, at least not alive."

Isobeau's composure, a fragile thing, began to crack. She shook her head and looked away from her brother. "Please… do not speak of him, not now," she begged softly. "I have spent the past several hours attempting not to fall to pieces so I took to writing a song to Titus instead to distract myself. Atticus said that I had no right to feel grief for a man I had only known a matter of weeks. He said that he found my tears at Titus' passing insulting, so I have stayed to my rooms in order to write a song to Titus to express how I feel. But… but I am not strong enough to speak of him so please don't."

Tertius' expression tightened. "Atticus told you that?"

Isobeau nodded. "He did," she said, marginally agitated in her restless movements, as if she didn't know what to do with her hands or body. Everything about her was on edge. "He came to tell me that upon his deathbed, Titus asked him to marry me and take care of me. I sent Atticus away; I do not want to marry the man. I cannot think on such things right now."

Tertius knew his sister could be temperamental and even sharp at times; Atticus could be the same way. He could only imagine how a conversation must have gone between them regarding the volatile subject of Titus' death. He cocked his head curiously. "You told Atticus that you did not wish to marry him?"

"I did."

"How did he react?"

She shrugged, averting her gaze. "He was unpleasant and bitter," she said. "Tertius, after we return to Wolfe's Lair to bury Titus, will you please take me home? I want to return to Isenhall. I do not want to say here in the north any longer. I do not like it here. Without Titus, there is no reason to remain."

Tertius scratched his head, thinking on his sister's request and realizing that he was somewhat irritated with it. In fact, he was *quite* irritated with it. "Are you truly so selfish, Iz?" he asked her. "Look around you. Northumberland's army has been badly defeated in a battle that turned decidedly against the king. Henry Percy was killed alongside Titus, and alongside thousands of other men, and all you can think of is returning home to Isenhall because you do not wish to remain here any longer. More than that, you have blatantly refused a marriage proposal from Atticus de Wolfe. Do you understand that his brother made that request of him? With is dying breath, Titus asked his brother to take care of you and you have *refused* that request? What on earth is the matter with you that you would be so selfish and short-sighted?"

By now, Isobeau was looking at her brother with a mixture of remorse and sorrow on her features. "How is that being selfish and short-sighted?" she wanted to know. "I do not wish to have another husband!"

"Your husband has made provisions for you," Tertius pointed out hotly. "The man thought only of you with his last breath and you have the bad manners to disobey him? Worse yet, you shut yourself up in this room while pain and devastation go on all around you and rather than lift a finger to help, you write songs to your dead husband. I am ashamed of you, Isobeau Adelaide de Shera."

It wasn't often that Tertius spoke firmly to her, or called her by her full name, but he was certainly doing it now. The more he spoke, the more regretful and confused Isobeau became, mostly because he was making sense. She trusted Tertius and he had always been good to her. She respected his opinion. Therefore, his latest statements had her in utter confusion and despair.

"What would you have me do, then?" she asked, on the defensive. "I cannot do anything to ease the pain and devastation."

Tertius abruptly stood up and grabbed her by the hand. "Aye, you can," he said. "You will go down to the great hall and you will tell the surgeon that you are there to help. The man has his hands full with the wounded and dying, and the least you can do is offer your services to comfort them. A kind word or a comforting touch will make a world of difference to those men who are suffering, Isobeau. Stop behaving like a selfish child and do something with yourself. Go help those in need."

Isobeau frowned as he pulled her towards the door. "But I do not know anything about tending wounded," she said. "I have never had a strong stomach for blood, Tertius, you know that. It is even worse now that...."

She stopped herself before she could say anymore. She didn't want Tertius to be the first one to hear of her pregnancy. But the more she thought about it, there was really no one else to tell. The only man she wanted to truly tell was dead. It was like a stab to her gut to realize that Titus would never know his son. It had been something she had tried not to think about because the mere hint of the recollection magnified her grief tenfold. Muddled in thought, she wasn't paying much attention to Tertius as he yanked open the chamber door.

"Now that *what*?" Tertius demanded, although his tone suggested he didn't much care. "Stop with your excuses, Izzy. Go down to the hall and help. There will be time for mourning Titus but locked away in your room like this... it is not a fitting way to honor his memory. Titus deserves a wife who will put aside her pain and show her strength by helping the men who fought at Titus' side. You are strong, little sister. I know, for I have seen it. Go down into the hall and do your duty, as Lady de Wolfe."

He was being kinder with her now, not as angry as he had been before. Isobeau paused in the doorway before he could pull her out into the darkened corridor beyond. When Tertius turned to look at her, wondering if she was just being difficult about it, he was somewhat surprised to see the soft, perhaps resigned, expression on her face.

"I... I did not think on it that way," she said. "You are quite right, Tertius. I have not been honoring Titus' memory this afternoon. I thought I was by writing a song to him but... but I suppose I should have been more thoughtful about it. I did not even think to help Titus men. That is not something I have ever really had to do."

Tertius sighed faintly, relieved that the strong and reasonable sister he knew was starting to come around. She could be stubborn, a dreamer even, but she wasn't unreasonable. He knew that Titus' death had her reeling; he could see it in her eyes. It was his intention to force her to focus on something else to help ease the sting of his death.

"I know," he said. "You have never been a wife before and therefore do not know how to behave with your husband's men. But you are now the widow of a great knight and you are expected to show your strength to honor him. I know you can do it, Iz."

Isobeau wasn't entirely sure but she would not dispute her brother. His confidence in her, in turn, gave her confidence. Besides, she had little choice. She didn't want to disappoint Tertius and she especially didn't want to disappoint Titus. Maybe there was more to being a wife than simply marrying a great knight and having his son. The way Tertius phrased it, it made sense. It was time to grow up, just a little.

"I hope so," she said. Smiling weakly, she let him pull her out into the corridor. "You know how I am around blood. I grow dizzy simply at the sight of it."

Tertius snorted. "You are a de Shera," he said. "De Sheras descend from the ancient Romans of Britannia who used to bathe in the blood of their enemies."

She made a face. "They did not!"

Tertius loved teasing her; she reacted quite humorously to his taunts most of the time. "Aye, they did," he insisted. "Therefore, you are a Master of Blood. It should not bother you in the least, so go down to the hall and do what you can to comfort the wounded. Make me proud, Izzy."

Isobeau nodded, noticing he came to a halt when they reached the stairs that led to the floor below. "Are you not coming, too?"

Tertius shook his head. "I have spent weeks in conditions so horrific it is best not to speak of them," he said, his dark eyes reflecting the horrors of his memories. "I have settled the men and the wagons, and now I plan to take a few moments to settle myself. Mayhap some food and a hot bath. I have not been warm in weeks."

It was then that Isobeau could see the exhaustion in her brother's face. He was a strong man and didn't often show his weariness, even when it was well-earned, so she was sympathetic to his statement.

"Go, then," she told him. "I will help the surgeon for a time and then come back to check on you."

Tertius shook his head. "No need, little sister," he told her. "Go about your duties as Lady de Wolfe. I will see you later."

With that, he gestured for her to move down the stairs and she did. Tertius watched her until she disappeared from view, the weary expression fading from his face. True, he was weary, but he also had someone to see. Atticus de Wolfe had evidently had words with Isobeau and Tertius wanted to get to the bottom of it. Atticus was his friend, and his sister's husband's brother, but he could also be a rude and arrogant whoreskin when he set his mind to it. He wanted to make sure all was well between Atticus and Isobeau, especially if Titus had asked his brother to marry his widow. That, more than anything, concerned him; if the two of them were to marry, he didn't want bad blood from the start.

When he was sure Isobeau was on her way to the great hall, Tertius went in search of Atticus.

I find your tears at his passing insulting to say the very least.

He was going to give the man a chance to explain his words to Isobeau before he slugged him in the face.

"I HAD HEARD you were in here."

Atticus heard the familiar voice, turning to see Warenne entering the dank confines of the vault. They were on the lower level of Alnwick's gatehouse, deep in the vaults that usually housed Alnwick's prisoners. Today, however, they housed the dead. Titus was in one of the cells and the earl was in the other. It was very cool down here and would protect the bodies from the rot that was already overtaking them.

"Aye," Atticus replied, watching Warenne as the man came to stand next to him. He then returned his attention to Titus, studying him just as Warenne was. "Kenton put the earl and my brother down here because the cold will preserve the bodies better. I have been spending my last few hours with Titus, trying to convince him to take back his request of me to marry his wife. So far, he has refused."

Warenne gave a half-grin to the attempt at humor. "Silent, is he?" he said, inspecting Titus' greenish cast and the eyes that were already becoming sunken. His sobered. "He looks terrible."

"I know."

"He must be buried as soon as possible."

"I am well aware of that."

Warenne knew he was. Unable to stomach looking at the rotting corpse that the mighty Titus de Wolfe had become, he moved over to a stone bench in the cell and sat heavily. He was weary, like the rest of them, but unable to sleep. There was too much to do.

"Kenton, Wellesbourne, de Russe, and Alec le Bec finally have the men settled," he said, changing the subject away from Titus' state. "I told them to report to you down in the vault for further orders. Is there anything else you need done, Atticus?"

Atticus was starting at his brother's sunken face. "I can only imagine they have completed everything that needed handling," he said. "The men are settled, the dead have been set aside for burial, the wounded are being tended, and the castle is bottled up. What more could there be?"

Warenne's gaze drifted to Titus, thinking of the obvious. "There is the matter of de Troiu and de la Londe," he said quietly. "They all know what has happened. What they will want to know is how they can help you find these men and punish them."

Atticus looked over at Warenne. "Vengeance is mine," he said, his voice low. "I would not expect them, nor would I want them, to set aside their loyalties to Northumberland and seek justice for my brother. I must do this alone, Ren. This is not a group activity."

Warenne shook his head. "You cannot deny them their sense of anger against de Troiu and de la Londe," he reminded him. "These men as much as betrayed all of Northumberland when they decided to seek converts for Norfolk and Edward's cause. They simply happened to approach Titus first; it could have been any of them. They are hurt and angry, too, Atticus. You cannot take that away from them."

"He is *my* brother."

"Would you prefer they didn't care, then?"

The last two sentences were quickly spoken, overlapping. Atticus frowned at Warenne. "I am seeking to kill them, Ren," he said plainly. "When I say that I must seek justice for Titus, it is to track down those two devils and kill them. I will not bring them before any magistrate or court; I will dispense justice as I see fit. That being said, I cannot pull all of the Northumberland knights into my revenge. That is an unfair expectation to presume all of them will follow me to punish these men and commit murder on behalf of the de Wolfe bloodlines."

Warenne could see his point but he still disagreed. "You are not pulling them with you," he said. "They loved Titus, too, or did you forget that?"

Atticus hadn't. All of Northumberland's knights had loved his brother. But he was convinced that he and he alone was the only one who could seek justice for his brother. His gaze returned to Titus.

"I do not know what I am going to do without him," he said, the reflections of grief in his voice. "My father will be devastated when I tell him."

Warenne crossed his big arms, leaning back against the freezing cold stone. "What about his wife?" he said. "How is Lady de Wolfe? I understand that she and Titus were quite fond of each other."

Atticus struggled not to make a face. "I have no idea why," he said, distaste in his tone. "She is a disagreeable, stubborn woman. I have no idea how my brother came to love her, but he did."

Warenne snorted softly, with humor. "Is she beautiful?"

Atticus looked at him. "Have you not seen her?"

"Nay."

Atticus shrugged and turned back to Titus. "She is an incredibly beautiful woman," he admitted. "I thought so the moment I set eyes on her. So did Titus. I have never seen finer. But she has a terrible personality to go along with that beauty."

Warenne put a hand over his mouth so Atticus would not see him grinning. "And your brother wants you to marry that terrible beauty? Shocking."

Atticus couldn't help it now; he pursed his lips irritably, thinking on the shrewish Lady de Wolfe. "Surely he did not know what he was saying," he said. "His wound must have twisted his mind somehow. Surely he did not mean it."

Warenne fought off the giggles at Atticus' lament. "Even so, he asked you to marry her and you agreed," he said. "My best advice for you is to just do what you promised to do and be done with it. And if Lady de Wolfe gets out of hand, a good spanking will do wonders."

"So would fifty lashes."

Warenne burst out laughing. "She is a de Shera," he pointed out. "Unless you want the entire war clan of de Shera down around you, I would not lash the woman. And do not forget that she is also related to Anglesey, so I have heard. You do not want to invite the wrath of the Welsh warlords, do you?"

Atticus grunted, scratching his head irritably. "I should simply send her back to Isenhall Castle and forget about her."

Warenne shrugged. "Aye, you could," he said. "But you would not forget your promise to your brother. It would eat at you until you fulfilled it. So my advice, once again, is to simply marry the woman and be done with it. You will be unable to live with yourself otherwise."

He was right. Atticus wiped a weary hand over his face, pondering the mess he found himself in with regards to his brother's wife, when the sounds of boot falls could be heard on the stairs leading down into the dank and musty vault. The stone steps were slippery with cold and rot and at one point, someone slipped and fell. They could hear the voices of at least two men trying not to fall the entire way down the steps. When the first man finally appeared, he was holding steady to the man just behind him.

"Damnable steps," the knight in heavy armor hissed as he let go of his companion. "I nearly broke my bleeding neck!"

He was holding on to his heart, not his neck, as if genuinely terrified that he would have met such an end. Sir Adam Wellesbourne was a short, stocky, and muscular knight who more than likely would meet his end on a battlefield and not a flight of stairs, but he was dramatic with the best of them. Following on his heels, the man he had been holding on to, was his cousin, Sir Alec le Bec. A big man, young, with blond hair and bright, blue eyes, he was grinning at the shorter knight.

"You would not break your neck," Alec said. "With your girth, you would roll all the way to the bottom and bounce off of the walls, just like an inflated bladder."

As Adam snarled at his good-looking cousin by marriage, more men came down the steps. Sir Maxim de Russe, also a cousin to Wellesbourne and le Bec and the son of the great knight once known as Beast, Sir Bastian de Russe, eyed his cousins with some irritation. Maxim was quite young, like Adam and Alec, but he had a wisdom that went well beyond his years. He was also excruciatingly handsome and he knew it, making him palpably arrogant.

"Still your tongues, both of you," Maxim said quietly, gesturing to Atticus as the man sat next to Titus' body. "Have respect."

As Adam and Alec shushed each other, Kenton and finally Tertius appeared from the stairs. Now, all five Northumberland knights were in the vault along with Atticus and the earl, gathered for a debriefing and further orders.

Atticus glanced up at the men, now *his* men. With Titus gone, he was now in charge of Northumbria's army. Odd how that hadn't occurred to him until that moment; it had been six long days since the defeat at Towton but the fact that he was now in command really hadn't hit him until now. Now, suddenly, realization dawned and he didn't like the weighty feel of it. He didn't particularly want it. He had things to do, a future path cut out for him that had nothing to do with commanding Northumberland's armies. But for the moment, he would pretend the mantle of command had been easily assumed. They were all expecting such confident direction from The Lion of the North and he would not disappoint.

"I am told that the men are settled and the army disbanded for the moment," Atticus said, looking at Kenton. "Now that we are settled and returned, what kind of assessment can you give me on the dead and wounded?"

Kenton folded his enormous arms across his chest, his brow furrowing in thought. He looked exactly like his paternal grandfather, the great Richmond le Bec, in many ways – he had the man's substantial height and width, and he even had the same habit of cocking an eyebrow when particularly annoyed or thoughtful. He also had Richmond's legendary fighting ability; in fact, he was better. At least, Richmond had thought so. The man had been gone for several years but his legacy, and his power, remained. There was no one finer with a crossbow in all of England than Kenton le Bec.

"We carried at least ten thousand men into battle," he said. "The exact number I had when leaving Alnwick was eight thousand, nine hundred and fifty-seven, but we picked up men as we marched southward so the best estimate is that we were well over ten thousand. Out of that ten thousand, a little over three thousand have returned with us to Alnwick and that is not including Thetford's army."

Atticus struggled not to let his shock show but he couldn't help it; he hissed, pinching the bridge of his nose to ward off the massive headache that threatened.

"Less than half," he muttered. "We have returned with less than half our men."

Kenton nodded solemnly. "Surely you realized that."

Atticus stopped pinching his nose and nodded with great regret. "I suspected," he said. "What of the battle in general? I know it was a sound defeat for Henry, but do we have an idea of the overall losses?"

Kenton sighed. "You saw the retreat of our army."

Atticus nodded vaguely. "I saw an entire river filled with bodies," he said. "I was part of the contingent that held off the charging Yorkists to allow our men to fall back. I finally had to give up or surrender my own life. With Norfolk bringing in fresh troops, there was no choice."

They all knew that; Towton had been an ugly, nasty defeat, something none of them had spoken of during the entire trip north. There had been no need, as they had mostly been concerned with reaching the safety of Alnwick. But now that they were safe, the terrible defeat at Towton was becoming even more terrible as they discussed the losses for the Lancastrians. Even for the seasoned knights, some of the news was quite shocking and the reality of their status now, as the defeated, was grossly depressing.

"So the tides are now turned against us," Kenton said quietly. "We are now enemies to the new king and you know that Edward is going to demand the surrender of Alnwick. Northumberland led those armies at Towton and the Percys secure the north. Edward is going to make sure we are neutralized."

Atticus knew that. His thoughts shifted from those of Titus as he considered the immediate future for Alnwick and her inhabitants. That weight of command he had felt moments earlier was now heavier than before.

"I know," he said. "But he will not come tomorrow, or even next month. It is my sense that Edward will wait until he settles in to London and establishes his court before he makes any demands of surrender to any of us. He does not have the manpower to retaliate so soon, so for the time being, we are safe."

"Then why bottle up Alnwick?" Adam Wellesbourne wanted to know. Adam was more a follower than a leader, but he was a skilled knight and fearless in a fight. "Our gates are closed and we have double guards upon the walls. Why all of the protection if Edward will wait to move against us?"

Atticus glanced at him. "Because there is no guarantee that Edward will not move against us in some way," he said. "He has men in York and in Richmond that he could send to us and there is always the threat of Norfolk since he is nearby. With that in mind, I will send word to Scotland to see if we can solicit reinforcements from the Scots. Henry's wife, Margaret, is allied with the Scots so there is the possibility. But I will be truthful when I say that we will make no sudden movements, in any case. We will bottle ourselves up and wait. That is the most prudent stance we can take."

"Where *is* Henry?" Adam asked quietly.

Atticus shrugged, looking at Warenne, who addressed the group when all attention shifted to him. "We believe he will flee to Scotland if he hasn't already," he said. "His allies are there. What happened at Towton turned Henry into a fugitive in his own country. Our lives, our very livelihoods, will change from this moment on, my good lords. We are now the enemy."

He hadn't said anything they didn't already know; they nodded in resignation, sighed wearily, shifted around on their legs, and leaned against walls. The men were restless and weary; Atticus was well aware. They were nervous, too, nervous of what was to come.

For the moment, however, the situation was quiet and he intended it should remain that way. He was preparing to dismiss the knights so they could seek much-needed rest when Warenne spoke quietly, interrupting him.

"What of the new earl, Atticus?" he wanted to know. "Young Henry Percy may have other plans for his army. Mayhap you should consult with him before making any decisions."

Atticus sighed heavily. "He is a twelve-year-old boy," he said, embittered that he now had to answer to a child he didn't much like. Young Henry Percy, the new Earl of Northumberland, was a spoiled and petty lad as far as Atticus was concerned. "He has no idea what to do in a situation such as this so we will do it for him. He has enough worry now with assuming the mantle of his father. I will counsel him and his mother and make sure they understand the necessity to sit tight and wait. We must not make any rash moves."

"And then what will *you* do, Atticus?" Alec le Bec interjected, his young face lined with fatigue and concern. "We know what de Troiu and de la Londe did to Titus. Surely you do not intend to stay here, bottled up in Alnwick, whilst de Troiu and de le Londe remain free and unpunished for what they have done. What will you do now?"

It was a swift change in subject but a question Atticus had been expecting, one he suspected they all wanted to ask him. He was surprised it took them this long. The conversation preceding the question had only been polite chatter. The real reason the knights were all here was to find out what Atticus intended to do about his brother's murderers. He glanced up, looking at the serious faces around him, and he knew that he was going to have a fight on his hands when he declared his intention to seek justice for Titus alone. He could see that they all expected to have a piece of that vengeance.

"I will take my brother home for burial," he said quietly, looking to Titus' oddly-colored face, "and then I shall track down de Troiu and de la Londe and punish them for this unforgiveable act of treason. I will make them pay with every bone in their body for what they did to my brother, I swear it."

A few feet away from him, Kenton cleared his throat softly. "Titus was our commander as well as our friend, Atticus," he said quietly. "I know that we cannot all go with you but if you would choose one or two of us to accompany you, we would all like to eagerly volunteer to go."

Atticus shook his head, looking up at his men. "I know that," he said. "I will be honest and tell you that I knew this question was coming and I am prepared for it. I would have never believed de Troiu and de la Londe capable of turning against us but they have. That betrayal alone is an affront to us all, but such things happen in time of war. Men fall victim to greed or fear, or both, and behave in a manner that is out of character for them. I care not what their reasons were; all I care about is the fact that they tried to turn Titus as well and when he refused, they killed him for it. That, my friends, is an affront to me and the entire de Wolfe lineage. I cannot let it go unanswered and I know you understand that. However, this is something I must do alone. I cannot take all of Northumberland's knights with me on my quest for vengeance. With the earl gone, you are needed here, now more than ever, but this is something I *must* do. I will return when I can but until that time, Kenton and Tertius will be in command."

Kenton grunted in displeasure, shaking his head and averting his gaze but having the good sense not to dispute Atticus. The truth was that he understood. The younger knights, however, weren't so restrained. As Adam and Alec grumbled unhappily, silenced by Maxim, Tertius spoke.

"Although I am honored that you would leave me in command, Atticus, Kenton can do it without me," he said. "Titus was my sister's husband. He was my brother, the only brother I have known. I have a stake in this as well and for my sister's sake, I must accompany you."

Atticus looked at Tertius, seeing utter stubbornness in the man's expression. But he didn't like the fact that Tertius was trying to claim some of his vengeance. He shook his head.

"You will stay with your sister whilst I accomplish my task," he said. "If something happens to you, then Lady de Wolfe will not only have lost her husband but her brother as well. I am certain she would not take it well."

Tertius cocked an eyebrow. "And if something happens to you, she will have lost another husband," he countered. "Did you not promise Titus that you would marry her? I do not think she would take well to losing a second husband, either."

Atticus' features tightened with anger. He could see that Tertius was trying to manipulate him and he didn't like it one bit. Tertius was his friend but he was also quite envious of Atticus, as if there were some rivalry there. Usually it didn't bother Atticus but at this moment, it bothered him a great deal.

"Marriage to your sister is incidental to my quest for justice for my brother," he said. "It is true that I promised Titus I would marry her, but that has no bearing on anything. No offense to your sister, Tertius, but I am only marrying her because my brother asked it of me and for no other reason than that. I will leave it to you to take care of her whilst I am away."

Tertius frowned. "She is *your* wife," he said. "I will not nursemaid her. If you are going after de la Londe and de Troiu, then I am going with you."

"You are staying here."

Warenne, seeing that the two knights were on the verge of a battle, quickly stood up and put himself between Atticus and

Tertius. He wanted to break their focus on one another for he was positive that Atticus, in his emotional state, would not hesitate to lash out at Tertius. They'd seen enough blood already over the past few days.

"Gentle knights," Warenne said pleasantly, trying to stave off the downward spiral of emotion. "Nothing is going to happen this night, so I would suggest we all retire to rest and eat. We can resume this conversation in the morning if you wish, but Tertius, I will say this – if Atticus does not want you to accompany him, then you will not. This is his fight, not yours. That goes for all of you; if Atticus does not want your company in his quest for justice for Titus, then you will obey his wishes. Is that understood?"

The Northumberland knights weren't particularly happy about that order, especially Tertius. In fact, the man turned and left the vault without another word. It was clear how displeased he was, upset that he wasn't allowed to share in the vengeance and perhaps in doing so, share in some of the victory. Tertius could be selfish that way. Warenne watched him go before turning his focus to the others around him. He especially looked at Kenton.

"Take the men out of here, le Bec," he told him quietly. "Make sure they are fed and rested. You will eat and rest also. I will not require you until morning."

Kenton nodded, acknowledging the order, before herding the younger knights from the vault. As they clamored up the slippery stairs, with Wellesbourne slipping yet again, Warenne waited until they had left and all was silent before finally turning to Atticus.

The man was still sitting by his brother, staring at his brother's sunken features. Warenne suspected that he needed to take charge with Atticus or the man would spend all of his time down in the vault, staring at Titus until the man's flesh rotted away and his bones turned to dust. It was very clear that Atticus could not or would not separate himself from his brother, at least not at the moment. It was a sad realization, sadder still to know that Atticus de Wolfe was so grief stricken over his brother. Warenne went to Atticus and put a hand on his broad shoulder.

"Now," he said softly, "your men are taken care of. There is nothing you need worry over until morning. For right now, you have tasks you need to accomplish, not the least of which is marrying your brother's widow. From our earlier conversation, I am assuming your relationship with the woman is marginally adversarial so it is my suggestion – nay, my request – that you make amends with her. You said before that you had no idea why your brother had fallen in love with such a petulant woman. Do you trust your brother's judgment, Atticus?"

Atticus nodded, glancing up at Warenne. "I do," he said. "Of course I do."

Warenne smiled weakly at the man. "Then assume he found something in her to love," he said. "Mayhap you could find the same thing. If at least not to love, then mayhap to like. In any case, you must make the attempt. This marriage will be what you make out of it and if you are to be linked to the woman for the rest of your life, then mayhap you should start by coming to know what Titus liked so well about her. Fair enough?"

He made a good deal of sense whether or not Atticus wanted to admit it. His gaze returned to Titus' features and, remembering how the man had been driven to tears when thinking on the wife he would leave behind, all of Atticus' resistance started to drain away. Perhaps Warenne was correct; if Titus found something to love in the woman, then perhaps there was something there, after all, beyond the stubborn petulance. Atticus was obligated to find out.

"Fair enough," he finally grunted, stiffly standing up from his seat next to Titus. "I am still not entirely happy about this."

Warenne laughed softly, directing him towards the vault stairs. "I know," he said. "But you know this would make Titus happy and I know you want to please your brother, so make every effort to establish a rapport with Lady de Wolfe. And stop being so bloody stubborn about it."

Atticus made a face at him as they hit the stairs but refrained from commenting. He'd already said all he had to say about the subject. As they ascended the steps up to the ground level of Alnwick, the colors of sunset and a few angry, black clouds greeted them, the promise of nasty weather moving in from the east. The great hall, with its glowing lancet windows, beckoned in the distance, looking somewhat inviting even though Atticus knew that was where the wounded were being cared for. That vast and great hall was surely anything but inviting at the moment. He thought perhaps to check on his men before heading into the keep once more to see to Lady de Wolfe.

The thought of encountering the woman again didn't please him but, as de Winter had said, perhaps he needed to try to come to know the side of her that Titus had fallen in love with. There had to be something there. Perhaps then he wouldn't be so resistant to the marriage. It wasn't as if he had much choice in the matter.

With thoughts of the beautiful harpy of a woman on his mind, he headed towards the great hall.

CHAPTER FOUR

> Ionian scale in C – Lyrics to Leave No More
>
> A bird sang sweetly to me, on a morning bright with rain:
> Said the bird so sweetly to me, lovers know no pain.
> My heart, my joy, is bound to you, like a hero from ancient lore:
> My heart, my joy, dream of the day when you will return to leave no more.
>
> —Iseobeau de Shera de Wolfe, 15th c.

THE MAN WAS dying.

Isobeau knew this because the surgeon told her so, but it still didn't prepare her for the actual experience. He was a young soldier and had only been in the service of Northumberland for a few months, following in the footsteps of his father and uncle. He was so very young, barely seventeen years of age, but one of the Yorkist arrows had pierced his torso, tore through his gut, and emerged on the other side. But the young man was strong; he had lived longer than he should have. At the moment, he had a raging fever and his innards were filled with poison. It was only a matter of time.

There was nothing to do for the young man, a lad barely having reached maturity, so she sat next to him and held his hand as he spoke of the mother he loved and the little sisters he missed. They lived in town but because of the fighting that had gone on lately, his father had sent them into the country with relatives. The young man didn't know where and his father, whom he had served with at Towton, had been killed. Therefore, all he could do was remember his mother and sisters, and tell Isobeau a story about a pet goat that didn't much like him and used to chase him around the yard.

Isobeau had never been exposed to anything like this. She had lived a happy and protected life at Isenhall, so the realities of battle were quite shocking. It was baptism by fire in the worst possible sense, dealing with death on a nasty and brutal level. The great hall was filled with the dying and the wounded, and the smell alone was enough to shake her already weak constitution. It smelled like rotting limbs and old, congealed blood.

The surgeon, the very same man who had tended Titus in his last hours, was exhausted and harried. He'd been working for almost a week straight with little sleep, ever since the battle, but he was still determined to help all of the men he could. Watching him in action bolstered Isobeau's courage; she admired the old man for his perseverance and it helped her to persevere as well.

Something that bolstered her even more was to see Lady Percy in the hall attending the men. The woman had just lost her husband as well, yet she had put her stark grief aside, knowing it was her duty to help the wounded. Their eyes met, once, across the smoky room and Lady Percy forced a tremulous smile at Isobeau, who smiled in return. But Lady Percy quickly returned to an older man who had lost a limb, a man who was crying out in pain. Isobeau admired Lady Percy greatly as she ignored her own anguish to help others. Isobeau vowed, to the best of her ability, to do the same. But surrounded by the wounded and dying as she was, it took a great deal to bolster her courage and not run screaming from the room.

"M... m'lady?" the young man spoke softly to her.

Distracted from her thoughts, Isobeau smiled down at him. "Aye, Gilles?" she replied. "Is there something I can get for you? Water, mayhap?"

The young man shook his head. "Nay, m'lady," he said, hesitantly, because it was difficult to speak. "I was hoping... my sisters and mother cannot read, m'lady, but I was hoping you could tell them that my last thoughts were of them. Tell them that my father died bravely and that I died bravely, too. I think it will make them feel better to know that."

Isobeau gazed down into his pale, stubbled face and realized she was fighting off tears. It was so very tragic to see the young man before her cut down before he had ever truly begun to live. She squeezed his hand and nodded. "Of course I will," she assured him gently. "What are their names? I must find them and give them the news."

"Hartha," the young man said. "My mother his Hartha. My sisters are Joi and Desmelda."

"Hartha, Joi, and Desmelda," Isobeau repeated. "I will not forget."

"Swear it?"

"Of course I do. I never forget a name, so I shall remember their names and find them all. I will even give them some coins to help them. Would that please you?"

The young man smiled gratefully. "Indeed, m'lady," he said, haltingly. His smile faded. "It... is difficult to speak, m'lady. I... would rest now. Just for a while."

Isobeau could sense that the young man's life was draining away. He was much weaker than he had been only minutes earlier. Saddened, she squeezed his hand once more. "Please rest," she told him softly. "Conserve your strength. If you like, I can sing to you. Would that make you feel better?"

The young man could only smile at this point and he did, faintly, and Isobeau took it for permission to sing. She thought quickly on a song, any song that might distract him from his pain. Settling on one she had written for Titus' return because it was the only one she could recall quickly, she sang softly, for his ears only.

"A bird sang sweetly to me, on a morning bright with rain;

Said the bird, so sweetly to me, lovers know no pain.

My heart, my joy, is bound to you, like a hero from ancient lore;

My heart, my joy, dream of the day when you will return to leave no more."

It was such a gentle song, one Isobeau had so hoped to sing to Titus the day he returned. But instead, all she could do was sing it to a dying soldier who had been under her husband's command. There was something incredibly ironic in that thought as she gazed down at the young man as he breathed his last breath. But there was a smile on his face, perhaps a smile at the tender song a young woman had sung to him that had helped transition him into the next world.

Perhaps Isobeau would never know why he was smiling but she felt as if, at the moment, she had done something kind and generous to help the young man. She had eased his suffering the best way she knew how. Her eyes filled with tears at the loss and the waste, and thoughts of Titus' loss filled her mind as well. So much loss and death on this day and the tears, so close to the surface, had returned. The young man's hand, in hers, released its hold and she knew that he was gone, so she carefully placed his hand upon his chest and made the sign of the cross over him.

"Go with God," she murmured, wiping the tears from her cheeks. "O Lord; unto your hands I commit his spirit. Be merciful."

Her work with the young man was finished but her gaze lingered on him, suddenly wishing she had sent him with a message for Titus. He would be seeing him in heaven, after all. As she prepared to leave the young man's side, a quiet voice caught her from behind.

"It was kind of you to relieve his suffering as you did. I know this young soldier; he was a good fighter."

Startled, Isobeau's head jerked around and she found herself looking at Atticus standing a few feet away. He was still in heavy mail and pieces of armor, still in the dirty tunic he had probably been wearing for days. He appeared weary and worn but she had no sympathy. Considering their last meeting, her defenses immediately went up and she looked away to gather the bowl and rag that she had brought with her.

"He is far too young to have died in battle," she said stiffly, motioning to the nearest servant to let the man know that the young soldier was dead and should be carried away. "He should be at home with his parents, dreaming of the young farm girl in the neighboring village. He should not be here with a hole in his chest."

Atticus stepped aside as she pushed past him, presumably on to the next man she could help. "In a perfect world, he would still be at home tending to his family and farm," he said. "But this is not a perfect world. He died valiantly for the king's cause."

Isobeau came to a halt and looked at him. "Is that what death is?" she asked. "Valiant? Is that how my husband died – valiantly? The result is still the same, Sir Atticus; he is dead and I am widowed at the young age of twenty-one years. I will have to raise his son alone when I had hoped for my child to have his father to guide him. That is what this war means to me, so do not paint a glorious picture of valiant death and expect me to accept it."

Atticus reached out to grab her arm. "Child?" he repeated, his dark-circled eyes wide. "You are with child?"

Isobeau yanked her arm from his grasp, realizing she had divulged information to Atticus that she had hoped to divulge to Titus upon his return. It had simply slipped out in her emotional state and she snorted wryly when she realized what she had said.

"I suppose it is right that you are the first man to know," she said. "Since I cannot tell Titus, I have told you. Aye, I am with child. Thank God for his mercy for at least I shall have something to remind me of Titus for the years to come. Or am I not allowed to be thankful for Titus' child just as I am not allowed to grieve for him?"

Atticus was staring at the woman, struggling to digest the fact that she was pregnant. *A son for Titus.* He was astonished; thrilled for Titus, but astonished. Had Titus known, he would have shouted his happiness to the rooftops. He knew the man would have been ecstatic. Atticus was torn between the joy of her news and the distinctly standoffish look in her eye.

"My lady, mayhap we should go and speak somewhere," he said, trying to ease the tension between them. "I fear that when I came to you this morning, I had been in the saddle for six days and then days of battle before that. It was my exhaustion speaking this morning. I would be grateful if you would overlook my bad manners and give your permission for a rational conversation."

Isobeau was surprised by what could be construed as an apology. From The Lion of the North, she hadn't expected it. It was well-known that Atticus de Wolfe was a man who did not apologize, in any situation, and his sense of righteousness was common knowledge. Titus had told her about it often enough, making Atticus seem arrogant and unforgiving. She hadn't been around Atticus to know otherwise, but her impression of Atticus was most definitely one of conceit and power. He'd proven that this morning. Still, it seemed to her as if he were at least trying to be pleasant. She wasn't sure if she should trust him or not.

"I have men to attend here," she said hesitantly, looking around the hall with its layer of wounded upon the floor. "Mayhap… mayhap later."

Atticus knew the men needed help and he didn't want to pull her away from her work, but he realized he very much wanted to speak with her now that he knew she was carrying Titus' child. It seemed that his attitude towards her changed at that very moment, not strangely enough, because she carried a living link to his dead brother. In her, Titus wasn't dead, after all. In her, there was hope that the man lived on.

"I would be grateful, my lady," he said. "In fact, I came into the hall to see to my men. If you are not opposed, I should like to accompany you as you tend them."

Isobeau didn't know what to say to the man so she simply lifted her shoulders, a non-committal answer. She knew that Atticus took it as permission because he was following her now as she moved to the nearest man who was begging for water. Setting her bowl and rag aside, she quickly went to the nearest bucket of fresh water, dipping a cup into it and carrying it back to the wounded soldier with a heavily bandaged torso.

As she returned, Atticus was leaning over the man, speaking with him. She bent over the man to help him drink as Atticus brought her a stool to sit upon. Eyeing Atticus curiously, if not suspiciously, she sat down and continued to help the man drink.

"Thank you, my lady," the wounded man breathed. "You are very kind."

Isobeau smiled at the man. "What more can I do for you?" she asked. "Would you like me to help you with anything further?"

The man licked his lips. "I am hungry," he admitted. "Could… could I have something to eat?"

Isobeau wasn't sure and she looked to Atticus, uncertain, but he shook his head. "Nay, Gus," he told the soldier. "You have a belly wound. You cannot eat. In fact, you should not even drink but Lady de Wolfe was kind enough to provide you with some water."

Isobeau looked rather stricken, as if she had just done something terribly wrong, but Atticus smiled reassuringly. It was a surprising gesture as far as Isobeau was concerned because she had never once seen him smile; the gesture changed his face dramatically. He had straight white teeth with slightly prominent canines, giving him a rather dazzling and handsome appearance.

He was a handsome man. In fact; he had dark, rather stiff and spiky hair, and hazel eyes that appeared gold in certain light. Titus had the same colored eyes but his hair had been lighter, as had his coloring. Atticus was dark all over; dark hair, seemingly darker skin, and if she were to admit it, he was far more handsome than Titus had been. More than that, he was very tall and very muscular – he was at least a head taller than Titus and had the broadest shoulders of any man she had ever seen. There was a good reason why Atticus was called The Lion of the North; he was, quite simply, fierce. He was a handsome and nearly beautiful man who bordered on myth. He was the stuff legends were made of.

Aye, all of this was Atticus de Wolfe. She had noticed before, of course, but she'd never truly thought about it until this moment because her focus until that moment had been on a husband she clearly adored. Now, she found herself looking at the man she would be marrying next, the brother she barely knew. Just as Atticus seemed to be amending his attitude towards her, perhaps now she was allowing herself to see him just a little bit differently as well.

"Lady de Wolfe is merciful, m'lord," the soldier said, breaking into her thoughts. "I… I heard what happened to Sir Titus. I heard those bastards killed him."

The smile faded from Atticus' face. He didn't know why, but he didn't want Isobeau to hear the circumstances of Titus' death. Perhaps it was the polite man in her trying to spare the details or perhaps it was even that he didn't want to hear them again. Any mention of the betrayal, the murder, made him feel as if he were hearing it again for the first time. He wasn't strong enough to keep hearing it. With sorrow, he shook his head.

"Those responsible will pay," he said simply. "For now, let us speak on more pleasant things. You have been in Northumberland's service for many years, have you not? I seem to remember that you were injured a few years ago in battle. This injury should not set you back much; you will recover."

The old soldier nodded although it was clear his thoughts were still on Titus. "It is a sorrowful thing to have lost the earl, too," he said, evidently unwilling to discuss anything else. "At least he did not meet the same fate as Sir Titus; betrayed and murdered. What happened to the men who killed Sir Titus? Did you punish them, m'lord?"

Before Atticus could reply, Isobeau turned to him. "Betrayed and murdered?" she repeated, perplexed. "What is he talking about? Who betrayed Titus?"

Atticus glanced at the woman. "When we speak later, I will tell you the circumstances," he said quietly. "Finish what you are doing now and we will speak later."

Isobeau set the cup down, facing him with building agitation. "You will tell me now," she said. "What does he mean?"

Atticus could see there was no way she was going to let the subject go. Undoubtedly, it was a distressing subject for all concerned and she was nearly the only person at Alnwick who didn't know the circumstances behind Titus' death. It wasn't fair to her but the truth was that Atticus simply hadn't been given the opportunity to tell her. Now, however, the opportunity had arisen.

Reaching out, he took her by the arm and guided her towards the entrance of the great, smelly hall.

"Outside," he said quietly.

Isobeau allowed him to lead her out of the hall and into the evening beyond. The smell of roasting meat was floating about the compound but due to the wounded in the hall, no formal meal was served. Men were gathered in groups throughout the inner ward, sitting against the walls as they slurped down their supper, and men upon the battlements were not eating as they vigilantly watched the countryside for any sign of threats. As soon as they were clear of the hall, Isobeau pulled her arm from Atticus' grasp and turned to him.

"Now," she said firmly, "what is all of this about betrayal and murder? Will you please tell me?"

She wasn't being belligerent but she was being firm. Atticus had been trying to formulate a reply that didn't sound too harsh, or too horrific, but he couldn't seem to do it. The circumstances surrounding Titus' death had been nothing short of harsh and horrific. Clearing his throat softly, he began.

"In order for you to understand what has happened, you must understand the dynamics of politics right now," he said quietly. "Henry had the throne, as the rightful king. Northumberland supports Henry. After this most recent battle, Edward now sits upon the throne. Do you understand that so far?"

Isobeau nodded seriously. "I do."

Atticus continued. "I would assume you know Simon de la Londe and Declan de Troiu?"

Isobeau nodded again. "I know who they are," she said. "They are knights sworn to Northumberland. Why do you ask?"

Atticus paused while a soldier passed within close proximity of them. He waited until the man faded out of earshot. "Unbeknownst to us, de Troiu and de la Londe were solicited by John de Mowbray, Duke of Norfolk," he said. "Norfolk somehow convinced the two knights to support Edward and he further convinced them to seek out converts from Northumberland's ranks. The first knight they approached was my brother, who refused. In order to silence Titus so the man could not tell anyone that de Troiu and de le Londe were now traitors, they tried to kill him. That is how Titus became mortally wounded. It was from men he had once trusted."

Isobeau was looking at him with wide eyes, her hand over her mouth to somehow hold back her horror. "Sweet Mary," she whispered, blinking back tears. "His own men tried to kill him?"

Atticus nodded, his jaw ticking faintly. Speaking of the incident was bringing his hurt and fury up all over again. "Aye," he replied, his voice soft and hoarse. "They tried and they succeeded."

"Are you for certain they did this terrible thing?"

"Titus told me himself with his dying breath," Atticus replied. "It is therefore my intention to seek de Troiu and de la Londe and punish them for what they did to my brother. I hope you can understand that, my lady. It is something I must do."

The hand came away from her mouth, the tears spilling over. "*Understand* it?" she repeated, aghast. "I encourage you to do it, Sir Atticus. If Titus did indeed name his killers, then it is your duty to find them and punish them. You will find them and you will make them pay, do you hear?"

Atticus was mildly taken aback by her attitude. He had never in his life heard of, or even seen, a woman who was in support of vengeance or killing or punishment. "You do understand that I mean to kill them, do you not?" he asked, just to be clear.

Isobeau nodded vehemently. "Indeed I do," she said, wiping furiously at the tears on her face. "The murderous blackhearts. They must be punished for what they did."

Atticus was quite surprised at what he was hearing from her. Women, to him, had always been rather indecisive and needy creatures, but Isobeau certainly wasn't that at all. She was strong-willed, stubborn, and as he could see, passionate in her views. She understood exactly what he had to do and she was not apt to fight him on it. In fact, her support of his duty was encouraging. He realized that it meant a good deal to have her approval on the matter. An inkling of respect for the woman began to sprout.

Come to know what Titus liked so well about the woman, Warenne had said.

Already, Atticus was coming to see a flicker of it.

"Then know that after we return Titus to Wolfe's Lair, I will leave to pursue de Troiu and de la Londe," he told her. "You will remain at Wolfe's Lair with my father. You will be safe there until I return."

Isobeau was still wiping at the tears that refused to stop flowing. It was clear that she was shaken, angry even. "I have not yet met your father," she said. "Titus spoke quite highly of him. I am looking forward to meeting him but I wish the circumstances were not so terrible. But won't your father want to go with you, too, to punish these men?"

Atticus shook his head. "My father is old now," he said. "I do not believe he has been out of Wolfe's Lair for ten years. He does not travel well due to the affliction he has with his joints. They are swollen and he cannot move very well."

Isobeau pondered that information. "Then if he cannot go with you, I will," she said decisively. "This is as much my vengeance as it is yours. Oh, I know you told me that it is not my right to grieve Titus but you were wrong. So very wrong, Sir Atticus. I adored Titus and he was very good to me. What those knights did… they took away my future and my child's father. If anyone has a great stake in this, it is me. I will not be any trouble, I swear it."

Atticus was shaking his head before she even finished her sentence. "My lady, I cannot take you on this journey," he said, watching her face turn red with anger. "It will be very difficult and the fact that you are with child will only make it harder. You must remain behind and take care of yourself and the baby."

Isobeau wouldn't let him deny her so easily. "Think on it this way," she said, deliberately attempting to coerce him. She wasn't one to be denied easily. "When I go with you and help you punish these men, then Titus' son, through me, will also have a hand in punishing those who killed his father. That will bring him great satisfaction in the years to come."

Atticus was still shaking his head; he'd never truly stopped. "My lady, I understand that you feel your own sense of vengeance, but I cannot take you with me," he said, more firmly. "Even for the sake of Titus' son, I cannot take you with me. It would be foolish to risk you and the child in such a way and I suspect that Titus would be quite angry with me to allow it. Nay, then, I will not do it."

"Please, Sir Atticus. I am begging you."

"I cannot. I *will* not."

"But I must go!"

"I am sorry, but you cannot."

Isobeau could see, plainly, that he had no intention of allowing her to accompany him but she could also see that he wasn't being stubborn about it more than he seemed to truly believe it was in her best interest. But that wasn't good enough for Isobeau; she was seized with a distinct sense of revenge on behalf of Titus, to punish the men who had killed him. Atticus denying her what she felt was her right was extremely frustrating. Frustrating, but not the end. Not as far as she was concerned. Still, she hung her head, upset and distraught, and struggling not to weep again.

Atticus could see that the woman was despondent but he wasn't going to back down from his stance. It was ludicrous for the woman to expect to accompany him on a trip wrought with hazard. Still, her bravery was to be commended. It was apparent to him that the woman had little fear of trying to track down dangerous men; at least, in theory she had little fear. The reality of such a thing would more than likely prove to be quite different. He reached out and grasped her gently by the elbow.

"Come with me," he said quietly. "It is cold out here. Let us go inside where it is warm and you can rest."

Isobeau balked. "Nay, not now," she said. "I… I want to see my husband. I have been waiting all day to see him. Did you find out where he has been taken?"

Atticus hesitated, thinking of the slightly greenish tinge to Titus' face and his rather sunken appearance. He wasn't sure it was a good idea for Lady de Wolfe to see her husband in such a way but he was also fairly certain he had no choice. She had every right to view her husband's body.

"I did," he said. "He is down in the vault along with the earl."

Isobeau gazed up at him with her green eyes. "Will you please take me to him?"

"Now?"

"Now."

Reluctantly, Atticus nodded and politely took her elbow again as they made their way across the muddy, half-frozen ward towards the gatehouse. The angry, black clouds that had been moving in at sunset were now gathering overhead in a vast, pewter blanket, preparing to storm. Isobeau glanced up at the clouds as they walked.

"You should know that I will ask you again tomorrow if I can go with you," she said to Atticus. "You cannot deny me forever."

She said it in a rather imperious way and Atticus fought off a grin; he couldn't tell if she was serious or not. Either way, it was rather humorous. "In fact, I can."

"I will ask you daily. Mayhap even hourly."

"Then you are in for a good deal of frustration."

"We shall see."

He frowned, glancing at her. "Do you think to badger me and beat me down until I submit?" he asked. "If that is the case, then you will be sorely disappointed. I do not fold."

Isobeau cast him a sidelong look. "To men, you do not," she said. "But it is different with women. It is bred into knights to grant a lady's request. You will not be able to deny me forever, I say."

"I suppose we shall find out."

"Aye, I suppose we shall. Do not feel too badly when you finally grant my wish."

"I will not grant your wish at all."

Her eyes narrowed at him. "Would you care to wager on that, Sir Atticus?"

He looked at her, astounded. "Wager?" he said, outraged. "I will make no bet with a lady and I am ashamed that you would even propose such a thing."

Isobeau scowled at him just as he was scowling at her. She even stuck her tongue out at him. Atticus held out about two seconds longer before swiftly turning away, breaking into a grin and hoping she hadn't seen it. *The little vixen*, he thought. Even so, her gesture had been quite humorous. He couldn't remember feeling the urge to laugh like that in a very long time. As of late, there had been nothing to laugh about.

Come to know what Titus liked so well about the woman. Already, he was starting to.

The gatehouse loomed ahead and Atticus directed her to the left side of the gatehouse where the stairs to the vault were housed. They were slippery, and narrow, and he held her arm tightly as she descended the stairs in her heavy, linen skirt. Slowly, they made their way to the bottom of the steps where it was very dark except for a single torch burning hot and low in an iron sconce. It gave off little light against the darkness.

Atticus let go of Isobeau's arm and removed the torch from the sconce, leading her towards the cell where Titus' body was located. Atticus could pick up a whiff of decay and he wondered if Isobeau could smell it, too, but if she did, she gave no indication. She was tucked in behind him closely because of the darkness and when he finally came upon Titus' decaying form, he held the torch up and away so she couldn't get a clear look at the color of his skin. He hoped to spare her somewhat. Stepping aside so she could see, he silently indicated Titus' stone-cold corpse.

Atticus wasn't able to catch Isobeau before she fainted dead away.

CHAPTER FIVE

> Ionian scale in C – Lyrics to The Warmth
>
> The warmth is you, in my heart and soul:
> The warmth is you, until the day grows old.
> The warmth is you, my dearest love:
> You are a gift from the heavens, from God above.
>
> —Iseobeau de Shera de Wolfe, 15th c.

Doncaster
The King's Head Inn

"YOU ARE GOING to lose some feeling in your face," the old surgeon said as he packed up his catgut thread and needles. "Your wound was open for quite some time, m'lord. You should have had it sewn sooner."

De la Londe could do nothing more than shrug his shoulders at this point; there really wasn't much he could say to any of it. The wound that Titus had inflicted upon him nearly a week before hadn't been properly tended until now for a variety of reasons, ones he didn't care to discuss. Mostly, it was because the freezing weather had frozen the blood and beard on his face and that alone had stopped the bleeding.

During the battle at Towton, there hadn't been time to do it. He'd kept his face wrapped with the piece of embroidered linen he'd stolen from de Wolfe. But six days later, he'd been forced to have it cleaned and tended because it was starting to fester. Hair had grown into it, as had dirt and debris, so the cleaning of the healing wound had been a harrowing experience. The surgeon had done his best but it was still a mess and de la Londe had been running a fever for two days. It would perhaps get worse before it got better.

But that was, in fact, the least of his concerns at the moment. Sitting in a room at an inn that had been confiscated in whole by the Duke of Norfolk, John de Mowbray, both de la Londe and de Troiu had bigger worries on their mind. De Mowbray, in fact, was in the room with them, as were several of de Mowbray's knights and a lesser baron from Surrey that had once been aligned with Warenne de Winter. In the past six days since moving south from Towton after the decisive York victory, much had changed in the worlds of de la Londe and de Troiu, and all of it revolved around de Mowbray.

"We will be leaving tomorrow morning," de Mowbray told the surgeon as the man moved stiffly for the chamber door. "I will ensure that he sees a surgeon in the next town we come to. We will keep check on the injury."

The surgeon was a big man, older, once muscled but now gone to fatty. He had been a knight once, too, years ago before he injured his sword hand and had been forced to turn to another profession to survive. The surgeon's gaze moved between de Mowbray and de la Londe.

"It is not the injury that is the issue, my lord," he said. "It is the fever. I gave you powdered willow bark for that; make sure he takes it at least four times a day in a cup of wine."

De Mowbray nodded. "He will."

The surgeon still didn't leave, a knowing glimmer to his tired, old eyes. He looked around the room, at the powerful and exhausted men. They smelled of war and he knew the smell very well.

"I heard about the battle to the north," he said. "Towton, wasn't it? Men passing through town a few days ago were speaking of it. They said it was a massacre for the Lancastrians."

De Mowbray remained impassive. "It was a defeat for them.

Aye."

The old surgeon nodded at the confirmation. "I didn't ask you when I came to tend the knight, but I assume he received the wound there?"

De Mowbray lifted a bushy eyebrow. "Indeed he did," he said. "Thank you for your service."

The surgeon had already been paid so it was only a matter of pushing him out of the door, which de Mowbray did. A stubby profile of a man, John de Mowbray was a powerful duke and a brilliant tactician. It had been his cunning that had turned the tides at Towton. Now, he was heading to London with his army because the new king had asked him to come. Edward, in fact, had already left for London and was a few days ahead of de Mowbray. The colors of the ruling house had decisively changed.

The king was determined to clean house of any remains of Henry's loyalists and set up his own court at Westminster. His plans also included taking over the Tower of London as well as Windsor Castle. He was infiltrating deep into the heart of England and wanted de Mowbray with him. But de Mowbray was slowed with a bigger army, and wagons of wounded that had been sent back to Norfolk, and he wasn't in any particular rush to reach London. At the moment, he was more concerned with gaining backing for Edward from the remnants of those who supported Henry. With Henry running for Scotland, de Mowbray would strike at the defeated supporters.

Which was where de la Londe and de Troiu came in. As de Mowbray shut the door behind the surgeon and bolted it, he turned to the two knights who had once been very close to Northumberland. They had been bought with relatively little effort and now that he had them, de Mowbray intended to use them.

"It seems that we have not truly had the opportunity to talk before now," de Mowbray said. "Days of travel have left us all exhausted and scrambling for closure, but now that we have a roof over our head and some privacy, I should like to discuss what happened with Northumberland's men. I already know that Titus de Wolfe is dead and you told me that you did not have the opportunity to speak to the others, but that is all I know. You will now give me the details. I would hear what happened in-depth."

De la Londe, even though he was having trouble speaking, answered him. "It was too chaotic to give you any details after the battle, my lord," he said. "It is true that Titus de Wolfe is dead but not before he did this to my face. This happened in a battle to the death. When we gave him your offer, he became enraged and tried to kill us both. We had no choice but to kill him."

De Mowbray sat in a nearby chair, accepting a cup of wine from one of his men. "Indeed," he said seriously. "I am sorry that Titus chose to die rather than serve Edward. But what of Atticus? You were not able to speak with him?"

De la Londe resisted the urge to look at de Troiu; for the past few days, they had discussed what they would tell de Mowbray about their inability to recruit other Northumberland knights. They couldn't tell the man the truth – that they had fled after they'd killed de Wolfe, so de la Londe had been given a few days to come up with a plausible lie. More than that, he had a suggestion that might help them all.

"We were not able to find Atticus," he said. "My lord, you must understand that we could not risk being seen as the men who killed Titus de Wolfe. If that were to happen, there would have been questions that we could not answer without consequences. At the time Titus was killed, the battle was just commencing. Men were called to arms. We went to arms, too. There was no longer the time or privacy to try and relay your offer to any more of Northumberland's men because by that time, they were all heading into battle."

De Mowbray was listening carefully. "I see," he sighed heavily.

"That is disappointing, I must say. I was hoping you would be able to at least speak with Atticus. The Lion of the North would be a fine weapon in Edward's arsenal. The king has asked for Atticus personally, you know. It is imperative that we somehow communicate with him. Now with Titus dead, he has no reason to remain with Northumberland any longer."

De la Londe shrugged. "With Titus dead and Henry Percy dead, Atticus is now in command of Northumberland's army," he said. Then, his expression took on something of a sly glint. "But that does not necessarily mean we cannot have him. It simply means we must be cunning as we go about it."

De Mowbray was interested. "You know the man," he said. "You know his heart and his loyalties. How can we sway him to Edward's cause?"

De la Londe glanced at de Troiu, then, seeing the man's silent nod of encouragement. Tell him what we discussed. De la Londe continued.

"Both Titus and Atticus are very close to their knight corps," he said. "Le Bec, de Russe, and Wellesbourne serve under them. If we could possibly convince one or more of those houses to pledge loyalty to Edward, it might help sway Atticus' position. Wellesbourne Castle is not far from here, to the south near Warwick Castle. Even though Warwick has switched loyalties from Edward to Henry and back again, Wellesbourne has remained staunch in Henry's cause. Adam Wellesbourne's father, Andrew Wellesbourne, knows me. He knows that I serve with his son. Andrew is old now and, according to Adam, remains at Wellesbourne most of the time, but he has command of over a thousand men. If we could convince Andrew to side with Edward, we may be able to sway Wellesbourne for our cause. If Andrew swears fealty to Edward, it is my suspicion that Adam will, too. With Adam out of Northumberland's stable, we move to le Bec next."

De Mowbray was coming to see the brilliance of the scheme. "Wellesbourne is married to a granddaughter of le Bec and a daughter of Bastian de Russe," he said thoughtfully. "Bastian de Russe is still alive."

De la Londe shook his head firmly. "He was a guardian to Henry when Henry was very young," he said. "Because of that, I cannot see Bastian de Russe swearing fealty to Edward. In fact, he may try to kill us if we try to convince him. Nay, my lord, I believe that trying to convince Wellesbourne, and mayhap Stefan and Gannon le Bec, is the only chance we have of gaining fealty of some of the great houses in Edward's favor. If the House of Wellesbourne and the House of le Bec join Edward's cause, then de Wolfe might follow. At least he might be willing to listen."

De Mowbray was somewhat dubious about le Bec. "Richmond le Bec's wife is a daughter of Henry of Bolingbroke," he said. "I doubt you'll be able to convince the sons to side against their own blood."

"We can but try, my lord."

That was true. It would be something of a triumph if they were even able to sway Wellesbourne. If Sir Andrew was convinced, then it would seriously weaken that entire le Bec-de Russe-Wellesbourne unity, which was a very powerful front. But there was something even more than that lingering on de Mowbray's mind.

"I am not in the habit of putting all of my hopes in one scheme," he said. "As encouraged as I am by your approach to Wellesbourne, let us return to the subject of Atticus. Now that Titus is gone, I am assuming Atticus will return his brother home for burial. The entire de Wolfe family resides at Castle Questing, does it not? Tell me what you know of Atticus' immediate family and where they live."

De la Londe thought a moment. "Atticus' father is the second son, brother to Baron Killham of Castle Questing," he said. "Atticus has spoken many times of his father and of his home, Wolfe's Lair. It is a garrison for Questing. Atticus' father has lived there for many years. It is where Atticus and Titus were born, so I would assume Atticus will return Titus to Wolfe's Lair."

"Do you know where this garrison is?"

De la Londe nodded. "Near Hawick."

"That is Scotland."

"It is indeed, my lord."

De Mowbray thought on that a moment. "Mayhap whilst you go to Wellesbourne Castle to convince Andrew Wellesbourne to side with Edward, I will send another contingent of men to Wolfe's Lair," he said pensively. "If Atticus is there, then mayhap we can open a dialogue with him about his support for Edward now that Henry is in defeat. I will tell him, of course, of Andrew Wellesbourne's switch in loyalty because I am quite certain your mission to Wellesbourne will be successful. Mayhap if Atticus believes Wellesbourne has sworn allegiance to Edward, it might be enough for him to consider it."

De la Londe sighed with doubt. "It will take more than that to convince Atticus, I fear," he said. "It would be wise to wait and work through his knight corps first. Once we have their loyalty, or at lease loyalty from some of them, that would be more persuasive for Atticus."

De Mowbray scratched his neck, thinking on all of the ways he could convince Atticus de Wolfe to support Edward's cause. "Is Atticus' father still alive?"

"He is as far as I know."

De Mowbray cocked his head thoughtfully. "Then mayhap we use the father to convince the son."

De la Londe wasn't sure what, exactly, the duke meant but he knew instinctively that it could not be good. "I would be wary, my lord," he said, his voice low. "With Titus gone, Atticus is bound to be very protective of his father. If I were you, I would be very careful what I did to Solomon de Wolfe. If you unleash The Lion's rage, there will be no stopping Atticus. He will come after you."

De Mowbray pretended not to care, although deep-down he cared a great deal. He did not want The Lion of the North on a vendetta against him. "Your concern is noted," he said. "You have your orders, de la Londe. Tomorrow, you will depart for Wellesbourne Castle while I send a contingent of men to Hawick. As soon as you are able to speak with Andrew Wellesbourne, I will expect your victorious news."

"Where will you be, my lord?"

"In London."

De la Londe simply nodded, collecting a cup of wine and drinking some of the willow powder that the surgeon had left. He wondered if the powder would also take away the uncertain feeling he was having, as if suddenly realizing he was in far deeper than he had imagined he ever would be. Accepting de Mowbray's bribe had seemed like a simple thing at the time until the conversation with de Wolfe had turned deadly. Truth was, de la Londe felt very badly about Titus. The man had been a friend and fair commander. But he had convinced himself that the rewards from de Mowbray had been worth the price of Titus' life.

Less and less, however, it was starting to seem that way. He was seriously coming to wonder if the entire situation and his treachery were about to catch up with him.

ISOBEAU WAS VAGUELY aware of light in the room. She stirred a bit, realizing she was lying on her belly when her eyes flitted open and she could see the angle of her head. She could also see a pair of big legs near her bed, legs clad in worn leather breeches. It would have looked like any man's legs except she recognized the boots with an "S" carved into the strap. With a groan, she lifted her head.

"What are you doing here, Tertius?" she said, grumpy, putting her face in her hands in a miserable gesture.

Tertius, seated next to his sister with one big boot up on the table and the other on the floor, looked up from the watered ale in his hand.

"Is this the gracious thanks I receive for spending the entire night by your side to make sure you came to no harm?" he said, incensed. "You ungrateful, little cow. I will leave this very moment if you do not show me more gratitude."

Grunting, Isobeau rolled onto her side, struggling to acclimate herself. She began to look around strangely. "What on earth happened?" she asked, trying very hard to recall her last conscious thought. "I was in the hall and then I spoke with Sir Atticus out in the ward. And then… then…."

Tertius knew what the "and then" was. Atticus had told him after the man had carried the unconscious Isobeau up from the vault and put her to bed. In fact, Atticus had remained with Isobeau until just before dawn when the man, exhausted beyond endurance, had finally gone to bed at Tertius' insistence. Aye, Tertius knew what the "and then" was. He was rather hoping Isobeau would not remember.

"It was a very strenuous day for you," he said, taking his big boot off the table. "You were exhausted. Today will be a better day, I am sure."

Isobeau was still trying to recall what had happened when suddenly her eyes flew open wide and she slapped a hand over her mouth in a mortified gesture.

"Titus!" she gasped. "Tertius, it was Titus! Sweet Jesus, he was *green!*"

Tertius, regretful that she finally remembered, stood up and went to her as she burst into quiet tears. He patted her shoulder comfortingly.

"I know," he said softly. "I am sorry you had to see that. Atticus should not have allowed it."

Isobeau wiped her eyes. "He did not have a choice," she sniffed. "I asked him to take me to Titus. Actually, I demanded he take me to him."

Tertius sighed heavily, dropping his hand from her shoulder. "Why would you do that?"

She looked up at him, still wiping her eyes. "Because he is my husband and it is my right to see him," she insisted. "I... I had to see him, Tertius. I had to know that he was truly gone."

Tertius understood, somewhat. "We all told you he was truly gone," he said. "Did you not believe us?"

Isobeau nodded, sniffling delicately, trying not to think of her green-tinged husband. "I did," she said. "But I had to see for myself."

Tertius lifted his eyebrows and moved away from her, towards the table where there was food and drink. "And so you did," he said. "But it would have been better to remember the man as he was and not his state the very last time you saw him. Sometimes you should not be so stubborn, Izzy."

Isobeau watched him as he brought her a hunk of bread; she waved it off, nauseous. "Did Atticus tell you that he intends to go after the men who killed Titus?" she asked.

Tertius looked at her with a mixture of disapproval and distress. "How would you know that?" he asked, his eyes narrowing suspiciously. "Did Atticus tell you the circumstances surrounding Titus' death?"

Isobeau nodded. "He did," she said. "But he was not going to tell me. A wounded man in the hall spoke of it and I made Atticus tell me the truth. He is going to find de la Londe and de Troiu but he will not take me with him."

Tertius threw up his hands in relief. "Finally," he hissed, "the man is showing some sense. Of course you should not go with him,

Isobeau. He will not even let any of the knights go with him, me included. I asked to go on behalf of you but he would not allow it."

Isobeau frowned. "He acts as if he is the only one with a measure of vengeance to be had," she said. "He acts as if I have no say in this at all."

"You don't," Tertius said sternly. "Let de Wolfe do what he is bound to do. You cannot stop him and he will not let any of us go with him, so there is nothing we can do about it. But trust me when I say that de la Londe and de Troiu will be found and they will be punished. Atticus de Wolfe will make sure of it."

Isobeau's gaze lingered on her brother a moment longer before looking away, rubbing her belly gingerly. She wasn't feeling very well at the moment.

"Mayhap you and I should go alone," she muttered. "If Atticus will not let us accompany him, then mayhap we should simply go alone. You can find these men and you can kill them."

Tertius glanced at her. "I will not take you, either," he said. "De Wolfe told me that you are with child. Do you really think I would drag my pregnant sister all over England? You are mad, Isobeau. Atticus is leaving today to return Titus to Wolfe's Lair and you will go with him. Then, you will remain at Wolfe's Lair whilst he does what needs to be done."

Isobeau looked at him with some guilt in her expression. "I am sorry I did not tell you about the baby sooner," she said, shrugging. "There has not been the opportunity."

He waved her off, as if it was of no consequence. "Have you sent word to Papa yet?"

Isobeau shook her head. "I have not."

"He will be eager to know."

She pursed her lips irritably. "He will want me to name my son after the de Shera tradition of Roman names for the males," she said. "I will not do it."

"Titus is a Roman name. Name him after his father."

She faltered, fighting off a grin. "That is the only reason Papa allowed me to marry Titus," she snorted. "He bore a Roman name."

Tertius grinned. "I fear you will not have a choice in naming your son."

She conceded the point. "Then I shall name him something grand like Julius Caesar de Wolfe."

Tertius burst out laughing. "Where did you hear of that?"

She watched her brother laugh. "From Papa, of course," she said. "You know how he felt it necessary for us to know of our ancient Roman heritage."

Tertius continued to snort although he was relieved that his sister seemed to be feeling better. The color was coming back to her cheeks. But now he was feeling rather exhausted, having sat up watching over her all night. Now that the sun was rising over the misty morning, he was seriously thinking on seeking his bed.

"I am sure when the time comes that you will honor both our heritage and your husband's," he said. "For now, I do believe I will try to get some sleep. I've been up all night watching over you and am starting to feel my exhaustion. Will you be all right for a time?"

Isobeau nodded. "I will."

Tertius pointed to the big wardrobe in the corner. "Since Atticus is leaving today to return Titus home, you should pack," he said. "I will have your capcases brought out of storage and I will send some servants to help you. Is there anything else you need?"

Isobeau shook her head. "Nay," she said. "Aren't you going with us?"

Tertius rubbed his weary eyes. "Nay," he said. "I must remain here, especially with Northumberland so weakened. Let things settle here a bit and I will come to you at Wolfe's Lair when I can."

Isobeau understood. Her gaze lingered on Tertius for a moment, her big and tall brother with the shaggy head of light brown hair. She loved him dearly and a separation from him was not particularly appealing. She would miss him.

"Thank you for being a good brother," she said softly. "I am sorry you had to sit up all night with me."

Tertius was already heading for the door. "It was not just me," he said. "Atticus was here until just before dawn. In fact, he seemed rather concerned about you. That is how I found out about the child, you know. He thought you may have hurt yourself and the child when you fainted. You feel well enough, don't you?"

Isobeau stood up, rubbing her belly. "I feel fine," she said. "Tired mayhap. And a bit hungry, although I cannot decide if I actually feel hungry or nauseous. Sir Atticus really stayed here all night?"

"He did."

Isobeau's thoughts lingered on Atticus as Tertius bid her a farewell and left the chamber. When the door shut softly behind him, Isobeau continued to think on Atticus de Wolfe. Her conversation with the man from the previous evening had been rather pleasant and she hoped they were past the nastiness that had plagued their exchange when he'd come to tell her of Titus' death. She truly didn't want to be at odds with the man, especially when she had an ulterior motive in mind. Perhaps it was time to ply him with honey in an attempt to wheedle her way into his quest to find the men who had killed Titus. Certainly, butting heads with him would not work. He was, perhaps, even more stubborn than she was.

You should know that I will ask you tomorrow if I can go with you.

It was tomorrow, after all.

Nothing had changed. She wasn't going to let him go without her. For Titus' sake, she was determined to have satisfaction, too.

"I HEARD YOU were departing today, Atticus," Warenne said as he entered the hall where Atticus was sitting at the scrubbed feasting table, enjoying cold beef and cheese to break his night's fast. "I saw the men bring Titus' body up from the vault and put it on a wagon."

Atticus, worse for wear after having only managed to get a couple of hours of very heavy sleep, drank deeply of his boiled fruit juice. He wouldn't drink watered wine or ale in the morning because it made him sleepy.

"Aye," he replied, grumpily. "It is at least a four day ride to Wolfe's Lair in this weather."

Warenne sat down next to him and confiscated the half-loaf of bread from Atticus, tearing it apart and using a knife to slather white butter on it.

"Fortunately, the weather is clear for the moment," he said. "But the snow on the ground will prove to be difficult. Hopefully, the skies will hold until you reach the Lair."

Atticus nodded, shoving beef in his mouth. "Hopefully."

Warenne eyed Atticus as he at his bread. "And Lady de Wolfe?" he asked. "How does she fare this morning?"

Atticus shrugged. "She was sleeping last I saw her," he said. "Unfortunately, I am going to have to wake the woman. I want to leave within the hour. When are you leaving, Ren? Surely you do not plan to stay at Alnwick too much longer."

Warenne shook his head. "Nay," he replied. "We are leaving as well. My army will head south, back to Thetford, while I will go with you to Wolfe's Lair."

Atticus looked at him sharply. "Why are you coming with me?"

Warenne swallowed the bite in his mouth. "Because you have need of me," he said quietly. "I will be truthful with you, Atticus. I do not intend to let you go after de la Londe and de Troiu alone. The two of them managed to kill Titus and he was no slouch of a knight. My fear is that they will use the same tactic they used against your brother on you, and I could not stomach that. So Kenton and I will be going with you whether or not you like it."

Atticus stared at the man. "You insult my abilities as a knight by assuming I cannot handle two armed men on my own."

Warenne shook his head firmly. "It is not slander and well you know it," he said. "Think on it this way, Atticus; if I were bent on revenge by going after two heavily armed men who had already killed a very capable knight, would you let me go alone?"

Atticus frowned. He didn't answer right away as he looked back to his meal. "Probably not," he grumbled. "But you are different. You are a soft and pampered earl and you cannot do something like that on your own. You would call upon a seasoned warrior like me to do it for you."

Warenne fought off a grin. "So now you insult me by calling me soft and pampered?"

Atticus couldn't hold a straight face. "Well, you *are*."

"Would you care to go outside with me so I can show you just how soft and pampered I am?"

Atticus snorted. "Nay," he said flatly, "because you would cheat and order your knights to fight me in your stead. Although I am confident I can best them, I have no desire to go up against Conor de Birmingham, Gerik le Mon, or Ackerley Forbes. You have a trio of powerful de Winter knights at your disposal. I am no fool; Forbes alone would try to cut me off at the knees."

"Then you admit you need help against more than one armed knight."

"I admit nothing."

"That is a true tragedy because you are going to have my help whether or not you want it. If you do not permit Kenton and me to ride with you, we will simply follow you at a distance, so you may as well accept our presence whether or not you want it."

Atticus was genuinely annoyed at the man. "Kenton must remain in command of Northumberland," he said. "He is needed here."

"You have Tertius to command Northumberland. He is competent."

"Aye, he is, but Kenton technically outranks him. And *I* command le Bec, not you."

"That is true, but in matters of rank, I outrank *you* and I have ordered Kenton to go to Wolfe's Lair."

Atticus sighed heavily and shoved the remainder of his beef into his mouth. What Warenne said was true and Atticus could see that his argument was at an end. There was nothing more he could say and his frustration was evident. "If you were not an earl, and a de Winter, I might tell you what I really think of you," he muttered.

Warenne was thrilled that Atticus wasn't fighting him on the matter any longer, or worse, actually fighting him off with weapons. He knew Atticus well and knew the man wasn't beyond brandishing a weapon when provoked. Warenne wasn't afraid to push the man, mostly because of his entitlement – he knew Atticus would respect that above all else.

Still, he felt very strongly that he needed to accompany Atticus on his quest for revenge and he'd pulled Kenton le Bec in on his plans. As good as Atticus was, and he was among the best, Kenton was possibly even better in combat by sheer strength and size alone. He was a monster with a sword and that was what Warenne wanted for Atticus should the need arise. The men who had murdered Titus were certainly not to be underestimated.

"You may tell me someday what you think of me when all of this is through," Warenne said. "But if you insult me too badly, I may have to punish you."

Atticus gave him a half-grin as he drained what was left in his cup. "With the mighty Lespada?"

"My heirloom sword has killed more men than you have."

"Of that, I have no doubt. But it is very old and I do not think you should be using it in battle. I have told you that before. It should be put in a place of honor and retired."

"Lespada is the sword of my forefathers. I carry it and no other."

Atticus chuckled, thinking on the very old but beautifully crafted sword that was carried by every first born male in the de Winter family. *Lespada* was a legend all throughout England, in fact, and it had belonged to Warenne since nine years of age when his father had died. He'd hardly been without it.

"I appreciate the tradition, of course," Atticus said. "But when I punish de la Londe and de Troiu, it will be with my brother's weapon and not yours. From now on, I carry Titus' sword and no other. That way, my brother is still with me. When I punish those two traitors, it will be with Titus' blade."

Warenne sobered somewhat. "That is fitting," he said. "You honor Titus in your actions; killing his murderers with Titus' sword. Marrying Titus' wife. When is the wedding, by the way?"

Atticus' frustration returned and he rolled his eyes, standing up from the table. "After I bury my brother," he said. "Can I not even put the man in the ground first before I claim his widow?"

Warenne stood up with him. "Of course you can," he said. "But remember what I said. Marry her quickly. The more you delay, the more the possibility that you will never wed the woman, and that is not what Titus would want. Atticus, you must understand that I only have your best interests at heart. It is as I have said before – if you do not marry his widow as you promised, you will forever lament the fact that you did not fulfill your brother's dying request. You would not be able to live with yourself. So you must marry her very soon. I am going to make sure that you do."

Atticus knew that. He knew that Warenne was only trying to be a good friend. He scratched his neck. "You should know that Lady de Wolfe and I have had a pleasant conversation last night before she took ill. You told me that I should see something in her that my brother loved."

Warenne was encouraged. "And?"

Atticus shrugged. "And… and I might have seen a glimpse of it. It is possible."

Warenne simply grinned. "That is good to know, Atticus. Mayhap there is hope, after all."

Atticus didn't say anything, mostly because he didn't know what to say to that. He was embarrassed to have admitted as much as he had. But he knew his secret was safe with Warenne.

Together, they quit the hall and met up with the knights out in the knight's quarters, a stone outbuilding that had been built into the inner wall of Alnwick. Thoughts shifted from Lady de Wolfe to those of the status of Alnwick and its future in the hands of the Percy family. Atticus reiterated the fact that he believed Edward would demand the surrender of the castle so, with the new Earl of Northumberland present at the meeting, they made plans to abandon Alnwick and move the inhabitants to Warkworth Castle that the Percy family also owned. A massive castle along the coast wasn't considered particularly strategic and plans were made to move there.

Satisfied that the future of the Earl of Northumberland was mapped out, and leaving Tertius in command of its once mighty army, Atticus was better able to focus on returning Titus home for burial and on the quest for justice he now faced. After the meeting with his knights, he found himself standing at the wagon where Titus' body was placed, now properly housed in an oak casket that the castle craftsmen had made for it, telling his brother of the plans they had made for Alnwick. He didn't know why he did it, only that it was habit with him to discuss everything with Titus, but it seemed somewhat unsatisfying speaking to a wooden box. Still, he spoke to it, knowing that wherever Titus was, he heard him.

With business concluded, there was no more time for delays. Atticus sent word up to Lady de Wolfe of their imminent departure for Wolfe's Lair and was mildly surprised when capcases began arriving down to the inner ward almost immediately. Evidently, the woman had already been informed of his plans. But he was also mildly perturbed that no less than seven capcases had been brought down, all of them stacked on the wagon next to Titus' body. It was fitting considering it had been Titus who had bought so much for his new wife and Atticus found himself laughing at his brother's expense, for now the man was surrounded by women's finery in death.

Perhaps it served Titus right to spoil the woman so but, in some small way, Atticus could understand why he would spoil her. When Lady de Wolfe finally emerged from the keep dressed in a beautiful, blue surcoat with a matching fur cloak, her hair arranged in a lovely style and some color to her cheeks, Atticus could understand a great deal of Titus' infatuation with the woman.

He found that he couldn't take his eyes off her, either.

CHAPTER SIX

> Ionian scale in C – Lyrics to My Sweetest Heart
>
> My sweetest heart... my lovely heart.
> The years will come... the years will go...
> But still you'll be... my own true love...
> Until the day... we'll meet again...
>
> —Iseobeau de Shera de Wolfe, 15th c.

THE FIRST DAY of travel had been marred by melting snow, muddy roads, and great, brisk winds that blew off the sea several miles to the east. It kicked up the mud and puddled water, spraying it up onto their legs as the party from Alnwick made their way towards the borders between England and Scotland and Wolfe's Lair.

Isobeau had heard of Wolfe's Lair enough from Titus, the compact castle along the borders that had belonged to the de Wolfe family for over one hundred years. Castle Questing, the main seat of the de Wolfes, was further to the north and Wolfe's Lair, whose real name was Rule Water Castle, was actually a garrison that had held a long stretch of the borders for many years. Solomon de Wolfe, the younger brother of the seated Baron Killham and current occupant of Castle Questing, had been a fierce fighter in his younger years. Much like Atticus, the younger brother had earned himself something of a reputation over the older brother.

Of course, Isobeau had heard all of this from Titus. It had been clear from the first day they'd met that Titus adored his younger brother. Never did Isobeau sense any brotherly rivalry. With Titus, it had always been respect and adoration when speaking of Atticus. He seemed quite proud that his younger brother had earned himself such a reputation at a young age which, Isobeau had discovered, had started several years ago when Atticus had fought for the Duke of Somerset in Normandy. The very strong, very skilled young knight had made a name for himself fighting the French but when he returned home and swore allegiance to Northumberland, where his brother served, his reputation as a fierce warrior gained footing. He was a de Wolfe, after all, and the de Wolfes were known to be fierce fighters against the Scots but, in Atticus' case, his reputation also extended to the Yorkists and the civil wars that wracked the country.

On the first day of travel, in fact, the Earl of Thetford was more than happy to tell Isobeau all he knew about Atticus and the origins of the man's reputation as The Lion of the North. Isobeau listened politely as the earl told her how fabulous and heroic Atticus was but she eventually began to suspect that Atticus must have put the earl up to it. Perhaps the man was trying to make Atticus more appealing to her, as a future husband, but the truth was that he didn't have to make Atticus attractive at all. Isobeau's opinion of him was already favorable for the most part.

She could see him at the head of their small group, riding a big, heavy-boned, black warmblood that had belonged to the previous Earl of Northumberland. Since Atticus' charger died at Towton, Lady Percy had given Atticus the horse with her blessing. As Thetford prattled on about some battle a few years before where Atticus had been particularly brilliant, Isobeau's mind wandered to the parting at Alnwick earlier that day and how stoic Lady Percy had been. Her women, ladies-in-waiting who were rather flighty and silly, had wept openly but Lady Percy had been a paragon of strength. Her life had changed forever yet she had still been gracious and resigned. Isobeau had admired that the day before, in the hall with the wounded, and she had admired it more that morning. She, too, wanted to be a lady like that someday.

Her farewells to Tertius that morning had been of the hugging variety when her brother had brought forth her precious mare from the stables, the one Titus had given her. Although Tertius had expressed regret at not being able to accompany her to Wolfe's Lair, Isobeau knew it wasn't exactly the truth. She was quite certain that Tertius, who had always looked at Atticus as a rival, was thrilled that he was finally in charge of Northumberland's army whilst Atticus was off conducting his own business. Tertius liked power and he liked control, although not in an evil sense. He simply liked to be in charge and he viewed anyone else who liked to be in charge, or who was in charge, as competition. Under any circumstances, he always felt himself the best man for the job.

Therefore, she hugged her brother farewell and proceeded to follow Atticus, the Earl of Thetford, Kenton le Bec, ten Thetford men-at-arms, and a wagon bearing her capcases and husband's coffin out of Alnwick. Thetford's army followed them out, heading south and being led by the earl's three big knights, men that she'd heard Atticus call Trouble, More Trouble, and Lucifer's Brother. Thetford had laughed at that whilst the three knights had departed on the road south without knowing what Atticus had called them. But Thetford had laughed uproariously and even Kenton, perpetually stone-faced, had cracked a smile.

As they travelled down the road now beneath pewter skies, Isobeau's gaze lingered on her husband's brother at the head of the column as Thetford chatted about a particular incident at some bridge where Atticus had held off a charge of hundreds of men with only a few dozen soldiers. In all, Isobeau was coming to see that Atticus was something of a mythical god when it came to warfare. She only wished he had been omnipotent enough to save his brother when the man had needed it. She was certain Atticus had wished that also.

Because they had gotten off to a late start that morning, they traveled until well after sunset in order to make up for lost time. The weather, although mostly clear, remained cold and windy but Isobeau was very warm in her heavy cloak and gloves. The traveling hadn't bothered her at all until the latter part of the day when her lower back began to ache. She spent the next two hours trying to stretch it out as they plodded along. Furthermore, they were delayed at least three times when the wagon became stuck in a rut or a mud puddle, and everyone would rush to push it out. The roads were truly atrocious because of the mud and melting snow, so their progress had been slow.

They reached the fairly large village of Rothsburg later in the night, one that had a tavern right in the middle of the town that seemed to be the busiest place on earth. As their party rode up wearily, stopping in front of the tavern, Atticus went inside to secure lodgings while Kenton took the men-at-arms and the wagon to the livery they'd seen on the edge of town as they'd entered. As Atticus disappeared into the tavern with the poorly painted sign over the door proclaiming the Crown and Gull Inn, Thetford went to help Isobeau from her mare.

She gratefully accepted his help, sliding into his arms as he lowered her to the ground. But the ground was muddy, and smelled of piss, and she quickly gathered her skirts so they wouldn't drag in the rancid mud. Thetford, seeing that she was desperately trying to preserve her clothing, lifted the back of her fine cloak so it would remain unsoiled.

"Shall we go inside, Lady de Wolfe?" he asked her.

Isobeau was eager to get out of the cold and mud. She followed Thetford into the front door of the inn, smacked in the face by the musty, smelly warmth of the common room. It was very crowded, and loud, and the hearth billowed smoke into the room where it gathered near the ceiling in a blue haze.

Atticus was nowhere to be seen once they entered the establishment so Thetford took Isobeau politely by the arm and found a tiny table crowded next to the corner of the front window for her. They soon realized why it was empty, because there was a terrible frigid draft from the window, but Isobeau was so glad to be sitting on something that wasn't moving that she waved Thetford off when he offered to find her another table. In fact, Isobeau didn't find the table bad at all. It was away from the bustle of the room and she found that inviting.

"This is quite acceptable, truly, my lord," she told him. "In fact, if I stuff my gloves into the hole in the window, the draft will be gone."

The earl smiled at a woman who would not complain about an uncomfortable table. "As you say, Lady de Wolfe," he said. "But it would be no trouble to find you another table."

Again, Isobeau shook her head. "I am quite comfortable, my lord."

Thetford didn't argue with her. He looked around for another chair, snatching one from the table next to them that wasn't being used. He put it next to hers but did not sit; instead, he was looking around to see if he could locate Atticus.

"Will you please do me a favor, Lady de Wolfe?" he asked as his gaze sought out the knight.

Isobeau looked up from pulling off her gloves. "Anything, my lord."

He glanced at her. "I would be honored if you would call me Warenne," he said. "We have traveled an entire day together, after all. I believe we know each other well enough to not be so formal."

Isobeau offered a weak smile. "Of course," she said. "I would be honored. You may address me as Isobeau if you choose."

Warenne dipped his head graciously. "Thank you, my lady," he said, his attention soon turning to the room. "I am sure Atticus is securing food and drink for you. Is there anything else I can do to see to your comfort?"

Isobeau shook her head, covering her mouth to stifle a yawn." Nay," she said. "Thank you very much, however. You have been most kind since we left Alnwick."

Warenne smiled and pulled the empty chair towards him, sitting. "It has been an honor," he said. "Besides, if my wife was traveling away from me with some strange earl for company, I should hope he would be just as polite."

Isobeau's smile warmed. "You are married, then?"

He nodded. "Indeed," he said. "We have been married three years. My wife bore twin girls two years ago and is currently pregnant with our third child. I am praying it is a boy because two little girls have been a chaotic and rather noisy experience."

Isobeau laughed softly. "And you think a boy will not be?"

He shrugged. "I am willing to hope. It will be a boy, after all."

Isobeau shook her head at his optimism, grinning. "Then I wish you luck," she said. "And your wife? What does she think? Does she hope for a son, also?"

Warenne nodded. "My hopes are her hopes," he said rather imperiously, laughing when he saw the look on her face. He sobered. "I jest. Whatever my wife wishes is my wish also. She wishes for a healthy son; therefore, I do as well."

Isobeau wished for the same thing, knowing that Titus' wish would have been her own. At that moment, she wished more than anything that she was sitting with Titus, reveling in the joy of their impending child. It occurred to her that she never had the chance to tell him, fainting as she did the moment she saw his sunken, green face. It had been so ridiculous of her to do that. Sadness swept her and tears stung her eyes, thinking that instead of rejoicing over a baby, Titus was lying cold and dead in a hard, oak box. It just wasn't fair. Distracted with thoughts of her husband, she forced herself to answer the earl.

"I am sure a healthy son will be born to the House of de Winter," she said, trying not to sound too sad or disinterested. "You must return home soon so you do not miss the birth."

Warenne nodded, thinking on his wife, the lovely Madeleine Summerlin de Winter, when they both caught sight of Atticus as the man suddenly appeared at the far end of the room. He emerged from the kitchen into the smoke-filled chamber followed closely by two serving wenches bearing trays of food and drink. Warenne rose to his feet as Atticus approached.

"Ah," he said with approval as he noted all of the food. "A feast fit for a very hungry lady."

Atticus immediately noticed that the table Isobeau was sitting at was far too small for four people, as there would soon be when Kenton returned. Since there was only a lone man sitting at a much bigger table nearby, Atticus swapped out tables with the man and presented a larger and more appropriate table for their party. When the tables were finally situated and the food was set out, Warenne begged a momentary leave.

"I will return shortly," he told Atticus. "I must see to my horse and Lady de Wolfe's horse. They are outside in this icy weather and must be tended to."

Atticus shook his head. "I will do it," he said. "Sit and enjoy your meal."

Warenne waved him off. "You have not spoken with Lady de Wolfe all day," he insisted. "Sit and eat. I will tend to the animals and return as soon as I can."

Before Atticus could further protest, Warenne was already across the room and out the door. With a heavy sigh, one at the man's swift disappearance, Atticus sat in the chair the man had vacated.

"It is not appropriate that an earl should tend to his own horse much less tend to yours," he said, eyeing Isobeau as he began to cut into a large loaf of cream-colored bread. "He should have let me do it."

Isobeau was watching him as he cut the bread and placed a thick slice in front of her; she still wasn't over thoughts of Titus and the son he didn't know about. "He seems like a very kind man," she said. "He has been great company today."

Atticus moved on from the loaf of bread and began to cut hunks of meat from a boiled beef bone. "Thetford and I have been friends for many years," he said. "We fostered together, years ago. He is a good man."

"Did he foster with Titus, too?"

"Aye."

Isobeau thought's lingered on Atticus and Warenne and Titus, all of them fostering together, sharing adventures together. Then she thought again of her husband lying cold and alone in a strange stable, without any companionship now whatsoever. It was wrong that a man so loved was now so alone in death. She gazed at the food he was putting on her trencher without much enthusiasm.

"Where did everyone go?" she asked. "The wagon and Titus and my things. Where did they go?"

Atticus pointed in the general direction of the street with his knife. "We saw a livery at the southern edge of town," he replied. "Kenton has taken them there. He will have the men bring your trunks here, although I cannot see a need for all seven."

There was disapproval in his tone. Uncomfortable and sad, and with an aching back, Isobeau was increasingly aware that she needed to relieve herself, as they'd not stopped since leaving Alnwick that morning. More than that, she now knew where Titus was. She had to go to him, to tell him of their child and to make sure he wasn't alone. It wasn't fair that he didn't know what everyone else did and it certainly wasn't fair that he was alone. Eyeing Atticus, Isobeau knew he wouldn't let her go to him. He would make excuses to keep her from him, or worse, he would tell her that it was not her right.

Therefore, she had to get away from Atticus if only for a precious few minutes. As Atticus continued to dole out food, she stood up.

"Do you know where the privy is?" she asked.

Atticus stood up as well, knife still in hand. "I do not," he said. "But I will find out."

Isobeau waved him off; she was already moving away from the table. "I will ask one of the wenches."

Atticus wasn't so apt to let her go alone; he followed. "You will not travel by yourself, madam," he told her. "I will escort you."

Isobeau came to an irritated halt and faced him. "There are some things that women need to do in private," she said. "This is one of those things. I am sure the privy is out back and there are plenty of people about, so nothing will happen. I will scream if I need you."

Atticus wasn't swayed by the clipped tone. "I will escort you."

He took her by the arm but she pulled from his grasp and charged on ahead, asking directions to the privy from the first serving wench she came across. The woman pointed to the rear yard where there were animals and other implements used to run a tavern. Isobeau headed for the back door with Atticus on her heels but before she crossed into the cold, muddy yard beyond, she turned to him and held a hand out.

"Please," she said quietly but firmly. "I will tend to this alone. I ask that you return to the table and eat your meal. I promise I will yell if I need you."

Atticus was unhappy but he wasn't accustomed to not granting a lady's wishes. He looked around the yard outside, only seeing animals milling about, and a shack with a trench dug beneath it that dumped out into a stream that ran behind the tavern. He even went so far as to go out into the yard and throw open the door to the privy only to be greeted by a horrifically smelling hole in the ground with a hollowed-out stool poised over it. Satisfied there were no dangers lurking about, he went back into the tavern.

"Go on," he told her. "But if you are not back in two minutes, I will come looking for you."

Isobeau didn't reply. She slipped out into the dark, muddy yard and ran for the privy, slamming the door. It didn't take long for her to relieve herself, and use a nearby bucket of water to wash with, but when she was ready to leave, she barely opened the privy door to see if Atticus was still standing at the back door of the tavern. She didn't see him but she knew there was every possibility he was lurking about, waiting for her.

But she didn't want to go back into the tavern, not at the moment. She wanted to find Titus and tell him what she had not had the opportunity to tell him, what her fainting spell yesterday had prevented. She wanted to spend a moment with him. A brief moment was all she wanted, a last moment with her husband before they put him in the ground forever.

In the darkness, she dashed out of the yard gate and into the street beyond.

WARENNE RETURNED TO the tavern to find the entire structure in chaos.

People were running from the building as if the devil himself were inside, demanding their souls, and the closer he came, the more he could hear yelling and banging about. Curious, and on guard, he unsheathed the sword at his side, the sword of his forefathers, *Lespada*. The ancient blade glimmered wickedly in the weak light as he stepped into the tavern, expecting a fight.

The first thing he saw was an empty room. Chairs were tipped over, meals half-eaten, and ale was spilled out over the floor. The dogs who usually congregated by the hearth were happy as larks as they wandered around the room, eating off vacated tables. Cautiously moving further into the common room, Warenne could see three serving wenches clustered in the back of the room near the kitchens as the tavern keeper hovered near them, evidently fearful of someone Warenne couldn't quite see.

There was a great deal of banging and crashing going on just out of his line of sight, back in the kitchens. As Warenne approached, on guard, Atticus suddenly appeared, sword in hand and a large pitcher of something liquid in the other. He hurled the pitcher across the room, smashing it against the wall on the other side and spraying wine everywhere.

"Do you understand that the next thing I throw across this room will be you?" Atticus bellowed. "If you do not tell me where she is, you will not have a tavern left when I am finished. Is that in any way unclear?"

Shocked, Warenne rushed forward. "Atticus!" he gasped. "What has happened? What are you doing?"

Atticus glanced at Warenne but his gaze quickly returned to the tavern keeper and the three wenches, who were, by now, huddled and weeping.

"Lady de Wolfe went to the privy a short time ago," he said, his eyes riveted to the employees of the tavern. "She never made it back inside the tavern. I checked the yard and the privy myself before she went in, and it was clear of danger, but she has somehow disappeared. I would wager to say that these people know who has taken her and if they do not tell me, I will crack a skull against a wall as easily as cracking that pitcher of wine."

Warenne sheathed *Lespada* immediately. "I know where she is," he said, reaching out to pull Atticus away from the thoroughly terrified people. "I just saw her. Come with me, Atticus, and leave these poor people alone."

Atticus looked at Warenne, shocked. "You just *saw* her?" he demanded. "Where in the hell is she?"

Warenne tugged on him. "With me," he ordered quietly. As he yanked Atticus along, he spoke loudly to the tavern keeper. "I will pay for the damages. It is a misunderstanding. Please make sure our rooms are prepared, as we will return shortly."

Puzzled, enraged, Atticus allowed Warenne to drag him out of the tavern but the moment they hit the muddy road outside, Atticus pulled Warenne to a halt.

"*Where* is she?" he asked, insistent. "The last I saw her was back in the tavern yard."

Warenne reached out and grabbed him again, pulling him along. "She is at the stable where the wagon is housed," he said quietly. "I was there bedding the horses down when she came in. She did not see me as she made her way to the wagon where Titus is. I was going to announce my presence to her but she climbed onto the wagon, sat on the coffin, and began to weep. The poor girl… I simply could not announce myself and embarrass her, so I slipped out through the rear and came to find you."

Atticus looked at the man at first with puzzlement but then with great relief. But that relief was quickly replaced by anger.

"She should not have run away," he said. "I thought she knew better than to run off. If she wanted to see Titus, why did she not ask me?"

"How did she know where Titus was?"

Atticus lifted his eyebrows at the foolish answer he was about to give. "She asked me earlier."

Warenne gave Atticus a long look. "You did not take her?"

"Nay. She did not ask."

Warenne sighed. "Atticus, forgive me, but it seems to me as if you have been incredibly selfish with regard to Titus," he said. "You treat that woman as if she has no rights to your brother at all. You said that Titus loved her. Do you think he would appreciate the fact that you have treated his wife with such disregard?"

Atticus was trying not to feel guilty as they crossed the last of the muddy road and ended up on mashed, frozen grass. The livery was in the near distance with the de Wolfe escort party milling around the livery yard near a cooking fire.

"I have not treated her with disregard," Atticus said, feeling as if he were defending himself. "I have been polite when the situation called for it."

Warenne sighed, shaking his head. "She was your brother's wife," he said, sounding disgusted. "You told me you may have seen a flicker of what your brother loved in her yet you continue to treat her poorly. I am ashamed of you, Atticus. This poor woman felt she had to slip away to see her husband because you would not take her to him. Is that truly what kind of a man you are? I would never have guessed it but your actions have thus far proven otherwise."

They had entered the livery yard by now and Atticus was feeling fairly well disgusted with himself, too. Hearing his behavior through Warenne's eyes made him think that perhaps he'd not been as benevolent and kind to Isobeau as he thought he'd been. Perhaps he had been selfish with his brother and hadn't even realized it. But he knew it wasn't because he had disdain for Isobeau; in fact, just the opposite. When he realized she was missing, he'd experienced fear such as he'd never known. He was still feeling the fear.

Through the small ventilation window of the livery he could just see the top of Isobeau's blond head; she was still up in the wagon. He couldn't hear her and she didn't seem to be moving around, but the sight of her was enough to make him realize what an idiot he'd been. Maybe he really had treated her poorly because he didn't feel as if she had a claim on grief for Titus. He was wrong; he knew he was wrong. Heart full of sorrow, he turned to Warenne.

"I never meant to treat her poorly," he said quietly. "Mayhap…

mayhap in a sense you are correct. I was being selfish with Titus, as if I am the only one who has claim to grieve for him. She does, too. I could see how enamored she and Titus were when he was alive. Mayhap… mayhap there is some jealousy there as well, that it was no longer simply me and Titus anymore. Isobeau was introduced into our lives and for the first time in his life, Titus was focus on something other than our common goals. It was terrible of me, I know. So what do I do?"

Warenne wasn't really angry at Atticus; he simply wanted the man to think about Isobeau and stop thinking about himself. He patted Atticus on the side of the head.

"Go in to that livery and apologize to her," Warenne said quietly. "Apologize for being selfish and terrible. Marry the woman tonight and make her happy as Titus wanted you to. If you truly want to honor your brother's memory, that is what you will do."

Atticus nodded, resigned. "I will," he muttered. "She wants to go with me when I seek out de la Londe and de Troiu, too. She accused me of being selfish about that, too. She said I acted as if I were the only one allowed vengeance in Titus' death."

Warenne shrugged. "You do act that way," he replied. "But fortunately, I did not listen to you. I will say this, however – just as you are allowed your vengeance, so is Isobeau. She has as much right to vengeance as you do. More, even. She was Titus' wife."

"Then you believe I should take her with me?"

Warenne lifted his eyebrows thoughtfully, perhaps indecisively. "I think you should consider it," he said. "She may resent you otherwise, for the rest of your life. I do not think you want that, do you?"

Atticus shook his head. "Nay," he confirmed. His gaze moved to the livery again; Isobeau's head had disappeared in the window. "But a quest for vengeance is no place for a woman. She may be hurt, or worse. Moreover, she is with child – Titus' child. How can I risk her and the child like that?"

Warenne shook his head. "Believe it or not, there are midwives all over England who can deliver a child when the time comes," he said sarcastically. Then, he grasped Atticus by the arm, his gaze intense. "She will not be hurt. Kenton and I will be there to aid you. We will also protect her. Stop treating his woman as if she does not matter, Atticus; she mattered to Titus a great deal. She has every right to mourn for him and she has every right to seek vengeance regardless of the fact that she is with child. I admire her strength for wanting to do so and you should, too."

Atticus knew he was correct. About everything, he was correct. No more protests, no more excuses. With a sigh, he turned away from Warenne and headed towards the livery.

"As you say," he said, sounding weary. "I will see if I can undo what I have done."

With Atticus in the lead, Warenne followed. The stable yard was mucky and slippery as they made their way to the wide entry door. Just as they reached it, Atticus came to a sudden halt and when Warenne opened his mouth to ask him why, Atticus shushed him. He gestured to the interior of the livery where there was some whispering and weeping going on. Not wanting to intrude, Atticus peered around the side of the entry door to hear better of what was happening inside that cold, dark structure.

"... and then she threw me!" Isobeau was saying, giggling. "Do not feel bad for it; I know you gave me the horse but it was my fault for not holding on tightly enough. She had been corralled in the barn since the big snow back in February, right after you left, and she was quite happy to be out. She was very frisky. I am riding her even now as we head to Wolfe's Lair. I am quite excited to meet your father, you know; I just wish... well, it does not matter. You are going home, Titus. Atticus is making sure of it. He is making sure of everything. He will punish those men who killed you. I only hope he does it with your sword... I do not know where it is but I shall ask Atticus. I am sure he knows. I hope he kills those men with your sword and that he then, in turn, passes your sword to our son. It would be such a great honor for our son to carry your sword. And that's another thing; what are we to name him? Tertius says I must name him a Roman name or my father will disown me."

She set off giggling again, stroking the lid of the casket lovingly as Atticus and Warenne watched. Isobeau was no longer sitting on the casket, she now knelt beside it. Her hands were all over it, touching it, speaking to Titus inside. As they watched, it looked as if she thought to lift the lid so she could look at Titus once more but she stopped herself. Defeated, she laid her forehead against the edge of the coffin lid.

She lifted her head. "I miss you so much," she whispered, her tone now very serious in contrast from the giggling that had been going on earlier. "I can still hear your voice and I can still see your smile as you waved farewell to me those months ago. You told me you loved me and I was too foolish to say it in return. I should have; God knows, I should have. Titus, I swear that if I had known you would not return to me, I would have never let you go. I would have found some way to keep you at Alnwick. It is not fair that we did not have a chance at a life together; it is not fair at all. And your brother... he says that you asked him to marry me and to take care of me. I am sure it was a noble thought, my love, but I must tell you that your brother wants nothing to do with me. I am afraid you have doomed us both to a sad and unhappy life with one another. It is therefore my intention to tell him that I release him from your request. Surely you did not mean to make him so miserable, Titus. It was selfish of you to ask. I know you do not want me to marry anyone else and I swear that I shan't. When we reach Wolfe's Lair, I will find the nearest church and tell the priest of my situation and beg that he admit me to the nearest convent. I will become a bride of

Christ. I would rather do that than marry anyone else."

With that, she trailed off and laid her head back on the coffin lid, simply laying there and perhaps dreaming of a life that would never be. Atticus, filled with sorrow and regret, turned to look at Warenne, who was gazing back at him with equal sorrow. They had both heard what Isobeau had said, now knowing what was in the lady's heart. It was tragic to say the least.

"That is not what Titus wanted," Warenne whispered. "You must speak with her, Atticus, *now*."

Atticus didn't hesitate. He went straight into the livery, leaving Warenne outside, and approached the wagon where Isobeau lay with the top part of her body across the coffin lid. She didn't hear him enter so he cleared his throat softly as he approached simply to warn her that she was no longer alone.

Isobeau's head shot up when she heard him, her eyes big on him. There was guilt and fear across her features as Atticus came to stand next to the wagon bed. For a moment, neither of them spoke; they simply stared at one another. Isobeau kept waiting for the man to explode at her but, so far, he'd given no indication he planned to. His expression was surprisingly calm, considering she had run off and lied to him. Maybe he was so calm because he was beyond fury and had terrible things planned for her punishment. Nervously, she cleared her throat.

"Sir Atticus," she stammered. "I... I did not mean to cause you any undue concern by leaving the tavern, but I felt compelled to...."

Atticus put up a hand, cutting her off. "You need not explain," he said quietly. "I am not angry. In fact, it seems as if I owe you a wide measure of apology, my lady. It occurred to me when you felt compelled to steal away to come and see my brother that I have not been very kind to you. For you to have to feel as if the only way to see Titus was to escape me, I have been a terrible man indeed."

Isobeau blinked, surprised by his reaction. "I... I simply wanted a few minutes alone with him," she said. "When you gave me the opportunity to see him back at Alnwick, I fainted. I have not spoken to my husband at all and I wanted to tell him of the child. And of other things. I think I told him everything that has happened at Alnwick since he left. I thought he would want to know."

She was tearing up by the time she finished, lowering her head and sniffling so he could not see her watery eyes. But Atticus knew she was weeping; he was coming to feel worse and worse about the way he'd treated her, especially after hearing what she had told Titus. There had been such joy in her words at first, and finally such sorrow. Was he really such a monster? Warenne had warned him of his behavior and now the words from Isobeau had suggested the same thing. Maybe he had been as selfish as they'd accused him of being. With a heavy sigh, he scratched his scalp wearily and sat on the edge of the wagon bed.

"He would want to know," he agreed with her, having difficulty looking the woman in the eye. "My lady, if I have been selfish and rude and terrible, then I apologize. I begged your forgiveness once but it seems as if I have not amended my ways. That will end, now. You do, indeed, have the right to grieve my brother and you do, indeed, have a right to your own sense of vengeance towards those who caused his death. I promised my brother I would marry you and I shall, and I hope to make as excellent a husband as Titus did. I shall endeavor to do so. I pray that you will accept my proposal of marriage and know that the man you have seen over the past two days is not indicative of the man I am. Grief can do odd things to one's soul. I am sorry you bore the brunt of it."

By this time, Isobeau was listening to him quite seriously, wiping tears from her eyes. "I do not know what to say, in truth," she said. "I told you that I do not want another husband. Titus should not have expected, nor have asked, us to wed."

Atticus grunted, leaning forward on the wagon. "I thought so, too," he said. "But then I tried to look at it from Titus' perspective. Actually, someone else made me look at it from Titus' perspective – if I had a wife I loved very much, it would be my first priority to ensure she was well taken care of. If the roles had been reversed, I am sure I would have begged Titus the same thing."

Isobeau regarded him carefully. There was some indecision in her expression now, as if she hadn't thought on Titus' standpoint until this moment. After a pause of deliberation, of reflection, her gaze moved to the coffin she was leaning against.

"He should not have asked you such things," she said quietly. "Sir Atticus, I release you from your vow to Titus. I know you do not wish to marry me and I do not wish to have another husband, so it is my intention to commit myself to a convent near to the place where Titus is buried. That way, I can visit him sometimes."

Atticus already knew of her plan considering he had overheard her earlier, so he had already planned out his reply. He was careful yet truthful.

"My lady, if you commit yourself to a convent, it would not be in your best interest or in the child's best interest," he said. "As soon as the baby is born, it will be taken away from you and turned over to a family to foster. Did you think you would be able to keep your son with you? They will not allow it in the convent."

She frowned. "Surely they would not separate a mother from her child."

He shrugged. "You would not be a mother," he said. "You would be a bride of Christ. Brides do not have babies."

Evidently, the thought of being separated from her child had not occurred to her and she was visibly distressed. "I will *not* let them take my child," she said flatly. "I would kill them if they tried."

He looked at her; she had such a delicate face with a little upturned nose, wide eyes, and beautifully arched brows. More than that, she had lips that were ripe and lush, inviting a man's lust. She was quite a ravishing creature, as he'd always noticed, but perhaps now he was noticing just a little more. She was an invariably strong woman, unafraid to stand up to him and unafraid to speak her mind.

So many pieces of a puzzle were coming together as he looked at her, disjointed pieces of the Isobeau puzzle that had been orbiting in his mind, things he realized about her but had never pulled together as a whole picture. He remembered the first time he ever saw her, telling his brother what a fortunate man he was to have such a beautiful bride. But after the wedding, he hadn't spent any amount of time around Isobeau because Titus occupied all of her time, as he should have. But in the past two days, they had been thrown together in unpleasant circumstances that would have destroyed a lesser woman. Isobeau had stood strong through it all. As a result, Atticus was coming to think she was fairly extraordinary.

Come to know what Titus liked so well about the woman, Warenne had said. More and more, Atticus could see it. He was finally coming to understand her, one piece at a time.

"As would I, my lady," he said quietly. "No one would take your child from you, my brother's child, and live to tell the tale, so it is my suggestion that you forget about the convent and marry me instead. If you do not, I fear I am in for something quite terrible. You would actually be doing me quite a favor."

Isobeau was still frowning as thoughts of baby-stealing nuns filled her mind. "Why?" she asked. "Whatever is the matter?"

Atticus averted his gaze, leaning against his brother's coffin and picking at the imperfections of the wood.

"I have... well, it is quite embarrassing to admit it, but I have women that follow me about," he said seriously, although he wasn't serious in the least. "Do you have any idea what a prize I would be to any woman? Not only am I a de Wolfe, but I have earned a reputation for myself as a warrior above men. I have some wealth, of course, but every father with an eligible daughter from Newcastle to Hastings is clamoring after me, demanding I wed their daughters. And *what* daughters! Fat, short, skinny, tall, in all varieties and shapes. The Earl of Dorcester, for instance, has *two* daughters and has demanded I pick one. The man has promised me half of Dorset if I do but in order to obtain such wealth, I have to choose between a woman with a mustache and her sister with no neck and a bald spot on her head. What am I to do?"

Isobeau forgot about baby-stealing nuns and was grinning at Atticus' distress. He was, in fact, pretending to be quite upset, but Isobeau sensed that he was mostly acting for her benefit. It was quite humorous, actually, because she had no idea that the man had such a personality. She had only seen him serious or angry, or both, so this comical side was unexpected. It was also attractive. She clucked sadly.

"That is truly a shame, Sir Atticus," she said with feigned concern. "I would think in such a case, you may want to take the woman with the mustache. She can always shave it off. Mayhap she would not be so bad if she did."

Atticus rolled his eyes, leaning his head against Titus' coffin in mock misery. He hoped his brother was hearing him because they had shared many a laugh over the same subjects, mostly Titus teasing him about the women that really did follow him around. With his striking dark looks and chiseled features, Atticus had more than his share of female admirers.

"Mayhap," he said, his voice muffled because he was leaning against his arm. "She is not unattractive in a way. If only her eyes focused in the same direction, she would be nearly pleasant to look at."

Isobeau put a hand over her mouth to stifle the giggles. "She is cross-eyed?"

"That is putting it kindly."

Isobeau couldn't help the laughter now. She put a hand on the coffin lid and leaned into it. "Titus?" she asked. "Do you hear your brother? He is attempting to coerce me into marriage with tales of cross-eyed maids!"

Atticus' grin broke through and he put his mouth against the coffin lid. "You will confirm whatever I tell her, do you hear?" he told his brother. "Tell her it is true! Tell her of the daughter of the Lord Mayor of Manchester and how the woman sent me gifts for three solid months. Tell her how I had to hide when the woman and her father showed up at Alnwick seeking to negotiate a marriage contract. Tell her how Percy had to entertain them for the night and then he tried to beat me afterwards because they were both terrible creatures with terrible manners. He blamed me for them setting foot in his beloved Alnwick."

Isobeau was giggling uncontrollably. "Lord Henry did *not* beat you."

Atticus nodded firmly. "He most certainly tried," he said. "He even threw a chicken bone at me. He was furious that I had brought those obnoxious people down upon him."

Isobeau was laughing so much that she was struggling to catch her breath. "It was not your fault," she said. "It was not as if you invited them."

Atticus pointed a finger at her. "I did not," he agreed, "but if you do not agree to marry me, I can only look forward to more of the same humiliation. Until and unless I have a wife, these ravenous females will never stop in their quest to acquire me as a prized husband. Therefore, my lady, I beg you… please consider my marriage proposal. It would make Titus happy and it would save me from a lifetime of shame."

For the past several moments, Isobeau had been swept up in Atticus' charm. She had no idea the man possessed such charisma, for he was a gifted and animated storyteller when he put his mind to it. If only this man, this charming and witty man, could be the man she saw from now on and not the bitter and nasty one. It was enough to give her hope that perhaps they could settle into a comfortable relationship with pleasant conversation such as they were having now. She was still torn, still indecisive, but that resistance was barely holding on. Her gaze lingered on the top of the coffin, thinking of the man inside, knowing that she, indeed, wanted to make him happy. And Atticus had a pledge to fulfill.

With a sigh, one of resignation, she finally nodded her head.

"Very well," she said. "If that is truly your wish, I will consent. I suppose you need someone to beat all of those women away from you."

Atticus smiled, one of genuine joy. "You are most gracious, my lady," he said. "But please know that your role in the marriage would be one of honor. I would never expect you to chase foolish women away. I would put you upon a pedestal whilst you watch me do it."

It was a kind thing to say, as if he meant she simply wouldn't be an excuse or a bit of baggage he happened to be tied to. But along with her consent, Isobeau was coming to feel as if a part of her life unfulfilled were slipping away from her, something she wasn't ready to let go. She put her hand on the coffin lid again, realizing she was fighting off tears. Visions of Titus and the last time she saw him alive filled her head.

"You do not need to put me on a pedestal," she said softly, stroking the coffin lid. "Sweet Jesus, this is all happening so quickly. The past few months of my life have been like a dream, so fast and fleeting. I married Titus and came to adore the man and just as quickly he was gone. Now I find myself pledged to you... Atticus, I do not want to forget Titus. I do not want to look back on this time of my life and think I only imagined it. Titus is worth remembering."

The smile was gone from Atticus' face. He, too, put his hand on the coffin lid, feeling the pangs of grief clutch at him. All humor aside, it was a horrible thing that had united them.

"He is worth that and more," he said hoarsely, realizing he had a lump in his throat at her words. "I will tell you something I have not told anyone. As Titus lay dying, he told me how proud he was to be my brother. I... I never got to tell him how proud I was to have been *his* brother. I realize I am the one who has earned the moniker; *The Lion of the North* they call me. I am a prideful man, my lady. I would bask in the adoration of others whilst Titus would stand in my shadow and applaud me just as others were. He never once showed any jealousy or envy. He was the first one to praise me. He was the rock upon which I stood to show my bravery and receive my accolades. But my rock is gone now and I am not entirely sure how I am supposed to go on."

He looked at Isobeau then, tears in his eyes. But she was far ahead of him in that regard; tears were streaming down her face as she felt his pain, deeply, for the very first time. Reaching out, she put a gentle hand on his arm.

"I miss him dreadfully," she whispered, fighting off a sob. "I know we were together for such a short time but in that time, I saw such perfection in him. I wanted to know him as my rock just as you knew him as yours, but that will never come to pass. I envy you your time with him, Atticus. Mayhap... mayhap someday you will tell me of the Titus you knew. Mayhap you will tell my child of his father, as you knew him. I hope you will."

Atticus averted his gaze, blinking back the tears that threatened to spill down his face. He sniffled loudly, struggling to compose himself.

"Of course I will," he said quietly. "I will tell my nephew how his father used to steal coinage from the knights he squired for and how, when caught, he was once put in the stocks for two days. I will also tell him how Titus risked his life to save a young page whose horse became stuck in a quagmire of mud and Titus slithered across the mud to secure a rope to the horse's saddle so we could pull them both free. Titus was both hero and devil, my lady. He was the greatest man I have ever known."

Isobeau wiped at her eyes, smiling faintly at Atticus as the man gazed upon Titus' coffin. In the weak light of the livery, illuminated only by the cooking fire directly outside in the yard, there was something very private and personal about the moment, sharing their common grief and coming to terms with it. Isobeau stroked the coffin one last time.

"I am at peace now," she said softly. "I have told Titus everything I wanted to say and I have a measure of peace. Thank you for giving me these few private moments with him and for not becoming angry that I ran from you."

Atticus touched the coffin lid one last time as well, giving it a pat, before pushing himself away from the wagon. "I was not angry that you ran from me," he said. "But I will admit that when I realized you were gone, I may have upended the tavern a bit. Just a little."

She looked at him, cocking an eyebrow. "A little?"

He shrugged, averting his gaze. "A lot."

Isobeau thought on that. "I see," she said. "Can I assume they will not welcome us back now and that we will be sleeping in the livery along with the animals?"

He cast her a long glance, his eyes twinkling. "Would that upset you?"

She threw up her hands. "Of course not," she said mockingly. "Why sleep in a warm tavern when I can just as easily sleep in a freezing livery stable amongst the pigs? 'Tis every woman's dream, I say. Thank God for Atticus and his ability to provide me with luxuries."

Atticus gave her a half-grin, holding out a hand to her. She was still up on the wagon bed and she took his hand as he carefully helped her off. Her hand was soft and warm in his big, rough palm. He rather liked the feel of it there.

"I am not entirely sure they will not welcome us," he said. "If they do not, I can always upend the tavern again. I will get you a warm bed one way or another, my lady."

She looked at him, drolly. "Perfect."

Atticus laughed softly at the wry expression on her face. As he led her from the livery, he was coming to think that Isobeau's choice to run from the tavern that night had evidently been something of a fortuitous happenstance. It had given them a chance to speak, to be honest with one another, and to bond just a bit more over their common grief.

Come to see what Titus saw in the woman. Those words kept echoing in Atticus' head, words of wisdom that had helped him come to understand the aura and mindset of Isobeau de Shera de Wolfe. What he saw, he was coming to appreciate. He hoped that they would have a warm and civil relationship towards one another in the coming years but he seriously wondered if he would ever stop viewing her as Titus' wife and come to see her as his own. It was a thought he had.

He further wondered if Isobeau would ever stop seeing him as her dead husband's brother and start viewing him as her husband.

Only time would tell.

CHAPTER SEVEN

> Ionian scale in C – Lyrics to I dreamt that you loved me still
>
> I dreamt that you loved me still
> And loved me forever and a day.
> From beyond the mellow sea
> I felt your spirit calling to me
> And I dreamt that you loved me still.
>
> —Isobeau de Shera de Wolfe, 15th c.

Rule Water Castle (known as Wolfe's Lair)

SOLOMON DE WOLFE was a very big man with a great, hairy beard and hands the size of trenchers. He had been dark haired back in his youth but age and ill health had seen his hair turn completely white while his beard was an odd shade of grayish-yellow. He knew the strange color was because his beard was dirty but he didn't care. He took great pride in telling the women of the local village that he ran a bit of hot water through his beard after a long day and made soup out of whatever bits of crumb and meat scraps were caught there. He loved to see the look of disgust on their faces. Much like his sons, Solomon had a wicked sense of humor.

Rule Water Castle hadn't been called by its proper name in decades, ever since the de Wolfe family from nearby Castle Questing had annexed the former Scottish garrison for the de Wolfe barony of Killham. Everyone in Northern England and Southern Scotland knew the place as Wolfe's Lair these days, an extremely fortified fortress that had a very odd look to it.

Much like infamous Hermitage Castle about a half-day's ride south, seat of the terrible de Soulis family, Rule Water Castle was built in much the same design. It was square, box-shaped, and four stories tall. The walls of the keep were also the exterior walls of the fortress, as it had no fortification walls at all. It did, however, have a moat that was fed by a nearby stream, a wide and muck-filled ditch that was at least ten feet wide, probably more in places, and had a retractable wooden bridge that crossed it.

The impression of Wolfe's Lair was one of intimidation. It sat on a flat plain, with rolling hills in the distance, and could been seen for miles. With its sheer, dark walls, it had the look of dread and danger about it. The entrance to the fortress was also much like Hermitage Castle in that it was a Norman arch, two stories tall, and had two enormous gates that had been forged from the strongest iron. These gates were thick, vastly heavy, and impossible to breach once closed.

The great gates protected the interior of the fortress, which included a hollowed-out bailey in the center. The stables, trades, great hall, small chapel, and kitchens were all on the lower level whilst the second level contained sleeping quarters for the soldiers. The third level contained living and sleeping accommodations for the family and the fourth floor was mostly the wall walk, a flat roof over the third floor that spanned the perimeter of the fortress.

Solomon ran Wolfe's Lair like his own personal kingdom. He was a firm man, fair and decisive, and he never backed away from a fight. He had peace with his neighbors for the most part but he wouldn't hesitate to send his garrison out if there was trouble. He had one hundred and twenty-seven men under his command, all of them loyal and seasoned, and Solomon enjoyed his life at Wolfe's Lair for the most part but he found in his later years that his thoughts weren't so much on war any longer as they were on women. There were a few wenches about he would chase and pinch, but that was as far as it went. The last woman he bedded had been his wife, twenty-eight years ago. He wanted that particular coupling to be his last memory of the act. He still missed Rosalie, very much.

Therefore, it was a peaceful kingdom that Solomon ruled and this spring day dawned cold and clear, like any normal day. The guards changed shifts upon the wall walk and at the front gates as Solomon rose and broke his fast with hard cheese and warmed-over stew from the previous meal. He hadn't slept well the night before and his wild hair was wilder, and his beard even more unkempt than usual. A good deal of Wolfe's Lair's function had to do with herds and herds of wooly sheep and as Solomon slurped up his stew, he was coming to think that it was time to assess his older herd, the one that was kept off to the north, to see if it was time to take them into town to discuss selling the wool to the local wool merchant.

But those thoughts of business as usual were interrupted by the sentries on the walls, taking up a cry of an approaching party. Solomon heard the cries but it didn't deter him from his food until a soldier entered and informed him that a wagon and several riders were approaching. He waved the soldier off and proceeded to finish his meal until the same soldier returned and informed him that his son, Atticus, had been sighted. That was enough to get Solomon onto his feet.

"Great Bloody Christ!" he exclaimed. "My sons have come home? Did you see them?"

The soldier was an older man who had served Solomon for many years. He knew how much the old man missed his sons, for it was something Solomon spoke of frequently.

"I saw Sir Atticus, my lord," he grinned. "I did not notice Titus but there are other riders. I am sure he is among them."

Solomon flew into a frenzy. "My clothes!" he bellowed as he raced to a pile of clothing that was over against the wall. He began picking articles of clothing up, inspecting them, sniffing them, and then tossing them aside. "I must dress to see my sons. What is this?

God, this stinks. And so does that. In fact, everything about me smells awful. Where is my soap?"

He was bellowing and the servants who tended the rooms and the hearths on that level began to race around, trying to find Solomon clothing that didn't smell too badly. Solomon wasn't the cleanest man in the world and a couple of minutes of sifting through tunics and torn breeches had them discovering at least one pair that wasn't ripped or stained. Solomon, wearing a worn sleeping robe at this point, pulled his breeches up, struggling to secure them as an old male servant, so old he could hardly move about well, tried to pull the sleeping robe off in order to help Solomon on with his tunic. The elderly servant pulled too hard, Solomon lost his balance, and fell onto his hip.

Angry, Solomon howled as he fastened his breeches and grabbed for the tunic the old servant was trying to give him. He pulled it over his head, rolled heavily to his feet, and began to make his way down to the courtyard with the elderly servant following after him, helping him dress in a fur-lined cloak. By the time Solomon began to descend the stairs into the central courtyard, the great gates of Wolfe's Lair were open and the party was entering the bailey. The first person Solomon recognized was his beloved second son, Atticus.

"Atticus!" he bellowed, waving his arms furiously. "Atticus, you have come home!"

Weary from four days of travel under terrible conditions, Atticus was unshaven and pale as he smiled weakly at his wild-looking father. Riding at the head of the party, he dismounted about the time his father came off the stairs. Arms reaching out to Atticus, Solomon ran as he hadn't run in years. He ran right to Atticus and threw his arms around him.

"My son," he breathed with satisfaction, feeling his brawny son alive and warm in his arms. "I have missed you every day since we last saw one another. How long has it been? At least two years."

Atticus was being squeezed to death by a smelly bear of a man with whiskers like thistles against his cheek. "It has been one year, ten months, and two days," he grunted. "I have missed you, too, Papa. How is your health? Have you been well?"

Solomon let go of Atticus long enough to cup his son's face between his two big hands, inspecting him, reacquainting himself with features that looked much as he had at that age.

"I am well enough," he said. "My joints are worse and some days I cannot walk, but I have good days and for that I am grateful. There is a physic in Hawick who comes and visits me every month. He gives me potions to drink in the hope that something will help, but so far, there is little relief."

Atticus nodded, not surprised to hear that his father's swollen, aching joint condition was not improving. It was the curse of the de Wolfe family and in Solomon's case had been getting steadily worse for years. He reached out and tugged gently on the wild and wooly beard his father was sporting.

"You look like a wild man," he said. "When was the last time you bathed and shaved?"

Solomon chuckled, embarrassed. "There is no one to bathe and shave for," he said. "Why should I?"

Atticus cocked an eyebrow. "Because you may have visitors you want to impress," he said. "Do you think it will please me to have people spread rumors about my father who lives like an animal?"

Solomon was still grinning sheepishly. "I do not live like an animal," he said. "I only look like one. But enough about me; let us speak on the reason for your visit. Why did you not send word ahead? I could have been ready for you."

Some of Atticus' good mood fled as Solomon inquired on the reasons for his visit. "I have come home for many reasons, not the least of which is to introduce someone important to you," he said quietly. "Now you are going to be embarrassed, looking like a barbarian who sleeps with the sheep."

Solomon's eyes widened and he smoothed at his white hair, trying to tame it, which was an impossible task. "Who did you bring?" he demanded. "And where is Titus? Why is he not greeting me?"

Atticus struggled not to tip his father off, to give him a clue as to the dreadful nature behind their visit. He wanted to tell his father about Titus in private but he wasn't entirely sure he would be able to. Solomon de Wolfe was a very sharp man and Atticus knew he had to come out with the truth, and quickly, or it would make matters worse. Solomon would grow suspicious and cause a scene. Moreover, it wasn't fair to put Solomon off, not even to take him to a private location to deliver the news. His father was, if nothing else, a loud and passionate man, and he did not like to be treated as if he were too weak to handle the truth. Atticus had seen that before. Therefore, he braced himself.

"Papa," he said quietly. "There is a great deal to tell you. We did not come simply to visit. I came to bring Titus home."

Solomon's brow furrowed. "Bring Titus home?" he repeated, puzzled. "What do you mean? Where is the man?"

Atticus had spent the past four days trying to figure how, exactly, to tell his father that Titus had been killed. He thought he had a fairly good speech planned but the moment he looked into his father's confused face, he forget everything he was going to say. Suddenly, he was five years old again and looking at his father as a child would. God, he didn't want to tell him. He wished he didn't have to. The pangs of grief began anew and he reached out, grasping his father by the arms.

"There was a very bad battle two weeks ago in a place called Towton," he said as calmly as he could. "It was Henry's forces against Edward's. We lost the battle, Papa, and we lost Titus in the fight. I have brought him home for burial, next to Mother."

It was a simple but straight-forward explanation. Solomon's reaction wasn't delayed; he understood the gist of Atticus' words instantly and had Atticus not been holding on to him, he would have surely collapsed. As it was, Atticus was having a difficult time holding on to his father who had suddenly seemed to lose every bone in his body. The man began to fold.

"Nay," Solomon breathed. "Not Titus. Not my boy."

Atticus nodded, trying to keep his father from collapsing completely. "It is true," he said, tears stinging his eyes at the sight of his father's grief. "I am so terribly sorry, Papa."

Solomon was bent over, holding on to Atticus as if the man could save him from the agony that was pulling him down to the cold, muddy ground.

"It is not possible," Solomon gasped. "Titus was strong… he was too strong for this. How could this happen?"

Atticus wasn't going to tell him that part of the truth. Perhaps later when he was calm, but not now. The knowledge that Titus had been murdered by men he was supposed to trust would have driven Solomon over the edge of sanity.

"Things like this happen in war," he said, holding his father tightly. "Titus was a warrior, the very best, but even the best can be felled. We are but mortal men, after all."

Solomon heard Atticus' words, mingling with the physical pain that was gripping his entire body. He could hardly think or move, images of his eldest son filling his brain.

"Titus," he murmured, closing his eyes as the tears streamed. "My beautiful boy. I cannot believe he is gone. Is it true, Atticus? Is it really true?"

Atticus nodded. "He is here, in the wagon. Would you like to see him?"

The idea of seeing Titus oddly fortified him. Solomon somehow found his legs as Atticus virtually propped him up. The old man's face was pale, his hazel eyes wide with grief, but he nodded his head to Atticus' question.

"Take me to him," he begged, saliva dribbling from his mouth. "Take me to my son."

Atticus had a firm grip on his father as he led him back towards the wagon. As he moved, Atticus caught a glimpse of Isobeau astride her leggy mare; she was watching the entire scene with tears in her eyes. When their eyes met, Isobeau closed her eyes and turned her head away because she knew they were going to open Titus' coffin and she did not wish to see her husband's corpse. The last time she had seen it, days ago, had been bad enough. She most definitely didn't want to see it now but she understood Solomon's desire to see his dead son. He had to reconcile himself with the man's death, no matter how unpleasant the reality was to be.

Atticus felt for Isobeau's sorrow, grief they had all be living with for days, now new and fresh as Solomon was informed of Titus' passing. As Atticus brushed past her, holding on to his father, he managed to brush her foot with his hand in a comforting gesture. When he opened the lid to the coffin and presented his father with Titus' two-week-old corpse, he stood back as Solomon burst into low, mournful sobs. He couldn't even watch; it was simply too painful. Stepping away to allow his father to grieve, he ended up standing next to Isobeau.

Up on the wagon bed, Solomon wasn't prepared for what faced him. Titus didn't much look like he remembered him, healthy and strong; instead, the man was an odd color of purplish-green with sunken features. Reaching into the wooden box, he touched his son's face, weeping, begging him to wake up and speak to him. When Titus didn't obey, Solomon practically climbed into the coffin, collected Titus into his arms, and clutched the man against his chest.

Atticus could no longer look away at that point. His father had Titus half-lifted out of the coffin, sobbing over him, and Isobeau was gasping softly at the horror of it. She'd turned her head slightly at one point to see what Solomon was doing, as she could only hear his sobs, and she had been greeted with her husband's limp body being pulled out of the coffin by his father. Horrified, she quickly turned away, gasping at the grisly and tragic nature of what was going on. It was incredibly sorrowful, on so many levels, the grief of a father who had outlived his son.

"Atticus," Warenne had walked up behind Atticus and was now whispering in the man's ear. "Let me take Isobeau inside. She does not need to see this."

Atticus, tears in his eyes and a vice around his heart, nodded faintly. "Third floor," he told him. "Ask the servants where to put her. Then you will return to me, please. I am not entirely sure I will be able to handle my father alone."

Warenne nodded, turning to motion to Kenton, who was at the rear of the party. When he caught Kenton's attention, he pointed to Atticus and Kenton understood. Warenne wanted the man to remain with Atticus in case the man needed assistance. As Kenton dismounted and made his way to Atticus, Warenne turned to Isobeau.

"Come along, my lady," he said, all but pulling her off the mare. As she slid down into his arms, he set her to her feet. "Let us go inside where it is warm and you may rest."

Weeping softly as she still lingered over the sight of her dead husband being held by his father, Isobeau kept her head down and her eyes averted as Warenne took her towards the flight of stairs that Solomon had come from. It was a flight of narrow stone steps that went up to the third floor, the family apartments, and Warenne stopped the first servant he came to in order to explain his business and seek shelter for Isobeau. The servant quickly took them down a narrow corridor, with thin window that overlooked the courtyard, until they came to a chamber situated at the north side of the fortress.

The servant opened the door, allowing Warenne and Isobeau entrance. The room was surprisingly well lit, with small, narrow windows facing both north and east that provided an ample amount of light into the otherwise very dark chamber. But it was as cold as sin, with a black hearth, and Warenne immediately ordered that a fire be lit.

Isobeau, weary and distressed, wandered into the low-ceilinged chamber and sat at a table that had three sturdy-looking chairs. But that was practically the only furniture in the room other than a narrow bedframe with no mattress on it. Warenne, still standing by the door, was studying the chamber with a critical expression. When the servant who had shown them to the room returned with kindling for the fire, Warenne began barking orders.

"This chamber is a disgrace," he said. "You would truly think to put Titus de Wolfe's wife here? There is no bed, nothing of comfort. Lady de Wolfe requires a bigger bed and a fine mattress stuffed with fresh straw. Where are the rest of the house servants? They must be brought here immediately. I have tasks for them to carry out."

The poor servant was rather harried with Warenne barking at him and he struggled to light the fire and call out to other servants he knew to be nearby. The very old man who was Solomon's Chamberlain came to help but Warenne took one look at the feeble, old man and told him to go find stronger servants. The elderly servant did, and soon there were three men and two women hovering in the corridor, waiting for orders from the man who had introduced himself as the Earl of Thetford. When Warenne saw the crowd in the corridor, he took charge.

"You," he said, pointing to a toothless woman with dark hair and oily skin. "You will assist Lady de Wolfe in whatever she needs. I want a bath sent up to her and food, immediately. And, you –," he pointed to the round woman with rosy cheeks standing next to the toothless servant, "– will make sure that a mattress, free of vermin, is stuffed with fresh straw and delivered to Lady de Wolfe along with clean linens, pillows, and anything else that will make her comfortable. Is this clear? Excellent. Now go about your business."

The women scattered but the men were still standing there and Warenne pointed to them. "You heard what I told them," he said. "Lady de Wolfe requires a bath and a bigger bed with a fresh mattress, so get on with it. Bring it as quickly as you can."

The men fled after the women and Warenne could hear hissing and scuffling going on as they hurried to carry out his orders. Meanwhile, the servant who had originally shown them the room was making progress on a fire in the hearth as Warenne turned in Isobeau's direction, seeing the woman seated at a table, her elbow on the tabletop and her head resting on her propped-up hand. He made his way to her.

"You should have all the comforts that Wolfe's Lair can provide," he told her. "Will you be all right while I return to Atticus? He is concerned over his father and asked me to return to him as soon as I settled you."

Exhausted, Isobeau waved him off. "I will be well on my own," she told him. "Thank you for assisting me. In fact, thank you for being such a comforting travel companion. Your presence has been much appreciated."

Warenne smiled faintly, giving her a gracious bow, before quitting the chamber. Isobeau's attention lingered on the door after he was gone, her weary mind reflecting on the scene down in the bailey. She was trying to forget what she saw, how Solomon cradled Titus' decaying remains, and how tragic it all had been. She was so very weary of reliving the grief every day, like a scab that was constantly being torn off to reveal new and fresh blood. She was bleeding fresh blood for Titus every day, still. After her farewells in that dark livery in Rothsburg, she was more at peace with Titus' passing but not nearly as resigned to it as she would have liked. Still, she missed him.

Odd, it seemed, because she had been separated from Titus more than she had actually spent time with him. The truth was that they'd only spent a couple of weeks together before he'd gone to war, so having him gone, passed on, and not around her on a daily basis was the norm in her life. She was used to him being gone. Even so, as she'd told Atticus, she would not forget him. She couldn't.

The fire in the hearth began to blaze quite brightly and the old servant fed it more wood, creating a rather bold blaze that began to heat up the cold room quite adequately. Once the fire was snapping, the old servant left the room and closed the door softly behind him, leaving Isobeau alone in a darkened, strange room in a castle where her husband had grown up. She wasn't the most comfortable she had ever been but at least she wasn't on horseback any longer. Her lower back was still aching and she'd had cramping in her legs and back since they'd left Alnwick, and she was exhausted to the bone, so even as she sat at the old, scrubbed table, she lay her head down on the tabletop just to rest for a moment.

She was asleep before she realized it but when she woke up to extreme cramping a short time later, there was blood everywhere.

"How is your father?" Warenne asked Atticus. "Any better?"

Warenne had found Atticus, Kenton, and Solomon inside Wolfe's Lair's small chapel that was built into the west side of the fortress. It was a long, skinny chamber with an altar at the far end covered in a fine silk cloth, and several burial vaults built into the walls of the chapel as well as sunk into the floor. The families that had inhabited the fortress prior to the de Wolfes had several family members buried in the vault, now joined by five de Wolfe members including Solomon's wife. Soon, Titus would join them.

"I am not entirely sure," Atticus said, his eyes on his father, who was still laying across Titus' coffin near the altar of the chapel. "It was all I could do to get him to put Titus back in his coffin and close the lid. I am afraid if we do not bury my brother tonight that my father might try to pull him out of his coffin again."

Warenne peered through the dimly lit chapel, seeing Solomon as the man knelt next to the coffin, his upper torso splayed across it. "Have you sent for a priest?" he asked.

Atticus nodded. "I had Kenton take care of it," he said. "He sent two men riding for Hawick. It is about an hour away on a swift horse so I imagine we will see a priest by this afternoon. At least, I hope so."

"Indeed."

Atticus' gaze lingered on his father a moment longer before turning to Warenne. "Where is Isobeau?" he asked. "How is she?"

Warenne threw a thumb in the general direction of the courtyard, just outside the door. "She is in a chamber having a bath and food brought to her," he said. "You should see to her shortly, Atticus, just to make sure she is well. I am not entirely sure how well she digested your father pulling Titus out of his coffin, so mayhap you should see to her comfort. I can watch over your father until you return."

Atticus nodded but his gaze moved to his father, who was now speaking to the coffin, to Titus, much as Atticus and Isobeau had done those days past. It seemed like an eternity ago when they had bonded in that cold livery, coming to terms with the course their lives had taken. The next three days traveling to Wolfe's Lair had been quiet between them for the most part; they had barely spoken but it wasn't intentional. There simply hadn't been the time or much of an opportunity. Atticus had been focused on moving them as quickly as possible to his ancestral home and Isobeau had simply followed along, uncomplaining and quiet.

Therefore, Atticus was coming to think that he should, indeed, see to Isobeau simply to make sure she was well enough. He didn't want her to think he was neglecting her. Now that they were at their destination, there was time enough to rest and focus on the next step in their lives, including his pursuit of de la Londe and de Troiu. He had not yet discussed that with Isobeau on a level that might see her joining him, as Warenne had suggested. Over the past few days, he had grown accustomed to the idea of taking her with him; more than that, he was quite certain Warenne would not let him leave her behind.

"Very well," he said. "I will see to her for a moment. Where is she?"

Warenne motioned to the north side of the fortress. "On the third level," he said. "She is on the north side."

Atticus knew the labyrinth of rooms at Wolfe's Lair and had a good idea where Isobeau had been settled. "Thank you," he said, eyeing his father one last time. "My father knows you and you know him. Do what you can for him while I am away but whatever you do, don't let him take Titus out of the coffin again. I am afraid my father may unwittingly damage the body in his grief and then he would wallow in that guilt for the rest of his life."

Warenne nodded, keeping an eye on Solomon as Atticus headed out of the chapel. Out in the yard where a very cold wind was whipping through the grounds, Atticus came across Kenton, who was disbanding the escort party and having Isobeau's capcases removed from the wagon. Just as Atticus passed by, Kenton called out to him.

"Atticus," he said. "Shall I have Lady de Wolfe's capcases sent up to her or would you have me wait?"

Atticus paused, eyeing the collection of very nice cases that Titus had purchased for his new wife.

"Have them sent up now," he said. "I will take one or two with me, for I am going to see her now."

As he bent over to test the weight of the cases, finally selecting two that weren't too heavy, Kenton reached down and collected the heaviest one.

"I will go with you," he said. "It will give us a chance to discuss plans for the next few days."

Atticus eyed Kenton, now holding the biggest and heaviest case. "Come on, then," he said. "Since you must show off your Herculean strength, let us make sure your display does not to go waste."

Kenton's lips twitched with a smile. "Then you admit I am stronger than you."

"I admit that you *think* you are."

Kenton fought off a bigger grin. "I am the one with the bigger case."

"That is because I am smarter than you are. I took the lighter cases so I would not break my back," Atticus pointed out. "Good Christ, how many cases does one woman need?"

Kenton, now following Atticus up the narrow stone steps, glanced over his shoulder to count the cases that had remained behind. "At least seven."

Atticus pursed his lips irritably at the glib reply, stomping up the steps. "When we leave this place, I will make sure she travels much lighter," he said. "I will not be lugging around seven capcases all over England."

They had reached the second level and mounted the steps for the third. "Then we are not going after de la Londe and de Troiu?" Kenton asked.

Atticus nodded. "We are indeed," he said. "But Lady de Wolfe is coming with us. It… it is her vengeance as much as it is mine, I suppose. Titus was her husband as well as my brother. Thetford seems to think it is important that I take her and allow her a measure of vengeance also."

They had reached the third floor and it took Atticus a moment to realize that Kenton had not responded. He turned to look at the man only to notice that Kenton seemed lost in thought. When Kenton saw that Atticus was looking at him, he merely shrugged.

"If it is your wish that she accompany us, then she shall," he said.

Atticus came to a halt, peering at the man strangely. "You do not think she should go with us, do you?"

Kenton averted his gaze. "It does not matter what I think," he said. "You have deemed that she should go and she shall."

Atticus still wasn't moving forward, shifting the weight of the cases on his broad shoulders. "That is not an answer to my question," he said. "Why do you think she should not go?"

Kenton grunted. He didn't want to give his opinion because Atticus had enough opinions with Thetford criticizing his every move. At least, that's what Kenton thought. He'd seen Warenne and how he'd given Atticus his opinion on the situation at every turn. Kenton respected Thetford a great deal but he'd seen how the man had tried to order Atticus about even on personal decisions and Kenton didn't like that in the least. He scratched his head.

"I am not entirely sure it is relevant," he said. "Can we get moving? This case is getting heavy."

Atticus blocked the corridor and wouldn't move. "That is your misfortune for picking the heaviest case," he said. "You will tell me what you think of all of this, Kenton. You and I have known each other a long time and you were particularly close with Titus. I cannot imagine any of this is easy on you, either."

"It does not matter."

"It matters a great deal to me. Speak."

Up until that point, Kenton had kept his gaze averted but when Atticus commanded him to spill forth his opinion, he looked the man squarely in the face.

"Do you really want to know what I think about all of this?" he asked, his eyes alight with emotion. "I was with Titus right before de Troiu and de la Londe approached him. Titus and I had been discussing positioning the right flank and I remember seeing de Troiu and de la Londe in the distance, heading in our direction. But I moved on to carry out Titus' orders. Had I stayed, then those two bastards would not have done what they did to him. I blame myself that I was not there to help Titus fend them off. Therefore, I have personal stake in all of this, too. You are entitled to vengeance for your brother's sake because he was, in fact, your brother; mayhap Lady de Wolfe is entitled to vengeance, too, because he was her husband. But I am entitled also because I was the last one to see him whole and healthy. This guilt that I feel has been eating away at me since the day Titus died."

Atticus signed heavily. "Kenton, it was not your fault," he said. "There was no way you could have known their intentions."

Kenton was struggling to remain stoic and stone-faced. "I realize that," he said. "But the fact remains that had I stayed, I could have prevented this. Therefore, when you face de Troiu and de la Londe, it will be with me by your side. Do not ask me to remain with Lady de Wolfe and protect her; I want revenge, too, Atticus. That is why I am here, why I did not remain behind at Alnwick to command the troops. I came for the same reason you came – to seek vengeance."

Atticus gazed into the eyes of the man he felt a closeness to. If there was a third de Wolfe brother, then it was Kenton. Beastly big, handsome, intelligent, and loyal to a fault. Atticus understood the man's position very well. He understood the guilt because he had that particular guilt, too. *I should have been there to help Titus.* Aye, he understood all too well.

Patting the man on the side of the head, Atticus shifted the weight of his cases once again and continued down the corridor with

Kenton in tow. Now that things were finally spoken, there was an understanding between them. This vendetta Atticus harbored was not one of single-minded necessity; it would seem there was yet one more person determined to obtain justice for Titus. More people wanted a hand in punishing de la Londe and de Troiu and Atticus realized that he was pleased at Kenton's attitude. One more person to share the bond of revenge with, in righting a terrible wrong done against Titus. Aye, Atticus wasn't displeased in the least. He was coming to understand that Titus hadn't only touched his life; the man had touched many lives. Many felt pain at his passing.

They neared the north side of the fortress where there were four chambers, including Solomon's master chamber. The corridor was low-ceilinged and dark, and Atticus threw open the first door he came to only to be met with a dark and cold chamber. Continuing on, he came to the next door in succession and opened that one, too, but no Lady de Wolfe. Moving further down the corridor, they came to the chamber that was next to his father's chamber, a chamber that had once belonged to Atticus' mother. Knocking softly on the door, he waited for a response.

There was no voice that bade him to enter but he did hear something fall over, perhaps furniture of some kind. It sounded like wood falling. He rapped again.

"Lady de Wolfe?" he called. "Isobeau? May we enter? We have your cases."

Still, no distinctive reply. But then he heard a gasp, and perhaps even a groan. Puzzled, Atticus lifted the latch and pushed the door open.

Isobeau was standing beside a small table in the room next to a toppled chair. Her fur cloak was across the table and she was clad in the pale blue traveling dress she had worn since leaving Alnwick. But Atticus immediately noticed that she had blood-stained hands and he dropped her two cases just inside the door, rushing to her side.

"What happened?" he demanded with concern. "Did you hurt yourself?"

Isobeau looked up at him, extremely pale and distressed. "I... I am not sure," she said. "There is blood."

He could see her hands but he didn't see any blood on her body other than the hands. "Where?" he asked, growing increasingly apprehensive. "Where did the blood come from?"

It was then that she turned around and he saw it on the back of her dress. There was a big, dark, red stain right on her bottom and smears against the fabric where she had tried to pull her dress around to look at the mess. Atticus' heart sank.

"Good Christ," he hissed, putting his hands on her because she seemed to be weaving about unsteadily. He turned to Kenton, who was standing back by the door. "Find a physic immediately. Lady de Wolfe has injured herself badly."

Kenton fled. He hadn't really seen what Atticus had seen but it didn't matter. What concerned him was that Atticus' voice seemed to be tinged with fear Kenton had never heard from the man. It was alarming. As the big knight dashed off, Atticus began bellowing for servants. There was still no bed, and no food, or anything else of comfort, and Atticus snarled at the elderly servant who appeared, demanding a mattress for Lady de Wolfe. The old man explained that they were stuffing a fresh one for Lady de Wolfe, per Thetford's orders, but Atticus bellowed at them to produce one immediately. When the fearful servant made it clear he could not comply, Atticus swung Isobeau into his arms and charged out of the chamber, straight into his father's room next door.

Solomon's chamber was a smelly, dirty mess, but at least it had a bed she could lay upon. Atticus ordered the elderly servant to strip his father's bed and find something clean to lay atop it so Lady de Wolfe could have a relatively unsoiled surface upon which to lie. The only thing that was even remotely clean in Solomon's pigsty of a chamber was an oiled cloak used to guard against the rain. It was a very big cloak, relatively clean, and the old servant laid it over the lumpy old mattress used by Solomon as Atticus deposited Isobeau gently atop it.

Isobeau's eyes were closed, her face ghostly pale, as Atticus stood over her. He needed to at least make an attempt to stop the bleeding but he knew, in his heart of hearts, that there was nothing to be done. He suspected the bleeding was coming from her womb because of the location of the stain and he further suspected he was witnessing the death of his brother's child. Horrendous, horrific guilt swept him.

"My lady?" he leaned over her, whispering. "Are you in pain?"

Isobeau's eyes fluttered open and she looked up at him with her great eyes, dark as a hot summer sky. They seemed oddly bright within her ashen face.

"I am not any longer," she said softly. "I was, but it went away."

Atticus was feeling increasingly terrible about the circumstances, realizing the woman had been in great discomfort but had not mentioned it to him. Perhaps she didn't think she should. For whatever reason, she had kept her agony to herself and hadn't complained. He hadn't noticed anything odd about her because he had been too preoccupied with his own troubles. He sighed heavily, distress on his features.

"How long were you in pain, Isobeau?" he asked her, unable to keep the sorrow from his voice. "Why did you not tell me?"

Isobeau's gaze lingered on him a moment longer before closing her eyes, turning her head away. "It was not terrible pain," she murmured. "My back ached all during our journey from Alnwick but I assumed it was the fact that I was on a horse from sunrise to sunset. It was nothing odd. But then… right after the earl brought me to rest, I had terrible pains in my stomach and then there was blood. I do not feel much pain anymore."

Atticus didn't know what else to say. He was utterly devastated, now because he had failed to protect Titus' child. He had forced Isobeau into a difficult trip, knowing her delicate condition, and now he was seeing the results of his bad decision. He should have left her at Alnwick but he knew, in the same breath, that leaving her behind had never been an option.

The loss of the child was one more shattering incident in a string of days that had seen many such things. For a man who had known only success and fortune in his life, the series of setbacks had left him reeling. He felt as if he were no longer on solid ground, a very bad sensation when he planned to face off against the two skilled knights who had murdered his brother. He felt unsteady and unsure. But perhaps there was more to life than this vengeance he harbored; he was starting to see that there was. There was his father, his friends, and even Isobeau… but he would not go back on his vow. He had a promise to fulfill and he would see it through or die trying. There was no alternative.

Thoughts of vengeance faded, however, as he gazed down at Isobeau's face. She was his priority at the moment and he was rather chagrinned that it had taken a health scare of this magnitude for him to realize that. For days, the woman had essentially been an afterthought. His priorities, his focus, had been elsewhere. But that situation was something he intended to change.

There was nothing more he could do until the physic arrived, so he pulled up a chair next to the bed where Isobeau lay dozing. He felt so utterly helpless and sad. Isobeau's hand, limp and lifeless, was lingering by the end of the bed. Atticus stared at it for some time before reaching out to gently collect it. Perhaps it was to comfort her, or perhaps it was even to comfort himself. For whatever the reason, Atticus sat there, holding her hand, for the rest of the morning until a tall, skinny man with a satchel in his hand arrived under Kenton's escort.

Atticus jumped up when the man entered the chamber, describing what the lady's issue was. After checking the man to make sure he had no weapons on his body, and even rummaging through the satchel he was carrying to see what was inside, Atticus allowed the man access to Isobeau. When the physic went to work, Atticus moved away from the bed, standing over near the chamber door. He wanted to afford Isobeau some privacy. When the physic helped her to sit up so he could remove her clothing, he left the room completely.

Standing in the corridor outside his father's room, the very room he had been born in those years ago, he thought it was a rather fitting place for Titus' son to know his end. So much life and death had happened in that chamber. Feeling depressed and hollow, he stood against the wall, just next to the door, straining to catch wind of what was going on inside. He couldn't hear any sounds at all. Kenton was standing across from him, next to a small lancet window that allowed ventilation and light into the corridor, and he turned his attention to the man.

"Where did you find the physic?" Atticus asked.

Kenton drew in a long, deep breath, the sign of an exhausted man. "In Hawick," he said. "He is the same physic that tends your father. The man's wife and mother are following behind in a wagon; they should be here shortly. I thought you might feel more comfortable with womenfolk to tend Lady de Wolfe because, God knows, there are only men at this place."

Atticus appreciated the foresight. "Indeed," he replied. "Thank you for your consideration of Lady de Wolfe's needs."

Kenton eyed him. "What is the matter with her?"

Atticus looked up at him, an expression of sorrow on his face. He wasn't sure how to delicately phrase the issue so he simply came out with the truth.

"I suspect the lady is no longer with child," he said quietly, lowering his gaze.

Kenton simply nodded, averting his eyes and looking at his boots much as Atticus was. "If that is true, then I am very sorry for you," he said quietly. "But I am sorrier for Lady de Wolfe. First Titus, now her child."

Atticus sighed heavily, reflecting on what Isobeau was being forced to endure. "I promised my brother I would take care of her," he said. "I do not seem to be doing a very good job of it."

Kenton glanced at him. "You did not cause this," he said. "Whatever has happened is the Will of God. You must have faith that everything happens as it should, and in the end, everything is as it should be."

Atticus grunted. "I am not particularly fond of God's Will at the moment," he said. "So much has happened that I feel as if I am sliding into a pit and have yet to see the bottom. I pray our misfortunes end at some point and we hit bottom. I should like to come up again."

Kenton understood. "You shall," he said. "Sometimes it takes a bottomless pit for us to appreciate the view from the top. In any case, Lady de Wolfe will be in good hands. There is nothing more you can do for her. In fact, I would suggest you return to the chapel and relieve Thetford of the duty of watching over your father. They have been there all morning."

Atticus knew that. He didn't particularly want to leave Isobeau, as he was anxious for news of her condition, but he knew at some point he was going to have to see to his father.

"Has the priest arrived for the burial mass?" he asked.

Kenton nodded. "I saw him when I returned with the physic."

Atticus processed the information. "Then with the priest here, we would do well to bury Titus right away," he said. "I will speak with my father about it. In fact, I will insist. Meanwhile, you will remain here in case the physic needs anything. Send word to me as soon as the physic finishes his examination. I would like to know of Lady de Wolfe's condition."

Kenton waved him off and Atticus headed down the low-ceilinged corridor en route to Wolfe's Lair's small chapel and his father. Kenton watched the man go; he swore he could see a cloud of doom and sorrow hanging over Atticus, a very unusual thing, indeed. As Atticus had said, much misfortune had befallen them since that terrible day on the battlefield of Towton.

The Lion of the North, a mighty and fearsome man, was suffering through some damnable luck at the moment. But Kenton knew, as did everyone else who knew Atticus de Wolfe, that a spell of bad fortune could not cripple The Lion.

If anything, he would emerge stronger than before. It was just a hunch Kenton had.

CHAPTER EIGHT

> *Ionian scale in C – Lyrics to Light*
>
> *Of all of the brightness the sunshine brings,*
> *Your face is the only light I see.*
> *In the sky, I can clearly see,*
> *Your loving eyes gazing back at me.*
>
> *—Iseobeau de Shera de Wolfe, 15th c.*

Wellesbourne Castle
Warwickshire

WELLESBOURNE CASTLE WAS a little over seven miles south of Warwick Castle, seat of the Earl of Warwick, and the history between Warwick and Wellesbourne had always been one of allied harmony until the last few years. With Warwick allied with Henry one day and Edward the next, that allegiance had been put to the test. Andrew Wellesbourne remained a staunch supporter of the true king of England, one of the more powerful barons in Henry's arsenal.

It was well known in military circles that the Wellesbourne army was eleven hundred of the best trained and best supplied men in all of England. They were usually the strike force, put out front in the event of a battle because they were usually very successful in surviving, and then countering, an enemy assault. They had not been at Towton because four months prior, they had seen major action in another massive battle at Wakefield in Yorkshire that had seriously weakened the Wellesbourne lines.

Andrew had been given permission to return his army home to regroup and he was in the process of doing just that. He'd lost almost three hundred men at Wakefield and through recruiting in the neighboring shires, he had managed to reclaim those numbers and more. Now, Andrew had new recruits that were seeing serious training every day. When Simon de la Londe and Declan de Troiu rode through the gatehouse of Wellesbourne in friendship, Andrew had no reason to think their visit was anything other than a welcomed social call.

Wellesbourne was a congenial man with dark hair and dark eyes, features his son Adam had inherited. He was an old knight, but still quite powerful and spry even at his advanced age, and was still very active upon the field of battle. Andrew Wellesbourne took no issue with being in the middle of a fight. In fact, he welcomed it. Therefore, as the evening feast commenced, Andrew shared his table with de la Londe and de Troiu as an associate and fellow knight, not as a man who had once held a sword.

It was a companionable meal that started out with the dreadful news of Towton. Andrew had heard pieces of news as told to him by travelers who had been to the north, or who had heard of the defeat from others, so it was something of a shock to hear the truth from de la Londe and de Troiu. It was even more of a shock to hear of Henry Percy's death and of Titus de Wolfe's death. Andrew had particular trouble swallowing that one; he knew Titus and considered the man a friend. Based on the information from Towton, the pleasant evening meal turned into a depressing and serious affair.

But that was what de la Londe had planned all along. In fact, he'd had days to plan on what, precisely, he was going to tell Wellesbourne to ensure he had the man's attention when he brought up the subject of swearing fealty to Edward and the best thing he could come up with was to try and gain the man's sympathy. If he believed Adam had already turned to Edward, if there was some way to build up knightly angst against his own allies, then there might be a chance. De la Londe proceeded carefully.

"As you can imagine, my lord, the entire country is in upheaval after the battle at Towton," he said seriously. "I have never seen so many dead. Someone said at least twenty thousand men and animals. And look at the wound to my face – that should tell you how brutal the fighting was."

Andrew drew in a long, pensive breath, closing his eyes briefly as if to ward off the horror. When he opened his eyes again, it was to the badly damaged face of de la Londe. "Unfathomable," he muttered. "And Henry Percy with them."

De la Londe nodded. "Northumberland, Andrew Trollope, and others," he said. "Lancaster is all but defeated. We have heard that Henry has fled into Scotland where he will more than likely remain. Henry is finished and Edward now takes the throne. If, for no other reason, I am glad to make that statement because it means the death and destruction is over. Mayhap men's lives will be spared now that the dominant king has emerged."

Andrew was watching him from across the table, over the glow of the flickering tapers. "The battles will never be over so long as a usurper sits upon the throne of England."

De la Londe could see, in that moment, that convincing Wellesbourne to join Edward's cause was not going to be a simple thing. Not that he believed it would be, but he had hoped the gloom and doom of the defeat at Towton might give Wellesbourne pause to think. De la Londe sipped at his wine.

"I suppose you have to think about it from the point of view for the good of England," he said, smacking his lips at the tart taste. "Henry is quite mad. We know he is quite mad. Because he is mad, his wife, Margaret rules for him. That means, essentially, a French whore rules England. That does not sit well with me or many other men. Edward, at least, is not mad and he does not have his French wife ruling in his stead. He is skilled, an excellent warrior, and possesses a keen mind. Those are all attributes of a man I would wish to have sitting upon the throne of England."

Andrew should have sensed something was afoot but he did not; he simply viewed de la Londe's statement as his opinion. He shrugged his big shoulders.

"Possibly," he said. "But the fact remains that he is not the rightful king."

De la Londe cocked an eyebrow to make a point. "Edward has a very strong claim to the throne. More than that, he has more support than Henry does. It is only a matter of time before Henry, and his supporters, are completely wiped out."

Andrew considered that for a moment. More than that, he was now starting to suspect something. He wasn't sure yet, but it was clear that de la Londe was advocating Edward for the sake of the argument. Calmly, he poured himself more wine.

"Is that what you truly believe, Simon?" he asked.

De la Londe nodded, glancing at de Troiu, who hadn't imbibed any alcohol the entire meal. De Troiu's mind was still quite clear and when he caught de la Londe's expression, he spoke up.

"Towton was a disaster," he said. "So many dead, including Titus de Wolfe. It was a horrible scene. There are not many Lancastrian supporters left and there is a great deal of talk among those who remain about ending these wars and throwing their support behind Edward. Now with Northumberland gone, his ranks of knights are discussing what is to be done now. There is now a twelve-year-old boy at the helm of Northumberland's armies and the lad is not a military leader like his father was. It has caused the Northumberland knights to rethink their loyalties, including Adam."

Andrew's head came up and his dark eyes focused intensely on de Troiu. "My son?" he questioned. "What has Adam said?"

De Troiu cast de la Londe a long look, a purposeful move, as if to imply he did not want to tell Andrew the truth. It was an obvious gesture that only made Andrew more suspicious of their motives.

"Like the others, he is considering supporting Edward," de Troiu said softly. "He has sent us here to ask you to consider the same."

Andrew sat back in his chair, surprised. "He has?" he asked. "Why did he not come personally?"

De la Londe spoke, an off the cuff answer because he had not expected Andrew's question, nor had he expected de Troiu's suggestion that Adam had asked them to approach his father on a change in loyalties. That was not how he and de Troiu had originally discussed approaching the subject and he silently cursed de Troiu for changing the rules of the game mid-stream. Now, they were forced to come up with believable answers in a hurry.

"Because he was injured at Towton," de la Londe lied. "He cannot travel. He asked us to come in his stead."

Andrew looked stricken. "Why did you not tell me he was injured when you first arrived?"

De la Londe shook his head. "It is not a terrible injury," he assured the old man. "But it is best that he not travel for a time. The physic wants him to rest. We are all considering swearing fealty to Edward's cause, Andrew. In fact, Declan and I have already sworn fealty to him. Adam and the others will soon follow. We need you with us, Andrew. As it is, you support a mad king who has very little support. If you attend battle for him again, you will be terribly overwhelmed. I do not want to see you slaughtered if I can help it and neither does your son."

Andrew simply sat there, digesting everything he'd been told. His son had been injured, the king's supporters had been defeated at Towton, and now knights that he had known and fought with for years were telling him that, out of necessity, their loyalties were shifting. That in of itself held warning for Andrew; he had accepted these knights into his home as allies. Now, they were telling him that it might not be the case. If they were not allies, they were enemies. He was very concerned with enemies in his home.

The more he thought about it, the more it disturbed him. Why did they not tell him of Adam right away? Why wait until the end? The manner in which the news was delivered suggested that de la Londe and de Troiu were trying to play on Andrew's sympathies. In fact, the entire conversation seemed to be designed to play on his sympathies. Death, destruction, and a mad king... as Andrew pondered all of these factors, he realized that he was becoming enraged. Quite enraged. How dare these men come to Wellesbourne under the flag of friendship, only to inform him that they were, in fact, traitors to Henry? Was anything they had told him even true?

Andrew Wellesbourne was many things but he was not a fool. He was a warrior and warriors knew what needed to be done. With that in mind, he began to carefully lay his trap.

"Then I suppose I must consider it," he finally said, regarding his cup. "It sounds as if Henry's cause is dying."

De Troiu nodded, relieved that Wellesbourne wasn't up in arms over the course the conversation had taken. He had suspected resistance, anger at the very least, but Andrew seemed to be seriously pondering their offer. Perhaps their coercion had worked, after all.

"After Towton, there is not much hope," he replied. "I suppose it is good that you were not there. You may have known serious casualties among your own men."

Andrew pretended to contemplate that statement when, in fact, he was contemplating much more that had nothing to do with switching loyalties to Henry. He glanced up, seeing two men-at-arms at the door to the great hall of Wellesbourne but he knew there were more armed men about, including his two knights, Juston de Royans and Jasper de Llion. De Royans and de Llion had been part of the meal at the onset but had soon left to complete their duties for the night. It was rather unfortunate, for Andrew wished the knights had remained to hear what de Troiu and de la Londe had to say. But they would hear it soon enough.

"You could be right," Andrew said, peering into the wine pitcher and pretending it was empty when it was really about a quarter full. "It is certainly something I shall think about, especially if Adam is so inclined. Let me summon a servant to fetch more wine and we shall continue this line of conversation. I am also interested to know how badly my son was injured."

He stood up, taking the wine pitcher with him. As he headed for the entry, presumably to summon a kitchen servant when the hall seemed to have several of them lingering about, de la Londe turned his head slightly in de Troiu's direction.

"Why did you tell him Adam had asked us to demand his change in loyalty?" he hissed, covering it up by lifting a cup to his mouth. "He will want to send word to Adam. What then?"

De Troiu pushed a piece of candied fruit into his mouth. "Hopefully by that time it will not matter," he muttered. "Hopefully Norfolk will have extracted complete loyalty from Wellesbourne and the matter will be settled. You know that Norfolk will want to come and visit Andrew if the man shows any interest in Edward's cause."

De la Londe sighed heavily with doubt, and took a couple of big gulps of wine. Then he looked around the great hall of Wellesbourne, a two-storied monstrosity with a minstrel gallery above.

"Have you thought about what you are going to do when these wars are over?" he asked quietly, his mind wandering to something other than war. "My family is originally from Rouen. I've no desire to return there. Norfolk promised Titus lands in Westwick but since Titus cannot accept, mayhap he will give them to me. I would be happy to settle in Norfolk."

De Troiu shrugged. "My family is from Northumberland," he said. "I was born at Deauxville Mount Castle. It will be mine when my father dies."

De la Londe glanced at him. "Then you have no need for the wealth Norfolk can provide."

"I will take anything he gives me."

De la Londe snorted into his cup. Further conversation was cut short, however, when Andrew reappeared and took his seat on the opposite side of the table. When de la Londe and de Troiu looked at him, expectantly, he grinned.

"I am having some of my private wine brought up from the vaults," he said. "It is wine I only share on special occasions and I would assume this is one of those times. Now, tell me more about my son. What has happened to him?"

De la Londe and de Troiu looked at each other, each man expecting the other to reply since neither of them really had an idea what to say, but de Troiu made it clear he had no intention of answering. He wasn't the one who had told Wellesbourne his son had been injured. That being the case, de la Londe had no choice but to speak.

"An archer strike," he said in a vague description. "There were thousands of Edward's archers that day. The physic expects him to fully recover."

That answer seemed to satisfy Andrew for the most part. "I see," he said. "I will have to tell his wife. Audrey is here at Wellesbourne, you know. She is pregnant with their third child."

De la Londe nodded; he had caught a glimpse of the woman when they had arrived, a lovely blond with a big belly. "He has two older boys, does he not?"

Andrew nodded. "Matthew is ten and fostering at Kenilworth along with his brother, Mark, who his eight," he said. "Matthew will be a great knight. He is bright and big and cunning. I am not entirely sure about Mark yet, but time will tell."

De la Londe and de Troiu simply nodded. De la Londe drained the last of his wine whilst de Troiu found interest in the candied fruits on the table. Andrew watched both men with a hawk-like stare, his dark gaze moving between the pair, knowing what was coming for them. With the excuse of having more wine brought from the storage vaults, he'd sent a servant running for de Royans and de Llion. He soon expected his knights in the hall, heavily armed, and he was counting the seconds with great anticipation. De la Londe and de Troiu had declared themselves to be enemies. He would treat them as such. But he had to trap them before they could make the first move against him.

"You have not yet wed, have you, Simon?" Andrew asked, making conversation until help arrived. "I seem to remember hearing you had a contract marriage. Or mayhap it was someone else; I cannot recall."

De la Londe shook his head. "It was not me," he said. "That was Titus. He married a de Shera."

Andrew was impressed. "The Lords of Thunder," he murmured. "The family is old and distinguished. They are related to the hereditary kings of Anglesey as well as the House of de Wolfe, if I recall correctly. So Titus married a cousin?"

De la Londe shrugged. "A very distant one, I think," he said. "Truthfully, I do not know much about the de Wolfes and the de Sheras. Titus' wife, the former Isobeau de Shera, seems pleasant enough. She is quite beautiful."

Andrew thought on the widowed young wife. "Tragic," he said. It was then that he noticed de Royans and de Llion appear in the entry, fully armed. Since de la Londe and de Troiu had their backs to the hall entrance, they could not see what Andrew saw. Therefore, he sought to keep their attention. "Now, tell me more about your opinion of Henry's future following Towton. You are proposing that I make a very big decision. I would have all of the information necessary to make the best decision possible."

De la Londe spoke up, encouraged that the man was asking such questions and completely oblivious to the threat stalking up behind him. "You must understand the scope of the support that Edward had at Towton," he said. "Warwick was there, no less. It would seem to me that if Warwick is supporting Edward, then the man must be worth that measure of respect."

Andrew lifted an eyebrow, his focus on the two men in front of him even though he could see de Royans and de Llion coming up behind them in his periphery. He didn't want to tip them off. "Indeed," he said. "But let us be frank; all Warwick wants is power and he will support the king most likely to give it to him."

De la Londe opened his mouth to reply but was cut short when de Royans brought the hilt of his broadsword down on the back of de la Londe's skull. De Troiu had no time to react at all before de Llion was smashing him against the back of the skull, too. Both men fell in a heap to the ground, wallowing at the feet of the knights who had just disabled them. Victorious, Andrew leapt to his feet.

"Excellent," he hissed, moving around the table to get a better look at his unconscious victims. "The vile bastards."

Juston de Royans, a big man with blond hair, peered curiously at Andrew. "What has happened, my lord?" he asked, concerned. "We received your message to incapacitate these men at all costs. What goes on in here? Did they threaten you?"

Andrew frowned at de la Londe, who was trying very hard to wake up. He kicked the man in the head to still him. "Lying bastards," he said. "They came here under the guise of friendship and fed me lies. More than that, they have declared their support for Edward. Put them both in the vault and make sure they are secure. Consider them enemies, is that clear?"

De Royans and de Llion were rather surprised at the news, looking down at their victims as they splayed across the dirt floor. More men-at-arms were now entering the hall, pulling de la Londe and de Troiu off the ground. De Llion went with the prisoners to secure them in the vault but de Royans remained behind. He was still quite confused.

"Support for Edward?" de Royans repeated, astonished. "I do not understand. They are Northumberland knights."

Andrew nodded, disgust in his manner. "I know," he said. "But there is something afoot in Northumberland's world, something terrible, and I will know the truth of it. I must send word to Adam immediately about these two traitors and find out what is really going on. De la Londe tried to tell me that everyone in the north is swearing fealty to Edward but I know that is not true. It cannot be. Send me the fastest messenger we have, someone who is not afraid of rough travel. This will be a perilous journey but it must be done."

"I will go, my lord," de Royans said. "I can make it there quickly. I will see for myself what is happening in Northumberland and report back to you."

Andrew considered the offer. "I do not like sending one of my two remaining knights to the north, but I suppose it makes the most sense," he said. "You are strong and courageous, and can make the journey with little trouble. Very well, Juston; you will go. Ride to Alnwick and find out what in the name of Christ is going on up there. If you can, bring Adam home. I am not entirely sure I want him with Northumberland any longer. Tell my son that I want him to come home."

De Royans was just as confused as his liege was about the entire situation; Andrew was speaking of things that didn't seem possible, but if Andrew Wellesbourne said there was trouble afoot in Northumberland's world, then Juston believed him.

As Andrew followed his men out of the hall, following the prisoners with the intention of making sure, with his own eyes, that they were locked away, de Royans headed to the knight's quarters to begin collecting his possessions. It would be a long and difficult journey to the north, one he didn't relish. But, as Wellesbourne had said, strange dealings were afoot and the truth must be uncovered. There was betrayal in the air.

Wolfe's Lair

DREAM OF ANGELS, my sweet, as they rock you softly to sleep...

Isobeau had been repeating those lyrics in her mind, over and over, a song she had written for the child she no longer carried. No one had to tell her that she was no longer pregnant; she knew.

Half-asleep, she struggled to wake up. The physic had given her something to drink that would make her sleep; whatever it was affected her greatly. Her eyes lids felt as if they weighed as much as a full-grown horse because try as she might, she could hardly lift them. Her eyes kept rolling back into her head. But she fought it, the lethargy, and pushed herself over onto her left side.

"M'lady?" came a thin, frightened-sounding female voice. "M'lady, you shouldn't move. Lie still."

Isobeau struggled to open at least one eye and it worked, somewhat. She found herself looking at a young woman with missing teeth and oily skin. The servant hovered near the end of the bed, the chamber illuminated by the fire in the hearth, so all Isobeau could really see was the woman's shadowed face. Isobeau licked her dry lips.

"How long have I been asleep?" she murmured.

The servant woman twisted her hands nervously. "A long time, m'lady," she said. "The sun has just set. M'lady, you shouldn't move around!"

Isobeau ignored the woman, struggling to clear the cobwebs, trying to recall her last coherent memory. She remembered the cramping of course, and the blood, and the physic who had forced her to drink the potion that put her to sleep. After that, she remembered nothing.

"Where is the physic?" she asked. "What did he do to me?"

The servant woman fled to the door, jerking it open and calling for someone named Piney or Pliney. Isobeau really didn't know. She tried to look around, for she had no idea where she was and she didn't recognize the chamber. But she noticed one thing right away; it smelled terrible and she was laying on an oiled cloth. It wasn't particularly comfortable, either. As she struggled to prop herself up on an elbow, the tall and skinny physic entered the chamber. He had hands that looked like skinny skeletal bones and wisps of white hair around his pointed head. When he saw that Isobeau was trying to sit up, he rushed to her and gently, but firmly, pushed her back down again.

"Nay, my lady," he said politely. "You will remain down. You must rest now."

Isobeau was on her back, gazing up at the man. He still had his hands on her and she didn't like it. "Remove your hands," she commanded. "Who are you?"

The physic took his hands away. "I am Pliney," he said. "I am Sir Solomon's physic."

Isobeau eyed the man, or tried to. She still felt as if her eyelids were extremely heavy. "What did you give me?" she said. "I cannot seem to keep my eyes open."

The physic nodded. "That is the drug," he said. "I gave you a potion of poppy. It will take away your pain and allow you to sleep. You need a good deal of rest, my lady. Your body must recover."

Isobeau thought on that a moment, coming to realize what he meant. She'd known it the moment it happened, the moment she had awakened. But she needed to hear it from the physic.

"I am no longer with child," she whispered. It was not a question.

The physic shook his head. "Nay, my lady."

Isobeau sighed heavily, fighting off the tears. "Was…," she began, stopped, and started again. "Was there anything left of the child? Was… was he very big?"

The physic shook his head. "We stripped you of your clothing, my lady," he said, watching Isobeau as she realized she was in an article of clothing that did not belong to her. "I inspected everything that was on the dress and there was nothing I could see. You must have been very early in your pregnancy."

Isobeau nodded, gazing up at the ceiling and thinking that her son was now with his father in heaven. "No more than six or seven weeks at the very most," she said. "It was not very advanced."

The physic suspected as much. "Then it is God's Will that this should happen, my lady," he said. "You must trust in the Lord that he knows what is best."

His words inflamed her. "Best?" she repeated, raising her voice and trying to push herself off the bed. "How is the death of my child for the best? I have only just lost my husband and now my child? I have lost my entire family, you fool. How can this be for the best?"

The physic was used to dealing with the high emotions of illness or loss, or at least he thought he was. He had yet to come across anyone with Isobeau's fire. "I am not God; therefore, I would not know," he said. "Now your son will not have to grow up without his father. That is a blessing."

Isobeau was utterly outraged. "Get out," she spat. "Get out before I throw you out. You are a barbaric, foolish idiot and I want you away from me!"

The physic backed up but he did not leave. "My lady, you must calm yourself," he said. "You must not get excited."

Groggy and weak, Isobeau rolled onto her side. There was a table next to the bed with a dirty wooden cup on it, a knife, and part of a shriveled apple. She lashed out a hand and grabbed the first thing she could, which happened to be the knife. She hurled it at the physic, barely missing the man. Rather than remain in the room if the lady was starting to throw weapons, the physic quickly vacated along with the toothless servant. Isobeau threw the cup at them just for good measure. When the door slammed, she collapsed back on the uncomfortable bed and cried.

The tears were cleansing and comforting. Isobeau cried tears for the child, tears for Titus. She comforted herself with the knowledge that their son was with his father now and the two of them had each other. The physic had been right about that particular point and she was at peace with the idea. But she herself had no one. She'd never felt more alone in her life.

Head aching, and feeling unsteady, she forced herself from the bed, wiping at her eyes. She didn't want to lie on the smelly bed any longer; she wasn't sure where she wanted to go or what she wanted to do, but she wanted to find Atticus. Somehow, all roads pointed to him in her mind, as nearly the only familiar person in her world, and she wanted to find him. She knew he wasn't far away, for he never seemed to be far away. As she staggered to her feet with the intention of leaving the chamber to hunt for Atticus, the door suddenly flew open.

"Isobeau!" Atticus gasped, rushing to her and grabbing her before she could fall on the ground. "Jesus Ch... you must return to bed immediately."

He sounded harried, concerned. He very carefully swung her into his arms and took her back to the smelly, oil-cloth covered bed, but the moment he attempted to lay her down, she balked.

"Nay," she gasped, putting her hand down to prevent him from laying her on the mattress. "Please... I would rather lie on the floor than that bed. It smells and is horribly uncomfortable."

Atticus, who had just run up three flights of stairs when a panicked servant told him that Lady de Wolfe was having a fit, looked down at his father's horrible bed and knew that she was correct. He had simply wanted to lay the woman down somewhere to calm her down. He still wasn't over his fright at the news of her fit and, with his heart still pounding against his ribs, he stood straight with her in his arms and turned for the door.

"I believe they are nearly finished with your chamber," he told her. "I'll take you there. We did not move you there sooner because the physic told us that you should not be moved at all."

Exhausted, and feeling a good deal of comfort in Atticus' arms, she laid her head against his big shoulder. "That physic is a fool," she uttered. "I do not want that man near me again. Will you make sure of it?"

Atticus took her out into the corridor, careful not to bang her head against the stone walls. "If that is your wish," he said. "But why? What did he do?"

She sighed, feeling quite calm now that Atticus was with her. It was both surprising and amazing that the sensation of being held in his arms should soothe her soul and her fears so much. She'd never known anything like it, ever. Somehow, she knew that she was safe and that everything would be all right as long as Atticus held her. He gave her peace.

"He told me that the loss of the child was God's Will and that I should be grateful," she murmured. "I do not want him near me again. If I see him again, I may have to kill him."

Atticus fought off a grin because he could hear humor in her weak tone. "I see," he said. "Well, I shall make sure if it, then. I should not want you to be forced to kill."

She nodded, or at least attempted to. "It would be messy, for I have never done such a thing," she said. "I would have to guess on the best way to kill a man. His brains would be in one place and his heart would be in another."

He laughed softly. "That sounds quite messy, indeed," he said. "I shall make sure he is kept away. Are you feeling better, then?"

Isobeau put her arms up around his neck, pulling herself closer to him, a gesture that was not lost on Atticus. She was warm and soft in all of the right places as far as he could tell. It was a rather enticing position he found himself in with her but he quickly chased those thoughts away. He was both embarrassed and intrigued by them.

"I am very tired," Isobeau said softly. "The physic gave me something to drink and it has made me very sleepy. It was probably poison, whatever it is."

They entered the chamber Isobeau had originally been put in, but now it was much different from the sparse chamber it had been before – servants had brought in a larger bed and a new mattress set upon it, now being sewn shut by an older, female servant. There was a roaring fire in the hearth, several sheep hides on the floor for warmth, and all seven of her trunks had been stacked neatly in a corner. There was also a pile of what looked like linen on the table and the elderly male servant who serviced Solomon's chamber was going through the linen, inspecting it and sniffing it. It was clear he was looking for clean things to put on the mattress.

When the servants heard Atticus and Isobeau enter, the old woman with the big, bone needle in her hand looked to them rather anxiously.

"M'lord," she said, her heavy Scots burr evident. "We hadna the straw nor grass tae stuff the mattress with. We must have that for the livestock. Instead, we stuffed it with wool from the spring sheer. 'Tis quite comfortable."

Atticus didn't put Isobeau down yet. He eyed the mattress. "That should do nicely," he said, looking over at the old man standing by the table. "What are those? Clean linens?"

The old man nodded. "These belonged to your mother, Sir Atticus," he said. He had been with Solomon many years and knew the family well. "They have been stored away. Lord Solomon does not know I have brought them out. I fear he will be angry. He does not like his wife's things touched."

Atticus thought of his father, still in the chapel with Titus. The priest from Hawick was there, and Warenne and Kenton were in the chapel, too. In fact, they had been in the process of trying to convince Solomon that Titus should be buried this night when the panicked servant had come for Atticus. He had wanted to hold the burial off until Isobeau was strong enough to attend but he had no idea when that would be and Titus could no longer wait to be put into the ground. Therefore, there had been a strong movement underway between him and Warenne to convince Solomon to bury Titus this night. That was still the plan as long as Atticus had anything to say about it.

Atticus thought of his father and how broken he was over Titus' death. The man never had recovered from the death of Rosalie, as indicated by the elderly servant. Atticus honestly wasn't sure if his father would ever recover from Titus' death. Atticus wasn't so sure he would, either.

"I know," he said after a moment's reflection. "But I do not think he would mind it if Lady de Wolfe used Mother's things since there is nothing else of feminine comfort to provide. Hurry and prepare the bed, now. There is no time to waste."

The old man began scurrying, grabbing the clean linens and rushing towards the bed where the female servant had just finished stitching the mattress shut. Between the two of them, they managed to adequately make the bed up with old but clean linens and even two old, silk pillows that had belonged to Atticus' mother. By the time they were finished, it looked rather inviting.

Isobeau, meanwhile, watched all of it from Atticus' arms. She was not really sleepy now as much as she was simply weak and exhausted. Her head was still against his shoulder as she watched the servant woman smooth out the faded coverlet that was beautifully embroidered but creased in places where it had been stored for years, folded up.

"Your mother had beautiful things," she said softly. "What a lovely silk coverlet."

Atticus' gaze lingered on it. "I remember that coverlet," he said. "She slept in this room because my father snored so badly she could not sleep otherwise. That coverlet used to cover her bed and I can remember, as a child, laying upon it as she would sing to me."

Isobeau's head came up and she looked at him. "Your mother sang?"

He met her gaze, thinking she was far too close. Her lush, pillowy lips were too inviting and he found himself chasing off thoughts of interest once again.

"She did," he said. "She had a lovely voice, as I recall."

"What did she sing?"

He shrugged. "Songs for children," he said. "I seem to remember a fairy song. Something about dilly, dilly. I remember telling her to sing the Dilly song."

Isobeau grinned. "I know that song."

"You do?"

She nodded, lifting her sweet soprano with the lyrics:

"Dilly, dilly, lady fairy, how shall you fly? Long to the day as slumber grows nigh;

On gossamer wings, you touch the stars.

On the wings of angels, you steal our hearts.

Come touch my heart, O fairy dove,

And take me from the world above."

By the time she finished, Atticus was looking at her in shock. "Where did you learn to sing like that?" he demanded softly.

Isobeau smiled, averting her eyes modestly. "Didn't Titus tell you that I sang?"

"He never mentioned it."

"I write songs, too."

Atticus smiled faintly, impressed. "I would like to hear one of your songs."

Isobeau was rather coy about it, shrugging with modesty. "I am sure you will soon," she said, her smile fading. "I... I wrote several songs for Titus while he was away and I was hoping to sing one of them at his burial. Do you think the priests will allow it?"

Atticus nodded, his gaze lingering on her. "I will make sure of it," he said quietly. "I am sure my brother would be very touched."

The servants finished with the bed at that point and gestured to Atticus to lay the lady upon the faded silk coverlet. Atticus gently set Isobeau down on top of the bed with linens that used to belong to his mother, thinking it was especially appropriate for Isobeau to sleep upon the same linens that had touched his mother's skin. He knew his mother would have been pleased with finally having a daughter. She had wanted one badly, so much so that she had died giving birth to one. Rosalie and her infant daughter had been buried together, in fact, but it was something that hadn't been mentioned since her passing. It was too painful for Solomon to hear.

As Atticus lingered over thoughts of his mother and coverlets and infant daughters, Isobeau was inspecting Rosalie's fine bed covering; she ran her hand over faded silk that had once been red. Now it was an uneven shade of pink. But her interest soon shifted from the coverlet to what she was wearing; it was oversized and unfamiliar. Somehow, she had been stripped of her bloodied traveling clothes. *We stripped you of your clothing*, the physic had said. She didn't even remember changing. She lifted her arms, inspecting the garment.

"Who does this belong to?" she asked. "I do not seem to recall putting it on."

Atticus eyed the linen gown. "I am not entirely sure," he said, "but your clothes were ruined and the servants came up with something. I would suspect they raided more of my mother's things for something to dress you in."

Isobeau stopped inspecting the heavy garment and craned her neck back to look at her trunks, over against the wall. "My things are here now," she said. "I can change into something that belongs to me."

Atticus put a hand up to prevent her from climbing off the bed in her weakened state in the hunt for familiar clothing. "Mayhap you should wait," he said. "You should rest and I am sure my mother would not mind you wearing one of her dressing gowns. When you are feeling better, I will have hot water brought to you so that you may bathe and dress properly if you wish."

Isobeau gazed up at him, smiling gratefully. "I would appreciate that," she said. "I actually feel much better than I did when I awoke. Whatever the physic gave me to help me sleep must be wearing off."

He eyed her, as if he wasn't convinced. "Surely you do not feel completely well," he said. "You were… that is to say, you were very sick. It seemed that you lost a good deal of blood."

He was trying to be delicate about it and Isobeau chuckled. "I am weary, that is true," she said. "But I feel better. I could eat something, I think."

Atticus was pleased to hear that. She also seemed to have some color back into her pale cheeks, which was encouraging. He felt like saying something warm to her, something almost silly and sweet, but he refrained. The woman had just been through a terrible emotional and physical event, and any foolish romantic notions he might be entertaining were sorely out of place. All he knew was that he was content to be with her and vastly relieved she was feeling better. More relieved than he realized. As he gazed at Isobeau's blond head, watching her as she inspected the embroidery on the coverlet, he heard a voice in the chamber door behind him.

"Is everything well with my lady?" Warenne said as he entered the chamber, his gaze moving between Atticus and Isobeau. "When you ran off with the servant, Atticus, we feared the worst."

Atticus turned to his friend. "She is well enough," he said, gesturing at Isobeau who was now smiling up at Warenne. "Ask her yourself."

Isobeau nodded her head before Warenne could speak. "I am much better, thank you," she said. "I appreciate your concern."

Warenne knew what had happened with the loss of the baby; they all knew, all but Solomon, who wasn't even aware that his dead son's wife was at Wolfe's Lair. The time for introductions would come soon enough but it would have to wait until the man overcame his initial grief and madness. Warenne had never quite seen such grief from a father over the death of a son. He was glad to have left the chapel in search of Atticus, leaving Kenton behind to watch over the bereaved Solomon. There was something inherently heartbreaking and depressing about watching the man suffer. Moreover, there was a reason why he had come in search of Atticus and he hastened to come to the point.

"I am glad to hear that, my lady," he said, feeling that it would be unseemly of him to mention the loss of the child. Perhaps some things were better left unspoken. Therefore, his gaze shifted to Atticus. "I came to tell you that your father has agreed to bury Titus this very night. I would suggest we go about it before he changes his mind."

Atticus grew seriously. "Saints be praised," he replied. "Is the priest prepared?"

"Prepared and waiting," Warenne responded. "He did not want to commence with anything without you."

Atticus nodded swiftly and was about to follow Warenne from the chamber when he suddenly came to a halt, turning to look at

Isobeau. She was gazing back at him, her eyes wide in her pale face. The color had gone from her cheeks again and he could see the emotion in her eyes. He could see the return of her sorrow.

"Isobeau, I am sorry...," he began, stopped, and started again as he grasped for words. "I know you do not feel well, but I am afraid we must take this opportunity to bury Titus. He must be put in the ground as soon as possible and if my father is willing at this moment, then we must do it."

Isobeau waved him off as she began to climb off the bed, very weakly. "He should have been buried days ago," she said. "He should have been buried before I saw him back at Alnwick. If you will give me a few minutes, I will dress and go with you."

"But...."

Isobeau cut him off with a deliberate look. "I will go," she repeated, more firmly. "You will not bury my husband without me and he must be buried; therefore, I must go. Give me a few minutes and I will be ready."

Atticus didn't have the heart to argue with her. The woman deserved to be at her husband's burial. She deserved to say her final farewells.

"As you wish," he said softly. "Do you require any assistance? Should I send one of the servants in to help you?"

Isobeau nodded as she found her feet and unsteadily began to make her way across the floor towards her trunks.

"Please," she said. "And hurry. I am sure your father will not wait."

Atticus glanced at Warenne, who simply shrugged; they both knew that they could not, in good conscience, deny the woman the right to attend her husband's funeral no matter how weak she was. Therefore, Warenne quit the chamber, calling for the servants, as Atticus stood near the door, watching Isobeau as she struggled to pull out a couple of her smaller trunks.

Quickly, he moved across the room and helped her, gently pushing her aside as he pulled out her trunks, all of them, and threw open the lids so she could get to the items she needed. He didn't even think about the fact that she had seven of them, a number he had complained about. To scold her again didn't even cross his mind. He had just finished opening the last trunk when the servant with the oily skin entered and rushed to help Isobeau as the woman began to pull things out of her trunks. She was moving as quickly as she could in spite of her weakened state; Atticus could see that. He returned to the chamber door.

"I will be waiting in the corridor when you are ready," he told her. "You need not rush. Do not strain yourself."

Isobeau turned to look at him and he could see that she was trying hard to be brave for what she was about to face. The finality of the burial was coming to weigh on both of them, the final farewell to Titus de Wolfe. It was a mood that now hung heavy in the air.

"I will only be a few minutes," she told him again. "I will be ready soon."

Atticus didn't reply. He simply left the chamber and shut the door, affording her some privacy. He waited in the low-ceilinged corridor for her but the truth was that he hadn't waited an overamount of time; she was swift in her dress as she said she would be, but all the while as he waited in the corridor, Atticus found himself asking his brother for guidance. He'd never missed it so much as he did at that moment.

I am so sorry about your son, Titus, he found himself saying. *Please know that if it had been within my power, I would have given my life if it would have saved his. But there was nothing to fight and no sacrifice I could have made that would have saved him. Please forgive me for what has happened.*

He knew, wherever Titus was, that the man had already forgiven him but that didn't lessen his guilt. Moreover, there was something more he was starting to feel guilty about when it came to Isobeau.

Would it be wrong of me to want to marry your wife now because I found something in her that you must have liked? Because, I am certain, I've found it....

CHAPTER NINE

> Ionian scale in C – Lyrics to May God Keep You
>
> May God's good grace be upon you:
> May He grant you the strength to stand tall.
> May God keep you embraced to his bosom:
> Until we meet again in this life or within his Holy Hall.
> Never have I adored as much as I do now:
> Never have I seen such light.
> Never have I know such serenity.
> Never have I cherished such a knight.
>
> —Iseobeau de Shera de Wolfe, 15th c.

TITUS' BURIAL IN the small chapel of Wolfe's Lair had been a somber and intimate affair. The crypt behind the altar that Rosalie de Wolfe was buried in contained another one next to her, meant for Solomon, but Solomon chose to put Titus there instead. Therefore, Titus was laid to rest next to his mother and infant sister in the great, stone de Wolfe vault. The entire mass had reeked of the scent of fresh rushes, dirt, and decay, making it a rather odd and somewhat nauseating experience.

Isobeau had remained surprisingly stoic through the mass as the tiny priest had intoned the burial service. Dressed in a dark blue surcoat and matching cloak of heavy, blue wool, she sat upon a small stool that Atticus had brought for her. She was calm and sedate.

The real issue had been Solomon. He had no idea who the strange woman was entering the chapel on Atticus' arm and when

Atticus introduced Isobeau as Titus' widow, Solomon wasn't sure if he should shun the woman or embrace her. They could all read his indecision in his expression. He knew of Titus' marriage, of course, but he'd not been able to travel to the ceremony down near Coventry. Now he was finally meeting Titus' de Shera bride and he wasn't sure how he felt about it. It was nearly too much for him to comprehend and, overwhelmed, he'd simply greeted the woman and walked away.

So the service had been conducted with Solomon quietly weeping over the crypt where his wife and daughter and eldest son lay and everyone else stood near the altar. Isobeau hadn't listened to the priest at all; her attention was on Solomon as the man mourned his family. She very much wanted to stand next to the crypt, too, and whisper final farewells to Titus, but she felt that by doing so she would be intruding on Solomon's grief. Not even Atticus was standing near the crypt, perhaps to leave his father alone to grieve. Therefore, with an aching heart, she allowed Solomon to grieve alone as well.

As the priest droned on, Isobeau found her thoughts wandering to the last time she had seen Titus. It had been a cloudy day, cold and windy, and she had stood upon the steps of Alnwick's keep, watching the army assemble in the inner bailey. Titus and Atticus had been walking among the men, issuing orders and making sure everything was prepared for departure.

Whereas Titus would offer a kind word or even a smile to the men, Atticus would remain serious and stern. And the way he walked; *he stalked*. He stalked like a predator, like a lion would. As she remembered that day, it occurred to her that there was perhaps one more reason Atticus was called The Lion of the North. The man stalked like one. That had not occurred to her before. Glancing at Atticus as he stood, head bowed in prayer, she was coming to think there were many things about the man that were mysterious and deep.

"My lady," the priest said, but Isobeau was still looking at Atticus. "Lady de Wolfe?"

Isobeau hadn't realized the tiny priest was speaking to her until he addressed her a second time. By that time, everyone had turned to look at her, including Atticus, and she was hugely embarrassed that she had been caught daydreaming. She smiled weakly at the priest.

"Sirrah?" she answered.

The priest gestured in the direction of Titus' crypt. "It is my understanding that you wish to sing a lament for your husband," he said. "Now would be the time."

Isobeau hesitated; what she wanted to sing for Titus wasn't a lament. It was a love song she had written for him the night before he departed but had been too embarrassed to sing it for him. Now she was singing it at his funeral and there was particular irony in that. Now he would only be able to hear it after his death. She wondered if he would have liked it.

It was difficult not to feel some measure of guilt because she should have sung the song for the man when he left. Perhaps it would have comforted him. Rising from the stool, and the least bit embarrassed that everyone would now hear the song she'd meant for Titus alone, she swallowed her embarrassment and went to stand next to his crypt. She ignored Solomon, partly because the man was ignoring her. But she mostly ignored him because her focus was on Titus, as it should be. She had words to sing to him, words that would send him off into the afterlife. Laying her hand on the cold, stone crypt, she lifted her crystal-clear soprano into a magnificent acapella song.

"May God's good grace be upon you;
May He grant you the strength to stand tall.

May God keep you embraced to His bosom;
Until we meet again in this life or within His Holy Hall.
Never have I adored as much as I do now;
Never have I seen such light.
Never have I known such serenity.
Never have I cherished such a knight.
May God keep you and protect you, my dearest Titus."

When she was finished, one could have heard a pin drop. Even Solomon had stopped weeping, staring at his dead son's wife in astonishment. Isobeau leaned forward, kissed the stone, and quietly made her way back to her stool. The entire time, she kept her head down and her gaze averted, as if she didn't want to see the expressions facing her. Somehow it was easier to pretend that only Titus had heard the song if she didn't see the other faces just yet.

But she had cast something of a spell, a spell that was fragile and haunting and beautiful all at the same time. Solomon felt that spell the most, surprisingly. He followed the subdued young woman from the crypt.

"My lady," Solomon said, awe in his voice. "The song you sang… it was beautiful. I have not heard it before."

Isobeau forced a smile at the man. "That is because I wrote it for Titus," she said. "It was meant only for him."

Solomon seemed to approve; his entire mood seemed to change. "You have given me comfort."

Isobeau touched him reassuringly on the arm. "I am glad, my lord," she said. "I… I hope we all have great comfort now."

Solomon seemed rather interested in her now, now that she had sung so beautifully for his son. He had been in his own world for so long that it was strange to see him so lucid and curious. As Warenne paid the priest for his services, Solomon reached out and took Isobeau's hand.

"I am sorry that I have been such a terrible host since your arrival," he said. "I pray you can forgive a grieving old man. But you are grieving too, are you not? This cannot be an easy thing for you."

Isobeau glanced at Atticus, who was paying attention to the conversation closely. He seemed quite interested in his father's sudden turn-about behavior. She returned her focus to Solomon.

"It is not," she said. "And I am sorry that you and I had to meet under such circumstances. I am sorry that you could not come to our wedding. Those were much happier times."

Solomon continued to hold her hand, his old, yellowed eyes inspecting her from the top of her long, blond head to the bottom of her dark surcoat. As if just seeing her through new eyes, because he essentially was, he thought she was an exquisite creature.

"I do not travel these days," he told her. "As much as I wanted to go to Coventry, my old bones would not have withstood the travel. I, too, am very sorry I was unable to attend your marriage to Titus. It was heartbreaking for me."

Atticus stepped in before his father could go on another emotional tangent about missing Titus' wedding, which was more than likely about to happen. Atticus knew his father well. "Do not fret, Papa," he said. "You will be able to attend my marriage. We will be married right here at Wolfe's Lair."

Solomon looked at his youngest son with surprise. "What is this?" he demanded. "A marriage, you say? *What* marriage?"

Atticus tried to be calm and reasonable in his delivery; he hadn't yet had the chance to tell his father of Titus' request to him and he was categorically uncertain as to how the man would react. Solomon tended to react first and think later. He honestly wasn't sure how the man would take the news.

"When Titus lay dying, he made a request of me," he said quietly. "He asked me to marry Isobeau and that is what I intend to do. He wanted her taken care of. He said he could not stand it if she was to marry another."

Surprisingly, Solomon didn't react overly. He actually appeared thoughtful. His gaze moved between Atticus and Isobeau as he pondered Atticus' statement. Then, he scratched his yellowed, graying beard.

"I can understand his concern," he said. "I would want my wife taken care of, too."

Atticus was quite surprised that he hadn't met with any resistance. "Then you approve?"

Solomon shrugged. "It is what Titus wanted."

Evidently, it was as simple as that. Atticus tried not to let his astonishment show at his father's easy acceptance of what could be construed as an odd, if not marginally distasteful, situation. *Marrying his dead brother's wife.* Oddly enough, Solomon had accepted the request far more easily than Atticus had at first.

"Do we have your blessing, Papa?" he asked. "Obviously, I have Titus'. It would mean a great deal to have yours."

Solomon looked between Atticus and Isobeau. Mostly, he was looking at Isobeau. "My lady?" he asked her. "I would like to know how you feel about marrying Atticus. Are your affections so easily transferred?"

It could have been construed as an insult, but Isobeau viewed it as an honest question from a grieving father who was in a very strange position. He'd just lost one son and now his surviving son was about to marry the dead son's wife. She did, however, think it odd that the man asked her opinion. She was chattel and nothing more, so she wondered why he even cared to know. After a moment, she shook her head.

"They are not, my lord," she replied. "Atticus has not asked for my affection. Only my hand."

Solomon was satisfied with her frank reply. His gaze lingered on her a moment. "Did you love my Titus?"

Isobeau lifted her eyebrows, smiling faintly. "Everyone loved your Titus," she said. "He was a great man."

Solomon pondered her answer, thinking on her and Atticus and Titus. Titus had something Atticus didn't, and that was emotion. He had a tender heart; *too* tender. Atticus had well learned to control his emotion but Titus never had. Solomon suspected that was what made the man so endearing to others and especially his wife. But Atticus… he was the perfect warrior. No emotion, only duty.

Solomon wondered if Lady Isobeau realized that about the man she was marrying. If she didn't now, she soon would – Atticus was nothing like Titus. He was hard, immovable, unbreakable. Out of the corner of his eye, he caught sight of the priest who had conducted Titus' funeral and a thought occurred to him. He turned to the tiny man in the smelly, woolen robes.

"You will perform a wedding mass before you leave," he told him. "Prepare your sacrament."

Atticus looked to Isobeau in surprise and she seemed equally stunned. Atticus reached out and grasped his father by the arm.

"Papa," he said quietly. "I fear this is too much for Lady de Wolfe. She has only just lost her husband and…."

Solomon threw up his hands in an impatient gesture. "Why should this be too much?" he wanted to know. "You promised that I could witness your wedding, Atticus. There is no better time than now. I see no reason to delay."

Frankly, Atticus didn't, either, but he was genuinely concerned about Isobeau's feelings. She was physically weak, and undoubtedly emotional, so Atticus thought remarriage on this day of days might be a little much for her. But he also remembered what he had told her; *I will not marry you until my brother is in the ground.* Titus was now officially buried, and truth be told, there was no reason not to marry the woman. The situation, at the moment, was optimal. With a sigh of resignation, he turned to Isobeau.

"My lady?" he said politely. "Are you agreeable?"

Isobeau looked between Atticus and Solomon, thinking much the same thing Atticus was – that there was no reason to delay. There was no point. Given the situation, she didn't view the marriage as an emotional event, merely one of duty, and she had already established that she was agreeable to marrying Atticus. She nodded to the question.

"Aye," she replied. "I am agreeable."

Atticus still seemed concerned. "Are you feeling well enough to do this?"

Again, Isobeau nodded. "I am."

With a faint smile, perhaps one of both encouragement and pleasure, Atticus extended a hand to her. When she placed her small, soft hand in his big, rough one, Solomon grabbed the priest by the arm and practically yanked the man back over to the altar where Atticus and Isobeau were now standing. As the tiny man began to intone the marriage mass from his dog-eared book of liturgy, one he had copied himself when he had been a seminary student, Atticus found his attention drifting to the crypt beyond the altar where his brother now lay.

There was great finality in the marriage ceremony, perhaps more finality than there was in the funeral mass. The funeral simply commended Titus' soul to God, a final motion in a death that had been dragged out for almost two weeks now. Titus' actual death had only been the beginning of a long journey of his passing that had brought them all to this point. Now, the marriage ceremony binding

Titus' widow to his brother was sealing the deal.

Titus was dead and gone and now they were all expected to move on with their lives without him. Atticus knew, as he'd realized from the start, how difficult that was going to be. His missed his brother more every day. His gaze lingered on the crypt as he said his vows and then his attention finally turned to the woman that was now his wife.

Isobeau....

Now, she was his.

Farewell, Titus....

CHAPTER TEN
~ THE NEW BEGINNING ~

> Ionian scale in C – Lyrics to *A Day of Dreams*
>
> *A day of dreams is upon me still,*
> *And I see your face in the sky.*
> *My heart knows only that it misses you still,*
> *Until the time goes by.*
>
> —Isobeau de Shera de Wolfe, 15th c

IT WAS JUST after dawn.

Atticus had spent most of the night watching his new wife sleep, pondering the turn his life had taken and feeling the loss of Titus to his bones. Yesterday had been a pivotal day for him, burying his brother and getting married all in the same stroke. But in the same breath, he knew that he had to push his grief and heartache aside. He had a task to accomplish, and a new wife to know, and he couldn't do it with the constant sorrow of Titus' death hanging over his head.

Today, his new life with Isobeau began and his determination to bring de la Londe and de Troiu to justice was stronger than it had ever been. Something was screaming in his soul about it, demanding his brother be avenged louder than he'd ever heard it. His thoughts had moved between his brother's murderers and his new wife throughout the night and by the time the sun began to peek over the eastern horizon, de la Londe and de Troiu had won over. He could think of little else.

After he and Isobeau had married yesterday morning, he'd escorted her back to the chamber that had been prepared for her, the chamber that had once belonged to his mother, where she had lain down to rest and ended up sleeping all day and all night. Even now, as dawn broke, she was still asleep, her body recovering from the trials and tribulations it had been forced to endure. Through it all, Isobeau had remained strong, at least as strong as she could. She had never complained or lamented her situation, a manner that Atticus found admirable. He'd seen that quiet resolve from the woman since the beginning but the sheer strength of character was coming to impress him. Ever since that night in the stable at Rothsburg, he had seen the woman in a new light.

In spite of everything, he was glad he had married her.

But a new day was breaking and, much like him, Isobeau would be forced to face her new future. There was something they had to do, a purpose to their lives. They would need to move south, following Norfolk's trail, in their search to locate de la Londe and de Troiu. Atticus was, in fact, planning a meeting with Kenton and Warenne this morning to plan that very journey and for the past hour he had been trying to figure out how to discourage his father from joining them. It was true that Solomon didn't travel, and hadn't for ten years, but these were extenuating circumstances. It was possible the old man would try, which would only drag them down. That thought concerned him.

"Did you even sleep last night?"

It was a soft, female voice that spoke, interrupting his chaotic thoughts. Atticus looked over to see that Isobeau was sleepily gazing at him. When their eyes met, he smiled faintly, watching her lips bloom with a lovely smile. It was a glorious thing so early in the morning, on this day that started their new life together. As Atticus looked at her, any lingering grief he had for his brother slipped away. If there was joy to be found in the darkness of his sorrow, he was looking at it.

"I may have," he said quietly, a glimmer of humor in his eye. "I cannot recall."

Isobeau stifled a yawn and lifted her head. "Surely you are weary," she said. "I will rise and you may sleep in this bed for a time if you wish. I will sit outside of the door and make sure everyone is quiet."

He laughed softly. "Although I appreciate the offer, it is unnecessary," he said. "How are you feeling? You slept a long time."

Isobeau couldn't stifle the second yawn that caught her by surprise. "How long?"

"All day and all night."

She sighed, thinking on the very long and restful sleep. The truth was that she felt much better than she had in quite a while. "Then it is little wonder that I am so famished," she said. "Would it be possible to have some food brought to me?"

Atticus was on his feet already, moving for the chamber door. "I will have them bring a feast," he said. "You slept through the meal last evening so I would imagine that you are quite hungry."

Isobeau yawned one last time, her eyes lingering on the man she had married as he opened the door and sent the nearest servant running for the kitchen. She reflected upon him the first time they'd spoken at Alnwick, when they had discussed Titus' death and the man's subsequent request for the two of them to marry. Atticus, at that time, had been a hard and bitter man but those particular traits seemed to have left him as of late and she was thankful. Ever since their discussion back in that cold, dark, livery stable, discussing their lives over Titus' coffin, Atticus had seemed much different towards her. Almost... kind. And sweet. Well, perhaps not exactly sweet, but there were times when she thought he might have a propensity towards that particular trait. Like now; he had been quite kind and friendly as she awoke from a deep sleep. Almost as if he was glad to be there.

But no; Isobeau knew he was marrying her out of a sense of duty alone. Still, if the man remained kind to her, she could grow used to such a thing and learn to accept it. She could learn to accept him even though she truly had no choice in the matter. She hoped they could at least have a pleasant association. She didn't expect it to be anything like her relationship with Titus so pleasant was the best she could hope for. Anything more seemed impossible. Confusing, even. But… even the least bit attractive.

Do you transfer your affections so easily? Solomon had asked her. Isobeau had never considered herself one to share her affections with anyone other than her husband, but Atticus was her husband now. Perhaps in time, there might be affection. She wondered if she would be an awful person for allowing that to happen.

Lost to her thoughts, she noticed when Atticus entered the chamber again and she sat up in the bed, immediately realizing she was in her clothing from the previous day. She brushed at the now-wrinkled dress.

"Sweet Jesus," she muttered. "I am still in the garments I wore yesterday. You must think me a terribly slovenly person for sleeping in my finery."

Atticus gave her a half-grin. "As I said, you were clearly exhausted," he said. "It was a difficult day for you."

"And for you."

He shook his head, averting his gaze as if an inherent sense of guilt forced him to. Guilt for allowing Titus' child to come to harm, guilt for his inability to protect Isobeau from forces beyond his control.

"I would say it was considerably worse for you," he said quietly. Then, he eyed her. "Are you sure that you feel well?"

"I do."

"I do not need to summon another physic or a midwife to tend to you?"

Isobeau knew what he meant and her heart hurt, just for a moment, thinking on the child she had lost. She sighed softly. "You do not," she told him. "I feel well, indeed. Please do not worry so."

Atticus wasn't sure what to say to that; if the woman said she felt well then he would not be rude and press her. So he simply nodded his head and changed the subject away from the unhappy occurrence of yesterday. "I instructed the servant to bring you warmed water as well so that you may wash if you wish," he said. "Is there anything else you require to begin your day?"

Isobeau shook her head. "Nay," she said quietly, her gaze lingering on him. She, too, wanted to move the conversation away from the tragic event of her lost child, something neither one of them could do anything about now. It was best not to dwell on it because there was so much to be hurt over as of late. But she had cried her tears. At some point, they were going to have to move past the pain. "I... I suppose this is a terrible way for a new bridegroom to spend the eve of his wedding, watching his bride as she passes out on the bed like a drunkard."

He laughed softly. "It was not so terrible," he said, his eyes rather warm. "I can think of worse ways to spend an evening."

She snorted, smoothing at her mussed hair. "If that is true, I cannot think of one."

"I can."

She simply grinned, perhaps a bit embarrassed at his moderate flattery, and rose wearily from the bed. It took her a moment to get her balance before she headed over to her capcases lined up against the wall. She noticed that he was watching her and she paused as she opened the first case, looking to the man with some sincerity.

"I did not have much opportunity to speak with you yesterday on the event of our marriage," she said, "but I would like to say that I will do my best to make this a pleasant association. I would say that it is for Titus' sake, because it is he who wished for our marriage, but it really has nothing to do with Titus at all. I say it because we are married now and will be together for the rest of our lives, and I should like for our association to be pleasant and peaceful."

Atticus pondered her statement for a moment. He realized that he wanted to say something more about it, as if he wanted it to be more than simply pleasant or peaceful, but he held his tongue. It was too soon to say such things, so he succumbed to the appropriate answer.

"As should I," he said. "I told you once before that I would endeavor to make a good husband. I will hold to that vow."

With a little smile, Isobeau turned to her capcases and began rummaging around for something to wear for the day. Atticus lingered over by the door, watching her. He liked to watch her. In fact, she had the most beautiful hands he had ever seen and he found himself fascinated by the way she moved. Every movement was fluid and graceful. He found himself moving from her hands to her torso, eyeing the woman's incredible figure of full bust and slender waist, thinking that all of that tender flesh now belonged to him.

He tried not to think on the fact that his brother had once touched that same flesh; there, he'd said it. Was it perverted that he would be lusting over her, tasting what Titus had tasted, joining his body to the woman in the most private sense where his brother had once been? Perhaps that dilemma, more than anything, had been bothering him. He was sharing the same woman his brother had loved and he was expected to perform as a man should perform with her. He was expected to impregnate her with his children as Titus had done. Was it wrong? Was it strange? Perhaps it was only to him, but it didn't matter now. He was married to her and she was his wife. He was allowed to do as he pleased. Already, the woman was drawing his lust, as misplaced as that might be.

A knock on the chamber door jolted him from his thoughts. He opened the panel, expecting to see a servant bearing food, but it was Kenton in the corridor instead. One look at Kenton's face and Atticus knew that something was amiss.

"You must come," Kenton said, his voice low. "We have sighted riders heading for Wolfe's Lair."

Atticus could hear the concern in the man's voice. "Have you identified them?"

Kenton nodded. "One of them is wearing a Norfolk tunic," he answered, keeping his voice down so that Isobeau could not hear. "You must come."

Startled at the mention of Norfolk, and seized with both curiosity and rage, Atticus fled the chamber, slamming the door in his wake and charging down the corridor with Kenton on his heels. He found that the information had him unstable, furious, and he struggled to contain his emotions.

"How far out are they?" he asked Kenton.

They had reached the steps that led down to the second level. "Very close," Kenton replied. "They should be reaching the gates by now."

"And you are only now telling me?"

"We did not see Norfolk's colors until a few minutes ago. Until then, we had no idea who they were."

"Has my father been notified?"

"We sent a man to rouse him."

Atticus was still agitated that he'd not been notified sooner but he let it go. Kenton would not have deliberately withheld anything from him. Descending the stairs into the freezing cold bailey, icy and shadowed in the early dawn, they made their way to another flight of stairs that led up to the gatehouse and the wall walk where dozens of men were gathered, evidently watching the approaching party.

Atticus had to push his way through men in order to reach the vantage point on the wall where he could see the entire moor spread out before him, facing off to the south. The sun was just peeking over the horizon at the point, reaching golden fingers onto the frozen landscape, illuminating but not warming.

Almost immediately, Atticus could see a group of six heavily armed men approaching the gatehouse, including two well-equipped knights of the highest order. It was then that he grew incredibly suspicious; more than that, he could feel the familiar scent of battle in his nostrils. Whenever he saw heavily armed knights, he couldn't help it. It was in his blood.

Warenne was standing closer to the gatehouse, right on the edge of the wall walk as the riders drew close to the gatehouse and pulled their agitated mounts to a halt. Steam was rising from the heated horses as Atticus came up behind the young earl.

"Norfolk," Atticus growled in Warenne's ear.

The earl nodded in agreement, his eyes never leaving the men below. "I know," he said. "You will let me handle this, Atticus. Knowing you as I do, you will be flying off this wall and murdering all six of those men before a word is even spoken. Leave this to me for now."

Atticus didn't say a word; he didn't have to. His silence was enough of an agreement for Warenne. Tension as thick as the ice floes in the streams weighed heavily upon the men of Wolfe's Lair as they gazed down at enemy riders. Theirs was an unwelcome appearance.

"Tell me your business immediately," Warenne shouted off the wall. "Who has sent you and why have you come?"

Six frozen faces looked up at Warenne and both knights flipped up their visors. The only things revealed were their eyes; their faces were wrapped up in layers of wool against the cold. The biggest knight, however, unwrapped the wool from around his mouth and nose so that he could speak clearly.

"I have come on business on behalf of the Duke of Norfolk," he said. "I did not expect to see you here, Warenne. What are you doing at a de Wolfe outpost?"

Warenne, who was cool and collected even in the worst circumstances, visibly tensed. He stared at the knight for several long seconds, processing the voice, the words, before the light of recognition finally appeared. His features twisted with disbelief.

"Shaun?" he said, obviously surprised. "What are you doing representing Norfolk?"

Sir Shaun Summerlin grinned ironically at his brother-in-law. "Father and I have been serving Edward for over a year," he said. "Had you come home at any point in time over the past two years, you would have known this. My sister knows it."

Warenne was feeling disoriented and sickened at the mention of his wife, Madeleine. "I *have* been home," he said flatly. "Maddie made no mention of such things. If she knew, she would have told me."

Shaun shook his head. "Not if it meant your ire towards her family," he said. "If Mad did not tell you, then she did it to protect you and to protect us. She does not like discord, especially between family members."

Warenne's mind was reeling with the very real possibility that his beloved wife had withheld vital information from him about something that was quite possibly very important to him and his cause. But he couldn't dwell on that now; whatever was between him and his wife was his business alone. He would not shout it out for everyone to hear. He struggled to overcome his shock and disappointment.

"It is of little matter," he said, downplaying the seriousness of Madeleine's lack of trust in her husband. "What matters now is what your business is here. I would know now."

Shaun knew that Warenne was off-balance by his appearance but that was of little concern to him at the moment. He gestured to his bulky companion. "You know Rik du Reims, of course," he said. "His family is East Anglia."

"I know him."

"We have ridden a very long way to speak with Solomon de Wolfe. Will you announce us?"

Warenne leaned onto the frozen stone, peering down at his brother-in-law and the man's noble companion. "I will when you tell me what your business is with him," he said. "De Wolfe is an old man who buried his eldest son yesterday. Surely you are aware of that, Shaun. Norfolk paid two Northumberland knights to betray all of Northumberland's knight corps. When Titus tried to stop them, they killed him."

Summerlin lost some of the confidence in his expression, now replaced by a hint of sorrow. "I had heard of Titus' death," he replied. "But those knights tell a different story. They were defending themselves against Titus and killed him in self-defense."

Warenne turned to look at Atticus and was met by, perhaps, the most steely expression he had ever seen. The Lion of the North was gazing back at him as hard and as unmovable as Warenne had ever seen the man. He was mostly looking to Atticus for a response or a comment on the circumstances surrounding Titus' death but when he received nothing, he returned his attention to Shaun.

"Be careful how you proceed, Shaun," he said calmly. "The Lion hears everything you say. If he charges, I cannot stop him."

That information seemed to surprise Summerlin. "Atticus de Wolfe is here?" he asked. "Then I would speak with him as well. My message is for him, to be truthful. We did not know he was at Wolfe's Lair."

"He is. Be advised."

That bit of knowledge seemed to change Summerlin's tactics. He didn't seem nearly as smug as he continued. "If he is listening, then I come bearing greetings from John de Mowbray, Duke of Norfolk," he said. "The duke sends his warmest greetings and his sincerest condolences on the passing of Titus de Wolfe. It is with this in mind that he has sent me to speak with Solomon and Atticus on a most urgent matter. I have been instructed to only divulge details of my purpose directly to the recipients so that is as much as I can tell you. Will you please announce me to Solomon and Atticus?"

Warenne sighed faintly, unsure what more to say. He turned to Atticus again only to discover that the man was no longer standing next to him. Panicked, he demanded to know where Atticus had gone but no one could seem to tell him. Even Kenton was missing, which was a sure sign that something very bad was about to happen. When Atticus and Kenton traveled in a pair, death wasn't far off. As Warenne sent the de Wolfe soldiers scattering in search of Atticus and Kenton, the great gates of Wolfe's Lair began to crank open.

Startled by the noise of rattling chains and creaking wood, Warenne and the men upon the wall strained to catch a glimpse of the gates and were not surprised to see Atticus emerging.

"God, no," Warenne breathed. Then, he lifted his voice. "Atticus, go back inside! Do you hear me?"

Atticus heard his friend but he soundly ignored him. At the moment, all of his attention was focused on the six Norfolk men in front of him and particularly on the knights. They were big men, of the highest order, but that only served to fuel Atticus' bloodlust. He knew Kenton was behind him, standing in the open gate, watching the four men-at-arms in case someone decided to be clever and pull out a crossbow. Kenton had a crossbow of his own trained on the group. With that confidence, Atticus was able to have his complete focus on his prey.

And, yes, they were prey.

"I am Atticus de Wolfe," he said calmly. "You will tell me your business now."

Summerlin wasn't surprised to see that Atticus had emerged from behind the walls of protection. From what he'd heard about The Lion of the North, there were no walls that could adequately contain or protect him. Atticus de Wolfe was something of a myth, immortal and swift. He inspected the very big knight who had announced himself as Atticus.

"The Lion of the North," Summerlin finally said, some satisfaction in his tone. "Somehow, I thought you would be nine feet tall with swords instead of arms."

Atticus remained cool, focused. "In the heat of battle, I am all you have imagined and more."

It was a fairly arrogant statement but Summerlin rather liked it; he fought off a grin. "We've not formally met, my lord. I am Sir Shaun Summerlin," he said, then indicated the knight next to him. "My companion is from the Earls of East Anglia, Alrik du Reims. We have been sent by de Mowbray to speak with you on a matter of utmost importance."

Atticus gazed up at the knights in the deepening light of dawn. "I do not speak with men on horseback," he said. "Dismount."

With some hesitation, they did. Now, Summerlin and du Reims were on level ground with Atticus but somehow, Atticus seemed bigger. Larger than life. Summerlin pulled off his helm and propped it on his saddle, peeling off the layers of wool to reveal a handsome, square-jawed face and shaggy, blond hair.

"Is this acceptable?" he asked.

Atticus didn't respond directly. "State your business."

"May I approach?"

"Stay where you are."

It was clear that Atticus was not the least bit friendly; Summerlin did not expect the man to be. "De Mowbray extends his sorrow at the passing of Titus de Wolfe," he said. "He wanted me to relay that to your father."

Atticus' lips flinched in a hint of a sneer. "Spare me your platitudes of condolences," he said, his voice low and threatening. "De Mowbray bribed two of Northumberland's knights to swear fealty to Edward and when they approached my brother with betrayal in their hearts, my brother denied them and they killed him for it. If they told you they killed my brother in self-defense, then they lied. My brother told me upon his deathbed what happened. De la Londe and de Troiu killed my brother because he refused to swear fealty to Edward and, based upon that betrayal, it is my intention to track those two knights down and kill them. If anyone stands in my way, I will kill them as well. Is this in any way unclear?"

Summerlin was a seasoned knight. He knew how to negotiate and he knew how to deal with threats. He understood that de Wolfe had lost his brother and he knew the man was grieving, but he also believed every word. Atticus de Wolfe, as far as he knew, did not issue threats. He made promises that he kept.

"I was not aware that Titus lived after his wounds were inflicted," he said evenly. "Clearly, we were told that Titus was killed by men defending themselves against him. Since none of us were present when the event took place, mayhap there is truth on both sides of the tale."

"My brother's deathbed confession is the only truth."

Summerlin nodded faintly; he wasn't going to argue the point. In fact, there was no use in delaying what he had come to relay. Better to get to the point.

"As you wish," he said to Atticus. "Will you summon your father so that he may hear Norfolk's proposal?"

"Nay. Get on with it."

Summerlin could see that Atticus had no intention of showing any manners in the situation; therefore, he decided his manners were misplaced as well. His behavior turned cold and professional, just as Atticus' was. It was time to discuss the reason behind his visit. The time had come.

"Norfolk has sent me to propose an alliance between the House of Norfolk and the House of de Wolfe," he said. "Specifically, an alliance between Wolfe's Lair and Norfolk. Surely you realize that Edward is now king and Henry has fled the country with his whore wife. There is no longer any reason for a house as fine as that of de Wolfe to serve a king with no honor. It is Norfolk's wish to extend a hand of friendship and peace to you. If you agree, I have one thousand men encamped over two miles away that Norfolk offers to you to reinforce your ranks. I have also brought supply wagons with me and coinage to bolster your supplies and wealth. It will be an equitable agreement. However, if you refuse, Norfolk has instructed me to lay siege to Wolfe's Lair, confiscate it, and make it an outpost for Edward. Do you understand these terms as I have relayed them to you, Sir Atticus?"

So there it was – motives as plain as the sun in the sky. Norfolk was now moving on Wolfe's Lair. Titus had denied the man's offer and had died for that denial. Now, de Mowbray was going to the heart of the House of de Wolfe, to the Lair, and he was trying to infiltrate it any way he could.

Atticus respected a man who was to the point, and Summerlin had been quite clear. His gaze lingered on the man a moment before turning around and moving for Kenton. He murmured something to the big knight, who then disappeared into Wolfe's Lair. Atticus, however, remained by the open gate, his gaze still on Summerlin. It would not do to take his eye off the prize. As he lingered by the open gate, Warenne suddenly appeared.

"Atticus, what are you doing?" he asked, urgency in his voice. "What did he say to you?"

Atticus' gaze beheld Summerlin standing several feet away. "He has offered us money, supplies, and men if we will swear fealty to

Edward," he told the earl. "If we refuse, then he has one thousand men camped about two miles away who will lay siege to Wolfe's Lair in an attempt to claim it for Edward."

Warenne sighed heavily, his attention shifting to his brother-in-law. "You know that Summerlin is my wife's brother," he said in a low voice. "Atticus, I would not dream of telling you how to conduct your business, but whatever you do, if you can spare Shaun, I would consider it a personal favor."

Atticus knew who Summerlin was; he had heard the conversation between Warenne and the knight upon the wall.

"I will do what I can," Atticus said. "But if he tries to kill me, I will have no choice."

"I understand. What are you planning on doing?"

Atticus looked at him. "We have been threatened, Ren," he said. "What would *you* do?"

Warenne could only sigh heavily again, raking his hand through his dark hair. "Should I prepare the man for battle, then?"

"That may be wise."

Warenne was deeply upset by the situation. His focus moved to Summerlin once again and without saying a word to Atticus, he was suddenly heading in Summerlin's direction. He simply couldn't let the situation spiral out of control without trying to ease it. For everyone's sake, he had to try.

"What in the name of God are you doing?" he hissed at Summerlin as he drew close to the man. "You have sincerely come to Wolfe's Lair to threaten the House of de Wolfe? Is de Mowbray truly that stupid? Does he not realize that by attacking Wolfe's Lair, all of Castle Questing and, more than likely, all of the north will come down on him? This is not a war de Mowbray can win."

Summerlin's gaze was steady upon his brother-in-law, a man he truly liked. "Ren, do you not understand that Edward is king now?"

he replied with equal passion. "Henry is gone; the man has fled the country. That being the case, any man who supports Henry is the enemy of the King of England. We cannot have enemies embedded within our own country."

Warenne hissed unhappily. "You are speaking of de Wolfe," he said. "That family is the core of England's heart. They are not enemies."

"They are if they support Henry."

Warenne threw up his hands in frustration, stomping about as he struggled not to wrap his fingers around Shaun's neck. He threw a finger in Atticus' direction.

"That man is The Lion of the North," he said. "He is smarter and more cunning and more passionate about truth and justice and England than you could ever hope to be. If he decides to move against you, I cannot stop him. I cannot protect you. Go away, Shaun; go away and take your men with you. Get out of here before something terrible happens and I am forced to tell my wife that I watched her brother die."

Shaun looked at Warenne with a mixture of sympathy and anger. "Madeleine has gone back to Blackstone Castle," Shaun told him. "She is no longer at Thetford. She has taken the children and has returned to the home she was born in. She lives under my father's roof, Ren. You may as well swear fealty to Edward because you shan't have your wife back if you do not. Father will not let her return to you."

Warenne stared at the man, struggling to conceal his shock. "You must be mad."

Shaun shook his head. "Not in the least," he said. "Go back to Thetford and see for yourself."

Warenne was reeling. He stepped back, away from Shaun, struggling to process what he'd been told. It was true that he'd not been home in quite some time but that was necessitated by the battles he had been involved in. He hadn't a choice. It had been something that had been a terrible rub between him and his wife but the knowledge that his lovely Madeleine had gone back to her father had him shaken to the core. Had she so little faith in him? Had she simply given up? Without anything more to say, Warenne made his way back to Atticus. In fact, by the time he reached Atticus, he simply walked past the man and didn't say a word. He continued on into the innards of Wolfe's Lair in complete silence.

Atticus, taking his eye off his prey for a brief moment to watch his friend walk by him, took some concern with Warenne's silent manner. It wasn't like him in the least. Thinking that Summerlin must have said something terrible to upset the man, his rage returned as his focus once again moved back to Summerlin.

There was going to be blood to pay.

Atticus was in the process of studying his opponent when Kenton suddenly appeared by his side, pushing the hilt of a big, heavy sword into his hand. Atticus looked down to see that he was holding Titus' sword, a masterfully crafted piece of equipment that had been Titus' pride and joy. As Kenton took up station by the open gate again, crossbow in hand, Atticus made his way, very slowly, towards Summerlin.

"Although I understand and appreciate that you are under Norfolk's orders, you must understand that by carrying out those orders, you are now in my line of fire," Atticus said steadily. "I have sworn vengeance against those who killed my brother and I warned you what would happen to those who stood in my way. You are now standing in my way. I will give you the opportunity to leave, now, but that grace will only be given once. If you refuse to leave, and take your men with you, then I shall be forced to do what is necessary. Do you comprehend?"

Summerlin didn't flinch nor did he change expressions. He remained surprisingly calm for a man who had just had his life threatened. "I do, my lord."

"Will you leave peacefully?"

"Alas, I cannot. I must carry out Norfolk's orders."

"Then you understand what this means for you."

"I understand that you are refusing Norfolk's offer."

"That would be a fair assumption."

Summerlin didn't back away, not even when Atticus came to within a few yards of him. He simply stood there, facing the man who had earned a reputation as a cunning fighter and brilliant military commander. He was waiting for Atticus to rush him and he believed himself properly braced.

Not wanting to provoke anything, he stood as still as stone and bade du Reims to do the same as Atticus began to stalk a slow circle around him, studying him from in front and behind. Atticus wasn't wearing a lick of protection. In fact, all the man had on was a heavy, woolen tunic, breeches and boots, and a very big broadsword in his left hand. Summerlin's senses were heightened as Atticus got in behind him, studying him and inspecting him. But The Lion made no move against him; he was watching, waiting, and biding his time.

"What did you say to Thetford that upset him so?" Atticus asked from behind.

Summerlin turned his head slightly so he was speaking in Atticus' general direction. "His wife is my sister," he said. "I told him that she has returned to the home of our father."

He heard Atticus snort faintly. "And you hoped that would sway Ren to Edward's cause?"

"I had hoped nothing. I simply told him the truth."

Atticus was still standing behind the knights in a move designed to unbalance them and make them very nervous. "I want you to listen to me and listen closely," he said. "My knight by the gate has the crossbow trained on your companion, du Reims," he said. "If you look upon the walls, there are several soldiers with crossbows trained on your men-at-arms. If they move, they will be killed. Is this clear so far?"

Summerlin glanced to the wall without moving his head. He could, indeed, see armored men with nasty-looking crossbows trained upon them. Cursing himself that he had allowed his party to walk into a trap, he was starting to feel some disgust.

"It is clear," he said, knowing his men heard him. "Is this how you treat guests?"

"You delivered a violent ultimatum. Therefore, you are not a guest."

"I could have brought the entire bloody army to your doorstep."

"But you did not. Now, I will deliver an ultimatum of my own."

"I am listening."

"I am going to take you and your men hostage and exchange you with Norfolk for de la Londe and de Troiu."

Summerlin did turn to look at him, then. "It will not do you any good," he said. "The two knights you seek are not with Norfolk."

"Where are they?"

Summerlin turned back around. He wasn't going to tell him. It was information that would betray those two knights and, subsequently, Norfolk. Now, the true test of wills would begin.

Atticus didn't think that Summerlin would willingly supply the information but he was fairly certain that the knight knew where de la Londe and de Troiu were. If he didn't know, he more than likely would have said so; therefore, his silence was telltale. As he lifted Titus' sword to poke Summerlin in the back with it, a silent threat and a hearty suggestion that he tell what he knew, du Reims caught the movement of the blade and panicked.

Seeing the flash of the sword from his periphery, du Reims moved to unsheathe his sword, thinking a battle was at hand. The problem was that he wasn't fast enough to adequately gain his weapon. In cold armor and bogged down by the weight on his body, he simply couldn't move fast enough.

Atticus, seeing that Summerlin's companion was going for his weapon, shifted Titus' sword quickly and went for an immediately disabling move; since du Reims had his back to him, Atticus went for the most crippling and most obvious part of the body. Using the razor-sharp tip of Titus' sword, Atticus sliced through both of the man's ankles, at the heels, severing both of the major tendons that controlled the feet and, consequently, the legs. It was one of the weakest parts of any suit of armor and also on the human body, hence the name Achilles' heel. Tendons severed, du Reims fell like a stone.

But the fight was on. Summerlin, believing that du Reims saw danger that he didn't, moved to unsheathe his own weapon. As Atticus disabled du Reims, Summerlin brought forth his weapon and moved swiftly away from Atticus, giving himself room to maneuver. The Norfolk men-at-arms, thinking the knights were under attack, began to move but they were subsequently cut down by the archers on the wall and by Kenton, who was still near the gate. In a hail of arrows, the four soldiers went down and their mounts fled. Now, all that was left of the Norfolk party was carnage and one able-bodied knight.

Atticus faced off against Summerlin, who had his broadsword out and was currently on the defensive. The big, blond knight was now in a fight for his life and his previously pleasant manner was gone. Now, there was a deadly gleam in his eye as he beheld his enemy.

"I did not believe you capable of attacking me from behind, de Wolfe," he said, sword leveled in Atticus' direction. "I thought you were a man of honor."

Atticus, too, had his sword defensively postured. "I did not make the first move," he said evenly. "Your knight did."

"He would not have acted without cause."

"Mayhap not, but in this case, I was not poised to strike."

Summerlin couldn't chance taking his eyes off of Atticus to look at du Reims, who was lying on the ground several feet away, grunting in pain. "What did you do to him?"

"He will not be able to walk for quite some time."

"Then at least let me take him to a physic."

Atticus shook his head. "Not until I gain the answers I seek," he said. "Where are de la Londe and de Troiu?"

"I will not tell you that."

"Then your companion is going to be lying there in pain for quite some time. That was what de la Londe and de Troiu did to my brother, in fact. Left him to die. Those are the men you are protecting."

Summerlin's jaw ticked. "I was told your brother attacked them."

"He did not."

"You do not know that. You were not there."

"My brother told me the truth."

Summerlin grunted in frustration. "So you would let a fellow knight linger in pain because you want answers to a question I will not give?" he said angrily. "What kind of man are you, de Wolfe? I see nothing honorable in this behavior."

That set Atticus off. He unexpectedly charged Summerlin, delivering several vicious blows against the heavily-armored knight who was slowed down by the fact he was laden with freezing armor that weighed a great deal. Atticus, with no protection, moved faster and lighter, and within the first few rapid-fire blows, had Summerlin overwhelmed. It was quite clear that Atticus was the superior fighter. As Summerlin staggered back from the heavy thrusts, Atticus leapt up into the air, lashed out a booted foot, and caught Summerlin squarely in the chest. Off-balance, and unable to catch himself, the knight toppled heavily onto his back.

But the fight wasn't over. Even with Summerlin down, Atticus went on the offensive, chopping at him, catching him in the hand and on the back where the seams of the armor were weak. Blood spattered from cuts onto the hard, dead ground. When Summerlin tried to rise, Atticus kicked him in the head and sent him crashing to the frozen earth. Half-conscious, Summerlin still struggled to get up and defend himself but Atticus stepped on his right wrist, so hard that Summerlin heard bones crack before he let go of the sword he was still trying to grip. Atticus reached down and yanked the sword from the man's grasp, tossing it several feet away. Shoving a knee into Summerlin's neck, he grabbed the man by the hair and lifted his head.

"Now," he growled. "Tell me what I want to know or there will be two knights lying in pain upon these frozen moors. Where are de la Londe and de Troiu? My patience wears thin, Summerlin."

In pain, and at a distinct disadvantage, Summerlin struggled between the innate sense of self-preservation and the unwillingness to divulge Norfolk's information.

"This is not what honorable men do," he breathed. "They do not cheat in battle."

Atticus yanked his hair, snarling in his ear. "Do not speak to me of honor when you serve a man who paid knights to betray their friends," he said. "Norfolk solicited Northumberland knights to betray their comrades. When my brother did not agree to their terms, they killed him. The men you are trying to protect killed my honorable brother because he would not betray his fellow knights. He would not betray *me*. I know Norfolk wants me worst of all; by all that is holy, I know it. So do not speak to me of honorable behavior when the very man you serve is a snake in the grass, seeking out the next victims of his deceit and treachery."

Summerlin didn't want to concede Atticus' point but he knew there was truth to it. Norfolk continued to work in secrecy and deceit in order to gain men for Edward's cause. He'd known before Towton that Norfolk had secretly solicited support from de la Londe and de Troiu, so everything Atticus said was true. He grunted as Atticus' knee grinded into his neck.

"If I tell you where they are, Norfolk will know I have spoken," he said. "I… I have a wife and a young son at Arundel Castle. If I betray Norfolk, they will suffer."

"He will not know you have given me any information unless you tell him."

"There is no one else to tell you *but* me. He will know."

Atticus continued to press his knee into Summerlin's neck for a few moments longer before abruptly releasing the man. As Summerlin collapsed onto the ground, unarmed and battered, Atticus stood a few feet away.

"Summerlin," he said, "as I see this situation, you have little choice in the matter. Either you tell me what I want to know, or I will lock you up in the vault of Wolfe's Lair and you will never see your wife and child again."

Summerlin pushed himself up on his bloodied hands, rolling onto his side and eventually into a sitting position. His ears were still ringing from Atticus' kick to the head and he struggled to shake off the bells.

"If you lock me up in the vault of Wolfe's Lair, my army encamped over the hill will eventually come looking for me," he said. "They will lay siege to Wolfe's Lair. Are you prepared to withstand an extended siege?"

"If they lay siege, I will throw your dead body over the wall onto them."

"Then you will never learn the answers you seek."

"Then tell me what I want to know and I will be merciful."

They were at a stalemate. Summerlin had no doubt that Atticus would do as he said he would and he didn't particularly want to be locked up in a freezing vault or thrown over the fortress wall. He was at a distinct disadvantage with no choice in the matter as he saw it; he wanted to live to see his wife and son again. He wasn't sure how he was going to explain his survival instinct to Norfolk, but he would think of something. He had no other alternative. With a heavy sigh, he looked up at Atticus.

"Do I have your word that you will release me?" he asked.

"If you tell me everything you know about de la Londe and de Troiu, I will show mercy."

"Do I have your vow?"

"I told you I would. That is good enough for you."

Summerlin wriggled his eyebrows; it would have to suffice. He glanced over his shoulder at the massive edifice of Wolfe's Lair, wondering what had become of his brother-in-law. He'd hoped to have an ally in Warenne but it was evident that he had been abandoned. He scratched his head with a bloodied hand.

"The last I heard, the knights you seek were heading for Wellesbourne Castle," he said, defeat in his tone. "Norfolk sent them there to try and elicit a promise of fealty from the older Wellesbourne. Since the younger Wellesbourne serves Northumberland, Norfolk would try to sway the father with the hope that if the father swears fealty to Edward then the son will follow."

Atticus was quite interested in what he had to say. "Andrew Wellesbourne?" he clarified. "Norfolk is trying to gain the man's vow?"

Summerlin nodded. "I swear to you on my oath as a knight that my last information on the whereabouts of de la Londe and de Troiu are Wellesbourne Castle," he said. "I do not know if they are still there. I was sent north by Norfolk to submit his proposal to you and your father, which I have done. That is all I know."

Atticus was genuinely perplexed. "So he would try to gain Adam

Wellesbourne's fealty through the man's father?"

"It would seem so."

Atticus pondered that information, turning to Kenton, who was standing over near the gates with the empty crossbow in his hand. He waved Kenton over. As the big knight came near, Atticus relayed to him what Summerlin had told him and Kenton was clearly just as bewildered as Atticus was. In fact, the usually stone-faced knight sneered as he mulled over what he'd been told.

"What would make Norfolk so determined to destroy Northumberland's knight corps?" he asked, more of a musing than an actual question. "There are several battle lords that are loyal to Henry, so why single out Northumberland? What purpose could he have?"

Atticus turned to look at Summerlin, who by this time had his attention on du Reims. The knight with the severed tendons had managed to roll himself into a sitting position also, but he was essentially crippled after Atticus' attack. Atticus spoke loudly to gain Summerlin's attention.

"Why does Norfolk want so badly to destroy Northumberland's knights?" he asked him.

"I know."

The voice came not from Summerlin but from the gates of Wolfe's Lair. Atticus, Kenton, and even Summerlin turned to see Solomon lumbering from the gates. The man was moving slowly and painfully, as he usually did in the morning with the disease that caused his joints to ache and swell. Atticus went to his father to help the man.

"What are you doing here, Papa?" he asked, grasping his father by the arm. "I have handled the situation. Go back inside and go to bed. I will come in when this has all been settled."

Solomon waved him off. "Nay," he grumbled. "I must speak now. I heard your question. It seems to me that I know why Norfolk is intent to destroy Northumberland's ranks."

Atticus was puzzled. "How would you know this?"

Solomon fixed on his youngest son. "Because three years ago, when Henry was upon the throne, Norfolk was still a supporter of the king, as were we," he said. "The man sent me a missive at that time – he wanted Titus for his youngest daughter in marriage but I refused. Titus had already been pledge to the de Shera heiress so Norfolk wanted you instead. Again, I refused. I told him that my sons were not meant for de Mowbray stock. I am sure he was insulted because I never heard from him again. Dear God... that may be why Titus was approached first. Norfolk was still trying to bring him into his fold and killed him when he refused."

Atticus was somewhat horrified by the revelation. "Why did you not tell us of this?" he demanded, although it was without force. "We knew nothing of Norfolk's overtures to wed Titus or me to his daughter."

Solomon shrugged, suddenly looking very old and very weary. "There was no reason to tell you," he said. "Besides, you were away serving Northumberland and I rarely saw you as it was. Why waste breath on talk of Norfolk? It certainly did not seem worth mentioning until now."

Atticus didn't press his father but what the man told him was certainly food for thought. It would explain Norfolk's obsessive behavior when it came to the destruction of Henry Percy's stable of knights. There was a great deal of odd dealings but nothing distracted from the fact that now, Atticus had his answer. *Wellesbourne Castle.* Now, he knew his next destination. He looked over his shoulder to Kenton, who was still standing over by Summerlin and du Reims.

"Keep du Reims and send Summerlin back," he told him. "We will keep du Reims as insurance that Norfolk's army will not attack Wolfe's Lair. If they do, I will do to du Reims what I threatened to do to Summerlin – throw his dead body over the wall and onto his men. Make sure Summerlin understands this."

Kenton nodded, turning to Summerlin, who had heard Atticus' directive. It was clear that Summerlin realized he should have been shrewder when dealing for his release – he should have included du Reims as well. Nothing was ever mentioned about releasing du Reims. Disgusted with himself, with the situation in general, Summerlin knew he had no room to negotiate. The best he could hope for was de Wolfe's mercy.

"Will you at least make sure du Reims is tended?" he asked.

Kenton, who was closer to him, grunted. "We are not animals," he grumbled. "The knight will be well tended."

Summerlin glanced at his dead soldiers, bleeding out over the frozen earth. "Will you also bury my dead?"

Kenton cocked a dark eyebrow. "I told you that we are not animals," he said, his voice hard and gritty like shards of steel. "Go back to your men now and return to Norfolk. Tell him that Wolfe's Lair is still held for Henry and that will not change."

Weary, and in pain, Summerlin rolled to his feet and stood for a few moments, unsteadily. His head was still swimming from Atticus' blow. Glancing up to the wall, he caught sight of Warenne near the gatehouse, as he had seen the man when he had first arrived, but he made no move to acknowledge the man. He knew, without a doubt, that they were at odds, and this entire meeting on the frozen moors outside of Wolfe's Lair had gone very badly for all of them. With no mount and four dead men-at-arms around him, Summerlin began the long trek back to his encampment.

Kenton and Atticus watched the man go. In short order, Kenton ordered several men to collect du Reims and take the man into the fortress, which they did. Solomon followed. Meanwhile, Atticus was still standing with Kenton near the half-open gates, watching Summerlin stagger off into the distance.

"Now what?" Kenton asked Atticus. "Do we ride for Wellesbourne?"

Atticus nodded. "Absolutely," he said. "We will leave today. Make sure the horses are prepared and that we have adequate supplies. It will take us two or three weeks at best, depending on the weather and how fast we can move, so I intend to start right away."

Kenton didn't say what he was thinking; *they have probably already moved on.* Nay, he didn't say that at all. He knew that would not be well-met by Atticus so he simply nodded and went about his business. Already, Kenton felt as if the situation were out of their control, especially with Norfolk's ulterior motive now revealed. Did the man truly want Atticus in his fold or did he simply want him dead? They would have to be on their guard constantly.

A bad situation was only going to grow worse.

CHAPTER ELEVEN

> Ionian scale in C – Lyrics to Home
>
> home, my sweet, where e'er ye roam,
> to home my heart ye come,
> The world is a cruel and darkly realm,
> but yer hearth will remain yer stead.
>
> —(possibly by) Isobeau de Shera de Wolfe, 15th c.

ISOBEAU HAD NEVER seen anything like it in her life. After hearing the servants fearfully whispering about an envoy from Norfolk at the gates of Wolfe's Lair, she had wrapped herself up in a heavy, woolen cloak and followed the trail of whispers, nervous servants, and uneasy soldiers to the wall walk of the fortress. She had seen the crowd of men gathered up near the gatehouse and she had seen Atticus and Kenton as they left the compound and went outside the great gates.

It seemed odd, everyone watching what was going on outside of the walls by the gatehouse. Inherently curious, Isobeau mounted the stairs to the wall and had moved among the soldiers for a view of what was happening. Strangely enough, no one questioned her or tried to stop her; they simply moved aside when she came near. That aversion afforded her a very clear view of Atticus' battle with the enemy knights.

At first, she had been terrified but the more she watched, the more fascinated she became. It had truly been a sight to behold. At first, Atticus seemed to only be speaking with the six men who had ridden to the gates of Wolfe's Lair but that all changed in a fraction of a second. Where there had once been six men, a hail of arrows left only two, and Atticus has completed a skilled and cunning move to disable one of the remaining knights so that there was only a single healthy man to face him. But that man, too, quickly succumbed to The Lion's talent as a knight. As Isobeau had watched with shock and awe, Atticus had effectively subdued the second knight so that the man was at his feet, begging for mercy. At least, that was what it looked like.

Isobeau had never seen anything like it.

It had been a terrible and tense situation but in the end, the remaining knight had been sent away while his companion, injured, had been carried into Wolfe's Lair. After that, the show was over and the men on the wall seemed to disburse as Isobeau made her way down the slippery stone steps to the inner ward of the fortress. De Wolfe soldiers were carrying the injured knight into the great hall whilst Atticus, now with Solomon clinging to him, entered the enclosure. The great gates closed, creaking and groaning, behind them.

Isobeau watched the very big, very silent knight, Kenton, move off towards the stables whilst Atticus and Solomon seemed involved in deep and quiet conversation. Solomon kept shaking his head, putting his hands on Atticus' face, seemingly very distressed over what had occurred.

In silence, Isobeau watched the two men, feeling like an outsider and wondering what had happened. Thinking perhaps that she should return to her chamber, as she was feeling quite cold and still somewhat weak from the events of the previous day, she turned back for the stairs that led to her chamber when she heard Atticus' voice call to her.

"My lady?" he said. "Isobeau?"

Isobeau came to an abrupt stop, whirling around to see Atticus heading towards her. His expression was warm in spite of his nose being red, pinched by the cold, and he reached out to gently take her elbow as he came up on her.

"What are you doing out here?" he asked. "The last I saw, you were warm and cozy in your chamber."

She gazed up into his handsome face, thinking it rather surprising that a man she had seen easily disable two heavily armed knights not moments before was now here by her side, appearing completely unflustered and calm. As if he hadn't been in a fight for his life mere minutes before. Cool, collected... it was a testament to The Lion's faith in his talents. Above all else, he would survive no matter what.

"You left so abruptly I thought that something might be amiss," she said after a moment. "When I heard the servants whispering about a Norfolk escort, I had to come and see what was happening."

His warm expression faded somewhat. "What did you see?"

She shrugged. "Enough, I suppose," she said. "I saw you fight those two knights. Why did you do that? Were they truly from Norfolk?"

He sobered, glancing over his shoulder at his father, who was being escorted into the great hall by a few servants who had learned to take care of the man. Solomon was fortunate in that he had a small army of servants who would tend his every need and that was why neither Atticus nor Titus every truly worried about the man. His servants of the body were very loyal. With his father taken care of, Atticus was able to focus on Isobeau and he grasped her elbow, leading her back in the direction of her chamber.

"Come along," he said quietly. "Let us break our fast and I will tell you all."

Isobeau gathered her skirt so it wouldn't drag over the muddy, frozen ground as she permitted Atticus to escort her. "Should I not have come?" she asked him, sensing his morose mood. "I did not mean to do anything wrong if you did not want me to leave my chamber."

He shook his head, carefully leading her up the old, stone stairs. "You did not do anything wrong," he said. "And those men were, indeed, from de Mowbray. It would seem that the man is attempting yet again to gain the loyalty of the House of de Wolfe, at the very least. At the very most, he wants all of Northumberland's knights."

Isobeau was listening with interest. "Why would you say that?"

They reached the second level and began taking the steps to the third. "Because I have learned that the men who betrayed and murdered my brother have gone to Wellesbourne Castle in an attempt to coerce Adam Wellesbourne's father into swearing fealty to Edward," he said. "These are very complex times, my lady, made worse by Norfolk's subversion. He does not seem to be willing to take a straight denial in exchange for the question of loyalty to Edward. Now, he is going to work on the families of the knights in order to elicit an oath for Edward."

Complexity was an understatement; even Isobeau sensed that. There was far more to Norfolk's dealings than met the eye but she understood clearly from Atticus' statement that de la Londe and de Troiu were now said to be at Wellesbourne Castle. The men who had killed and betrayed Titus had evidently been sighted or tracked. At least now they had a location or some clue as to their whereabouts. She felt some excitement and relief at that.

"Then we are going to Wellesbourne Castle to confront those who betrayed Titus?" she asked.

Atticus nodded as they reached the top of the steps and headed into the corridor that led to the sleeping chambers. "We are, indeed," he said. "I have Kenton pulling together our supplies and mounts. We will leave as soon as you are ready."

Isobeau thought quickly on packing what she needed, struggling to ignore the massive chill throughout her body. She just couldn't seem to get warm this morning and the thought of riding out into the icy weather was not particularly appealing to her, but she would not beg off. She was determined to see her task through of seeing the men who killed Titus punished, just as Atticus was.

"I can be ready very soon," she assured him. "I will pack a small satchel. Will that be too much to take?"

They reached her chamber door and Atticus opened it. "If it can fit on your saddle, it is not too much," he told her. "We will travel swiftly and lightly, so keep that in mind when packing."

She unfastened the heavy, woolen cloak, laying it upon the table. "Will I be able to ride my mare or would you prefer for me to ride something more hearty?"

Atticus shrugged. "The mare seems strong enough."

"She is, but I have never taken her on a long journey. I do not know how she will react."

Atticus' gaze lingered on her a moment. "I am more concerned with how you will react," he said quietly. "Are you sure you feel up to this?"

Truth be told, Isobeau wasn't. She was very cold and feeling oddly weak. She knew it was because of what happened yesterday and she also knew that she more than likely should not be up and moving around. She should be in bed because her body needed rest. But she didn't want Atticus to go without her and she didn't want to delay him if she couldn't travel, so she did what she had to do. She lied.

"I feel well enough," she told him. "I will pack right away and we can leave."

Atticus didn't question her even though she seemed somewhat pale to him. She simply didn't look well. But he didn't argue with her. Instead, he went to the table where her cloak lay, to the food that the servants had brought. He sat heavily and began pulling at a warm loaf of crusty bread, cooling quickly in the chill temperatures.

"Did you eat anything?" he asked.

Isobeau already had a satchel out and was selecting things to pack. She looked at him as he stuffed bread into his mouth.

"Not yet," she said. "I will after I have packed for our journey."

"I will make sure that you do."

She turned back to her packing. "How far is it to Wellesbourne Castle?"

Mouth full, Atticus poured himself some watered wine. "It will take us a couple of weeks at the very least to reach it," he told her. "It is much further south."

"Near Coventry?"

He nodded. "It is very near Coventry."

Isobeau paused, hope on her face. "Do you think it would be too much to stop at Isenhall Castle and visit my father?"

Atticus shrugged. "That can more than likely be arranged if you wish it," he said. "But my business at Wellesbourne will come first."

"I understand."

They fell into silence after that, although it was not uncomfortable. Isobeau was packing and Atticus was eating. But eventually Isobeau's movements slowed as she thought of the men she had seen Atticus battle so effortlessly. She couldn't seem to push the event out of her mind. It had been both a horrifying and thrilling spectacle, something she had never before witnessed.

"Those men you fought," she said, grasping for words and wondering if she should say anything at all. "You did not have any armor on. Were you not concerned that they might injure you?"

He looked up from his bread and cheese. "Were you?"

She shrugged because she truly didn't know what to say to that. "I do not know," she said honestly. "I suppose that I was frightened at first. I realize we have been married less than a day but I do not believe I am strong enough to bury another husband at the moment."

Atticus swallowed the bite in his mouth, wondering if he was reading too much into her words. Did she say such a thing because she knew she could care for him? Or perhaps she already did? He was absolutely terrified to say anything emotional to her, fearful that she would reject any sentiment. Their marriage was a business arrangement, after all. He was certain she saw it as nothing more than a duty.

"You will not have to," he said, taking a sip of his wine because he wanted to say much more than that. Putting something in his mouth was a way of preventing anything embarrassing from coming out. "In the cold, and in armor, they were not as agile as I was. I knew I could best them both but I had to move first and move quickly. There was really nothing more to it than that."

Isobeau turned to look at him; *really* look at him. Seated at the table in his woolen tunic, with the weak sunlight coming in through the window behind him, he had a rather ethereal look. Her heart began to beat faster as her gaze lingered on him, the odd weakness plaguing her body growing worse and better at the same time. There was a certain giddiness to it, something that seemed to be caused by Atticus. He was an exquisitely handsome man. She wondered if she would ever be able to tell him so.

"It was very brave," she finally said, taking her eyes off him because she had to. Her heart was beating so strongly against her ribs that she could hardly catch her breath. "But you sent one of them away while the other you brought inside. Why did you do that?"

He drained the wine in his cup. "The knight I brought inside is a hostage against any hostile action Norfolk might try to take against Wolfe's Lair," he told her. "I would not worry. I do not believe we will have any further trouble from the man, at least not here at Wolfe's Lair."

Isobeau looked at him. "But we could have trouble with him elsewhere?"

Atticus nodded, toying with his empty cup. "It is possible," he said. "But you should not worry overly."

She shook her head, packing in the last of what she intended to take with her, a lumpy bar of white soap and a comb. "I am not worried," she said. "But it seems as if Norfolk is going to great lengths to try and gain your loyalty."

Atticus grunted. "The man is an idiot."

Isobeau sealed up the satchel. "Mayhap," she said, leaving the satchel and moving to the table where there was bread and cheese and strips of jerky. She eyed the food, not particularly hungry. "But it seems to me that he is trying to get to the House of de Wolfe somehow. Mayhap Titus was only the beginning. Mayhap he means to destroy the entire house and everyone within it. Must we be looking over our shoulder for the rest of our lives, fearful that he is lurking in the shadows?"

Atticus could hear tension in her voice, not surprising considering the history with de Wolfe versus de Mowbray over the past few weeks. Much like his world, hers had been rocked lately, too. The poor woman had lost everything. She was standing near him and instinctively, if only to give reassurance, he reached out to grasp her hand but the moment he did so, it was as if a bolt of fire shot through him.

She was warm, that was true, but it was more than that; it was fire that surged through him like nothing he had ever known. Fire and ice and lust and passion, and everything in between suddenly flashed before his eyes. Instinct told him to drop her hand because the mere contact between them was shattering, but his emotions, those things he kept deeply buried, overcame his instincts and he squeezed her hand more tightly, feeling her flesh against his.

"He will not be lurking," he said in a strange, husky voice he'd never heard from himself before. "This is war, my lady, and men have many enemies. Norfolk will soon tire of me and find others. We will not live our lives in fear of a man who is not worthy of such regard."

Isobeau's focus was riveted to his face as he held her hand, tightly, as if the touch meant something to him. Her heart was racing again, brought on by Atticus' touch, and her breathing was coming in strange little gasps. It occurred to her that Titus had never brought on such a reaction. He had been kind and gentle, and his kisses sweet, but he had never set her heart to racing the way Atticus did. Part of her wanted to yank her hand away from him but a greater part wanted to grip him as he was gripping her, flesh against flesh, heat against heat. His touch was exhilarating.

"If… if you say so," she managed to stammer, realizing that she was fixated on the shape of his lush lips. She wondered what it would be like to kiss him. "If you say there is nothing to fear, I will believe you."

Atticus could hear her voice but he almost couldn't understand her words. She was standing up against him, her hand in his, and he'd never known anything so intoxicating in his life. His fingers caressed her hand, acquainting himself with the silken texture of her flesh, before he even realized he was doing it. There was something incredibly inviting and alluring about the woman, something that overwhelmed his senses. Before he could stop himself, he brought her hand to his mouth for a gentle kiss.

"Good," he murmured, kissing her hand again simply because he couldn't stop himself. "It would make me unhappy if you worried. I would have to ride to Arundel myself and kill de Mowbray simply to ease your mind."

He said it with a twinkle in his eye and Isobeau broke into a grin. "That seems rather drastic," she said, breathless.

He shook his head. "Not at all," he said huskily. "You are my wife. It is my duty and my pleasure to make your life as worry-free as possible."

Isobeau's cheeks flushed a dull red at his sweet flattery. *You are my wife*. Sweet Jesus, she loved hearing those words from his mouth but then in the same breath she felt guilty because she had never felt such joy hearing the same words from Titus' mouth. Overwhelmed, and thrilled, she averted her gaze because looking into his handsome face had her so giddy that she could scarcely breathe.

"You are too kind," she managed to say.

Atticus didn't reply. He was too swept up in her flushed cheeks and coy expression. God, but she was an alluring creature. She seemed to grow more beautiful by the moment. He kissed her hand once more, a final time, before releasing it, mostly because he was afraid of what would happen if he didn't. He wanted to pull her against him and kiss her in the worst way and he knew, if that happened, that he wouldn't be able to stop at a mere kiss. She was his wife and he had every right to her luscious body but after what she had been through the day before, it simply wouldn't do. It was wrong and tasteless on too many levels. He would be an inappropriate man indeed, filling her womb with his seed so soon after his brother's child had been lost. Confused, and feeling guilty for his overwhelmingly lustful reaction to her, he stood up from the chair.

"Then I will leave you to your meal and to finish packing," he said, heading for the door and realizing that his male member was semi-aroused against his breeches. He made sure his tunic was covering the bulge. "I have duties to attend to but I will return for you shortly. Dress warmly; it is cold outside."

Isobeau, still keeping her head down and her gaze averted because of her red cheeks, nodded. "I will be ready."

Atticus quit the room with a nod although Isobeau didn't see it; she wasn't looking at him. But the moment he shut the door behind him, she let out such a sigh that her entire body nearly deflated. It was relief but it was also a release, and the grin on her lips was unmistakable, a grin only for her, the secret longing for her new husband now fully revealed.

Isobeau was certain it was wrong, feeling as she did so soon after losing Titus, but the truth was that she and Titus had only known each other for two weeks before he departed for Towton. She'd spent much more time away from him than with him, and theirs was a relationship that had never truly developed past the initial stage. Had she loved him? It was possible that what she had felt for him would have developed into love, but as she thought hard on her feelings for Titus, she couldn't honestly remember feeling anything more than great fondness for him. Titus had been a warm and sensitive man and she admired that a great deal. But Atticus... God help her, Atticus was quickly forging his way into her emotions. He was searing and passionate and exciting. She couldn't stop him.

She wasn't sure she wanted to try.

You are only a duty to him, she reminded herself. *Only a duty!*

Would it be that way forever? She wondered.

With her satchel fully packed, she sat down in the seat that Atticus had vacated, feeling his warmth still on the wood. The realization made silly, giddy thoughts roll through her head. She stared at the cheese and bread in front of her, thinking that she really wasn't very hungry. She was tired more than anything, exhausted from the eventful past. Her head hurt and the odd weakness had not gone away. Rising from the chair, she made her way over to the bed and lay upon the faded silk coverlet that had once belonged to Atticus' mother. It was soft and warm and comfortable, and very quickly she fell into a deep sleep.

When she dreamt, it was with vivid images of Atticus.

Alnwick Castle

ADAM WELLESBOURNE, IN charge of the wall on this fine but cold evening as the sun set against the western hills of Northumbria, was the first one to see the lone rider approach from the south.

Alnwick had been bottled up tight since the return of the army from Towton nearly two weeks ago. No one went in or out, and there was the constant fear of Edward's army arriving and demanding the surrender of the fortress. They all knew that was coming; they simply didn't know when. With Edward's rule established after the victory at Towton and Henry on the run, the surrender of Alnwick was inevitable. Like a sinking ship, it was only a matter of time before it was scuttled. That being the case, the young earl spent most of his time with his mother these days, planning the move to Warkworth Castle as Atticus had demanded, while his knights, seasoned men that had served his father, had charge of the fortress, watching and waiting for the coming changing of the guard.

In such a case, it would stand to reason that things like lone riders grated on their fears. Tertius, having been in charge since Atticus left, was currently in conference with the young earl and the dowager countess as Wellesbourne signaled the approach of the lone rider. Since there was only one man, the man-gate that was built within the great gates of Alnwick opened, emitting two armed men on horseback who quickly intercepted the approaching rider.

Together, the trio then approached the gatehouse and by that time, Adam was there to meet them. Surprise registered across his face when he realized that he recognized the rider.

"De Royans?" he asked, incredulous. "Why are you... oh, God... my wife. Is Audrey well? Or is it my father?"

Juston held up a heavily gloved hand. "It is neither," he said. "They are both in good health."

Adam was so relieved that he nearly collapsed with it. "Thank

God," he muttered. But it only seemed to increase his puzzlement over de Royans' presence. "Then why are you here?"

Beneath his open visor and heavy, woolen scarf, Juston's blue eyes were riveted to Adam. "Because we received information that you are now sworn to Edward," he said. "Yet I find you here at Alnwick, manning the gatehouse with Percy soldiers. This is most confusing."

Adam was clearly perplexed. "Me?" he asked. "Sworn to Edward?"

"That is what your father was told," Juston replied. "He has sent me to Alnwick to discover the truth of it."

Adam's expression went from one of puzzlement to one of rage quite quickly. "Who told you such lies?" he demanded. "I have never declared for Edward nor shall I."

De Royans could see simply by Adam's reaction that the rumor was false. He had suspected as much and on his long ride north, he'd come to the conclusion that de la Londe and de Troiu were complete and utter liars. De Royans had known Adam for many years and the man was many things – rash, impulsive, fierce, and humorous – but he was not a traitor to the crown. Hearing Adam's denial simply confirmed it. He didn't doubt the man for a second.

"Take me inside," de Royans said, pointing at the gatehouse. "Unfreeze my bones and we will have a discussion, you and I. Your father wants to know what is going on, Adam. There are mysterious and unhealthy dealings afoot that you must be made aware of."

Adam already figured that much out; de Royans' very presence told him as much. Ordering the gate opened so they could all pass through comfortably without being restricted by the man-gate, Alnwick was once again bottled up tight as Adam took de Royans into the great hall.

By this time, word had spread of de Royans' arrival and they were joined in the great hall by Alec le Bec and Maxim de Russe. De

Royans had been traveling for days upon days and, in particular, he'd set out on this day well before dawn, traversing frozen moors in icy weather. Therefore, when it came to removing his clothing, the man could barely move and Alec and Maxim took to pulling stuff off of him. Even Adam got into the action, removing de Royans' ice-bound helm from his head and unwinding the crackling, icy, woolen scarf that had become sweaty, and frozen, and sweaty again over the days of travel. By the time the knight was unwound, unbound, and removed from most of his outer clothing, he simply sat there in the heat of the great hall and quivered.

"God's Bloody Neck," de Royans hissed a curse through blue lips. "Why has it remained so frozen this spring? The warmth should at least be making an attempt to return by this time of year."

Adam gave him a half-grin as he ordered the servants to lay out de Royans' things before the snapping hearth. "It is simple," he said. "God hates England. He is trying to freeze us to death."

De Royans' lips cracked into a smile. "That is possible," he said. "I believe he likes France and Spain more. It is warmer there."

The knights around the big, scrubbed table snorted with humor, lightening the mood. But soon enough, the mood darkened again as Adam faced his father's half-frozen knight.

"Tell me what has you traveling over miles of frozen land, Juston," he said. "Who said I had sworn fealty to Edward?"

A servant brought hot wine and de Royans wrapped his cold fingers around the cup, sighing with contentment at the heat. "A short time ago, Declan de Troiu and Simon de la Londe came to Wellesbourne Castle," he said. "They came on a mission from Norfolk, which was confusing enough until they mentioned that you had sworn fealty to Edward. Your father, sensing that something was afoot, had both knights thrown into the vault at Wellesbourne Castle until he could discover the truth. That is why he has sent me here, to learn what goes on here in the north. Why would de Troiu and de la

Londe say such things?"

Adam grunted with disgust, eyeing Maxim and Alec. Maxim, perhaps the most emotional knight of the group, plopped down on the bench opposite de Royans.

"They have become traitors to all we have known," he said, raking his hand through his black hair. "They murdered Titus de Wolfe."

De Royans' brows furrowed in concern, in horror, as Adam filled in the details. "As near as we can determine, the Duke of Norfolk somehow contacted the pair," he said. "In exchange for money, or lands, or both, he somehow coerced them into attempting to persuade Northumberland's entire knight corps into swearing fealty to Edward. The first knight they approached was Titus and when the man refused, they murdered him. Then they fled south, undoubtedly to flee Atticus' wrath."

De Royans sipped at his hot wine. "The Lion of the North," he muttered. "Where *is* Atticus?"

Adam accepted his own hot wine from the nearest servant. "He took Titus back to Wolfe's Lair for burial," he replied, sipping at the steaming brew. "The man is bent on vengeance, Juston. He wants de Troiu and de la Londe. You say that my father has them both captive at Wellesbourne?"

"He does indeed."

"Then Atticus must know. He will want to go to Wellesbourne Castle to dispense justice."

"And I will go with him," Maxim declared. "Titus was my mentor. I wanted to go with Atticus from the start but Thetford would not allow it."

Adam held up a hand to the hot-headed young knight. "Because Atticus was volatile enough without emotional knights tagging along with him," he said, bordering on scolding. "But Atticus must know that de Troiu and de la Londe are at Wellesbourne and someone must ride to tell him."

"Let me go," Alec said, standing over de Royans' shoulder. "I would consider it an honor."

Maxim stood up, his unhappy focus on Alec. "I told you that I wanted to go with Atticus," he said. "Why should you be allowed to go?"

Adam put up his hands between the pair before someone threw a punch, which had been known to happen between the cousins. They loved each other dearly but didn't hesitate to fight one another if the situation called for it.

"Cease," he commanded, glaring at Maxim before turning his attention to Alec. "I have a feeling that each one of us will volunteer to go to Wolfe's Lair to inform Atticus that the very men he seeks are at Wellesbourne Castle, so it is my inclination that only de Royans should go since he has seen de la Londe and de Troiu personally. He can verify with his own eyes to Atticus that those men are prisoners at Wellesbourne. Moreover, you know that we cannot leave Alnwick, not now. There is too much at stake."

Maxim growled unhappily. "Because Edward will march upon us," he said. "That will not happen for months, Adam. Do you truly believe Edward will march an army up here so soon after Towton? Men are wounded and battle lords scattered. Edward is in London. He has better things to do than worry about Alnwick!"

As Adam and Maxim started to argue, caused by the stress of being bottled up in Alnwick awaiting Edward's proverbial axe to fall on their heads, de Royans put up his hands to interrupt them.

"We heard news of Towton," he said loudly, distracting the two knights, "but we heard it from de la Londe's point of view. What has happened?"

Adam was still glaring at Maxim but answered de Royans out of politeness. "It was a route for Edward's forces," he said, sounding weary and unhappy. "Edward soundly defeated us. We lost Henry Percy among others. However bad de la Londe made it sound, the reality is that it was much worse. Be glad you were not there, de Royans. I have never seen such carnage or death in my life. It was hell."

De Royans listened seriously. Pondering the destruction, he shook his head in sorrow. "Then I am saddened to hear this," he said. "But I fail to understand why Henry was so badly defeated. He had superior numbers, did he not?"

Adam shook his head and spent the next hour explaining to de Royans the tactics of Edward against Henry. By the time he was finished, de Royans was counting his blessings that Wellesbourne had not been at the fight. He more than likely would have been one of the dead, too.

When tempers calmed, the evening was spent in a quiet meal with the knights of Alnwick, including Tertius, and also including the new earl, young Henry. The older knights deliberately kept the conversation away from Towton, or Atticus or Titus, or any reference to death in general. They told stories of past adventures, laughing at their foolishness or their cleverness, and passed the evening in a rare, jovial mood. As of late, there had been little to be jovial over and the meal had been a welcome respite in the midst of their stressful existence.

But the evening inevitably ended and there were tasks to be completed. Before dawn, de Royans was once again on the road, heading for Wolfe's Lair and the news that the very men Atticus wanted were safe and sound, locked up in the vault of Wellesbourne. He left behind several disappointed knights, a fearful young earl, and a castle that was once again sealed up to await her fate as the tides of the throne had shifted against them.

CHAPTER TWELVE

> Ionian scale in C – Lyrics to The Deepest Dream
>
> *I seem to awaken,*
> *As if from the deepest dream.*
> *But in this world of confusion,*
> *Nothing is as it seems.*
>
> —Isobeau de Shera de Wolfe, 15th c.

I T HAD BEEN an odd sensation, truly. Atticus had never had to think of anyone other than himself and after he'd left Isobeau in her chambers to finish packing, he'd headed down to the stables to inspect the mare she had mentioned. He didn't know why he should do such a thing, or even care, because the horse had brought her from Alnwick to Wolfe's Lair with no problems, but she had seemed concerned about the endurance of the animal which spurred his sense of concern as well.

Atticus had never had to consider anyone else before – their safety or their comfort. He was a selfish man but that selfishness had kept him alive and safe all of these years. Therefore, inspecting the somewhat skittish mare with the strange look to her eye, he decided that he didn't want Isobeau riding the beast for the long journey south.

He went on the hunt for a sturdy, less-skittish animal and came across a very big, very shaggy gelding that his father used. The animal was so calm that he had to slap it a couple of times, affectionately, to make sure it was even breathing. He was certain his father would not mind if they borrowed the animal and Atticus would feel much better with Isobeau on such a calm beast. His wife. He didn't want to have to worry about her safety on an already-perilous journey.

But there was another reason as well, something he didn't want to admit to himself because it sounded incredibly cruel and self-centered. He knew that Titus had given Isobeau the lovely mare and somehow, he didn't want that reminder of his brother around. Titus had asked him to marry Isobeau and he had done that. But he was coming to realize that he had to make a life with her; nay, he *wanted* to make a life with her, and a constant reminder of Titus would make that difficult. Perhaps it was selfish or perhaps it was understandable; in any case, he didn't want her riding the mare. He hoped that Titus, wherever the man was, would understand.

He had Kenton take charge of the great, hairy beast to prepare it for the journey as he checked on his own horse and completed other small duties that centered around their departure. As he was crossing the inner ward on his way back to Isobeau's chamber, he remembered about Norfolk's injured knight, a man who was now his hostage. Taking a detour, he headed into the great hall, the last place he had seen the man. He wanted to see the knight and to make his position, and the position of the hostage, abundantly clear. That was simply good manners in the complex and ruthless world of knights.

The great hall of Wolfe's Lair was a long, slender room that could easily house a hundred men at any given time. It had a sharply pitched roof and a great fire pit in the center of the hall, with small holes in the ceiling for the smoke to escape. The fire was burning low in the big pit and a haze of blue smoke hung up towards the ceiling, ribbons of smoke filtering out through the vents. The hall, usually so cold and dark, was fairly warm and well lit. As Atticus made his way deeper into the hall, he could see Norfolk's knight positioned against the wall nearest to the pit.

The man was tucked back in the shadows a bit and as Atticus came upon him, he saw his father's physic from Hawick and an older male servant tending the man. The knight noticed Atticus right away and their gazes met through the haze of smoke. Emotionlessly, Atticus was the first to speak.

"How do your injuries fare?" he asked as casually as one would ask about the weather.

Alrik du Reims was as emotionless as Atticus was. A big knight with black eyes and shoulder-length hair, he glanced at the physic as the man wrapped his left ankle tightly.

"The right leg is not as bad as the left," he told him. "The right one was only partially severed but the left one has been badly cut. The physic is attempting to straighten out the tendon by stitching it together with catgut. He is not entirely sure I will ever be able to walk properly."

Atticus felt absolutely no guilt even though he had been the one to inflict life-changing injuries upon the man. His gaze lingered on the physic as he man wrapped up the leg before his attention drifted to the room, the roof, the chamber in general.

"Since you cannot run off, I will have you moved to a more private and comfortable chamber," he said. Then, his focus returned to du Reims. "You understand that you are my hostage, insurance against anything Norfolk may attempt."

Du Reims nodded his head, resigned. "I understand," he said. "But I can tell you that my presence at Wolfe's Lair will not hold off Norfolk. We have our specific orders to gain your fealty or lay siege if you refuse. Summerlin will see these orders through."

"Then you will die."

"That is always a risk in this vocation."

Atticus had to admit that he was mildly impressed with du Reims' logical assessment of his situation. There was no fear there, no pleading, only acceptance. That respect opened the door for a measure of guilt at what he'd done to the man, or rather what he'd had to do to the man, but Atticus fought it off. There was no room for guilt in his profession.

Without responding or reacting, he turned away from du Reims and quit the hall, heading for Isobeau's chamber to see if she was ready to travel as she said she would be. Thoughts of du Reims were pushed aside as he crossed the cold bailey, now illuminated with the soft strains of morning, as his mind began to turn towards thoughts of Isobeau.

It seemed as if his mind was always very quick to think of Isobeau, no matter what situation he was in. As he mounted the steps to the upper floor, he couldn't help but think of his reaction to her when he touched her earlier. Her hand in his had been exhilarating beyond words, flames of passion and lust licking at him like he'd never experienced. Even to think on it now made his heart race and he was eager to see her again, to perhaps touch her hand again, or even more. Was it wrong that he wanted to kiss her, to taste this woman he had married? He was nearly to the top of the steps on the third level, wrapped up in thoughts of Isobeau, when Warenne suddenly appeared.

"Good Christ," Atticus hissed, putting his hand over his heart as he fell back against the door jamb. "You startled me."

Warenne smiled weakly. "That is not a statement you make often."

Atticus shook his head. "Not at all," he said. Gazing into Warenne's drawn expression, he sobered. "I am sorry for what I had to do to Summerlin earlier, Ren. I know that he is your wife's brother but the man all but threatened Wolfe's Lair and I had to assert my dominance. I hope you understand that."

Warenne waved him off. "Of course I understand," he said. "But Shaun's appearance meant much more to me than it did to you."

Atticus nodded, seeing the distress in Warenne's eyes. "I realize that," he said. "What did he say to you, Ren? Is there anything I can do?"

Warenne shook his head. "You know that I am related to Norfolk, of course," he muttered, raking his fingers through his dark hair. "He is a distant cousin on my father's side. My wife's family, the House of Summerlin, is sworn to him now. That was not the case only a year ago, but according to Shaun, it is the case now. He told me that my wife has left Thetford and returned to the home of her father to live under his roof."

Concerned, Atticus put his hand on Warenne's shoulder. "I am sorry to hear that, my friend," he said sincerely. "What will you do?"

Warenne lifted his eyebrows in resignation. "I must return home immediately," he said. "I… I have been thinking, Atticus. Mayhap I have not been a good husband, after all. I have spent my time fighting wars for Henry when mayhap the real war I should have been fighting is the one at home. I should have fought to keep my wife. If what Shaun said is true, and I have no reason to doubt him, then Madeleine is back with her father who is now a supporter of Edward. I am not entirely sure how to get her back."

Atticus' brow furrowed. "She is your wife," he said firmly. "She must come back to you. It is her duty."

Warenne smiled weakly. "You do not understand women, do you?" he asked. "Do you think it will make her happy to return to a husband who is at odds with her family? She will be miserable returning to me, knowing that I will be going to battle against her brother and father. I do not want my wife miserable, Atticus."

Atticus could see where the conversation was heading. He had a horrifying suspicion of exactly what Warenne was driving at. "Then what?" he asked, torn between disgust and sorrow. "Do you swear fealty to Edward?"

Warenne sighed heavily. "It may be my only choice."

Atticus dropped his hand from the man's shoulder. "So you

compromise your beliefs to make your wife happy?"

Warenne gave him a pointed look. "You have a wife now," he said. "Ask yourself that same question when you become fond of the woman. Judge me not, my friend, for you will find the same answer that I have."

Atticus didn't contest him, mostly because what Warenne said gave him pause. *Ask yourself that same question when you become fond of the woman.* God help him, he was already fond of her. But would he change loyalties in order to please her? Of that, he was not so certain. Confused, he turned away from Warenne but he didn't leave. He simply lingered a few feet away, pondering the situation Warenne found himself in. The truth was that he understood it, or at least he was coming to, and that scared him.

"I do not judge you," he finally said. "You told me once that I should come to know what Titus liked so well about Isobeau. In order to fulfill my promise to my brother and in order to make the marriage work, you told me that was what I had to do."

Warenne was looking at him in the dim light of the entryway. "And you told me that you found it."

Atticus nodded faintly, drawing in a deep and pensive breath. "Aye," he muttered. "I found it. I am fond of her. In fact, I believe it is more than that but I cannot be certain. She is a duty, a promise to my brother, and nothing more… isn't she?"

Warenne went to him, now the one to put his hand on Atticus' shoulder. "If you are asking that question, then I suspect you are feeling much more for her than you will admit."

Atticus let out a deep, pent-up sigh, as if all of his control suddenly left him. He slouched against the doorway. "It is not right," he hissed. "Ren, this is the woman my brother loved. I feel as if I am debasing his memory if I allow myself to entertain thoughts about the woman that are more than simple duty. I am attracted to her and hating myself for it."

Warenne squeezed his shoulder. "You should not," he said quietly. "Look at it this way, Atticus; Titus is dead. He is never coming back. You must make a life with Isobeau, as your wife, and not as your dead brother's widow. She is your wife now and she belongs to you. You are not debasing Titus' memory by feeling attraction or even love for the woman. Don't you think that is what he would want? Don't you believe he would be very happy if he knew the two of you loved one another and were happy together? Why should you feel guilt for that?"

Atticus could see his point and it made him feel marginally better, but he was still wrestling with the inherent guilt that an attraction to his brother's widow brought. But she was his wife now and that superseded everything, even the fact that she was Titus' widow. He turned to his friend, forcing a smile.

"As always, you are the voice of reason," he said. "But I cannot help the doubts that plague me. I hope they will go away in time, but at this moment, I am confused with what I feel and struggling to come to terms with it."

Warenne patted him on the shoulder. "You will come to terms with it, of that I have no doubt," he said. "But it is still too soon after Titus' death for you to feel otherwise. Still, you will come to accept what you feel for her and the guilt will leave you. How does *she* feel? Have you even asked?"

Atticus shook his head firmly. "Nay," he said. "I would not know what to say to the woman. I am sure she views our marriage as a duty and nothing more. She is fulfilling Titus' last request, as I am."

Warenne knew women a bit better than Atticus did. Moreover, he had seen the way Lady Isobeau looked at her new husband. He knew there was something there, something buried deep in the woman's heart, but he would not tell Atticus for the man would more than likely not believe him. He would have to discover it for himself.

"Mayhap someday you will ask her and she will be truthful," he said rather generically. "Meanwhile, I have some serious issues of my own to deal with, issues that are consuming me."

Atticus pulled his attention off of Isobeau and his feelings for her, looking to Warenne and seeing how saddened the man appeared. He felt for his friend.

"Whatever happens, Ren," he said quietly, "if I must face you in battle at some point because you have sworn fealty to Edward... know that I consider you my closest friend. I will not lift a sword against you, no matter what. Loyalties and politics cannot destroy the bond between us."

Warenne forced a brave smile but his eyes were moist. "This is a painful situation for me."

"And for me. But do what you must and I will not love you less for it."

Warenne patted him on the cheek and dropped his hand. "Nor I, you," he muttered. "I must go home now and see if I can undo the damage done. I want my wife back. I want my family back. I am willing to do whatever is necessary to achieve that."

Atticus nodded. "I understand," he said. "Family above all. Were I in your shoes, I would more than likely do the same."

Warenne nodded, reaching out to grasp Atticus' hand one last time. For a moment, they simply looked at each other, a thousand silent words of brotherhood and friendship filling the air between them. There wasn't much more either of them could say but Warenne made one last attempt.

"I am sorry I will be unable to see your vengeance through with de la Londe and de Troiu," he confessed tightly. "But when you face them, Atticus... when you face them and you punish them... one of those sword thrusts to their bellies will have my name on it. For me, you will do this. Even if I am not with you there in body, I will be with you in spirit."

Atticus nodded, feeling sad and emotional at Warenne's departure. "I miss you already," he whispered. "Safe travels, my friend. I hope you are able to bring your wife back."

"As I am."

"If you need me, send word. I will come."

"I will."

Atticus let go of Warenne, watching the man head down the steps and down into the inner ward where he would collect his horse and belongings and be along his way. His heart was heavy for Warenne, knowing what the man needed to face. He had always been so proud of his wife and children, and now this.

When the Earl of Thetford faded from view, Atticus turned back for the darkened corridor and resumed his path to Isobeau's chamber. Still, his heart was heavy for his friend. Would he ever love his wife so much that he would do anything for her, too? At the moment, he couldn't discount anything and he labored to shake off the sorrows of Warenne de Winter.

Isobeau's door was shut and he rapped softly on it, calling her name. She didn't answer immediately and he knocked again, louder this time. He had to knock two more times before he heard the latch lift from the other side and the door slowly creaked open.

Atticus found himself gazing into Isobeau's oddly flushed face. She appeared very sleepy and his brow furrowed with concern as he stepped into the chamber.

"Are you feeling well?" he asked her. "Did I wake you?"

Isobeau stifled a yawn, covering her mouth. "I laid down to rest for a moment and fell asleep," she said. "But I am packed. I am ready to depart."

Atticus looked at her dubiously; he didn't like her pallor. She simply didn't look well. Reaching out, he put a hand to her forehead only to discover that she was quite warm. Seized with concern, he put his hand on her cheeks to realize that they were searing.

"Good Christ," he hissed. "You are on fire."

Confused, Isobeau put her hand to her own forehead even as Atticus was dragging her back over to the bed. "I am simply tired," she said, refusing to admit that she had a fever. "I will be fine. We can leave whenever you wish."

Atticus shook his head firmly and pushed her down onto the bed. "Lay down," he commanded softly. "I am going to fetch the physic."

Isobeau bolted to her feet. "Not your father's physic," she said, almost panicked. "I do not like that man."

Atticus was trying to calm her. "I know you do not," he said evenly. "But he is skilled. He will know what is the matter with you."

She frowned tremendously and tried to move away from him, but he grasped her by the arms. She tried to pull free. "He is a terrible, foolish man," she said, quite unhappy. "If you bring him here, I will not let him look at me."

Without even realizing it, Atticus tried to gently negotiate with her. He didn't like seeing her unhappy. "Sweetling, you must," he said. "I will be here the entire time. I will not leave him alone with you, I swear it, but you must let him examine you and discover what is the matter. You are running quite a fever."

Pouting and ill, Isobeau allowed Atticus to drag her back over to the bed. He gently pushed her down to sit on it, kissing her forehead as he did so. It seemed like the most natural of actions, a tender kiss to her hot forehead. He smacked his lips.

"Christ," he muttered. "'Tis as if I kissed a branding iron."

She was deeply unhappy with his comment and her hand went up to her hot forehead. "I am not *that* hot," she said. "Stop exaggerating."

Atticus saw an opportunity to tease her, however gently. He slapped a hand over his mouth as he moved to the door. "I am burned," he said, hoping he could at least make her laugh a bit. The truth was that he was extremely worried. "My lips will never be the same."

As he'd hoped, Isobeau fought off a grin and looked away. "It serves you right," she said. "Never kiss a woman unless you have her permission."

He opened the door to summon a servant, his hand still on his mouth. "I am your husband," he said flatly. "I do not need your permission."

Isobeau turned her nose up at him. "Is that so?" she said, collapsing back on the bed because she was, in truth, quite exhausted. "If someone has told you such a thing, they were sadly mistaken. You must not kiss a woman who does not want to be kissed. You could come away missing an eye."

He burst out in laughter, summoning his father's elderly servant from down the corridor and sending the man scampering off for the physic. As the old man fled, he shut the door and faced Isobeau, now lying on the bed with her feet hanging over the side.

"Would you really gouge my eye out if you did not want me to kiss you?" he asked, rubbing his chin and pretending to be serious. "I may have to rethink my views on a husband-wife relationship if that is the case."

Now that she was on her back, Isobeau was feeling extremely lethargic and tired. She did, indeed, have a fever and it was pulling at her, but not enough so that she wasn't enjoying the gentle flirtation between her and Atticus. It was the first time for such a thing and she didn't want to miss a moment of it, no matter how badly she felt.

"You have never been married before so you would not know," she said. "There is a proper way to do such things."

He put his hands on his hips. "You were only married a couple of months," he said, cocking a stern eyebrow. "Do not think yourself to be such an expert."

She tilted her head, looking at him. "I am more of an expert than you."

Atticus frowned, unwilling to admit she might actually have more experience at something than he had. But it was all in good fun. "My father has had more experience than either of us," he said. "I will ask him if I need permission to kiss my wife."

"Why not just ask your wife and be done with it?"

He cocked his head, conceding the point. Then, he made his way over to the bed, standing over her as she lay upon his mother's faded silk coverlet. The humor of the situation faded as he envisioned her spread across the silk, her blond hair splayed about her head and shoulders like angel's wings. His heart began to race, fluttering oddly in his chest.

"God, you're an alluring creature," he murmured as his gaze drifted over her. "You are quite beautiful."

Isobeau smiled at his words, warmed and thrilled by them. Hearing him speak made her think that perhaps he was seeing her as more than a duty after all. As she gazed up into his handsome face, she fervently hoped so. She very much wanted to be more than a duty to him.

"Are you saying that so I will give you permission to kiss me?" she asked softly. "If you are, it is working."

He broke down into a grin. "I did not say it to coerce you," he said quietly. "I said it because it was the truth. You are the most beautiful woman I have ever seen."

Isobeau was deeply flattered, feeling giddy. Something in his eyes glimmered, suggesting warmth and truth and... Sweet Jesus, could she even hope for more? Was it even possible?

"Then I give you permission to kiss me," she said very softly, whispering the words. "You need not ask permission if you feel the need. I will allow it, for always."

The smile faded from Atticus' face. Before he realized it, he was bent over her, his enormous arms braced on either side of her slender body, his head hovering above hers. All he could see at the moment was the most alluring, sensuous woman he'd ever known. His wife. There were brief flashes in his mind of Titus, but flashes that were quickly pushed aside by whatever he was feeling for Isobeau. How he came to feel for the woman so quickly, so strongly, was beyond him. All he knew was that he had an attraction to her stronger than he could control.

With great tenderness, he bent down and kissed her on the forehead. When that wasn't satisfying enough, his mouth slanted over her warm, dry lips, and suckled gently. Within the first few seconds of tasting her, however, lust as he'd never experienced bolted through him and his big arms went around her, pulling her up from the mattress and holding her against his chest as his lips devoured her.

She was soft, heated, and compliant in his arms, and he'd never tasted anything so sweet in his life. When her hands timidly moved to his face, clutching at him, that gentle motion drove him wild with excitement and he opened his mouth to her, his tongue snaking its way between her honeyed lips, now tasting her tongue as if it were the most delicious of morsels.

Isobeau whimpered, her body caving into him, and Atticus held her so tightly that he very nearly crushed her. Only when she pulled her mouth away from his, gasping for breath, did he realize how firmly, how powerfully, he was kissing her. He pulled back to look at her half-lidded eyes and kiss-swollen lips. Their eyes met and he felt something more than he'd ever felt, for anyone. Something within her green eyes reached out, grasped his heart, and devoured it.

At that moment, he wanted nothing more than to rip her clothes off and drive his swollen male member into her quivering, yielding flesh, joining himself with her until he spilled himself deep. And then he would take her again and again until this wild lust inside of him was satisfied.

But he knew he couldn't do that, not now. The last shards of control that he possessed brought him back to his senses, reminding him that she was ill and, for the first time in his life, he could not do as he pleased with a woman. He smiled weakly, apologetic that he had lost control, but that didn't stop him from kissing her one last time, gently, before letting her go.

"I suppose now you know what it means to give me permission to kiss you," he said, trying to make light of his powerful reaction.

Isobeau was back on the coverlet now, her heart beating so forcefully against her ribs that she was positive it was about to shoot out of her chest and fly across the room. She put a hand on her chest, subconsciously, as if to prevent such a thing.

"I suppose," she agreed, breathless. "Next time I shall be prepared."

His eyes glimmered at her. "I hope not," he said. "I rather like it when you are not prepared."

All Isobeau could do was grin; a silly, foolish, unrestrained grin. All Atticus could do was mirror her expression. But the physic arrived shortly thereafter and put a stop to all of the foolish grinning, yet the mood, the joy, lingered.

Perhaps there was to be more to this marriage, after all, than just a duty.

CHAPTER THIRTEEN

> Ionian scale in C – A Love so Noble
>
> A love so noble
> A love so kind
> A kiss so delicious,
> My heart mingled with thine.
>
> —Isobeau de Shera de Wolfe, 15th c.

1.8 miles southeast of Wolfe's Lair, near the village of Byrness

SHAUN WINCED WHEN the barber-surgeon threw the last stitch into his scalp where Atticus had kicked him and nearly knocked him out cold. When he'd finally returned to the main army encampment, he realized he had a two-inch gash on his scalp that had been bleeding profusely. As he sat in his tent along with three knights, his senior commanders, and the barber-surgeon, all he could manage to feel was rage.

"I have no idea what he did to du Reims," he told the host of concerned faces around him. "De Wolfe cut him from behind in the legs and the man could not walk, so he entirely severed his knees or cut the back of his legs in general. The last I saw, they were carrying Rik into Wolfe's Lair because the man was unable to support himself. De Wolfe told me that if our army laid siege to the Lair, he would kill Rik and toss his dead body over the wall. I have no reason not to believe him."

The three knights facing him were seasoned knights who had served the House of de Mowbray for quite some time. Two of them were a father and son, Sir Ferris Aston and his son, Edmund, and the third knight was a legacy knight with Norfolk, meaning his father, grandfather, and great-grandfather had all served the House of de Mowbray. Sir Rafael Archer-Phipps was a big man with a crown of curly auburn hair and a rather nasty manner about him. Rik du Reims was his friend and he was greatly displeased with what Summerlin had told them.

"Bastard," Rafael hissed. "I do not care if he is called The Lion of the North; Atticus de Wolfe has my ire for what he's done to Rik. He cut him down!"

Summerlin tried to shake his head, made difficult by the barber-surgeon piercing his flesh. "Rik is not dead."

Rafael was exasperated. "But he was badly injured," he insisted. "Was there no way to save him? Did you have to leave him behind?"

Summerlin growled, unhappy at the question, unhappy at the barber-surgeon stabbing him in the scalp with a bone needle.

"Do you truly believe I would have left him behind if I'd had a choice?" he barked at Archer-Phipps. "Of course I had no choice. De Wolfe's archers had taken out the soldiers I brought with me and there was no guarantee that he was not going to take me out as well. Someone had to return to tell you what had happened and that someone happened to be me."

"We have orders to lay siege to the de Wolfe stronghold if they will not side with Edward," Ferris Aston spoke softly. The father-figure of the group, he was usually the one the men listened to. "We cannot return to Arundel and tell de Mowbray that we did not carry out his orders because we feared for du Reims' life. That is not an option."

The knights knew that, an ominous knowledge of a colleague's potential death hanging over their heads. No one wanted to send Alrik du Reims to his doom, but a worse option was returning to de Mowbray with the news that they had failed to carry out their orders. That would not be well met. Summerlin, eyeing Ferris as the barber-surgeon put the last stitch in his scalp, sighed heavily.

"Then Rik forfeits his life," he said simply. "If we have to make a choice between Norfolk's orders and du Reims' life, we must choose fealty to our lord over the life of a knight. I, for one, do not want to be known as a commander who disobeys orders. If Norfolk dismisses me, I would never be able to serve another lord. I would have no honor."

Archer-Phipps nearly exploded. "So you would not trade your honor for a man's life?" he demanded. "You may as well sink the blade into his chest yourself!"

Ferris held up a hand to Archer-Phipps before the man went on a rampage. "Enough," he said softly but firmly. "Do you think Shaun wants to do this? Of course he does not. But we do not have a choice. You know what Norfolk will do if we disobey him. Dismissal would be the least of the options. He has been known to flog men who disobey him, or worse, thrown them in the vault. There is no other option here and you know it; we must march on Wolfe's Lair. We must claim her in the name of Edward. These are Norfolk's orders and they will be obeyed."

Archer-Phipps, red in the face, turned away in disgust and worry even though he knew Ferris was right. Ferris was always right. Agitated, he paced the tent for a few moments before coming to a halt. "Why can we not negotiate for du Reims' release?"

Summerlin looked up at him. "With what?"

Archer-Phipps threw up his arms in exasperation. "I have coinage with me," he said. "Mayhap if we pool our money, we can buy his release."

Summerlin shook his head, itching at the stitches on his scalp. "The de Wolfes are already rich," he muttered. "They do not need or want our paltry few coins."

"But you can at least try!"

Ferris intervened again, putting himself between Archer-Phipps and Summerlin. "I will discuss it with Shaun," he said. "You and Edmund go and prepare the men. We will depart before dawn for Wolfe's Lair. Go, now; make sure everything is ready."

It was a distraction tactic and they all knew it, especially Archer-Phipps. He eyed Summerlin, Ferris, and Summerlin again, his expression suggesting he didn't believe they were really going to discuss du Reims' release, before quitting the tent after Edmund. The truth was that he didn't have to say a word because the mood of his movements, his countenance, said more than he ever could. He didn't believe them. They were liars. Alrik du Reims was as good as dead. When he was gone, Ferris turned to Summerlin.

"There was truly nothing to be done, Shaun?" he asked. "De Mowbray will not be pleased to have lost du Reims. His father is the Earl of East Anglia and a longtime ally of Norfolk. Moreover, he is a good man. He is the best man among us if you ask me. Are you sure there was nothing to be done?"

Summerlin shook his head, rising from the stool he had been sitting on. He was weary, beaten, and truth be told, embarrassed about what had happened. A single man with a sword had gotten the better of him and another knight, a man he considered quite skilled. He grunted, unhappy and defeated.

"I have never seen a man move so fast," he muttered. "One second we were speaking and in the next, du Reims was down and so was I. I have never personally fought against Atticus de Wolfe but it is clear to me why he has earned the reputation he has. I am ashamed to say that he bested me quickly. That has never happened before. As for du Reims, there was nothing more I could do. You know I would have exhausted all options if there had been any."

Ferris pondered the situation seriously, drawing in a long and thoughtful breath. "I know de Wolfe by reputation only as well," he said. "I have heard that he is ruthless and skilled, but never that he is barbaric and cruel. Mayhap there is a chance for du Reims. Mayhap we can appeal to de Wolfe's honor not to kill the man."

Summerlin snorted. "Talk of honor is what caused de Wolfe to strike," he said, shaking his head reluctantly. "I do not believe I want to take that tactic again."

"But we must do *something*."

Summerlin nodded, mulling over the mystery and man that was Atticus de Wolfe. "We will," he said. "Meanwhile, make sure the men are prepared. We depart for Wolfe's Lair before dawn."

Ferris quit the tent without another word, leaving Summerlin to ponder the course his mission had taken in silence. He was fearful to return to Norfolk to tell the man he was down one very good knight and without his objective of Atticus de Wolfe or Wolfe's Lair. He knew Norfolk would not accept failure easily. He more than likely would never trust Summerlin again with anything of importance. Either way, Summerlin's career as a knight might be over, at least in England.

He'd always hated France but he supposed he'd better change his mind. French lords were always looking for skilled English knights, even disgraced ones.

CHAPTER FOURTEEN

> Ionian scale in C – Lyrics to Hope
>
> Hope dims but it does not die,
> Hope remains when all else is gone.
> Hope is fragile but it cannot be broken.
> Hope is all I have now that I am alone.
>
> —Isobeau de Shera de Wolfe, 15th c.

Wolfe's Lair

IT WAS DAWN as Atticus stood at the lancet window overlooking the western expanse of the moor that surrounded his family's ancient fortress. The past day or two had seen temperatures warm significantly and the ice that formed on the ground overnight was quickly gone by mid-morning. In fact, temperatures had warmed quite rapidly, suggesting that spring was, in fact, on its way. It would have been wonderful traveling weather if, in fact, he had been able to travel. But those plans were temporarily on hold.

He turned to look at Isobeau, sleeping soundly in his mother's bed. *The remains of the child are poisoning her*, the physic had said. That was the cause of the fever. Evidently, when Isobeau had bled out her dead baby not everything had been evacuated, and the physic was forced to take steps that would help heal Isobeau's womb. He put some kind of a potion into her, rinsing her out, and made her ingest something else that would allegedly help her heal. *Colt's Foot*, he'd said. It all seemed mysterious and magic.

That had taken place yesterday. Even though Isobeau had remained brave through the entire process, it had been exhausting and painful and traumatic. After the procedures, she had fallen into a dead sleep and had remained that way for nearly twelve hours; Atticus knew because he'd never left her side, as he'd promised. The truth was that he didn't *want* to leave her. This woman he'd married, the one he was becoming so wildly attracted to, was quickly consuming his focus as if nothing else existed. He had a mission to complete, justice for his brother, but at that moment, those plans were on hold. He never thought he'd see the day when a woman would cause him to put aside a strong sense of duty. Perhaps a strong sense of affection, or more, was even more powerful than that. The truth was that he wasn't all that upset about it.

Turning away from the window and the breaking dawn, he made his way over to the bed, standing over it to gaze upon the woman he married. There was some color back in her face and she didn't look nearly as sick as she had. He was grateful. That foolish physic his father employed was skilled even if he was difficult to deal with.

Thoughts of his father then came upon him and he pondered his father's general mood and health over the past day or two. Solomon was still heavily grieving Titus and had taken to his bed for most of the day and night. He had been oddly quiet, too, which was strange for the usually very vocal man. Atticus was thinking on looking in on his father when there was a soft knock on the door. Quietly, Atticus went to answer it.

Kenton was standing in the corridor, his stubbled face grim. "Trouble, Atticus."

Atticus' eyebrows lifted. "What trouble?" he asked almost reluctantly. "The last time you were here with news, Norfolk's knights were on our doorstep. What now?"

Kenton gave him an expression that was droll and intense at the same time. It was an odd mixture. "Call me the bearer of bad tidings, then," he said. "You told Summerlin not to return, did you not?"

Atticus' brow furrowed. "He's back?"

"Back with Norfolk's army."

Now Atticus was stunned. "He's *back* with the army?"

Kenton nodded. "You told him that you would kill du Reims if he returned," he said. "Evidently, the man does not care about his comrade."

Atticus' features hardened, outrage in his eyes. "Surely you jest, Kenton. This is not funny at all."

Kenton shook his head, the irony of the situation not lost on him. "I do not have a sense of humor; therefore, I do not jest," he replied. "Summerlin is back with his army and they are preparing to mount an offensive against Wolfe's Lair."

Atticus' outrage turned to pure rage. "Then he will learn the hard way that I do not make threats I do not intend to carry out," he said. "Summerlin and his men are in for a brutal time of it."

Kenton understood. A threat, once given, could not be rescinded or Atticus would look like a weakling. "Much is his misfortune, then," was all he could say.

Atticus' mind was already whirling with the burden of command. Norfolk's army was here. His instincts took charge, the training that had been part of his life since a very early age, and he stepped out into the corridor and softly shut the door behind him. The scent of battle was already filling the air and he inhaled of it deeply; he fed off of it. He was in his element with it. The Lion was born for battle.

"Then we prepare," he said as he began to head towards the inner ward and, subsequently, the gatehouse. He wanted to see what was coming. "Are the men mobilizing?"

Kenton nodded. He was extremely efficient, already anticipating what needed to happen. "They are," he said. "Warenne has not left yet, you know. He ended up staying the night because it was late by the time he was fully prepared to depart. He is already positioning the men upon the walls."

"And my father?"

"I have not yet seen him."

They were now descending the steps that would lead down to the inner ward, which was alive with men and animals. Soldiers were moving all of the animals and supplies they could into the stables because of the sod roof. If Norfolk decided to send flaming projectiles over the wall, at least the roof would not burn and protect those beneath. Atticus passed a practiced eye over the commotion, assessing it, understanding the progress in an instant. Already, much had been done.

"Leave my father in peace for now," he said. "I will go and speak to him after I have fully assessed the situation. At the moment, I need to see the approach and positioning of Norfolk's army."

Kenton gestured to Atticus' torso. "You should dress for battle first in case they decide to employ the archers. Knowing Norfolk, they will be his initial assault."

Atticus eyed him. "You know that always comes last with me," he said. "The restriction of armor makes me feel less than agile."

Kenton shook his head. He had been fighting with Atticus for many years and he knew that. He didn't agree with it, but he knew the man's position. "You are the only knight I know who feels encumbered by protection," he said. "Someday that is going to cost you. You would fight naked if you could, Atticus."

Atticus grinned. "If I thought I could get away with it, I would," he said. "I move much better when I am not covered by great hunks of metal."

"You are an odd creature."

Atticus laughed softly as they made their way up the wall to the gatehouse where he could better see the approach of Norfolk's army.

The moment he was in position to gain a view of the eastern moors, he could see the army in the distance, lined up on the crest between Wolfe's Lair and the small valley that spread out before it.

In the light of dawn, Atticus studied the distant cluster of men and animals. There were trees in the distance, somewhat marring a clear view of the army, but he could see easily enough of it. They were moving forward at a slow pace. He pointed to the incoming tide of men.

"I see at least two siege engines," he said. "They will have little trouble rolling those to the wall of the castle but they will not be high enough."

"So they will bring in ladders," Kenton said. "Ultimately, that is what they will use to try and mount the walls."

Atticus agreed. "That is true, but they will have to be very tall ladders to reach the top, and ladders that tall are unstable," he said. His gaze lingered on the distant army a moment longer before turning away. "I will inform my father of what is happening and then I intend to pay a visit to du Reims. The man and I must speak."

Kenton watched him as he headed down the narrow stairs that led up from the ward. "Do you truly intend to kill him and toss him over the wall?"

"That is what he and I will speak of."

Kenton didn't press him and he didn't offer his opinion. Atticus had a better sense of knightly chivalry and honor than most, but all of this was tied into Titus' death so he wasn't entirely sure just how restrained, or how fair, Atticus would be in his judgement. Du Reims was a man who couldn't really fight back should Atticus go after him and it would be unlike Atticus to go to battle against a man who couldn't defend himself. He would consider that dishonorable. Still, the situation was different these days. Kenton would keep an eye on Atticus and how he dealt with du Reims because he didn't want the man to do anything that he would later regret.

Atticus, now at the bottom of the steps, wasn't oblivious to Kenton's thoughts. They were close and understood each other well. He knew Kenton didn't approve of the possible execution of du Reims and, deep down, Atticus wasn't entirely comfortable with it either. There was the little matter of honor with him, honor that would prevent him from outright murdering a disabled knight. Still, he couldn't let Summerlin's defiance go unanswered and they all knew it. Just how he dealt with that defiance would define this battle in particular. He was halfway across the inner ward when he heard Kenton's bellow.

"Incoming!"

Atticus dashed for the safety of the nearest shelter, which happened to be the stables. He had no sooner entered the smelly, dark confines when a series of arrows pelted the inner ward. Two men who had been scrambling for shelter had been hit but those were the only injuries. As Atticus emerged from the stable, looking at all of the arrows, he realized it could have been much worse, him included. Now he thought that perhaps he should don his armor before he did anything else. With the armory across the ward, he began running.

"Collect these arrows for our own use!" he yelled to the men around him, who began to scramble. "Take them up to the archers on our walls!"

Men were rushing everywhere, collecting the arrows that had been shot at them, as Atticus reached the other side of the bailey. There was a small tower in the southeast corner of Wolfe's Lair's curtain wall, and he immediately began donning his mail. He had stored it on a frame in the armory, a frame that held his hauberk as well as his plate armor and heavily padded tunic he wore underneath. A soldier who happened to be near the armory came to help him and between the two of them, they managed to get his armor on completely.

Now, fully protected, he continued on to inform his father and also Isobeau of what they would be facing. He was no sooner out of the armory when Kenton yelled again and a second round of arrows rained down from the sky. Atticus was moving up the exposed staircase that led to the upper floors when a shaft caught him in the back of his thigh.

Angered, and hardly aware of any pain, Atticus ripped the arrow free and tossed it aside for the men collecting arrows to retrieve. At the moment, he had more important things on his mind, but most importantly, furious that Summerlin should attack Wolfe's Lair after he'd spared the man's life and told him to go home. Evidently, his mercy had been betrayed.

He would not make the mistake a second time.

ISOBEAU HAD NOT been part of a siege before. Isenhall, her home, had been mostly peaceful her entire life so the event of an actual battle was something shocking. Shocking and eye-opening. It was an entirely new experience altogether.

Earlier that day, Atticus had come to tell her, dressed in full armor, that Wolfe's Lair was under attack. Awoken from a deep sleep but feeling infinitely better than she had from the day before, she'd listened to his information with some horror. *Norfolk had come back.* Atticus had instructed her to have servants bring supplies to her room and then barricade herself behind the sturdy, oak door until he came for her, and she did just that at first. The two female servants at Wolfe's Lair had brought supplies to her chamber and then had remained with her behind the barricaded door until sometime later in the day when a male servant came knocking on her door wanting to know if she had any needle and thread with her.

It seemed that there were several wounded in the hall, men who had been hit with arrows, and the physic from Hawick was running out of catgut. He needed thread and, as Isobeau questioned him through the closed door, it sounded as if he needed help as well. More wounded were coming in by the minute because Norfolk had taken to slinging things like spikey tree trunks and other damaging objects over the wall with a small ox-drawn trebuchet they'd brought with them. Part of the stable had collapsed from something heavy slung over the walls and some of the animals were injured. Panicked, thinking it might have been her mare, Isobeau collected her precious sewing kit and dashed out of the chamber with the female servants in tow.

What she saw shocked her to the bone. The inner ward of Wolfe's Lair had been pummeled with tree trunks and other large chunks of trees that had been hurled over the walls. Arrows littered the muddy ground. She could see de Wolfe men lining the wall walk, watching Norfolk's activity below, but they weren't doing much more than watching at this point. Norfolk was expending all of the energy. Isobeau didn't see Atticus, which was probably a good thing. With everyone's attention focused outside of the wall, Isobeau was able to move about rather freely.

Her first stop was the stable to check on her mare. The animal was quite snug and quite safe, crammed into a stall along with three goats and a small work pony. The horse seemed quite happy with the company. Satisfied her pet was safe, Isobeau proceeded across the inner ward to the great hall on the other side, entering the slender, long structure.

Immediately, she was confronted by several wounded men. They were all positioned over near the hearth, which was burning low and smoky, a haze of blue hovering near the ceiling. But it was warm and moderately comfortable, as Isobeau made her way deeper into the hall in search of the physic to offer her assistance. The men she passed, men who were lying on the ground, seemed to be fairly injured. One man still had an arrow sticking out of him while yet another man had the arrow out of his neck but was bleeding a great deal.

It was a daunting and intimidating sight. Isobeau began to rethink her offer to help, for she truly didn't know if she would be of any use, when the physic caught sight of her and immediately put her to work. The first man she was assigned to was the one with the profusely bleeding neck. Sickened by the sight of so much blood, Isobeau threaded her needle with the fine, silk thread her father had bought for her in Coventry and went to work.

As the afternoon progressed and she stitched up man after man, the task seemed to become a bit easier. After the first three or four patients, she began to get a bit of practice and was more at ease with it. This was her second experience helping wounded, but the experience back at Alnwick had been very different from this one. These men were freshly injured and freshly in pain. She wanted very much to help them and ease their anguish but she figured out early on that she was a bit squeamish when it came to plunging a needle into a man's flesh. The first time she did it with the man with the neck wound, she had put several tiny stitches into his skin when it probably only needed four or five stitches total. He had a big cluster of white stitches in his neck that looked strangely like flower petals.

But she soldiered on, gaining experience, remembering Lady Percy at Alnwick and how stoic and calm the woman had been. She tried to be that way, too. Nearing sunset, all of the men were tended, all fourteen of them, and another man was brought in that the physic from Hawick tended personally. At that point, the only aid needed was seeing to the comfort of the wounded so Isobeau wandered among them, encouraging them to be brave from the pain or giving them some water to drink. When she came to an older man lying away from the fire, off by himself, he seemed to be quite miserable from the arrow wound to his gut. He was shivering and sweating, and Isobeau knew enough about illnesses and wounds to know that the man had a fever. Kneeling next to him, she put a gentle hand on his arm.

"Sirrah?" she asked softly. "Would you like some water?"

The old man, eyes closed, stirred at the sound of her voice. Slowly, he turned his head in her direction and the wrinkled eyelids lifted. He stared at her a moment, blinking.

"Who are ye, lady?" he rasped.

Isobeau smiled faintly. "I am Lady de Wolfe," she replied. "I am Sir Atticus' wife."

A ripple of surprise moved across the old soldier's face. "The Lion?"

"Aye."

The old lips creased into a distant smile. "I knew him as a boy, m'lady," he said. "We are proud of him, we are. He has grown into a fine and famous man."

Isobeau continued to smile at the old soldier, unsure what to say to that. She wanted to agree, to perhaps heap praise upon Atticus for his reputation only, but she was embarrassed to do so, embarrassed that she was so willing to praise him after having been his wife for little more than two days. As if she had any right to be proud. But the kiss between them the day before, that heated gesture of liquid fire, was still enough to make her heart race every time she thought of it. Titus' kisses had been soft and warm and comfortable; being kissed by Atticus was like being burned by the sun.

"We are all very proud of him, of course," she said, lifting the wooden cup from the bucket of water she had next to her. "Would you like some water?"

The old man shook his head. "Nay," he said, raspy. "My time is drawing to a close. I was lying here dreaming of the times when I was a young man. I was thinking on me mum and pa. They died when I was young, ye know. I will see them again soon."

Isobeau sobered. "You mustn't speak like that," she said. "You will get well again. Lord Solomon's physic is very skilled. He will make sure of it."

The old soldier cast her a long glance. "Do ye sing, m'lady?"

Isobeau nodded. "I do."

"Will ye sing something for me?"

Isobeau nodded eagerly this time. "Of course I will," she said. "What do you wish to hear?"

"Old Rose the Whore."

Isobeau's eyes widened in shock. "I do not know any such song," she said stiffly. "Even if I did, I would not sing it. What else would you have me sing?"

The old soldier was giggling at her offended manner. "Do you know Tilly Nodden?"

Isobeau eyed him suspiciously. "You only want me to sing unseemly songs."

The old man put a hand on her arm. "That is all I know, my lady," he said. "I am a soldier and know a soldier's life. Do ye know Tilly Nodden?"

Isobeau frowned. "Well," she said reluctantly, "I have heard it a few times. My father had soldiers that would sing it."

The old soldier's eyes twinkled in the dim light. "It is a happy song," he said. "Would ye please sing it for me?"

Isobeau was very hesitant. "I cannot sing some of the verses," she insisted. "I *will* not."

"Then sing the chorus. Let me sing it with ye."

Isobeau opened her mouth to try to refuse him yet again because the chorus had some very dirty phrases in it when a deep, smooth voice interrupted.

"That is not an appropriate song for a lady to sing. Choose another song."

Isobeau looked up to see where the voice had come from and noticed, tucked back against the wall, a big man laying upon a pallet. He was actually sitting up, his back against the wall, and both of his legs below the knees were tightly wrapped. Because of the dimness in the hall, she couldn't really see his face but it began to occur to her who the man was. *The knight Atticus cut down.* She wasn't particularly frightened, but she was wary.

"Thank you, my lord," she said rather firmly. "I can make my own denials."

"You have not done a very good job."

She eyed the man in the shadows with some irritation. "I am trying to be polite with a wounded man."

"That is true, my lady, but he is taking advantage of your good heart by trying to coerce you into singing a bawdy song."

The knight was probably right. Frowning, and unhappy that she had very nearly sang that bawdy tavern song that spoke of a cross-dressing whore, she stood up and collected her bucket with water, making her way over to the knight in the darkness.

Isobeau could see the man's face better now. He was handsome, square-jawed, with black eyes and long hair that tumbled in waves to his shoulders. He was handsome in a barbaric sort of way and she eyed him curiously.

"You are the knight that my husband cut down," she said. "What is your name?"

The knight dipped his head politely. "I am Sir Alrik du Reims," he said. "You may call me Rik. No one calls me Alrik except my wife when she is cross with me. When she uses my full name, it is time to run and hide."

His humor softened Isobeau somewhat and she fought off a grin. "You are married, then?"

He nodded. "Indeed I am," he said. "I have a wife and three small daughters."

Isobeau knelt a foot or so away from him, scooping some water from her bucket and extending the cup to him. "Where do they live?"

Du Reims took the cup gratefully and drank. "At Arundel Castle," he said, smacking his lips. "My wife is actually from Sussex. I met her whilst stationed at Arundel."

Isobeau took back the empty cup. "Have you been away from them a long time?"

Du Reims' black eyes took on a distant cast. "It seems like ages," he said. "It has only been a few months, but it seems like ages."

There was such longing in his voice that it tugged at Isobeau's heart. She couldn't help it. She lowered her gaze, putting the cup back into the bucket. "I understand," she said. "It is terrible that this war should separate and destroy families. It seems that… forgive me. I meant to say that I will pray for your wife and your children's good health while you are away, even if you are my husband's enemy."

Du Reims leaned back against the wall, eyeing the extremely luscious Lady de Wolfe. He was not surprised to see that Atticus de Wolfe had such a beautiful wife; a man of such reputation was worthy of such a woman. But it also occurred to him that, in Lady de Wolfe, he saw the woman who would save his life.

Du Reims was no fool. He knew that Summerlin had returned with the army to lay siege to Wolfe's Lair. He had expected it, in fact, and up until Lady de Wolfe presented herself, he was resigned to the fact that this would be his last day on earth. He knew that at some point, Atticus would come to the hall and kill him just as he had promised. Du Reims was in no position to really defend himself, as he could not walk, so he had spent the better part of the day attempting to figure out how he could save himself. Now, he knew. He had to do what was necessary in order to exact his freedom and it was unfortunate that Lady de Wolfe was now part of that plan.

"Thank you for your prayers, my lady," he said. "May… may I have more water before you leave?"

Isobeau complied. Dipping the cup in the water, she approached du Reims and extended the full cup. He lifted his hand to her but instead of taking the cup, he snatched her by the wrist. The water went flying as Isobeau was yanked onto the man's lap. She screamed, and tried to pull away, but before she realized it, she was seated upon his lap and his big arm was across her neck in an extremely dangerous position. His lips were against her ear.

"Forgive me, my lady," he begged softly. "But your husband intends to kill me and I apologize that I must use you to negotiate for my life. I wish to see my wife and children again and you will be the means by which I accomplish that."

Terrified, Isobeau struggled and yelped as the servants in the hall realized she was in a very precarious position. Someone bolted from the great hall, running no doubt for Atticus.

"Please calm yourself," du Reims said quietly but evenly. "I will not hurt you, I swear it, but your husband must believe that I will. I want to go home and you must help me."

Isobeau was angry as well as terrified. She tried to pull the knight's arm away from her neck, which was an impossible feat.

"You will never make it out of here alive," she said, verging on tears. "My husband will see to that!"

Du Reims was quite calm as she squirmed on his lap. "Mayhap," he muttered. "But this is a chance I must take. I am very sorry to involve you in it."

Isobeau was trying very hard not to cry, for she was genuinely terrified. "I gave you water," she said angrily. "I tried to give you some comfort and this is that thanks I get? You are a beast!"

Du Reims sighed. "I am sure you have every reason to believe that," he said. "But the truth is that I am an excellent knight and an excellent husband. My wife's name is Catrina and her family is from

Cornwall. She is a d'Vant. I have three daughters. Charlotte is five years of age and very bright. Cassandra is four years of age and she wants very much to be like her older sister. She is a joy. My baby is Annabelle and she has seen two years. Annabelle was born with crippled legs but you have never seen a sweeter nor smarter child. I think it is Annabelle that I miss the most. She loves to sing songs to me, songs she makes up herself. They do not make much sense because she cannot speak very well, but they are the most beautiful songs I have ever heard."

By this time, Isobeau had stopped struggling. She was hearing of the knight's family, coming to understand why he would make such a desperate move as to take a hostage. He had children, including a crippled one, and she could tell by the tone of his voice that he loved them very much. As frightened as she was, she also found herself being sympathetic to the knight's plight. He was fearful, too – fearful he would never see his family again. But the fact remained that he had her in a very bad position. All he had to do was squeeze and her neck would be snapped.

"As much as you do not want to die, I do not want to die, either," she said, her lower lip trembling out of fear. "I only married Atticus yesterday. Before that, I was his brother's wife. I lost my husband at that terrible place called Towton and my life is in turmoil much as yours is. I do not understand war and pain and suffering and why men who want to be king would throw this country into turmoil in order to rule. So many men have died yet there is no definitive king upon the throne. I do not like any of this and I do not want to die for a cause I do not understand."

Du Reims could feel the seeds of doubt and sympathy sprouting; doubt in what he was doing, sympathy for Titus de Wolfe's widow. But he was determined to go home and Lady de Wolfe was an integral part of that plan. If Atticus was going to threaten him, then he had to play hard and dirty as well, starting with Lady de Wolfe.

"No one does, my lady," he said quietly. "You are correct. There is much turmoil right now. Men are uncivilized to each other all in the name of Edward or Henry. Before this, I was friends with many of the knights I now fight against. It is very difficult to fight against your friends."

Isobeau could feel his grip on her relax but she didn't try to bolt, for she knew he would only tighten up. Her only hope was to try and talk him out of whatever terrible deed he wanted to use her for. Perhaps if she could speak with the man and they could understand one another, he might see that holding her hostage to ensure his release was not the way to go about things. She had to try.

"Did… did you know Atticus before these wars?" she asked.

Du Reims shook his head. "Nay," he said. "I knew him by reputation only. My life is in the south and the de Wolfes rule the north. I have never had the opportunity to know much about the north of England except in these wars."

Isobeau thought quickly on what more she could say to him, anything to force him to speak so that they could understand one another. She had to make the man feel badly enough for what he was doing to her that he would let her go.

"Atticus and his brother grew up here, in the north," she said. "They fostered at Kenilworth, however. Did you foster in the south, too?"

Du Reims shifted behind her and his enormous arm, the one across her neck, eased. "I did," he said. "Okehampton Castle. My father is the Earl of East Anglia and Okehampton is an ally. At least, they used to be but like most of us in this war, friends one moment can be enemies the next."

She sighed faintly. "I am not your enemy, Sir Knight."

"My name is Rik."

"And my name is Lady de Wolfe. I do not want to die. Please do not kill me."

Isobeau heard the knight sigh. "I do not want to die, either," he murmured. "I want to see my children grow up. I want to see their children born. I love my wife and children, my lady... I want to see them again and your husband has threatened to prevent that."

Isobeau could feel the sorrow in his tone; there was great sadness there and great longing. She truly felt a good deal of compassion for the man but she wondered, after this action, if Atticus would allow him to leave unassailed. She doubted it. The man had laid his hands upon her and, by that action alone, forfeited his life. The fact was that they both knew it. Therefore, his desperation was fed.

As she opened her mouth to reply, the big door to the hall opened and men were filtering in. She couldn't see who they were simply because the light behind them made them silhouettes, men with weapons and armor outlined in the backlighting. But she knew, instinctively, that one of them was Atticus and as the men drew close, all three of them, she could see Atticus, Kenton, and Warenne on the approach. Kenton seemed to hang back, to fan out behind them, but Atticus and Warenne approached boldly.

Isobeau looked into Atticus' face, hope and relief and joy in her expression, but Atticus was focused solely on du Reims. He had yet to even look at her. Without a word, he marched up on them, seated on the ground against the wall of the great hall, and lashed out a massive boot, kicking du Reims in his damaged legs. The pain must have been horrendous because du Reims groaned, more than likely biting off a scream, and instinctively let go of Isobeau with his left hand, reaching down for his injured legs as if to hold them fast against Atticus' assault.

But his inability to control his reaction to pain and Atticus' advantage of a surprise attack had devastating consequences for du Reims. The moment he loosened his grip on Isobeau, Atticus reached down and yanked her forward, trying to break du Reims' grip on her. In the same motion, he thrust a nasty-looking dagger straight into du Reims' neck, plunging it so deep that it came out the other side. The man's main artery was cut as well as his windpipe. Dying, he fell over onto his side as Atticus pulled Isobeau completely free.

"Atticus, *no!*" Isobeau screamed. "Sweet Jesus, no!"

Atticus didn't even look at her. Warenne was beside her now, holding her fast, because it seemed to him that she was trying to run to du Reims to somehow help the man. But he was beyond help. Without thought or sympathy or regrets, Atticus removed the dagger in du Reims' neck and plunged it again into his chest. With the heart of the big knight punctured, death was immediate.

The only sound now was that of Isobeau's shocked weeping. She stood in Warenne's grip, her hand over her mouth as she looked with horror upon du Reims' dead body. It had happened so fast that she was still struggling to process it all. But it was then, and only then, that Atticus seemed to notice her. He looked her over closely, his gaze intense and still deadly.

"Did he hurt you?" he asked.

Isobeau looked at him, tears spilling over. "You did not have to kill him," she wept. "He only wanted to go home to his wife and children."

Atticus had absolutely no sympathy, not one ounce of pity or guilt for what he had done. In fact, Isobeau's tears seemed to irritate him.

"And so he will not," he said coldly. "He signed his death warrant the moment he touched you. What are you doing in the hall, anyway? I told you to stay to your chamber."

Isobeau couldn't stop the tears; they kept coming and coming. "I came to help," she wept. "I came to help the physic tend the wounded. I was giving the knight water when he grabbed me. He… he only wanted to go home, Atticus. You did not have to kill him."

Atticus' gaze lingered on her for a moment longer before turning to Kenton, who was gazing down at du Reims' bloodied body.

"Take him up to the wall," he told Kenton. "Throw him over the side. They will see that Atticus de Wolfe keeps his word."

Without hesitation, Kenton reached down to haul du Reims up. Isobeau, unable to watch, took off running. She heard Atticus call her name but she ignored him, bolting from the hall and running for the steps that led to the upper floor. But she didn't make it to the stairs before coming to a halt and vomiting into the mud in the middle of the bailey. Overwrought, she wiped at her mouth and continued her trek towards the stairs but before she could reach them, someone grabbed her arm.

Startled, she turned to see Atticus. When she saw who it was, she yanked her arm away from him, brutally, and stumbled back, falling onto the first step behind her.

"Do not touch me," she hissed. "Leave me alone!"

Atticus' expression remained emotionless, following her as she attempted to crawl up the steps to get away from him. "I will not leave you alone," he said. "Do you not understand what happened in there, Isobeau? I saved your life."

She was climbing up the stairs on all fours, struggling to get away from him. She was nearly hysterical at that point, laboring to control her breathing. She simply couldn't wipe the image of the dead knight from her memory, a man who had spoken so lovingly of his children. It was heartbreaking in more ways than one.

"Catrina," she gasped. "His wife's name is Catrina. He has three daughters – Charlotte, Cassandra, and Annabelle. Annabelle is crippled. You did to them what de la Londe and de Troiu did to me. You took their husband and father away, and you did not have to do it. You murdered him!"

She was shouting at him by the time she was finished and Atticus' emotionless façade was starting to crack. He was starting to understand what had her so upset, the taking of a man from his wife and children. She put it in context that both of them could understand; *you did to them what de la Londe and de Troiu did to me!* Aye, he understood that very well. But she didn't see the other side of it, the warring side, the side of honor where a man threatening another man's wife would guarantee that man's death. She understood none of what was in Atticus' heart.

"I was protecting you," he said, struggling not to let the emotion she was exhibiting bleed out onto him. *Infect him.* "Du Reims had nothing to lose; he was going to kill you. I had a choice to make between sparing his life and saving yours. Did you truly think I would let the man kill you?"

Halfway up the steps to the upper level, Isobeau came to a halt. She dry heaved as nothing was coming up. She refused to look at Atticus, standing on the step below her.

"He would not have killed me," she breathed, feeling ill and overwhelmed. "He was frightened, Atticus. All he wanted to do was see his wife and children again and you took him away from them. Now they will face the same grief that you and I have faced over Titus' death but mayhap that means nothing to you. Mayhap life in general means nothing to you. Is that the kind of man you are? Do you treat all life so callously?"

Atticus simply stood there, trying not to feel wounded by her words. Each one of them was like a dagger, impaling him, drawing blood. His heart began to hurt in a way he never knew it could ache. All of it was swirling around him, causing him pain and turmoil. He didn't know what to say because, God help him, she made some sense. He didn't like that she made sense.

"Go to your chamber and bolt it," he told her, his voice oddly hollow and raspy. "You will not come out until I tell you to, not even to help the wounded. Is that clear?"

Isobeau pushed herself off the stair, rising unsteadily to her feet. "But your men are suffering," she said, wiping at her tear-stained cheeks. "I can help them. Even if you are cruel and unfeeling, I am not."

He was deeply hurt by her words when they should not have bothered him at all. He'd heard worse. But coming from her lovely lips, her words stung. He wasn't used to being stung by someone he cared for and lashed out at her.

"Your desire to help men and disobey my orders is what got another man killed," he snapped, watching her turn sharply to him, utter distress on her face. God, he couldn't look at her. Her distress was eating away at him. He turned away and headed down the steps. "If there is anyone to blame, then blame yourself. Now, go to your chamber and stay there. If I have to tell you again, I will lock you in the vault until all of this is over."

Isobeau didn't say anything more, watching the man as he headed down the steps and into the muddy, bloody bailey. He was heading for the wall, back to his warring ways. Isobeau watched him as he walked, realizing he wasn't stalking as he usually did. His movements seemed to be labored, as if he were exhausted or as if... as if there were things on his mind. Perhaps guilt at killing a man he didn't need to kill.

She wondered.

What kind of man have I married?

Someone who killed for her without hesitation. Although she was still devastated by du Reims' death, shaken by the brutality of it, there was a part of her that was glad Atticus was willing to kill for her. Without hesitation, knowing she was in danger, he had done precisely that. He was following his instincts, instincts that had him protecting her above all else. *His wife.* Perhaps she shouldn't have become so angry with him. He was only doing what he had been trained to do.

With a heavy heart, she headed up the stairs and made way to her chamber.

The siege continued into the night and on into the next day.

CHAPTER FIFTEEN

> Ionian scale in C – The Fear
>
> *I speak of thee in hush'd tones,*
> *Fearful to hear the words.*
> *In time, it seems, that which I speak of,*
> *Will soon meant to be heard.*
>
> —Isobeau de Shera de Wolfe, 15th c.

THE SMELL OF smoke was heavy in the early morning air, damp and icy as the sun began to rise. Juston had been on the road from Alnwick for two days, now beginning a third day as the gray mists of dawn began to lighten with the coming of the new day. He was exhausted and very cold, but he knew that Wolfe's Lair was close by. He'd been there once before, years ago, and knew it was less than a three day ride from Alnwick, the legendary de Wolfe fortress nestled upon the contested England/Scotland border. He was frankly looking forward to spending the night in a fortress with food and warmth. He might even stay an extra day and sleep. Lord knew he'd had little of that as of late. He swore after this jaunt he was never going to travel so much ever again.

But Juston thought it rather odd that the smell of smoke was so heavy in the air. Upon these moors were clusters of trees, occasional forests, but everything was fairly wet and frozen from the particularly cold weather they'd experienced as of late. What he was smelling was quite heavy, as if an entire forest were burning somewhere. Smoke mingled with the fog, turned to moisture, and clung to his freezing armor. Plodding along the muddy road that was on an incline to the top of a hill, he had to direct his steed onto the grass because the animal kept slipping on the mud.

The grass, cold and dead, offered some traction to the horse's hooves as Juston directed the beast up the incline. By the time they neared the top, the road had become a little less slippery and muddy because all of the water was rolling down the hill. Reining the horse back onto the road, they moved the last several feet to the top of the hill in relative ease.

At the crest of the hill, the smoke was much heavier here, as was the fog. But immediately, Juston could see a big-walled fortress off to the west, set right in the middle of a frozen moor, that was clearly under attack. He could see men in the distance swarming around it, and at least two siege engines up against the walls. Somewhat startled at the sight, he immediately spurred his horse into the nearest cluster of trees so that he would not be seen and possibly set upon by those conducting the siege. He'd been in enough battles in his lifetime to know how men in battle mode thought. Everyone, even a lone traveler, was a potential enemy.

So he wedged his horse back behind some thick-trunked trees, watching the siege carefully. There were perhaps a thousand men, maybe less, trying very diligently to mount the walls of the enormous gray-stoned structure. He knew it was Wolfe's Lair because he recognized it; therefore, it stood to reason that someone was trying to mount the de Wolfe walls and from what he could tell, it most certainly wasn't Scots. They fought much differently from the English. Nay, this was a methodical and well-thought-out siege.

Someone was trying to get to the de Wolfes, including Atticus.

It made sense to Juston that the only one who would be foolish enough to attempt that was Edward or men loyal to Edward. But why attack Wolfe's Lair? The fortress was nearly unbreachable. As Juston watched, flaming arrows suddenly shot out from the walls of the fortress, aimed at those attempting to breach her. Juston couldn't see what the damage was because he was too far away, but he could imagine it was substantial. A nasty battle was commencing on this foggy day in April as Juston stood helplessly by to watch.

But no, he wasn't helpless, not in the least. Perhaps Wolfe's Lair wasn't close to being breached or perhaps it was – he couldn't really tell and he didn't want to move any closer. But he knew one thing… Alnwick, a huge supporter of the House of de Wolfe, was only two days away if he rode swiftly. He could summon assistance for Wolfe's Lair. It was the only option as he saw it because he certainly couldn't ride away and pretend he didn't see anything. What he saw was an ally under attack. He had to summon help.

Turning his beast back onto the road, he spurred the animal as fast as it would safely go, avoiding mud puddles and great slicks of dirt as he headed back the way he came. He had to make it to Alnwick, and quickly, because Wolfe's Lair needed assistance.

Exhaustion and cold forgotten, Juston de Royans made haste for Alnwick and Northumberland's mighty army.

"YOU SHOULD KNOW that I have sent word to my son."

In the near pitch-blackness of Wellesbourne Castle's vault, Andrew's quietly uttered words reverberated with ominous finality off of the moss-covered walls. De la Londe and de Troiu, who had been sitting in blackness and silence for days on end, flinched when they heard the words. Even though they had been spoken softly, because of their sensitivity to sound, it was as if the man had shouted at them. De la Londe groaned and rubbed at his painful right ear.

"Sent word about what?" he grunted. "And by what right do you keep us locked up in here like this? No light, no air. You have condemned us to hell!"

Andrew stepped into the vault, nearer to the iron-barred cell. He had a torch in his hand, dipped in fat and burning brightly with a heavy black smoke. De la Londe and de Troiu shied away from the fire as if the sun had just entered their world.

"And you think me unfair, do you?" Andrew asked bitterly. "You, who would come to my home and try to convince me that my son is a traitor? What you have received is not nearly as bad as you deserve, but your just reward will come once my son is notified of your presence here at Wellesbourne. I simply want to inform you of what was coming so that you can sit here in the dark and imagine all of the horrible things that will happen once my son arrives from Alnwick. And you know he will come."

De la Londe squinted up at Andrew in the weak light. "Adam is not the man to be feared," he said. "The man to be feared is de Mowbray. When he finds out what you have done to us, he will bring his army and raze Wellesbourne Castle. He will punish you."

Andrew was unmoved by the man's threat. "De Mowbray will not care that I have imprisoned two traitors," he said. "He knows as well as I do that men like you can be bought. Your loyalty is not worth the effort it takes to speak those vows and he will not waste the time nor the manpower to seek retribution on your behalf. He can easily find two more men to buy for his cause."

De la Londe glared at the man a moment longer before looking away, slumping back against the slippery stone that smelled of rot. "De Mowbray will not let us languish here," he said. "He will come and you had better be prepared."

Andrew snorted. "The only men who need be prepared are you and your companion," he said, "because I am quite certain that Adam will not keep this information to himself. When he tells the other knights that you have come to Wellesbourne spreading your lies, I would not be surprised to see more than one Northumberland knight upon my doorstep. They will all want to know why you have been spreading such lies, de la Londe. You are creating mischief and they will demand answers. I would suggest you think on a good answer."

De la Londe refused to look at him, instead looking at his lap and thinking on Wellesbourne's statement. *I would not be surprised to see more than one Northumberland knight upon my doorstep.* That bit of information did not please him, not in the least, but he could not worry over it. Dead men did not speak and with Titus dead, the knights of Northumberland would have no way of knowing de la Londe or de Troiu's role in Titus' death. They would not even know that de la Londe and de Troiu had sworn fealty to Norfolk. They would be coming in blind, which would work to de la Londe's advantage.

De la Londe had served Northumberland for several years. He had worked with, fought with, and died with these men who would be coming to seek answers from him. It was imperative that he concoct the best story he could in order to convince these men that he was not a traitor. He had been forced to side with Norfolk, to support the man. They had to believe had no choice in the matter and if the subject of Titus' death came up, he would disavow any knowledge of it.

Denial was the only thing he could do in that case because if they suspected he was responsible for Titus' passing, the wrath of The Lion of the North would be upon him and he would be hunted for the rest of his life. Clearly, that was not an option – he didn't want Atticus de Wolfe seeking vengeance against him. At the moment, for all de la Londe knew, no one had made the connection between him and Titus' death. He wanted to keep it that way.

He had to be the victim

"Let them come, then," he muttered. "There is nothing I can do to prevent it. But know that all of this… everything I have told you was because I had to. It was not of my free will."

Andrew was puzzled by the statement but suspected it was just another lie in a long line of de la Londe lies. He was an old man and had seen much, and was suspicious of everything, especially knights who would try to turn him against his own son.

"We shall see," he said after a moment. "When my son arrives, you are free to tell him why your lies about my son were not of your free will."

"There is much more to the situation than merely your son."

"I would like to hear that, as well."

De la Londe fell silent, refusing to say any more. He would wait until Wellesbourne left before speaking to de Troiu, in the darkness, and pulling together their plan. Now that they knew Adam Wellesbourne and the knights of Northumberland would soon be upon Wellesbourne Castle, they had to pull together a common defense. They had to convince their former friends and allies that the bonds of loyalty between them were not broken and that their association with Norfolk had been at great personal peril. More lies, to be sure, but there was little alternative.

They had to save themselves.

In the darkness, they awaited the arrival of their fate.

CHAPTER SIXTEEN

> Ionian scale in C – Lyrics to Memories
>
> *My eyes create a memory for my heart:*
> *My lips create a memory for my soul.*
> *A love that was never meant to be is stronger*
> *Thanks words can ever make it so.*
>
> —Isobeau de Shera de Wolfe, 15th c.

Wolfe's Lair

"WHEN IS THE last time you spoke to her?"

The softly uttered words came from Warenne. Atticus, trying to fix a long-shafted spear tip that seemed to be coming loose, heard the question and knew exactly who Warenne was speaking of but, in truth, he wasn't ready to acknowledge it. Doing what he'd done as of late, he simply ignored the question.

"Who?" he asked, then deliberately moved to change the subject. "Can you please have someone bring me more strips of leather? The smithy should have some. These spears are old but they are still serviceable. If Norfolk charges tonight, which all indications seem to be that we will have a second wave of their assault, then these spears will come in hand. So barbaric, though. I feel like a wild man pitching sharp sticks at my enemy."

Warenne was fully aware that Atticus didn't wish to speak of his wife; he'd spent six days refusing to discuss or address the woman. Ever since Alrik du Reims' lifeless body had been hurled over the massive stone walls, landing in a heap in front of his horrified comrades, Atticus had refused to even mention Isobeau's name. If Warenne hadn't known better, he would have sworn there was agony in Atticus' eyes over the situation with his wife. Warenne knew that Lady de Wolfe had been distraught over Atticus' killing of du Reims and he was fairly certain terrible words had been spoken between the two as a result, but so far, Atticus hadn't said a word about it. He kept his mouth shut.

But his manner was growing increasingly bitter and snappish as the days went on. He was professional and cool as always, and he had directed the defenses against Norfolk brilliantly, but as the days wore on, he seemed to grow more and more sullen. Warenne suspected it was because Atticus was greatly distressed over his wife. When he thought no one was looking, Atticus would glance back at the structure of Wolfe's Lair in the direction of his mother's former chamber where his wife now resided. He thought no one had noticed but Warenne had. Considering he was in anguish over what was happening with his own wife, Warenne well understood Atticus' pain.

But Atticus wouldn't speak of it and Warenne didn't press, not until this morning when Atticus had practically shoved his father aside when the old man got in his way. That was very unlike Atticus. Therefore, Warenne thought he'd better speak with Atticus and see if he could ease his mind, or at least help him reason through whatever he was feeling. For all of their sakes, it had to be done. The tension surrounding Atticus because of the siege, and because of issues with his wife, was growing to splitting proportions.

"I will have someone fetch the smithy," Warenne replied belatedly to Atticus' question. "He will bring the leather to you. Now, answer my question; when is the last time you spoke to your wife?"

Atticus didn't look up from his task. "The day du Reims died."

"Why have you not spoken to her since?"

"Because I have nothing to say."

"Not even to check on her well-being?"

"The servants would tell me if anything was wrong."

Warenne was becoming less understanding with Atticus and more irritated. Foolishness always upset him and at this moment, he was under the opinion that Atticus was either being extremely cold or extremely foolish. Reaching out, he stilled the man's hands as they wrapped a strip of leather around the wobbling spear tip.

"Enough of this, Atticus," he said, his voice low. "When I should be heading home to speak with my wife, whom I would move the sun and moon to be with, I am here, at Wolfe's Lair, watching you ignore a woman you are clearly fond of. Do not give me that look; I've seen that cynicism before. I've seen that aloof manner before, too. I have watched you ignore Lady de Wolfe for the past six days and I am offended by it. I am *deeply* offended by it. You have an opportunity to be with your wife, to resolve whatever issues are between you two, yet you have soundly ignored her. I would give anything to be in your position with my wife only a few steps away from me, but I am not. I must remain in this God-forsaken fortress and look at your ugly face all day long. I am sick of it, do you hear? Now, stop acting like a foolish squire and go talk to the woman you married!"

By the time he was finished, Warenne was rather animated, which was unusual for the usually-collected young earl. Had Atticus not been so surprised by his tirade he would have been offended by it. Or he would have laughed. As it was, he walked a fine line between defending himself and agreeing to Warenne's demands.

"It is not so simple," he told him, speaking hesitantly. "She does not wish to speak with me."

"How do you know if you have not tried?"

"She told me to stay away and leave her alone."

Warenne cooled somewhat. "So you are doing what you think

she wants you to do?"

"Of course. If she does not want me near her, I will comply."

Warenne let out a hiss and shook his head. "Do you know nothing about women?" he demanded. "She regretted what she said the moment it left her mouth. The longer you let this fester between you, the worse it will be."

Atticus averted his gaze, looking back to the unsteady spear tip. After a moment, he sighed heavily. "I do not wish to speak of this, Ren," he said. "I cannot be distracted from what is going on outside of the walls. Whatever is happening with Lady de Wolfe will have to wait until this is over."

Warenne watched the man fidget with the spear. "It may be too late," he said quietly, glancing off to the southwest, the direction he intended to travel home. "Trust me when I tell you that every day you delay may create damage that cannot be repaired. Unless, of course, she does not matter to you. Is it possible that you do not care what she thinks of you?"

Atticus merely shrugged. "It does not matter."

"To you?"

Atticus exhaled sharply and looked at him. "Why do you care?" he hissed, looking around to make sure no one heard their conversation. "I will not be distracted with talk of Lady de Wolfe. She believes me a murderer and wants nothing to do with me, so I have remained here on the wall, allowing her privacy in her chamber. That is the way of things, Ren. I would appreciate it if you would stop asking about it."

Warenne could see the pain in Atticus' expression as he spoke of Isobeau, but it was pain that Atticus would never acknowledge. Either he didn't truly recognize it or he was too proud to admit it. Therefore, Warenne backed off on his approach. He watched as Atticus returned to his spear, leaning against the stone wall behind him, noting that sunset wasn't far off. The earl's gaze was distant, reflective, as he gazed into the darkening sky.

"The moon will be full this night," he said casually, looking up to the surprisingly clear sky. "It will be as bright as day."

"I know."

Warenne glanced at him. "They will come tonight, you know," he said. "If it were me, I would launch a night attack with flaming projectiles and flaming arrows. Have you noticed that they've been collecting animal fat for days now? They have it simmering over a big iron pot off towards the far east of the encampment."

Atticus nodded. "I know," he said. "We have been soaking the roofs of the stables and outbuildings with water to ensure they do not burn."

Warenne looked at him. "What about men, Atticus?" he asked quietly. "Men burn."

"And the men will all remain inside, under cover, until the barrage is over," he replied steadily. Then, he paused and looked at his friend. "What are you driving at, Ren? What are you thinking?"

Warenne sighed faintly, looking off to the west and to the muted colors of sunset across the expanse of sky. "I am thinking that I should speak with my brother-in-law to see if we can resolve this," he said. "They can hold out indefinitely and we cannot. Already supplies are running low. Would you have your wife starve to death in a fortress under siege?"

Atticus wasn't particularly agreeable to what he was saying. "We can manage with what we have for quite some time," he said. "They'll not starve us out any time soon."

Warenne shrugged. "Mayhap not," he said. "But I want to go home and see my wife, and you have a task to see through. De la Londe and de Troiu are somewhere in this country and you must find them and make them atone for Titus' murder. We do not have time to be wasting here on the borders while Norfolk's knights lay siege. This needs to end."

Atticus stopped fussing with the spear and hung his head, thinking of his brother. He grunted ironically. "It all seems so long ago," he muttered. "Titus' death, my vow of vengeance. Nothing has gone as I have planned; not my determination to punish those bastards who killed my brother nor the marriage to Titus' widow that seemed like a very bad idea from the start. Now I find myself holding off a siege and married to a woman who wants nothing to do with me. This is not how it was supposed to be."

Warenne watched him carefully. "And you want nothing to do with her?"

It was a leading question. Atticus knew very well that it was a leading question, but his guard was down. He was feeling momentarily confused and vulnerable. After a moment, he shook his head.

"I believe that is the problem," he mumbled. "I… I cannot stop thinking about her. She is mine; she belongs to me. When I saw du Reims with his arm around her neck it was as if something inside of me snapped. I could not prevent Titus' death but I could prevent hers. I do not regret what I did, not for one second, but she does not see it that way. She thinks I am a murderer. I suppose that I am."

Warenne could see the weakness in a man he never knew capable of such a thing. "You care for her," he whispered. It was not a question.

Atticus, his head hanging as he looked at his lap, nodded once. It was such a faint movement that Warenne barely saw it, but it was there. "Aye," he murmured. "I do. I could not see her come to harm. I regret that she cannot understand that."

Warenne was thrilled to hear Atticus' confession but it also emphasized to him that whatever distress was occurring between him and Lady de Wolfe had to be rectified. Atticus was too afraid or too stubborn to approach the woman and she was more than likely too hurt or too angry to do the same. But Warenne had seen how Lady de Wolfe looked at her new husband; he knew in his heart of hearts that she felt something for Atticus. It was a pity that neither one of them was brave enough to speak of it.

Yet Warenne didn't have that particular problem. He had the advantage of being removed from the situation somewhat. Still, thoughts of Lady de Wolfe were heavy on Atticus' mind and it would be a true pity if something happened to Atticus in the coming siege and he had been unable to voice his thoughts to his wife. And poor Lady de Wolfe would have buried two husbands, never knowing how Atticus had felt about her. Warenne simply couldn't stand by and watch that happen.

Leaning forward, he kissed Atticus on the forehead and departed in silence, heading down the narrow stairs that led into the damaged inner ward, heading for the steps that led to the living levels of the fortress. If Atticus was going to be difficult about this, then the man needed help.

Warenne, wishing it was his wife he was about to go and speak with, was more than happy to provide such help.

SEVEN DAYS.

It had been seven days since Isobeau and Atticus had spoken to one another. Seven long and miserable days of angst, confusion, isolation, and sorrow, at least for Isobeau. They had been some of the worst days of her life in a long line of terrible days that had seen her suffer through much heartache and sorrow for many different reasons. But this latest brush with anguish between her and Atticus was particularly sad. The hope she had built up for the marriage and future was in danger of being destroyed.

She had remained in her chamber as Atticus had ordered. She hadn't moved from it. Therefore, it had become her prison as well as her refuge. She knew every line in the floorboards and every crack in the walls. She had packed and repacked her trunks several times. She had even taken to sweeping the floor and cleaning out the hearth simply to stave off boredom. The servants would bring word of the progress of the siege and it seemed that, for the past several days, things had been mostly calm with Norfolk's army simply camping around Wolfe's Lair and evidently rethinking their strategy. Atticus, she had been told, had rarely left the wall and had taken to sleeping in the gatehouse. The man was living and breathing the defenses of his ancestral home.

With the situation moderately calm, Isobeau's frenzied pacing and frantic packing and re-packing her trunks had ceased. The swift, agitated movements had been in response to her great worry for the situation and, although she wouldn't admit it, her fear for Atticus' safety. His swift actions against Alrik du Reims seven days past seemed like a lifetime ago and she'd awoken for the past two mornings wondering if she'd merely dreamed it. It seemed surreal and distant, and all of the sorrow and rage and fear she'd felt towards Atticus because of it had faded from memory. All that was left was an empty, hollow shell.

She didn't even know what her life was worth any longer or what it was meant to be. So much had happened since she'd been informed of Titus' death on that cold day those weeks ago that it seemed as if she'd lived a hundred years in a very short amount of time. One thing she did know, however, was that she was alone and the incident with du Reims had more than likely ruined any hope of her and Atticus ever having a pleasant marriage. She was positive he hated her and she, in turn, wasn't entirely sure how she felt about him. He was The Lion of the North, a knight who had gained a brutal reputation at a very early age. She'd seen evidence of that reputation quite clearly when he'd fought Norfolk's two knights and then again when he'd saved her from du Reims. He was a man to be feared, a man of brutality.

He was also a man she was most fond of. God, she ached for him.

Miserable and confused, on this seventh day after the siege of Wolfe's Lair had begun, she had arisen early to sweep her floor, make over her bed, and refold the scarves in one of her smaller capcases. The two serving women of Wolfe's Lair had slept in her chamber also and they had been free to come and go, moving about their usual business and, as Isobeau had heard, helping with the wounded in the great hall. She'd also heard that Solomon de Wolfe had risen from his bed and was now making a nuisance out of himself as he tried to take command of the fortress from Atticus. In a sense, she was glad she was confined to her chambers so that she would not add to Atticus' burden. Perhaps it was best that she had remained secluded and out of the way.

So she sat at her small table later in the day, having finished her monotonous chores, with the remnants of her meal around her, bits of cheese and a crust of bread. The oily-skinned serving wench had managed to find an egg beneath one of their frightened chickens and she had scrambled it for Isobeau, who had eaten it happily with bread that had been toasted. Her appetite was coming back after her brush with bad health and there was color in her cheeks once again. She looked entirely beautiful and delicious as she sat at the table and used some of the precious thread her father had bought for her on a sleeve she was embroidering on one of her shifts. It was something more to pass the time, something more to try and help her forget her troubles.

Working on the form of a dragonfly with pale blue silk thread, she was deep into her project when there was a soft rap on the door. Since it wasn't locked because the female servants were coming and going, she bade the caller enter.

Warenne stepped into the chamber, smiling weakly when he saw Isobeau's shocked expression. The sewing in her hands froze.

"My lord," she said, rising from her chair. "Is everything well?

Is… nothing has happened, has it?"

Warenne's smile grew at the sight of her; he was pleased to see that she was anxious at his appearance and he swore that she was going to ask about Atticus before shifting to a generic question. It was simply a feeling he had. Moreover, it was a pleasure to simply look upon her and he knew the sight would have softened Atticus' stubborn heart if he were only to see her, just for a moment, dressed in a dusky blue shade, her woolen dress was snug and clinging, emphasizing her utterly divine figure. In fact, Warenne had to make a conscious effort not to look at the beautiful, full breasts that were in his line of sight. He kept his focus on her face.

"Nothing has happened, Lady de Wolfe," he replied. "I have simply come to see how you are faring. Have you been well?"

Isobeau nodded, feeling a distinct amount of disappointment that the earl had come to see to her well-being and not Atticus. It was difficult to keep her disappointment off her face.

"I am quite well," she said, lowering her gaze and reclaiming her seat. She pretended to be disinterested in his appearance now. "And my husband? Is he well?"

"He is quite well."

"Did he throw that knight over the wall?"

"He did it many days ago. But you were already aware of that."

Isobeau could see that Warenne would defend Atticus' actions. She wasn't surprised. "What of the siege?" she asked, moving away from the events of the past. "Is it over?"

Warenne shook his head. "It is not," he replied. "Norfolk backed off for a few days but we expect a siege in earnest tonight beneath the full moon. It will be quite dangerous for us, in fact."

As he'd hoped, that seemed to jolt Isobeau. She stood up again, looking at him with great concern. "Is this true?" she said fearfully. "What will you do? How will we protect ourselves?"

Warenne shrugged. "We will simply take cover until it is over," he said. "You will remain here, of course. It is the safest place for you. But Atticus… well, as you know, he is directing the defenses of Wolfe's Lair and doing a marvelous job. He will be in the most danger because of his constant need to assess the situation. I am worried for him, actually."

Isobeau was quite clearly seized with fear for Atticus. She put her fingers over her lips in a gesture of great concern. "Sweet Jesus," she muttered. "He must take great care."

Warenne was trying not to smile at her reaction to Atticus being in danger because it was plainly obvious that she cared a great deal about it. She cared a great deal about *him*.

"I have tried to tell him but he will not listen to me," Warenne said, completely manipulating her emotions. "Mayhap… mayhap if *you* tell him, my lady, he will listen."

Isobeau seemed to back down somewhat. "He… he does not wish to hear it from me, I am sure," she said, averting her gaze and moving over to the table that held her sewing kit. "We said quite enough to each other on the day du Reims was murdered. I am sure he does not wish to speak with me, but I thank you for coming to tell me of the situation. I will pray for everyone's good health."

Warenne would not be deterred. "We say many things in fear or anger that we do not mean," he said, eyeing her. "I am sure that when you told him to go away and leave you that you did not mean it."

She looked at him, then. "Did he tell you I said that?"

Warenne nodded. "Aye," he replied. "That is why he did not come to see you himself. He is certain you never want to see him again."

Isobeau's gaze lingered on the man a moment before turning away, confusion and longing evident on her face. "I… I meant it at the time," she said, unsure of what to say. "But… my lord, I simply do not understand why Atticus had to kill the knight. I am positive the man was not going to harm me. But Atticus killed another woman's husband and after what happened with Titus... I am not sure I can forgive him for that. Already I feel that woman's grief and it eats at me. I know how she feels. I wish Atticus had not killed the man."

Warenne was careful in his reply but he was also honest. He prayed that Atticus would forgive him for what he was about to say. "Do you know what Atticus told me about it?" he said softly, watching her turn to him with interest. "He said that when he saw du Reims with his arm around your neck, it was as if something inside of him snapped. He could not prevent Titus' death but he could prevent yours. My lady, you must understand that Titus' death still affects Atticus, every moment of every day. He already lost someone he cared very deeply for in a situation where he was unable to protect him. He could not lose someone else he cared deeply for and not do anything about it. Does that make sense?"

Isobeau looked at him, stunned. Her eyes were wide and her hand went to her chest as if to ease the pounding of her heart, pounding at Warenne's words. "He... cares deeply for me?"

Warenne nodded in a gesture that suggested what Atticus felt for her was much more than that. "Aye," he whispered. "He does. Your anger with him over du Reims' death is tearing him apart. Will you please see him, my lady? If you care anything about him, will you please see him and tell him that you at least understand why he did what he did? He could not lose you, too."

Tears sprang to Isobeau's eyes. Her limbs went warm and fluid and weak with the very idea that Atticus felt something for her. There was joy and jubilation in her heart more than she could control.

"Are you certain of this?" she whispered tightly.

Warenne's smile returned. "I am," he said. "Will you please see him?"

Isobeau nodded, so firmly that her hair came out of its careful braid and swung across her face. "I will," she whispered fervently. "Tell him that I will see him. Tell him… tell him that I would welcome his visit when it is convenient."

Warenne felt more relief than he could express. Moving to Isobeau, he took her hands and kissed them both before quitting the chamber in his quest to return to Atticus. Everything will be all right now, he told himself. Atticus would be happy, Isobeau would be happy, and soon this entire madness would be over so he could return to his wife and try to make amends with the woman. All would be as it should be.

The colors of sunset were deepening across the sky as Warenne took the steps down into the inner ward, yelling at some men near the stables to take cover, as they were expecting Norfolk's attack at any second. In fact, Warenne was halfway across the ward when Norfolk let loose the first barrage of flaming projectiles, arrows that came sailing over the wall, raining a horrific and painful death upon the occupants of Wolfe's Lair. There were so many of them that the sky lit up as if it were daylight, and those caught out in the open had nowhere to go.

This included Warenne. In the middle of the inner ward with no cover, he was an open target when the arrows rained down upon him. He tried to make it to the armory, which was closest, but he wasn't fast enough to evade a heavy, fat-soaked arrow that hit him in the left eye and penetrated all the way to the back of his skull.

The Earl of Thetford was dead before he hit the ground.

CHAPTER SEVENTEEN

> Ionian scale in C – Man so Bold
>
> In days of old time passing,
> Among men, it was told
> There was a man of power
> A man uncommonly bold
>
> —Isobeau de Shera de Wolfe, 15th c.

THE GATES WERE on fire.

Whatever oil or fat Summerlin was using, it burned very hot and very long, and after the first wave of flaming arrows, Summerlin and his men had managed to get up against the big iron and oak gates of Wolfe's Lair and light the things on fire. A great pile of kindling and wood had been pushed up against the gates and ignited, and even now, a great, black cloud burned steadily into the brilliant night sky.

Atticus stood in front of the gates, watching them burn, as his men had a bucket brigade going, dousing the flames from their side. Wolfe's Lair had two big wells that provided more than enough water to battle the blaze but the fat that Summerlin and his men had smeared on the gates would not be extinguished. It was those areas, with fat spread into the old and pitted wood, that were burning hotly. The smell was almost overpowering.

The truth was that Atticus was worried. The gates were reinforced with great strips of iron about an inch thick, like bars on a cage, so even if the wood burned away, the bars would remain. They would still be protected. But if the fire from the burning wood burned hot enough, the iron would soften and that would be a problem. Therefore, it was important to keep water on the fire to lessen the heat generated by the flames.

Atticus, therefore, not only directed the water on the gate, he participated as well. He tossed great buckets of icy water on the burning wood. Kenton was upon the wall walk, directing the soldier to dump burning rocks and earth onto the men below. It was a common enough tactic and they heated earth in great cauldrons in the bailey before taking them up to the wall in buckets or baskets or anything they could find, dumping them out onto the Norfolk men below. The scorching earth and pebbles and layers of sand would get into the cracks of men's armor, seriously burning them. As Atticus manned the gate, Kenton rained hell from above.

Beneath the courageous façade, however, lay great sorrow and grief. Both men were struggling with the death of Warenne. Having been notified of the earl's death and then subsequently seeing the man's body in the inner ward had taken something out of Atticus' soul. First Titus, and now Warenne… he was struggling not to think on the loss of those closest to him, focused on what he must do in order to protect Wolfe's Lair. It would have been very easy to become disoriented by death, to let it claim his sound mind. He thanked God for Kenton, for the man was unbreakable and emotionless, a rock when Atticus felt like crumbling. When Atticus heard Kenton's bellows over the commotion of the siege, it reinforced his courage. All was not lost and he was not alone.

But there was something more on Atticus' mind as well; the more compromised the gates became, the more his thoughts turned towards his wife. Locked up in her room, he was glad for her safety but he knew that if the gates were breached, she would be in danger. Wolfe's Lair appeared to only have one way in or out, through the front gates, but the truth was that there was a tunnel that ran from the storage area beneath the great hall to the creek bed to the south of the fortress.

When Atticus had been a small boy, he and Titus used to play in that tunnel constantly but he had no idea if the tunnel was still open and viable. Somehow, someway, he would have to get Isobeau to the tunnel and the more he watched the front gates burn, the more he knew he would have to go to her whether or not she wanted to see him and take her to safety. He would have to take the woman and flee.

"Atticus," Solomon was suddenly standing next to him, interrupting his thoughts. "If we cannot douse the flames on the gate, the bars will start to soften. We must prepare the men for the breach."

Atticus looked at his father, a man he had shoved aside a few hours before when he felt his father was in his way. Solomon was old and slow, but his mind was still very sharp. Atticus suddenly felt very badly for the way he had treated his father. He reached out, putting a big arm around his father's broad shoulders in a gesture of comfort.

"They are already prepared," he said. "But you… you cannot withstand hand to hand combat these days, Papa. I have been standing here thinking about the old tunnel that leads to the creek bed off to the south. If the tunnel is still open, then mayhap we should think about leading my wife to it. I am hoping you might do this for me."

Solomon shook his head. "I will not leave my home," he said. "I was born here and I shall die here. I will not flee. But you must go, Atticus. It is you they want. You must take Isobeau and leave. Run, boy; run away and do not look back."

Atticus looked at his father, studying the man. After having lost Titus, and now Warenne, he was fairly certain he couldn't handle losing his father.

"Papa," he said softly. "You are all I have left. I could not stand to lose you. Therefore, you must come with Isobeau and me when we flee. But if you remain, then I will remain. I will not go without you."

Solomon looked at him and Atticus was struck by the defeat he saw in the man's eyes. The death of a son, now the siege of his home... Solomon was weary. He was an old man and he was weary of what life had dealt him as of late. But there was more to it than that; Atticus had never seen his father so... calm. Resigned, even. Perhaps Solomon was prepared to accept the end, which Atticus was not.

"You have a beautiful wife now," Solomon said quietly. "You and Isobeau will carry on the de Wolfe name. You will have many strong sons that will outshine the sun. We are descended from greatness, you know. William de Wolfe himself, the Wolfe of the Borders, is our ancestor. I imagine when I look at you that I see a great deal of him. You have his strength and his sense of honor. There is so much of William de Wolfe within you, Atticus. That must be preserved."

Atticus had heard that before from his father; *I see you as the embodiment of William de Wolfe*. He smiled faintly.

"William de Wolfe lived two hundred years ago," he said. "Whatever traits the man possessed, I am sure that generations of breeding have watered it down. What you see in me is a reflection of yourself. You are the greatest knight I have ever known, next to Titus. Whatever you see in me, it is you."

Solomon smiled, sharing a warm moment with his son as the gate began to burn even hotter now. De Wolfe men were trying frantically to douse it but the flames were shooting up the length of the gates, igniting the wooden frame that held it against the opening of the gatehouse. But even though the enemy appeared to be winning, and soon they would be overrun with Norfolk men who wanted to claim Wolfe's Lair for Edward, there was peace and joy between Solomon and Atticus. He patted his youngest son on the cheek with a big, meaty hand.

"You are my shining light, boy," Solomon said softly. "Never forget that. Now, go to your wife and take her to the tunnel. It is still open although we use it for storage these days. Take Isobeau and flee. I must know you are safe."

Atticus sighed heavily. "Papa, you are putting me in a terrible position," he said. "I will not leave you."

"You must."

"If the situation was reversed, would *you* leave *me*?"

Solomon frowned. "I would do what my father told me to do."

"Then I am a terrible son because I am not leaving."

"What about your wife?"

Atticus' staunch refusal took a hit as he was reminded of Isobeau. Soft, sweet, lovely Isobeau… she could not fall into the hands of Norfolk. He was fairly certain that Summerlin would treat her well, but he could not be sure of her fate. What a prize she would be to Norfolk or even to Edward. Could he risk her falling into the hands of the unscrupulous new king and his lascivious family? Nay, he could not. But he was greatly torn about leaving his father behind. He simply couldn't do it.

"I will take her to the tunnel and tell her to flee into the woods that are to the south," he said. "But I will not go with her. I will only join her after we have fought off Norfolk's assault."

Solomon's heart ached for Atticus, understanding his son would not leave him to face the aggression alone. He understood the loyalty, the unwillingness to leave the man he loved to battle for him. But time was growing short and there was no time for argument.

"Do you think she will go without you?" Solomon said, now moving out from under his son's arm and pushing at the man's chest as if to push him away. "We have discussed this; she has already buried one husband and it would be unfair, nay, *tragic* to expect her to bury another. You must go with her, boy. I have lived my life. I was married to a woman I loved. I had my beloved sons. My life has been lived. But you… your life has only just begun, now with a beautiful wife at your side. You must go, Atticus. It will kill me to have you linger simply because of me."

Atticus was starting to feel panicky, torn by his father's words. He wished to God that Warenne was here to advise him, but Warenne was wrapped up in an old coverlet and stored in the corner of the dark and cool chapel. Warenne wasn't here to tell him what he should do because Atticus' instinct was to remain with his father. He *couldn't* leave him. The more Solomon pushed, the more Atticus resisted.

"Papa, please," Atticus said. "You are asking me to choose between you and… and…."

"And your wife!" Solomon snapped. "You must take her and flee, Atticus. Time is shorter than you realize. Look at the flames; the iron frame is already beginning to soften. If you do not go now, it may be too late. You must save yourself!"

Those were the magic words as far as Atticus was concerned. He had no intention of saving himself and fleeing like a coward. But he would lead Isobeau to the tunnel. Then, he would return and fight off Norfolk as best he could. Feeling saddened but determined, he moved away from his father.

"I am going to take Isobeau and the servants to the tunnel," he said, pointing at his father. "But I will be back. If you are planning on fighting off Norfolk's assault, then I suggest that you arm yourself. Go the armory and collect your weapon."

Solomon bellowed at him, something gut-wrenching and painful. He told Atticus not to return; he begged the man. But Atticus wasn't listening. He was racing across the inner ward towards the steps that led up to the living levels. His heart was racing for more reasons than one. He was apprehensive to see Isobeau again, fearful that the anger and hatred in her heart for him had not yet dissipated.

He was fearful of seeing such animosity in the eyes of the woman he was so deeply emotional for.

Thoughts of her, now heavily upon him, weighted him down with worry and anxiety. What if she wouldn't come with him? What if she wouldn't even listen to him? He would have to become a brute, forcing her to do his will and try not to care that she would hate him for it. She already hated him. One more offense would not make a difference. It was with an extremely heavy heart that he put his foot on the first step. But a shout from the wall stopped him.

"Atticus!" Kenton roared. "Incoming!"

Atticus turned in the direction of the shout, watching as Kenton waved almost frantically to him. That wasn't like Kenton at all, for the man did nothing that conveyed agitation or fear. Deeply concerned, not to mention curious, Atticus shifted direction and ran all the way to the steep, narrow staircase that led up to the wall. He had to push men aside as he went, pushing through soldiers and archers, until he reached Kenton's side. He opened his mouth to ask Kenton to clarify his statement when Kenton pointed a finger eastward. That's all the man had to do; he simply pointed. When Atticus turned to see what he was pointing at, everything became instantly clear.

Northumberland banners, leading a mighty Northumberland army, were approaching.

Atticus would believe until the day he died that, at that moment, he had witnessed divine intervention in the form of an allied army.

"Tertius!"

Isobeau had very nearly screamed the name when her brother suddenly appeared in her doorway. Startled, she dropped her dragonfly embroidery and flew to her brother, throwing her arms around the man's neck and breaking into tears. She had never been so surprised, or so glad, to see anyone in her life.

Tertius had just fought his way through a weary Norfolk army to make it to the gates of Wolfe's Lair that, by the time he arrived, were twisted and smoldering and very difficult to move. But they managed to get one of them open, allowing Northumberland's army in as Norfolk's exhausted men scattered and fled south. It had been an extremely short-lived battle that had seen Northumberland, and Wolfe's Lair, emerge the victor. The de Wolfe standards still flew high above the battered gatehouse.

"Easy, Iz, easy," Tertius told his hysterical sister, giving her a squeeze before releasing her. "All is well. Everything is safe now."

Isobeau wiped the tears of joy and relief off her face. "You came!" she gasped. "Why did you come? Why are you here?"

Tertius looked her over critically. "Are you well?" he asked, avoiding her question for the moment. "You look rather pale."

Isobeau waved him off. "I am fine," she insisted. "What are you doing here?"

Having his question answered, and knowing that his sister had emerged from the siege of Wolfe's Lair unharmed, Tertius was inclined to provide Isobeau answers to her own inquiry.

"We were told that Wolfe's Lair was under attack and made haste to lend assistance," he said. "How long has this been going on?"

Isobeau shrugged, for she truly didn't know. It seemed like forever. "At least a week, possibly more," she said. "Is... is Atticus well? I have not seen him in a very long time."

Tertius nodded. "Not a scratch on the man," he replied. "Solomon, either."

"And Warenne? Kenton?"

Tertius seemed to sober. "Kenton is well," he said. "But Warenne is dead. You did not know this?"

Isobeau gasped in horror at the news. "I... I did not," she said, devastated at the passing of the Earl of Thetford. "I have been locked in this room for the past week. I have not been allowed to leave and no one has come to tell me anything, save Thetford. He... he was only here a short while ago. Now he is dead?"

Tertius nodded. "Aye," he said sadly. Then, he sighed heavily. "Losing Titus and now Warenne... it makes me want to give up war altogether and take up the life of a fisherman. I have seen far too many friends perish over the past few years, but the past few weeks have been the most costly. I am coming to wonder if these wars between Henry and Edward are worth the price we all must pay."

Isobeau was still lingering on Warenne's death, so deeply saddened by it. She wandered back over to her little table where her embroidery lay and sat heavily on the nearest chair. "He was such a giving and wise man," she murmured. "I am sure Atticus is... Tertius, where is Atticus?"

Tertius tugged at his mail gauntlet. "The last I saw, he was cleaning up pockets of fighting near the gate," he said. "I told you he was well."

Isobeau nodded. "It is not that," she said, thinking on the last conversation she and Warenne had shared. *He already lost someone he cared very deeply for in a situation where he was unable to protect him. He could not lose someone else he cared deeply for and not do anything about it.* She wondered if Warenne had ever made it back to Atticus to tell him that she was more than willing to see him. *To forgive him.* Since Atticus had not come to her yet, she suspected that perhaps Warenne had never told him. Her expression to Tertius was filled with urgency. "Please find Atticus and send him to me, Tertius. I must speak to him immediately."

Tertius frowned. "The man is cleaning up after a battle," he said. "He has better things to do right now."

Isobeau stood up. "If you do not send him to me, I will go out and find him," she said. "Please, Tertius. It is very important."

Tertius made a face at her but he wasn't beyond sensing the stress in her tone. Snarling at her, he turned for the door. "You are a demanding creature, Izzy," he said, unhappy. "I will send Atticus to you when he is finished and not one moment sooner. You should know that you cannot always have everything just the way you wish it."

Isobeau stuck her tongue out at her brother. "I love you very much, Tertius," she said. "But sometimes you are an annoying little snip."

Tertius shook his head at her, lingering in the doorway before he left completely. "And I love you, too," he said. "But you are a spoiled child."

"I hate you now."

"I hate you more."

Tertius left the chamber but not before Isobeau saw a grin on his lips. Grinning herself, she went to the door, watching her beloved brother head down the corridor and out to the steps that led down into the inner ward.

Once he was gone from her sight, she began to wonder if he would really tell Atticus to come and see her. She suspected he wouldn't, at least not right away, and that thought began to drive her into agitation. The battle was over, so Tertius said, so surely there was no danger any longer. Surely she could leave her chamber and find Atticus without any hazards befalling her. She simply couldn't wait any longer to speak with him; seven days had been far too long to wait.

She had to see him.

In silence, she left the chamber and headed out into the gentle dusk.

More death and more destruction.

At least, that was what Isobeau thought when she made her way down the steps that led into the inner ward. The big ward was badly damaged and dead men, men with arrows still in their bodies, were being piled up near the great hall. She could see at least a dozen or more, all being carefully lined up. She stood upon the steps for quite some time, watching the activity below, trying not to become ill at the sight of so much death, before shifting her attention to the stable off to her left.

The structure didn't seem to be any more damaged than it had been the last time she saw it and she made her way over to it to check on her mare. The horse was still where she had left it, crowded into an undamaged stall with a pony and three goats. The horse was gnawing on the wooden slats of the stall so she gave it some of the dried grass that was piled up in another stall. The mare and the pony and the goats descended on the grass, hungry. Leaving her animal friends feasting, Isobeau wandered back out into the ward.

It was difficult to tell if there was still fighting going on at the gate because there were so many men grouped around it that she couldn't really see what was happening. All she knew was that there were dozens of men, and knights on horseback, and she recognized Maxim de Russe and Alec le Bec. Alec even waved at her. She waved back even though her attention was focused on finding Atticus.

Men were moving about everywhere and she dodged groups of them as she made haste across the inner ward, heading for the great hall where she knew the wounded were. She tried not to think on the last time she was in the great hall, the day that Alrik du Reims was killed, but it seemed an easy enough thought to overcome when she wanted badly to see Atticus. She had to find him and she had to tell him… well, she wasn't quite sure what, exactly, she was going to tell him, but if what Warenne had said was true, then perhaps it was time for her to be truthful with the man she had married. All she knew was that she had to see him. She was lingering by the entry to the great hall, straining to catch a glimpse of the men inside, when she heard a soft, deep voice behind her.

"Isobeau?"

Whirling around, she found herself facing Atticus. He was in plate armor, without his helm, and he appeared positively exhausted. A dark growth of beard spread over his face and his beautiful eyes were ringed with dark circles. But it was what she saw within those eyes that had her breath catching in her throat; there was something very deep and very emotional there. Whatever it was brought tears to her eyes. She was so glad to see him that she very nearly crumpled.

"I heard about Warenne," she said, her throat tight with emotion. "I am so sorry, Atticus. I know he was your friend."

Atticus' gaze lingered on her. In fact, he couldn't stop looking at her. He'd happened to notice her when she came out of the stables and even though he had been at the front gate, directing the disposal of the Northumberland dead, he left the knights in charge and followed his wife all the way across the inner ward until she came to a halt at the entry to the great hall. Now, all of those words he had planned to say to her, or wanted to say to her, seemed to catch in his throat. He'd never seen anything so beautiful in his life.

"He was a dear and valued friend," he finally said. "I will miss him."

"As will I."

"What are you doing down here? It is quite a mess still."

She took a step towards him, her lovely face upturned to him, illuminated by the torchlight that was casting a warm glow over the inner ward. "Tertius came to see me," she said. "He said that Northumberland came to help us."

Atticus nodded. He wanted so very badly to reach out and hold her but he knew it wouldn't be well met. His arms fairly ached to touch her. "They did," he said. "A Wellesbourne knight, who was traveling to Wolfe's Lair to see me, came upon the siege and rode straight to Alnwick for help. Fortunate for us that he did or I have no idea what state we would be in now."

Isobeau grew serious. "Was Wolfe's Lair in danger of falling?"

Atticus nodded. "I believe so," he said. "In fact, before Northumberland appeared, I was coming to see you to take you to safety."

Isobeau's face lit up. "You were coming to see me?"

He nodded, seeing that she appeared rather pleased by the thought. "Aye," he said, wondering if he should say anything more. He was terrified to, terrified she would run off or, worse, reject him. Therefore, he restrained himself. "As I said, I was going to take you to safety."

Isobeau's face fell. "I see," she said, lowering her gaze and looking to the destruction of the inner ward. "I am glad that Northumberland appeared, then. I understand that your father is well also. He survived."

Atticus nodded, noting how depressed she seemed now whereas moments before, she seemed quite warm and receptive. "He is very well," he said. "Now I cannot keep him out of the clean-up efforts. He thinks he is in charge."

"Well, it *is* his fortress."

Atticus gave her a lopsided smile. "Aye, it is," he said, eyeing her. He cleared his throat softly and somewhat nervously. "You… you said that you came to find me?"

Isobeau looked at him; *really* looked at him. At that moment, she could do one of two things – she could simply tell him that she was pleased he was uninjured and leave it at that, or she could bare her soul and pray he didn't run off in horror. Since Warenne had led her to believe that Atticus felt something for her, she took a chance on the latter. But speaking of her feelings for the man was the most difficult thing she'd ever had to do in her life.

"I did," she said quietly. "I... I wanted to speak with you."

"What about?"

She looked at him sadly, perhaps with some chagrin. "Shall we pretend that I did not say such terrible things to you the last time we saw one another?" she said softly. "I, for one, cannot do such a thing. I cannot ignore the terrible things I said to you and... and I wanted to ask for your forgiveness. I understand that you were trying to protect me, Atticus. You saw danger and you did what you could to save my life. I should not have been so horrid to you about it. I should have trusted you and I am sorry that I did not."

At that moment, Atticus felt as if a massive weight had been lifted from his shoulders. He could breathe again. He smiled faintly at her, realizing that he felt more alive and joyful than he had in days, even weeks or months. Perhaps ever. Nothing he'd ever known equated with what he was feeling at her words.

"I am sorry, too," he said. "I frightened you and I upset you. I did not mean to do either of those things, but when I saw the knight with his arm across your neck, I knew that it was either his life or yours. Know that if I had it to do all over again, I would do the same thing. I could not let anything happen to you, Isobeau. It would destroy me."

Isobeau could feel her heart racing, that giddy feeling she was coming to associate with Atticus. Very boldly, she reached out to take his gloved hand and he instantly latched on to her, bringing her fingers to his lips. He closed his eyes tightly, her flesh against his mouth, and Isobeau instinctively put a hand to his cheek. A dam of some kind had broken and she could feel the emotions flowing from both of them, wrapping up around them like a vortex. Any hesitation she had at speaking her mind or her thoughts vanished.

It was time for total truth.

"As it would destroy me as well if something happened to you," she whispered, watching him kiss her hand. There was so much power behind his kisses that it brought tears to her eyes. "I have been so worried for you, Atticus, and I did not want anything to happen to you before I had the opportunity to tell you how I feel. I had the opportunity to tell Titus before he left and I did not take that chance. I will not make the same mistake twice."

Atticus opened his eyes, focusing intensely on her. "What do you feel?"

Her eyes were glimmering with every unspoken emotion she was feeling. "Shall I tell you?"

Atticus nodded. Then he shook his head. "How is it even possible that you should feel something for me?" he asked, bewildered and genuinely curious. "You loved my brother."

Isobeau smiled sadly, her palm still against his cheek. "I was very fond of him," she murmured. "Titus was a warm and wonderful man and mayhap in time, I would have loved him. But in hindsight, it wasn't love that I felt for him. It was simply a great fondness. I will always be greatly fond of him. But you... you are a man unto yourself, not to be overshadowed by a brother that everyone loved. What I feel for you has nothing to do with Titus and everything to do with you, as a man. My fondness for you grows by leaps and bounds. I look forward to the day when I can tell you that I love you with all my heart. I pray that does not repel or alarm you."

Atticus kissed her hand once more and the dropped it, cupping her face between his two big palms. He gazed into her eyes, trying to think of something sweet and warm and lovely to say to her but he could only think of one thing to say. It was the truth.

"I cannot remember when I have not loved you," he said softly. "It came upon me and suddenly I realized that it was true. I tried to tell myself that it was wrong to love my brother's widow but the truth is that you are *my* wife. You belong to me and I will love you, and only you, until I die."

Isobeau was swept away by his words, her heart beating furiously against her ribs and her limbs turned to liquid fire. She leaned into him and Atticus slanted his mouth over hers, kissing her so forcefully that he drove her teeth into her soft lip. He tasted her blood and, loving it, suckled her mouth harder. His arms went around her and he pulled her so tightly against him that he thought to crush her. But he didn't care; she was where he wanted her and where she belonged, in his arms, never to stray again.

It was a magical moment.

But they were not alone in it. Standing several feet away, Tertius, Kenton, Alec, Adam, Maxim, and Juston de Royans stood, watching Atticus devour his luscious and shapely wife. Juston turned to Tertius.

"Is *that* your sister?" he asked.

Tertius nodded, watching the woman being ravaged by her husband. "Indeed it is."

Juston lifted his blond eyebrows. "If I had known she was such a beauty, I would have pledged for her myself."

Tertius grunted. "I cannot think of her in those terms," he said. "She is still the skinny, freckle-faced sister I have always known."

All five knights shook their heads in utter disagreement but Kenton was the one who spoke. "Nay, she is *not*," he said. "A blind man can see what a prize she is. I am glad Atticus finally realized that. I was coming to wonder if he ever would."

Tertius, his gaze lingering on his sister and her amorous husband, waved a hand at the pair as if to dismiss them and their lusty display, and headed back to the gates where his men were collecting the dead. Kenton, Maxim, Alec, Adam, and Juston were still clustered in an exhausted group, watching Atticus and Isobeau for a few moments longer before turning away. They had their own duties to attend to. In truth, they had come to find Atticus to seek out direction on what he wanted them to do as far as cleaning up Wolfe's Lair, but they could all see that the man was indisposed. They would have to figure out their tasks without his direction.

"Does Tertius have any more sisters?" Juston asked Adam as they walked away.

Adam snorted. "He does not," he said. "But Maxim and Alec do. Mayhap they will put in a good word for you. But be advised that I have seen these women and they look just like their ugly brothers, so you may want to reconsider."

Alec, hearing Adam's comment, threw a pebble that hit the man in the neck. Angry, Adam shook his fist threateningly at Alec but his threats went largely ignored. The knights then dissipated into the deepening evening to help shore up Wolfe's Lair for the night while Atticus and Isobeau lost themselves in a kiss that would go down in history as possibly one of the best and purest in the true sense of the gesture. It was everything they ever knew it could be… and more.

After that, Atticus spent the next hour with his wife simply to make up for lost time before reluctantly pulling himself away from her to oversee the post-battle activities of Wolfe's Lair. At least for the night, there was no talk of battle, of death, or of war.

With Shaun Summerlin and his men on the retreat and Wolfe's Lair under a veil of peace, Atticus was able to relax somewhat. For the moment, he was worry-free. For a brief and shining moment, he allowed himself the luxury of life without battle or grief. For that brief and shining moment, there was only Isobeau.

Even though Atticus slept in his mother's bed next to his wife that night, he did not engage in his husbandly rights. He knew she was still healing from her recent miscarriage and he suspected that an act of that sort would be physically difficult for her, so he refrained. It was the first time in his life that he'd ever thought of someone else over himself. But he didn't regret it. In fact, sleeping with her in his arms was quite possibly the best thing he ever did.

Waking up to her soft, gentle singing was just this side of heaven.

CHAPTER EIGHTEEN
~ THE END IS KNOWN ~

> Ionian scale in C – Lyrics to The Lion
>
> He came from the north
> One starlit night
> A man called The Lion
> Much more than simply a knight
>
> —Isobeau de Shera de Wolfe, 15th c.

"WITH THE THREAT against Wolfe's Lair gone, I do not intend to delay any longer in my quest to ride to Wellesbourne Castle," Atticus said. Seated around the feasting table of Wolfe's Lair's great hall, he spoke to the knights sitting near him, including Juston de Royans. In fact, he was singularly focused on the man. "I realize you and I have not had any time to speak since the chaos of yesterday, but Adam mentioned briefly that you had been on the road to Wolfe's Lair specifically to see me when you came upon Norfolk's siege and went to summon help. I am in your debt for that action."

Juston, a cup of warmed wine in his hand, was exhausted from little sleep this morning after the siege but, like the other knights, he was focused and determined. He had a message to deliver to de Wolfe but from Atticus' statement, he was coming to think that Atticus already knew the whereabouts of de la Londe and de Troiu. He was moderately surprised to realize that.

"No need, my lord," he replied. "I was coming to tell you that

Simon de la Londe and Declan de Troiu came to Wellesbourne Castle but it seems that you are already aware of that."

Atticus cocked his head curiously. "The information I had, from Norfolk's knight no less, is that Wellesbourne Castle was their last known location," he said, grunting as he reflected upon the past several days and all that had happened. "Let me be clear on the situation; Norfolk's siege was the direct result of my refusal to swear fealty to Edward. But there is more to it; Norfolk sent two seasoned knights, Shaun Summerlin and Alrik du Reims, to inform me that Norfolk would have my oath or he would confiscate Wolfe's Lair. Naturally, I refused, but it seemed very odd to me that Norfolk knew where to find me. Logically, I would be at Alnwick, yet Norfolk came straight to Wolfe's Lair in search of me, as if someone told him to come here. Upon interrogating Norfolk's knight, I discovered that information for my whereabouts came from none other than de la Londe and de Troiu. I was told that their last known whereabouts was Wellesbourne Castle, according to Summerlin. That is why I said my destination was Wellesbourne Castle. Now, a knight from Wellesbourne Castle has come to Wolfe's Lair to speak with me, which is both strange and coincidental. What more can you tell me about de la Londe and de Troiu?"

Juston started to speak but Adam interrupted him. "Those bastards went to Wellesbourne to convince my father that I had sworn fealty to Edward," he said, angry. "They tried to convince my father to swear fealty to Edward also, but my father was smart. He knew there was something odd about the situation and he did not trust them, so he threw both of them in the vault and sent de Royans to Alnwick to find out what the truth of the matter was. Atticus, de la Londe and de Troiu are locked up in Wellesbourne's vaults. They have been there all along."

Atticus was stunned; pleased, but stunned. He looked to de Royans. "This is what you were coming to tell me?"

Juston nodded. "Indeed," he replied. "Upon my arrival to Alnwick, Adam and the other knights strongly denied de la Londe and de Troiu's assertions. They were lies, as Andrew Wellesbourne suspected they were. But what Lord Andrew does not know is that those knights killed your brother; Adam told me what happened with Titus. He told me of the betrayal, how they have sided with Norfolk and are trying to recruit all of Northumberland's knights for Edward's cause. If you will ride to Wellesbourne, I am sure Lord Andrew will happily turn the traitors over to you for your good justice."

Atticus understood everything now and he felt an extreme amount of relief in what he was being told. The men he sought to punish were being held in a dank, nasty vault at an allied fortress. It was an amazing stroke of good fortune and his gratitude ran deep.

"Now it is clear," he muttered with satisfaction. "I am more grateful than you can know for the information and for Andrew Wellesbourne's astute action to capture them. That has made all of the difference in the world to me. Now I will ride to Wellesbourne Castle and dispense justice for my brother."

The knights at the table, particularly Maxim and Alec, began to eye each other. The subject of accompanying Atticus hung in the air as an unspoken question and, once again, everyone was eager to go with him but no one wanted to speak up. Already the knights from Northumberland had been denied. Tertius, who knew very well what the sentiment was, finally broke the silence.

"I would assume Kenton and de Royans will go with you to Wellesbourne," he said. "Atticus, I will be honest when I say that every man here wants to go with you. We all have a personal stake in this. Titus was our commander as well as our friend, and what de la Londe and de Troiu did was betray all of us when they swore fealty to Norfolk. What happened to Titus could have happened to any of us; Titus was simply the knight they approached first."

Atticus looked around the table at the men he had fought with for many years. They were all close friends, brothers-in-arms, and he deeply respected every one of them. Here they sat, surrounded by wounded from the siege, exhausted to the bone from fighting off Norfolk on behalf of the House of de Wolfe, and still they wanted to help him. Their support had always meant a great deal to him but somehow, it meant more today, on this day of days after Titus' death and Warenne's death and the realization that he loved his new wife. There were emotions close to the surface for the knight known as The Lion of the North, emotions he was allowing himself to feel for the first time.

"I have learned a great deal over the past several weeks," he said to the group as a whole. "I have learned that Titus was not the only brother I have. I have several – Tertius, Kenton, Maxim, Alec, Adam, and, in particular, Warenne. I have always considered you all brothers-in-arms but not necessarily brothers of the blood… but now I consider all of you that as well, for only brothers in blood would risk their lives and show support such as you all have. When I left Alnwick, I only took Warenne and Kenton with me. I felt strongly that with Alnwick under threat from what I assumed to be imminent attack from Edward that your places were at Northumberland's fortress. But I no longer feel that way – Tertius, you are correct in your assertion that every man has a stake in this. We all have a right to see de la Londe and de Troiu punished. But I am the only one with the right to punish them. Therefore, if any man wants to accompany me to Wellesbourne, I will not deny you. But this vengeance, this right to punish, is mine alone. Is that clear?"

Every man around the table nodded except for Tertius. He was looking at the knights he would lose to Atticus' quest. He drew in a deep, thoughtful breath.

"One of us must return to Alnwick and since you left me in charge, I suppose that should be me," he said. "But I will certainly not stop any man who wants to go."

"I want to go," Maxim said immediately.

"As do I," Alec chimed in.

Kenton, eyeing the two younger knights, shrugged. "I am already going," he said, cocking his head in the direction of Maxim and Alec. "Moreover, if these two ladies are going, then I must certainly go to keep them in line."

"I am going," Adam said, serious. "I want to see my father and I am sure he wants to see me."

So the escort party was assembling, men determined to see their former friends and comrades punished. Men determined to support Atticus. De Royans, draining what was left of his watered wine, set the cup down.

"And I am going simply because I live there," he said, watching Adam and Maxim grin. He sobered. "If I know Lord Andrew, and I do, he has kept those two locked down in the black hole without any light or human contact. They will already be quite demoralized by the time we arrive which is far less than they deserve."

Atticus, realizing he had nearly all of his knights accompanying him to Wellesbourne, felt a great satisfaction in that. He felt bolstered by their support, as if he were an avenging angel supported by a gang of heavenly hosts, descending upon de la Londe and de Troiu to dispense his particular brand of fiery justice. In that respect, he didn't want to delay any longer. He had a task to fulfill and he wanted to get to it. Setting his wine cup aside, he rose to his feet.

"Then the end will come and the end will be known," he commanded, praying and hoping that his quest for vengeance for Titus was now coming to a conclusion. "You will share this end with me, good knights. We will know it together."

The knights nodded, each of them feeling a different sense of purpose than the man next to him. There were many reasons for this closure, as diverse as the needs of the men around the table. Kenton, across the table, stood up along with Atticus.

"When will we leave?" he asked.

Atticus looked around the table. "Be ready to leave in an hour," he told the group. "I intend to make arrangements to send Warenne back to Thetford and then see to my father and wife in that time. I will meet you all by the stables. Kenton, please see that my horse and my wife's horse are saddled and ready."

The knights stood up as well, intent on completing their tasks so they could be ready to leave when Atticus wanted to. Now, their path was set and the journey lay ahead of them, a journey that was several long weeks in the making. Finally, Titus would know justice. They would *all* know it because what Tertius said was true; de la Londe and de Troiu's move against Titus was purely by fate. It could have been any one of them. They all had a stake in this and there wasn't one man there not eager to watch Atticus dispense justice against those who had murdered his brother.

Vengeance was coming.

The Lion of the North was coming.

ISOBEAU WAS SITTING at the table in her chamber, her small harp in hand, doing something she'd not done in ages; she was writing music again. Now that all was well between her and Atticus, and Wolfe's Lair was at peace again, her heart was overflowing with songs for her new husband and she'd even awoken that morning with one on her lips. She must have been singing it in her sleep because when she opened her eyes, Atticus was propped up on an elbow, smiling down at her. It had been the most wonderful thing in the world to wake up next to him. Although it was certainly no slight against Titus, she'd never known such jubilation as she did when gazing into Atticus' handsome face. There was something magical about it.

She and Atticus had broken their fast together before dawn before he went out and about his duties, leaving Isobeau to dress leisurely. She'd had the oily-faced serving wench bring her warmed water and she proceeded to use her precious bar of white soap that smelled of lemon, washing herself as thoroughly as she could, before dressing in a linen gown the color of lilac.

The garment was long-sleeved, snug in the bodice, giving her a delicious silhouette. Braiding her long, blond hair and draping the braid over one shoulder, she had proceeded to remove her small harp from one of her larger capcases, pulled forth the box that contained the precious parchment that Titus had bought her, and the song writing for the day began. Once again, she was happy. It seemed as if she couldn't remember the last time she was actually happy.

So she composed whilst Atticus was away conducting business. She must have been making some noise at it because she was almost finished with the song she'd been composing in her sleep when there was a soft rap on the chamber door. She bade the caller to enter and when the door swung open, Solomon was standing in the doorway. He smiled timidly as she smiled brightly.

"Sir Solomon," she said. "Please come in. 'Tis good to see that you are well this morning."

Solomon entered the chamber hesitantly, lingering near the door even when he came in. The last woman he'd seen in this chamber had been his wife and it was difficult not to relive those memories. Therefore, he remained near the door, refusing to delve deeper into the reflections of Rosalie de Wolfe. At least, for the moment.

"I heard your music, my lady," he said after a moment "I have not heard music within these walls since… well, it has been a very long time. You play beautifully."

Isobeau was flattered. "I have always composed music," she said.

"Since I was very young it has been my favored diversion. Do you sing, Sir Solomon?"

He snorted. "Not in a way that anyone likes to hear," he said. "But you sing beautifully. I have heard you."

Isobeau smiled, placing her fingers on the strings. "Would you like to hear my newest song?"

Solomon nodded. "I would," he said. "It has been many years since there has been joy at Wolfe's Lair. I… I would like to feel joy again."

Isobeau strummed the strings softly, creating a gentle halo of music that rose up to fill the very room. "Did your wife play music, Sir Solomon?"

Solomon's gaze turned distant as he thought of the fair Rosalie. Now, he could no longer avoid her memories but he found that in discussing her, there wasn't the pain there used to be. Odd how that was. He felt warmth more than anything.

"She did, in fact," he said. "My wife had a clavichord that she would play quite often. I had one brought to her all the way from Italy and she loved it. Those were wonderful days when her music would ring throughout the fortress."

Isobeau's smile grew as she continued to strum her harp. "Do you still have the instrument?"

Solomon nodded. "It is in my chamber."

"Will you show it to me?"

Solomon almost seemed embarrassed to do so but he motioned for Isobeau to follow him and, together, they made their way into his smelly, cluttered chamber. Isobeau paused by the door, remembering this chamber from her first few days at Wolfe's Lair. It did not bring good memories for her. So she remained by the door as Solomon went over to a darkened corner near his wardrobe and pulled a drape of some kind off of a square object. Beneath it was revealed a small clavichord.

Even from her position by the door, Isobeau could see that the instrument was beautifully painted, dingy with age, but the lure of the clavichord brought Isobeau into the room and she went to it, admiring the beautiful craftsmanship of the piece. It wasn't very large, perhaps only two feet across, and there was a lovely seascape scene painted on the cover.

When she lifted the cover, however, the true beauty of the piece was revealed; inside the cover, an intricate scene was painted that seemed to depict ships at sea and sirens calling to them from shore. The keyboard was ebony and ivory, beautifully made, and Isobeau was in awe. Instinctively, she put her hands on the keys, as she had taken music lessons as a child and was quite proficient at several musical instruments, and she brought forth the first chords the clavichord had played in decades.

The clavichord was out of tune but not too terribly. Isobeau tightened a couple of the nuts that held taut the catgut strings and she played the chord again. It sounded much better. With a smile at Solomon, she began to play a song.

An old hymn filled the stale air of Solomon's chamber, music and beauty such as it hadn't heard in years. Solomon was torn between Isobeau playing Rosalie's clavichord, for only Rosalie had ever played it, and the beauty of bringing the instrument back to life again. The joy of his wife's instrument once again playing music won out and he stood there, eyes moist, as Isobeau touched Rosalie's beloved keys and sang *Veni Sanctus Spiritus,* a very old church hymn. After the hell of the past several days, of Titus' death and the siege of Wolfe's Lair, to hear that unexpected beauty brought the old man to tears as if reminding him that there was still some goodness and glory left in the world.

But the hymn eventually ended and Isobeau, ever the musician, moved to tighten two more strings that she felt were slightly out of tune. As she was tightening up the last one, with Solomon hovering over her and very curious as to what she was doing, they heard a voice in the doorway.

"I thought I heard music," Atticus said, noting the clavichord that his wife was bent over. "I had no idea you still had Mother's instrument. I've not heard that thing played in years."

Isobeau smiled at the sight of her husband, feeling her heart race simply at the sound of his voice. "Your father was kind enough to let me play it," she said. "It is a beautiful instrument."

Atticus stepped into the room, eyes only for Isobeau. There mere sight of her lightened his heart in ways he could not begin to describe. "And you play it beautifully," he told her. "I could hear you all the way outside."

Solomon ran his hands over the old clavichord. "Your mother adored this instrument," he said. "Do you remember, Atticus? Do you remember that she would play it for you?"

Atticus nodded. "I do," he said. "When I was very young. Odd how I'd forgotten that until this moment. Those were some of my better childhood memories."

Solomon was still inspecting the clavichord as if reacquainting himself with it. "Mayhap your wife would like to have it, Atticus," he said. "I would be pleased knowing that she would play it and love it as much as your mother did. As it is, it is simply sitting here rotting."

Atticus looked at Isobeau's jubilant face; he could see how thrilled she was at the offer. "That is very kind, Papa," he said. "Mayhap when we have settled somewhere, we will have a place for it."

Solomon turned to look at him, concern and curiosity on his face. "You will not live here?" he asked. "I thought you would return to Wolfe's Lair, Atticus. I will not live forever. When I pass, you must take your rightful place here. With Titus gone, there is only you to carry on Wolfe's Lair."

Isobeau looked at Atticus, who seemed genuinely torn. "You will not pass for a very long time," he told his father. "And we have all the time in the world to speak of this when I return from Wellesbourne Castle."

Solomon was puzzled. "Why must you go to Wellesbourne Castle?"

Gazing at his father, it occurred to Atticus that he never told Solomon how Titus had died. He hadn't consciously withheld the information but with all that had happened, and the grief his father had been going through, there simply hadn't been the opportunity to give the man the details.

Perhaps there was a part of him that didn't want to upset his father more than he already was about Titus; the man was dead. How he died was another matter altogether. When Atticus had brought Titus home, he'd merely told his father that they'd lost Titus at Towton. He never said how. Now, he had to tell him how his beloved oldest son met his doom.

It was only fair to Solomon that he know everything.

"Papa, there is something I've not told you in all of this," he said, trying to be gentle about it. "When I brought Titus home, I told you that he had been killed at Towton and that was the truth. But I did not tell you how his death came about. I suppose I simply did not want to burden you with it, not whilst you were grieving so terribly. But I find that I must tell you now. It is the reason why I must go to Wellesbourne Castle."

Solomon looked at his son warily, wanting to know yet not wanting to know. Did it matter? To Solomon, it did. He wanted to know his son's final moments.

"Tell me how he died, Atticus," he said quietly.

Atticus nodded, lifting his eyebrows with some resignation and sadness of what he was about to say. "Two Northumberland knights betrayed and murdered Titus," he said. "These men had secretly sworn allegiance to Norfolk and when they approached Titus and proposed swearing fealty to Edward, Titus refused and they killed him for his refusal. Now those two knights are at Wellesbourne Castle, in the vault, and I must go there and punish them on behalf of my brother. I swore to Titus that I would avenge him and that is exactly what I intend to do. I will kill those who killed my brother."

By the time he was finished, Solomon was looking at Atticus with big, horrified eyes. He didn't say anything right away, unusual for the usually vocal man, as he simply sat and digested what he'd been told. His shock, his sorrow, was obvious.

"Murdered," he finally muttered. "Murdered by men he trusted."

"Aye."

Solomon's features washed with incredible pain but he fought it; it was pain he'd already suffered through but now with the knowledge of how Titus had died, the pain threatened anew. The angst, so recently eased, was back with a vengeance.

"Great Bloody Jesus," he hissed after a moment. "I wish I could go with you. Damn these rotten joints that I cannot even exact justice for my own son!"

He pounded on his big leg as Atticus and Isobeau watched with concern, afraid that the latest information would send the man spiraling downward again. Solomon pounded, and he even groaned, but his head came back up and he looked to Atticus with eyes alight with revenge. Atticus had never seen such hatred in the man's eyes, ever. It was a shocking moment.

"Punish them, Atticus," Solomon hissed. "For me, for Titus, you will punish them and ensure every pain they feel, every agony they experience, has Titus' name on it. They killed my son and they must be made to suffer."

Atticus could see how agitated his father was and he put his hands out, clutching the man's big shoulders in a reassuring manner. "You know I will," he said softly, seriously. "I will make them pay with every last breath they possess. They will not get off easily, I swear it. Do you believe me?"

Solomon was nodding his head furiously, his bushy hair waving about. There were tears in his eyes, now trickling onto his face. "I do," he gasped. "You are The Lion of the North. That reputation was given to you at a young age but never has it meant as much as it does now. You were given that title for this one moment, Atticus – to avenge your brother against those who betrayed him. Let The Lion roar, boy. *Let him roar!*"

Atticus held on to his father, comforting the man, so very sorry that he was deeply upset all over again. Perhaps he should have told his father the circumstances surrounding Titus' death earlier, but it did not matter now. Solomon knew that his beloved son had been betrayed and his pain was again fresh. As Atticus put his arm around his father's shoulders, soothingly, he looked over to see how Isobeau was reacting to everything. He worried for her, too.

But Isobeau seemed remarkably composed. She was still standing near the clavichord and when she saw that Atticus was looking at her, she smiled faintly. It was a reassuring gesture, one of faith and trust, and a gesture not lost on Atticus. It fortified him. Quietly, she made her way over to him.

"Is it true?" she asked softly. "De la Londe and de Troiu are truly at Wellesbourne Castle?"

Atticus nodded, reaching out a hand to her. She took it immediately and he held her hand fast, caressing her flesh with his big fingers. "Aye," he said. "It is a miraculous series of events that have brought us to this place in time and I will tell you the entire story on our journey to Warwickshire, but for now, if you still intend to go with me, you must pack quickly and you must pack lightly. We leave within the hour."

Isobeau nodded and fled the chamber, heading back to her room and to her possessions there. She wanted very much to go with Atticus, for a variety of reasons, not the least of which was the fact that she simply didn't want to be separated from him. She wanted to be with him every moment and she wanted to share this experience with him. It was a vital part of their bonding, of their marriage in general. With de la Londe and de Troiu gone, there would be closure on Titus and a new beginning for them. They both needed that closure, that justice, and that satisfaction.

Atticus could hear Isobeau in her chamber next door, evidently destroying the place as she went to pack for her journey. Things were banging about and something fell. Solomon, distracted from his grief by the banging, looked up as if concerned for the woman but Atticus merely grinned.

"I hope she does not hurt herself in her attempt to pack," he jested, attempting to lighten the mood for his father somewhat. "It sounds as if she is tearing down the very walls."

In spite of himself, Solomon smiled weakly. "Women are flighty that way," he said, putting a meaty hand on his son's broad shoulder. He seemed more composed than he had been moments earlier. "Are you sure these men are at Wellesbourne, Atticus? Are you positive?"

Atticus nodded unhappily. "Evidently there is a good deal to the lengths they would go to sway men to Edward's cause," he said. "They went there to inform Andrew Wellesbourne that his son, Adam, had sworn fealty to Edward in the hopes of gaining Andrew's vow. Lord Andrew, suspecting betrayal and deceit, threw them in the vault and sent a knight to Alnwick to discover the truth of the matter. Of course it wasn't true, so now de la Londe and de Troiu are still in Wellesbourne's vault."

Solomon sighed faintly, pondering the situation before sitting heavily on the end of his lumpy, smelly bed. It was clear that he was deep in thought.

"It is fortuitous, then," he said. "As if God has had a hand in helping you find these men and punish them."

"I think so."

Solomon lingered on the two knights who had murdered his son. "Tell me," he said after a moment. "You were with Titus when he died, were you not?"

"Aye."

"Did he suffer greatly in the end?"

Atticus was reluctant to say anything about Titus' final moments. "Does it matter?" he asked softly.

Solomon shrugged, suddenly feeling quite weary and old. He rubbed at his knees, thinking yet again how he cursed them because he could not easily travel.

"I want to know what those men did to him," he finally said. "Did he suffer greatly?"

Atticus was glad Isobeau wasn't in the room. He found that he couldn't deny his father's request but he didn't particularly want her to hear his answer. Did he suffer greatly? If Atticus had a son who had been killed by others, he would have wanted to know the same thing. He would want to know what his son felt at the end of his life, if he was in pain or at peace. Perhaps it was something only warriors would understand, and Atticus understood his father's request well.

The man wanted the details.

"He was gored through the belly, twice," he finally said, his voice no stronger than a whisper. "By the time I saw him, he did not feel much of anything at all. His body was badly wounded, Papa. It simply shut down. Did he suffer greatly? I do not believe so. He was at peace in the end. He simply closed his eyes and was gone."

At that gentle but frank summation, Solomon lowered his head and wept quietly. Atticus felt very badly for his father, hearing the last moments of his son, but in a sense, perhaps the man would have some peace now. But it wouldn't be over until Atticus confronted those who committed the crime. Only then would they know complete peace.

Atticus kissed his father farewell later that morning when he departed Wolfe's Lair with Isobeau by his side. Kenton, Adam, Maxim, Alec, and Juston were with him as Tertius and the bulk of Northumberland's army headed back for home. Warenne, carefully cleaned and wrapped by Kenton and Adam, was placed in the same coffin Titus had used for transport and sent back to Thetford with twenty-five Northumberland men-at-arms for escort.

Atticus found himself kissing the coffin yet again, this time because his dear friend was inside. It was a truly sad parting for Atticus, who deeply missed Warenne and his wisdom. But he was glad that Warenne was finally able to go home even though it wasn't the manner in which Warenne had wanted. As Atticus lingered over the coffin, saying his farewells, he remembered that Warenne had once told him to make sure that when he punished de la Londe and de Troiu, one of those sword thrusts was meant from Warenne himself. Now, Atticus would make sure of it.

Under partially cloudy skies on a wind-swept day, all parties departing from Wolfe's Lair went their separate ways.

But all thoughts were with Atticus on his final journey for Titus.

There wasn't one man among them who wasn't praying for his success.

CHAPTER NINETEEN

> Ionian scale in C – Lyrics to Joy Comes
>
> Joy comes again
> Beneath the pale moonlight
> For joy to know an ending
> It must have dear blue sight.
>
> —Isobeau de Shera de Wolfe, 15th c.

Just north of Wellesbourne Castle
Mid-May

ISOBEAU WAS NOT hard pressed to admit that her backside was numb from the fifteen days of travel she had endured following Atticus from the extreme north of England to the area of mid-England she was much more familiar with.

Her mare had been extremely durable and easy to ride for the length of their trip south so it wasn't the mare's fault that her bum was both achy and numb. Still, she wanted nothing more than to dismount the horse and walk or even run, anything to ease up the pressure on her bum. Sometimes she tried rubbing it but she was surrounded by knights who, she had discovered, would watch her do it with great interest, so she stopped. They seemed to like it too much. Suffering in silence, she rode mile after mile with a sore arse.

While the knights were watching her, however, Isobeau was watching Atticus. The past several days of travel had been very good for the two of them in spite of the seriousness of their journey, and Isobeau had come to know a man who was very funny, very bright, and very quick to move no matter what the reasons or situation. He was brave beyond measure, unafraid of anything, and she gained new appreciation for the man she had married. The trip south with his comrades-in-arms had been an experience for her, witnessing the bonding of brothers-at-arms in a way she'd never had the opportunity to know. They would die for each other but they weren't beyond a vicious joke or two. She found that out fairly early on.

Traveling through the town of Morecambe, they had lodged for the night in an inn that had no separate sleeping chambers, only a big dormitory on the second floor. Atticus had been rather perturbed about that, not having a private room for his wife, so he sat and brooded about it for the majority of the evening whilst Alec, Maxim, and Kenton had gone in search of another inn that had more suitable arrangements. But there were none to be found, at least not locally, so the men had returned after their unsuccessful venture and throughout the course of the evening, the younger knights had proceeded to become fairly drunk. Especially Maxim.

The young knight was chasing serving wenches about in spite of Atticus admonishing the man, so when he jumped up yet again to go chase after a wench he'd been trying to snag most of the night, Atticus and Kenton took his chair, loosened one of the legs, and put the chair back where Maxim had originally left it. Maxim returned, drunk and upset at yet another unsuccessful hunt, sat down heavily, and the chair promptly collapsed.

Unfortunately, Maxim hit his head on the table behind them and knocked himself unconscious in the fall, and Kenton had hauled the man up and taken him to the dormitory where he slept off his drunkenness with great snoring choruses. Even though Atticus and Kenton had giggled about the broken chair leg, it would seem that Maxim had the last laugh when he snored heavily all night. Isobeau, wrapped snug in her bed next to her husband, had silently laughed at her husband for a joke that didn't work out for him. When Atticus realized she was laughing at him, he'd tickled her until she screamed for reprieve. Snoring, tickling and all, it had been one of the better nights of her life.

The journey south had seen great bonding between Isobeau and Atticus, and even though their purpose in traveling south was a serious one, Isobeau was grateful for the time she was able to spend with Atticus, time that saw them draw closer. The only trouble was that he had not touched her in the husbandly sense because they hadn't been given any real time alone.

The trip south had seen them either camp in the open or seek shelter in taverns where they'd always had to share a room with Kenton or another knight. They'd shared a few stolen moments of very heated and lusty kisses, moments away from the others, but it hadn't been nearly enough for a husband to be intimate with a wife. It had been both a frustrating and titillating problem, something Isobeau knew was eating away at Atticus. Having been married before, she knew when a man was aroused and Atticus seemed to be aroused around her quite often. She giggled while he groaned miserably.

But she pushed those carnal thoughts aside, knowing that the time would come at some point when he would claim his husbandly rights and eagerly awaiting that day. But this trip, this journey south, was for a singular purpose and on the morning of the fifteenth day, she had awoken alone in the bed she had shared with Atticus.

Lifting her head to look about, she noticed that the pallet against the wall was also vacant where it had once held Kenton. Both men were gone but in their wake they had left her a bowl of lukewarm water and a great hunk of cream-colored bread with a hard brown crust.

Isobeau had wolfed down the bread, washed in the water, and prepared for the coming day. In a durable traveling dress of brown wool that was heavy and comfortable, she had ridden behind Atticus for most of the day, refraining from rubbing her bum, and that was where she currently found herself. She was so concerned with finding a comfortable position on the saddle that when a distant castle came into view and Adam and de Royans suddenly spurred their horses forward, she was nearly pitched off her mare when the animal danced about excitedly.

Wellesbourne Castle had been sighted.

Isobeau could see it now on the horizon, a white-stoned castle that rose above the gently rolling, green hills of Warwickshire. Nestled near the River Dene, Wellesbourne Castle was a very tall but somewhat compact structure. As they drew closer, Isobeau drank in the sight of the fortress with its soaring walls the color of pearl. Great blocks of nearly white granite comprised the walls and, once inside the curtain wall, also comprised the keep. There were stables and trades off to the left in a surprisingly roomy bailey, knight's quarters and other apartments to the right as they were built against the wall, and in front of her was a keep in the shape of a quatrefoil at least four stories high. It was an impressive sight to say the least.

As Isobeau gawked at the sheer height of Wellesbourne Castle's keep, Atticus dismounted his beast and made his way over to his wife. He lifted his arms to her but she didn't see him, still gazing up at the top of the keep. Atticus grinned.

"I promise to take you to the very top so you can see the views of the countryside," he said. "But you must get off your horse first. Surely your backside must be sore."

Jolted from her observations, Isobeau smiled as she slid down into his warm, wonderful embrace.

"It is," she said. "How did you know?"

"How do you think we *all* knew?"

He snorted as he said it and Isobeau flushed with embarrassment as she rubbed at her bum. "Well, it *hurts*."

He stopped laughing and kissed her forehead. Even when her feet touched the muddy ground, Atticus kept her in his grasp. His gaze upon her was warm.

"Not to worry, sweetling, although you provided quite a titillating show for Maxim and Alec," he said, watching her make a menacing face at him. He grinned. "It will be a relief to sleep in a chamber of our own tonight, away from those frisky young knights. As much as I love and respect my men, if I have to hear Maxim snore one more time or be woken up by Alec fighting unseen assassins in his sleep, the top of my head will surely blow off from sheer frustration."

Isobeau laughed. "Kenton is the only one who does not make any noise when he sleeps," she said. "Many times I thought he was dead asleep but if I so much as breathed, he was instantly awake and ready to do battle."

Atticus was forced to agree. "Such are the instincts of a trained knight," he said, turning for the big keep with its wide stone steps when he heard voices.

The first thing he saw was Andrew Wellesbourne, greeting Kenton loudly, and right behind him he saw Adam hugging his blond-haired wife with great care. The woman was quite pregnant and Adam was trying to be very careful with her in his zeal.

Maxim and Alec were standing with Jasper de Llion, the big Wellesbourne knight having opened the gates for the party to enter. Atticus knew all of the Wellesbourne knights, including de Llion, because he had fought many battles with them and he realized he was rather proud to introduce Isobeau to them. It was the first time in his life, he realized, that he would take pride in someone other than himself. Even though their visit to Wellesbourne was grave, there were some joyous factors to it and Isobeau was one.

"Come, wife," he said. "Let us greet our host. I have a great deal of gratitude to express."

Isobeau took his arm as he led her between horses, heading for the keep where everyone was gathering. They could see Andrew and Juston in deep conversation. Isobeau leaned in to Atticus, speaking quietly.

"Those men, Atticus," she said, grasping for words. She couldn't even really bring herself to speak their names any longer. "Those men who killed Titus – now that we have finally arrived, will you see them this very moment? Or will you wait?"

Atticus had been asking himself that same question for fifteen days. Would he take immediately to his task? Or would he wait, planning his attack, making sure that when he faced them that he had a plan so that he was guaranteed ultimate victory? The truth was that he saw no reason to wait. The sooner he finished with what he must do, the sooner he and Isobeau would be able to move on with their lives. For Titus' sake, he didn't want to wait. Titus deserved justice and he wanted de la Londe and de Troiu dead before sunset, which was fast on the approach. Nay, he didn't want to wait at all.

"I will greet Lord Andrew and then see to my task," he told her. "You will retreat inside with Lady Wellesbourne. I will come to you when it is finished."

Isobeau came to a halt and he along with her. When he turned to look at her, curious as to why she had stopped, he could see the unhappiness in her expression.

"Nay, Atticus," she said firmly. "You said this would be vengeance for us both. I will be present when you administer justice to these men."

"Nay, you will not."

"It is my right to see this ended just as much as it is yours!"

Now he was the one frowning. "You may see their bodies when I am finished," he said. "Why should you want to see the actual punishment?"

She looked at him as if he were daft. "Why *wouldn't* I? I have come a very long way, too, and it was not to be shut up in a keep whilst you face life and death against men who killed Titus. Moreover, I want to be here... with you... whilst you administer justice. I want you to know that I am here to support you in everything you do."

Atticus didn't want to enter into a confrontation with her, not now. If she felt so strongly about it, then he would not deny her. But she had to know that what she was about to see what going to be very brutal. In fact, he thought to scare her a bit so that she might decide on her own to retreat inside until it was over.

"Very well," he said, although it was clear he was unhappy about it. "If you choose to watch, then know this will be a fierce event. These men will die, right in front of you, and not in pleasant ways. Are you willing to watch that?"

She was unmoved by his attempt to frighten her. "I hope they suffer tenfold any pain that Titus felt," she said, her voice tight with emotion. "I hope they feel his pain and beg for your mercy to end it. For what they did, they deserve nothing less."

Atticus was a bit taken aback at her passion when she spoke of the suffering of men. He could see that she meant every word. Before he could respond, however, Andrew Wellesbourne came upon them, reaching out to grasp Atticus in the joy of greeting.

"Atticus," he said, great satisfaction in his voice. "You have come. Adam and Juston just explained everything to me, why you have come and what de la Londe and de Troiu mean to you. So they killed Titus, did they? Somehow, I am not surprised. They told me that Titus was killed at Towton but they did not say how, the bastards. Now I know. They are traitors at the dirtiest and most unsavory level. I am deeply sorry for the loss of your brother, Atticus. My heart grieves for him."

Atticus greeted Adam's father fondly. "As does mine," he said, turning to indicate Isobeau. "Meet my wife, Lady Isobeau de Shera de Wolfe. She has accompanied me from Wolfe's Lair. Isobeau was born and raised at Isenhall, which is not far from here. Surely you know her father."

Andrew turned his attention to her, surprise and pleasure registering on his face. "My lady," he said. "Of course I know your father, Calpurnius. He is a friend and ally. I remember you, too, but it has been years since I last saw you."

Isobeau smiled at the man, looking rather chagrined. "I am sorry to say that I do not remember you, my lord," she said. "I was a foolish child and remember little from my childhood. Pray forgive me."

Andrew laughed. "I am a forgettable old fool," he said, looking between Atticus and Isobeau. "But please come inside and allow me to show you some Wellesbourne hospitality. You must surely be exhausted from your journey."

Atticus shook his head. "I will not sample Wellesbourne hospitality until my reason for coming here is complete," he said quietly. "Where are de la Londe and de Troiu?"

Andrew wasn't surprised that Atticus would not relax until the men who had killed his brother were appropriately punished. He was a knight, and he understood the heart of a knight. Therefore, he understood Atticus' position very well.

"In the vault," he said. "I have held them in that hellish, black hole since the day they arrived here last month. I have seen them twice since then and they knew that I had sent word to Alnwick to discover the truth of the madness they were trying to tell me. Imagine my son swearing fealty to Edward. I knew it was a lie! But now I have been told that their presence in my vault means much more to you, Atticus. I am privileged to deliver them to you so you may exact justice for Titus' death."

Atticus thought on that a moment. He looked around the bailey of Wellesbourne; it was cluttered with men, and a few animals over by the stables, but there was a great open area right in front of the gatehouse where their horses were gathered after having just arrived. The area in front of the gatehouse was open, with soft earth, and it was easily viewed from both the keep and the wall. He must have paused in thought too long because Isobeau nudged him gently.

"Atticus?" she said. "What are you thinking?"

Atticus' gaze lingered on the soft earth near the gatehouse. "I am thinking that I will wait no longer to seek justice for my brother," he said, turning to Andrew. "Bring de la Londe and de Troiu to me, my lord. I will wait for them here."

Andrew looked at the man, trying to gauge his mood and also what he intended to do. "You want me to simply bring them out to you?"

Atticus nodded. "Aye."

Andrew looked to Isobeau for a moment as if she could clarify the demand, but she seemed as puzzled as he did. He returned his attention to Atticus. "And what will you do?"

Atticus' expression was serious, deadly. "What needs to be done," he said. "Have weapons standing by so that they might defend themselves. This will be finished now, my lord. I have come a very long way and I will wait no longer. For my brother, I will dispense justice as quickly and as painfully as possible."

The Lion of the North had spoken. Andrew simply nodded, glancing somewhat ominously at Isobeau as he walked away, but Isobeau had no discernable reaction to her husband's words. It was clear that she agreed with him.

As Andrew moved, he gathered Adam, Jasper, and Juston, relaying Atticus' orders. They appeared a bit surprised but nonetheless resigned as Juston and Jasper headed to the vault on Andrew's heels but Adam remained behind. Kenton made a point of asking Adam where his father and de Royans were heading and when Adam told him, Kenton understood. He gathered Maxim and Alec, and together, the four knights moved to Atticus' side.

Already, it would begin. There would be no delays, no pleasantries, no relaxation for those who had traveled so far. Atticus had come with a purpose and that purpose would begin.

The time for reckoning was swiftly approaching.

THE LIGHT WAS blinding. He couldn't see. His eyes, from weeks in darkness, couldn't tolerate the sunlight at all. As de la Londe emerged from the black vaults of Wellesbourne and out into the daylight, he had his hands over his eyes because he couldn't see in the least. Next to him, de Troiu was actually folded over, eyes closed and head down. De Royans and de Llion had brought them up from the vault, roughly, shoving them up the moss-covered steps until they reached the blinding white light at the top.

De la Londe was fairly certain that the brightness had burned holes in his eyes as he blinked rapidly, covering his eyes, struggling to acclimate. De Royans and de Llion were still shoving him, out into the dirt of the bailey, and both he and de Troiu were staggering blindly.

De la Londe had no idea how far they actually staggered until de Royans and de Llion stopped shoving. At that point, de la Londe was able to see a little bit but he kept his eyes shaded. He saw dirt and he could see the legs of men standing around him. Off to his left was the gatehouse; he recognized the old iron portcullis. There were more soldiers standing over there, looking at him. Still blinking rapidly, he tried to lift his eyes to see more of what was surrounding him.

The first face he saw was that of Atticus de Wolfe.

Suddenly, de la Londe wasn't so blind. He found himself gazing at Atticus with astonishment, his mouth gaping as he beheld the stubble-bearded vision of a knight he knew very well. But in that split second of recognition, he knew why Atticus was here; at least, he thought he did. He knew that Andrew Wellesbourne had sent word to Alnwick to try and straighten out the lies that he had been told, so the truth was that de la Londe wasn't surprised to see Atticus.

In fact, he was prepared. Armed with the fabricated story he'd had a great deal of time to concoct in the black depths of Wellesbourne's vault, de la Londe reached out an arm in Atticus' direction.

"Atticus," he breathed. "Thank God you have come. You can help straighten out the misunderstanding with Wellesbourne."

Atticus gazed steadily at the two men who murdered his brother. It was a defining moment for him, one wrought with emotion, and he was rather proud that he hadn't charged them and cut both of their heads off. That was his first instinct when he had seen them emerging from the vault, crippled by the bright sunlight in their faces. He had wanted nothing more than to rush them and cut them to shreds. But he didn't; his composure held, although it was fragile. But the sound of de la Londe's voice threatened to shatter it.

"There is no misunderstanding," Atticus said steadily. "In fact, everything is perfectly clear. You know exactly why I am here."

De la Londe rubbed at his eyes, struggling to focus on Atticus with his still-weak eyes. "You have come to vouch for me, of course," he said. "I am a Northumberland knight, a man you have fought with for many years. And where is Titus? Is he here?"

Atticus' expression was darkening even though he was struggling desperately to remain calm. Still, something inside him, that terrible need to right a wrong, to make men suffer in payment for all of the suffering Titus had endured, begged to be released. *So much hate.*

Atticus felt so much hate that it began to control him. He couldn't stop it. Now, the time for vengeance was upon him and it was hate, and oddly enough love for his brother, that would see this through. Both of them seemed to be intertwined within him, feeding his soul. Slowly, he made his way towards the two men standing together near the gatehouse.

"I want you both to look at something," he said, holding up a heavy and well-made broadsword. "Do you recognize this?"

De la Londe blinked as he looked at the weapon. "A broadsword, of course," he said. "Why do you ask? Atticus, what is happening here? Why are Declan and I standing here like animals? Take us inside and feed us. We have been treated terribly since our arrival."

That was enough to snap Atticus, at least slightly. A massive fist lashed out and struck de la Londe in the jaw, sending the man reeling. When de Troiu, shocked by the sudden violence, threw up his hands to protect his head, Atticus lashed out a big boot and caught the man in the belly. De Troiu collapsed in the dirt.

Atticus stood over the writhing pair, resisting the urge to kick and punch them until there was nothing but bloody bits left. As de la Londe wallowed on the ground, Atticus put the tip of the broadsword under the man's chin, forcing his head up. Their eyes met and nothing short of hell could be seen in Atticus' tumultuous orbs.

There was death there.

"The more you speak your foolish lies, the more painful your death will be," Atticus snarled. "Whatever fabrications you have decided to tell me, be aware that I know the truth. This broadsword at your throat is my brother's, the one he used to defend himself with when you and de Troiu murdered him. It will now be the instrument used to send you to your death. *That* is why I am here, Simon. I have come for *you*."

Simon seemed to lose some of his confidence. He squinted up at

Atticus, rubbing his jaw and struggling not to let his fear show. *He knows!* He thought in a panic. *That is impossible! How could the man know when they made sure to kill Titus? Dead men do not speak!*

"Who told you such lies?" he demanded weakly. "Titus is dead, you say?"

Atticus, infuriated, lashed out another foot and caught de la Londe in the face. When de Troiu attempted to crawl away, out of the line of fire, Atticus grabbed him by the hair and threw him to the ground.

"Both of you will listen to me and listen well," he growled, watching the blood pour from de la Londe's nose. "When you kill a man, it is imperative you finish the deed so that he cannot tell others what happened. Fortunately, your inept skills against my brother allowed him to live for a short while and tell us what you had done before he mercifully passed on. I know that it was you two who approached my brother and demanded his oath to Edward. I know that when he refused, you gored him. I am here today because I swore to Titus I would avenge his death and that is exactly what I intend to do. Is this in any way unclear?"

De la Londe was looking up at Atticus with baleful eyes. His expression, pleading and innocent moments earlier, had now turned dark and murky. He barred his teeth, menacingly, giving one last attempt to deny his crimes and save his life. As he saw it, he had nothing to lose. He knew his life was now measured in minutes and he had to make every attempt to extend it.

"He lied," de la Londe hissed. "Titus lied!"

Atticus snapped. He threw Titus' broadsword aside and pounced on de la Londe, using his fists to beat the man within an inch of his life. De la Londe fought back although he was mostly trying to defend himself as Atticus mercilessly pounded the man in the face and around his head and shoulders. Every blow had Titus' name on it, every drop of blood vindication for his death. When de Troiu, close enough so that he was on the receiving end of a couple of brutal punches, attempted to crawl away, Atticus grabbed the man by the hair again and beat him in the neck and on the side of the head hard enough to daze him. As de Troiu hovered above unconsciousness, Atticus pushed himself off of de la Londe and went to retrieve Titus' sword.

"Give them weapons," Atticus snapped to Kenton and Adam, who were holding two broadswords. "Give them the weapons, I say! Let us be done with this now!"

Atticus was agitated, feeding off of battle and off of his sense of vengeance. Kenton, ever cool, took the broadsword from Adam and, with two in his hands, approached de la Londe and de Troiu. He kicked de Troiu to try and rouse the man.

"Get up," he rumbled. "If you want to at least have a fighting chance, then you had better get up and defend yourselves. Otherwise, Atticus will make short work of you."

The tension in the air was unbelievable, a splitting mood of anguish and hatred and grief, and all of it radiating from Atticus. They all felt it, most especially Isobeau; standing on the top step of the keep and well away from the fighting, as she had promised Atticus, she nonetheless had a full view of what was going on. There were tears in her eyes as she watched, tears for Atticus and tears for the grief and agony for Titus that were surfacing once again. The pain was returning, fresh as if it had never left.

But this was what Atticus had been waiting for since the day of Titus' death, the opportunity to avenge the man he loved so dearly. As brutal as it was, it was also healing. Isobeau knew that. The pain, fresh again, would be eased. Today, the healing would truly begin for Atticus and as difficult as it was to watch, it was also therapeutic.

For both of them.

They both needed the closure.

As Isobeau observed from the steps, hands to her mouth, Atticus had managed to calm his rage somewhat but not completely. He was growing impatient as de la Londe and de Troiu continued to stagger from his beating. He didn't want to wait any longer.

"Take the swords or I will gore you both at this very moment," he commanded.

De Troiu, regaining consciousness, tried to crawl behind Kenton for some protection, but Kenton kicked the man aside and threw the sword at his feet. Kenton then tossed the other sword at de la Londe and it landed in the dirt a few inches away from him. As Kenton moved away from the center of battle, de la Londe grabbed at the sword and clutched it defensively. His face, now bruised and bloodied, was fixed on Atticus.

"A dying man will say anything!" he bellowed desperately. "You will not even hear the truth of the matter? Then you murder two innocent men!"

Atticus resisted the urge to charge them again. They were such blatant liars that it sickened him. Still, he managed to pause and collect himself as best he was able.

"The truth is that you murdered my brother for refusing to side with Edward," he said. "That is the only truth. If you speak any more lies against my brother, I will cut your tongue out."

De la Londe cut short his reply, knowing that Atticus would do it. The man always carried out his threats. He therefore knew his life was at an end and he knew there was nothing more he could do to save himself except, perhaps, defer the blame. Maybe it would ease Atticus' anger; maybe it would compel him to be merciful. Maybe he could lie and cheat and worm his way out of this predicament altogether, for now, he was out to save himself. He didn't want to die.

"It was Declan," he finally said, pointing to de Troiu. "He was the one who stabbed Titus first. He brought about the first blow. It was not me. I would have ridden from Titus without killing him, but de Troiu struck first!"

De Troiu, still on the dirt a few feet away from de la Londe, looked to his comrade in horror. "You *bastard*!" he hissed. "It was *you* who provoked him!"

De la Londe was now in the losing game of Casting Blame. He and de Troiu were no longer united as the truth began to spill forth. In an effort to deflect the accusation, he turned to Atticus.

"Look at my face!" de la Londe jabbed a finger at the healing gash across the side of his face. "Titus did that! He moved against me first! De Troiu was only defending me!"

De Troiu, realizing that de la Londe was utterly out for himself, moved to plead his case to Atticus. "Norfolk offered Titus the manse at Westwick," he said. "He offered him productive lands and a title, but Titus refused. He knew we had already sworn fealty to Norfolk and he viewed us as the enemy. With God as my witness, Atticus, it was Titus who moved first. He slashed de la Londe's face. I was able to get in the next blow. Up until that moment, we had not drawn our weapons. It was Titus who drew first."

Atticus listened, unmoved. "Because you were traitors," he said simply. "He had every right to move against you and subdue you."

"And we had every right to defend ourselves!"

Atticus held up Titus' broadsword. "Just as you have every right to defend yourselves now," he said. "Get up and face me. I will not tell you again."

It was an order. But de Troiu knew, as did de la Londe, that the moment they picked up the swords, Atticus would kill them. It would be an honorable killing. In that respect, they weren't going to make it easy for him. Atticus de Wolfe was a man whose reputation was built on honor. Killing an unarmed man would be most dishonorable. With that in mind, de Troiu shook his head.

"Nay," he said, rising to his knees and refusing to collect the sword. "If you are going to kill me, then do it. I'll not pick up a weapon and pretend to give you a fight. We both know that there is no fight. Therefore, if you are going to kill me, then kill me unarmed."

Atticus knew what the man was attempting to do; an honorable knight would not fight an unarmed knight. But this was an extraordinary case; this was a punishment for a crime, not an honorable fight in the least. Giving de Troiu and de la Londe weapons to defend themselves was purely a courtesy. Given that Atticus was seeking vengeance against two murderers, there were no rules in this hunt. It was the hunter against the prey. The prey refused to arm itself.

Therefore, Atticus didn't hesitate to act. No sooner had the words left de Troiu's mouth than Atticus marched up on the man and shoved Titus' broadsword straight into de Troiu's sternum.

It was a shocking and brutal move. The first blood had been drawn as de Troiu collapsed into the dirt, bleeding out from a pierced heart. After that, bedlam reigned. De la Londe, seeing that Atticus had killed de Troiu without hesitation, grabbed the broadsword at his feet and swung it at Atticus, who was fairly close to him. The blade caught Atticus in the hip and, being that Atticus was quite typically not wearing armor, immediately drew copious amounts of blood.

In an instant, the battle to the death had finally begun.

Injured, Atticus turned on de la Londe and attacked the man. It was nearly even odds considering de la Londe had been beaten and battered, and his head was unsteady, but the swordfight that commenced was truly one to behold. It was a vicious battle across the compound as Atticus, bleeding profusely from a very large gash to his left hip, went after de la Londe with a vengeance.

Sparks flew into the air as blade met with blade, and men who had once been allies now tried desperately to kill one another. Upon the steps of Wellesbourne's keep, Isobeau was watching in fascination and horror as the knights around her, now witnessing a rather brutal and powerful battle, analyzed every movement of the fight. They could see already that Atticus was having some difficulty in moving with his usual grace because the gash to his hip was severe. Muscles had been cut. But the man didn't back off in any form. He was The Lion of the North, after all, and he had a reputation for skill and power. Now, he had a reputation for unwavering determination as well, even with the serious wound.

As all of the knights witnessing the event would later attest, the battle between Atticus de Wolfe and his brother's killer had truly been something to behold. It was a great battle that would be spoken of and passed down from generation to generation, for centuries to come.

It would cement The Lion's reputation for good.

Being that both men were excellent knights, however, it was a battle that went on longer than it should have. With Atticus' injury and de la Londe's bruising, the fierceness of the fight was a testimony to their individual strengths. De la Londe was clearly up to the task, but so was Atticus. In the course of their battle, the men fought their way over to the stables and they spent several long and terrifying minutes chasing each other through the yard, leaping over water troughs or dodging fences. At one point, Atticus nearly cut de la Londe's head off when the man barely ducked a slice that came in over the top of a fence post.

The knights watching the fight followed it as it moved from the stables to the kitchen yard. They were so involved in the battle that they had all but forgotten about Isobeau as the woman watched the fight with utter horror. It was a surreal performance of battle and skill by Atticus, weakened only by the wound to his hip, but it was clear that the wound was slowing him down. On and on they went, fighting their way into the kitchen yard, when de la Londe took hold of a long garden tool and hurled it at Atticus' head.

Atticus ducked the flying tool but the iron end of it still clipped him on the head, drawing blood. The sight of Atticus' blood on his head was all Isobeau needed to slide into full-blown panic; terrified her husband was going to be killed by the same man who had killed his brother, she could no longer stand by and observe. She had to do something. She understood now the depths of Atticus' angst at his inability to protect his brother, for now that she saw her husband bleeding and battling, it was as if something inside her snapped.

Snapped....

She would do anything to protect her husband, her love and her life, and she simply couldn't stand by and watch de la Londe defeat Atticus. Defeat would mean his death. This was something she could not allow. She could not bury another husband and she certainly couldn't bury Atticus.

She had to save him.

Following the knights as they followed Atticus and de la Londe around the corner of the keep and towards a walled-in garden, it looked to her as if de la Londe had the advantage. Atticus, with his bleeding head, seemed to be backing off a bit and taking a beating because of it. She couldn't watch de la Londe beat him into the ground and with that thought, the thought of Atticus' imminent death, everything else in her mind became a blur.

She had to save him!

De la Londe had his back to her now as he slashed down upon Atticus, driving him off-balance. Isobeau looked around for a weapon of some kind, anything to injure the man with and give Atticus the advantage, but there wasn't anything strong enough or sharp enough in her line of sight to complete the job. Her desperate gaze darted about until she came across a dagger shoved into a sheath on a belt that draped around Kenton's hips.

A dagger!

Now, she knew what she had to do. Rushing at Kenton, Isobeau snatched the dagger before the man even realized she had it. De la Londe's back was still to her as she burst through the crowd of knights watching the battle and threw herself at de la Londe's backside. Lifting the dagger, she plunged it squarely into the back of the man's neck. As de la Londe screamed and went down, she withdrew the dagger and stabbed him twice more, feeling him collapse beneath her and experiencing a very odd satisfaction as he folded. Words, words she couldn't even control, came hurling out at the dying man beneath her.

"For Titus, I hope you feel all of the anguish that he felt at your hand," she hissed into his ear. "For the grief and agony you caused me, let my voice be the last one you hear in this world and know that I hope you spend eternity in hell as Satan's handmaiden. And for Atticus, know that he will feel the ultimate satisfaction in your death. But hear me now; as you lay dying, know that it wasn't a knight who killed you. *It was a woman.*"

It was the ultimate insult to the felled man. She may have whispered more to him after that but she could not be sure. Someone was lifting her up and carrying her away, and the last she saw of Simon de la Londe was when a circle of knights surrounded him, watching him die in agony. It was the last memory Isobeau had of that event, of the moment when all that was controlled and fearful within her snapped enough so that she killed the man who was hurting Atticus. De la Londe's death, her own sense of vengeance against the man, was the last thing she remembered.

When her senses finally returned, the first face she saw was Atticus'.

He kissed her. And then he wept.

CHAPTER TWENTY

> Ionian scale in C – The Ending
>
> And now the tale has ended,
> And now the love has come.
> The Lion and his lady,
> Now, at last, are one.
>
> —Isobeau de Shera de Wolfe, 15th c.

THE NIGHT WAS soothing and surprisingly balmy. Night birds were calling to each other over the treetops and the moon, high and bright in the sky, cast silver light over the landscape. There was a sense of tranquility and peace, something Atticus hadn't felt in months. Years, even. He couldn't remember the last time he'd known such utter stillness and calm, as if nothing was amiss in the world.

It was a feeling he knew he could grow accustomed to.

"Atticus?"

A soft voice pulled him away from the lancet window and his view of the countryside. He turned to see Isobeau gazing up at him from her position in the big, comfortable bed. He smiled as he went to her, sitting on the bed beside her.

"How do you feel?" he asked quietly. "You slept a long time."

Isobeau smiled faintly. "Sleepy," she said. "How long was I asleep?"

Atticus stroked her blond head. "All day," he told her. "Do you remember that I brought you up here after the events in the bailey?"

Isobeau nodded, the smile fading from her lips as she recalled the dagger and the death that she had inflicted. *She had killed a man.* It was the first thing that came to mind but, strangely enough, she wasn't sorry in the least. She did what she'd had to do. She hoped Atticus would see it that way.

"I do," she murmured. "Are you angry with me for what I did? I... I want to say something before you berate me. I want to say that I understand now why you killed du Reims as you did. Atticus, I saw you in the bailey with blood on you and it seemed to me that de la Londe might actually best you. I could not stand by and watch that. I had to protect you. Can you understand that? I realize this was an honorable fight and I ruined it, but I do not regret it. You are alive and that is all that matters to me. Now, if you must still berate me, go ahead."

Atticus listened to her somewhat rambling speech. He could see she was upset, nervous even, and it softened his heart. He stroked her head again. "No one has ever cared for me as much as you do," he told her. "In answer to your question, I am not angry. Vengeance was your right as much as it was mine."

Isobeau, vastly relieved that he was not upset with her, shook her head. "I suppose there was some vengeance to it," she admitted. "When I drove the dagger into him, I imagined that it was Titus doing it. Perhaps I was an instrument for Titus' spirit in a sense. But more than that, I was protecting *you*. It had less to do with Titus and much more to do with you."

Atticus leaned down, kissing her on the forehead. He was deeply touched. "You are a strong and remarkable woman, Lady de Wolfe," he said. "I am honored to be your husband. I am honored that you would care so much for me that you would kill for me."

Isobeau reached up and put her hands on his face, her fingers in his dark hair. There was so much emotion swirling in her heart that it was difficult to grasp a single coherent thought. All she knew was what she felt for him… that she loved him. Aye, that was all she knew.

"I love you, Atticus," she finally whispered. "It was difficult to understand what, exactly, I felt for you all of this time, fearful that what I was feeling somehow overshadowed my relationship with Titus. I told you all of this before… what I feel for you has nothing to do with Titus and everything to do with you. To men, you are The Lion of the North, the fiercest and most cunning knight in all of Northumbria, but to me, you are my sweet and beautiful husband and I shall love you until I die."

Those were the words Atticus had been waiting to hear all his life. He hadn't realized that so much as he did at that very moment. To have Isobeau's love, love so deep that she would kill for him, was something few men ever knew. He was the most fortunate man in the world, of that he was certain.

At last, the vengeance that had clouded their marriage from the start was over. Those who had murdered Titus had been punished. Norfolk was defeated, at least for the moment. Now, it was just the two of them and nothing else. They were alone and the night was peaceful. Atticus could only think of one thing to do to celebrate their marriage and their new beginning. He felt as if he had been waiting all of his life for this moment.

His mouth slanted over hers, hungrily. Isobeau responded immediately, latching on to him, her hands in his hair drawing him down to her. Atticus fell over onto the bed, on top of her, and his arms went around her as he kissed her fiercely. She was sweet, delectable, and warm. But he wanted more.

His tunic began to come off and he realized that Isobeau was removing it. She was pulling it up over his head. She tossed it aside as he grinned at her, kissing her ferociously as he went to remove her from her gown. Fortunately, it wasn't restrictive and when the stays were unfastened, she easily slid out of it. Atticus threw it onto the ground. He very nearly jumped up and stomped on it. He'd been waiting to get the woman out of her clothing for days, weeks even, and he was thrilled to finally have his way. The shift followed next and at the sight of her nude and entirely delicious body, Atticus' roving hands and mouth descended upon a taut nipple.

Isobeau groaned as he suckled her, his heated mouth sending bolts of pleasure through her body. He was moving quickly, with great passion, but with great care. Nothing he did was painful or unpleasant. Every time he touched her, every time his tongue lapped at her, she experienced only the greatest of pleasure.

In the midst of his mouth to her breasts and belly, Atticus had somehow managed to remove his leather breaches. He almost jumped up and stomped on those things, too, things that would prevent his flesh from touching Isobeau's. They had made his arousals most painful as of late. Utterly nude against her, he savored the moment, their naked skin touching, and as his mouth continued to suckle her breasts, his fingers probed the dark curls between her legs. She was already moist and heated, her body preparing itself for his entry. He didn't keep her waiting.

Atticus looked Isobeau in the eye when he finally mounted her, thrusting his long, hard length into her warm and quivering folds. Isobeau groaned with pleasure, bringing her legs up, wrapping them around his thighs as he thrust into her. Her hands moved over his body, acquainting herself with the feel of his skin as her nostrils drew in the scent of his musk. The man was pure power and pure excitement, and she savored every thrust, every movement. The Lion was finally mating with his chosen female, his wife, and as they took their pleasure upon the bed, Atticus simply couldn't get enough of her. She was absolute paradise in his arms.

The wound on his hip, since stitched by Wellesbourne's surgeon, pulled slightly and caused him a slight amount of pain as his hips moved, but he ignored the discomfort. There was far more pleasure to override any discomfort. Isobeau's luscious body beneath him drew his lust, his hands on her heaving breasts, feeling the silken texture, until he could hold back no longer and his release came with a deafening roar.

The Lion's roar.

Feeling his tremors within her body, Isobeau was catapulted into a blinding climax of her own, nearly screaming with pleasure until Atticus covered her mouth with his own in order to silence her. He knew that everyone in the castle had probably heard them but he didn't much care; he was glad they heard him. It meant that life was good and normal again. It meant that grief was a thing of the past for them both and now, they could move forward into the light.

It meant that he loved Isobeau with all his heart.

Isobeau and Atticus remained in their chamber in Wellesbourne Castle all night and well into the day, making love no less than six times. Atticus only left the chamber to procure them food, which grinning servants gladly provided. The rest of Northumberland's knights, meanwhile, enjoyed a few days of good food and hunting, knowing they would not be returning to Alnwick until Atticus was good and ready, and given the noises coming from his chamber up at the top of Wellesbourne's keep, he might not be ready for a very long time.

But that was okay with them. Atticus and Isobeau had suffered through a long and painful journey to reach this point and to that regard, they deserved all of the joy and pleasure they were experiencing and then some. On that terrible day back in March when Titus had been killed, it had been the catalyst for something much larger for The Lion of the North, much larger than Atticus or even Isobeau could have ever realized.

On the night of their third day at Wellesbourne, Atticus stood in the lancet window of his chamber as Isobeau slept, gazing up at the stars and seeing a vast blanket of diamonds across the sky. They were glittering back at him, winking even, and he imagined he saw Titus in that blanket of stars, winking back at him. He even imagined he saw a smile. Atticus smiled back. For the younger brother of the murdered knight, finally, he was to know some joy.

Wherever Titus was, Atticus knew that he approved.

Atticus and Isobeau, at last, had found peace.

EPILOGUE

September 1467 A.D.
Wolfe's Lair (Rule Water Castle)

THE CHILDREN HAD been rolling around in the dust of the construction of a new wing of Wolfe's Lair and there was nothing Isobeau could do to stop them. Caius de Wolfe, at five years of age, thought it was an extremely good idea to cover himself in white stone-dust while his younger brother by a year, Leonidus, simply followed what his brother directed. The blond-haired children became white-haired children as their grandfather, Solomon, watched the whole thing and giggled like a fool.

"Solomon?" Isobeau was in the bailey, a very pregnant woman leading a two-year-old girl by the hand. "Where are the boys?"

Solomon was seated on a stack of gray stones that were prepped and waiting to be used to create the inner wall of the addition. He pointed to an area where the masons from Edinburgh were working, men who were spraying white stone dust onto the ground. Isobeau saw the stones, the dust, and then saw her two boys smearing the dust all over themselves. She growled.

"Caius!" she snapped. "Leo! Come to me, *now*!"

Mother's orders weren't meant to be disobeyed and the sons of Atticus de Wolfe were well aware of that. Promptly, the boys stopped rubbing white dust all over each other and skipped over to their mother, who didn't seem particularly happy that they were covered in stone dust.

"Mama, *look*," Leonidus said, grinning in a manner that was very much reminiscent of his father. "We are clouds!"

It was difficult to become angry at the child when he seemed so happy. Isobeau sighed. "But why are you clouds?" she said. "You know that your father's army has been sighted. He should be back any moment. And see how dirty you are."

Solomon put a hand on Leonidus' head, watching a great cloud of dust puff up. He coughed, waving the cloud away. "They are becoming clouds to fly in the sky," he said, smiling proudly at the boys. "You know how they are fascinated with birds. They know they cannot be birds, so they will be clouds."

Isobeau shook her head reproachfully, looking pointedly at Caius, the eldest. He was extremely bright and extremely curious and she was positive it was his idea to become a cloud so that he could float in the sky.

"Cai," she admonished softly; she didn't want to be too hard on him. "You know you cannot fly like a bird and know you cannot float like a cloud. It frightens me to death to remember the time I found you and Leo standing on the top of the stairs outside of your chamber, preparing to fly off like a bird. You must promise me that you will not do anything so foolish again. You will kill yourself if you do and I could not stand it. Please promise me."

Caius nodded solemnly, although they both knew he didn't mean a word of it. He simply did it to placate his mother. "I promise," he said. "Mama, will Papa be here very soon?"

Isobeau nodded, turning to look at the gatehouse, shielding her eyes from the sun. "He should be here very soon," she said. "I would like for you to greet your father when he arrives but not covered from head to toe in white powder."

Solomon stood up, stiffly. He wasn't moving particularly well these days but he could still handle two small boys. At least, most of the time. His entire life revolved around his grandchildren – Caius, Leonidus, and little Morgana. He loved the children dearly. But Caius and Leonidus reminded him very much of Titus and Atticus, from long ago, so he spent nearly every waking minute with those two, watching them explore and learn and cover themselves in white dust so they could be clouds. So late in his life, he never imagined he would know such joy. Five years ago, he believed his life was over. He could have never guessed that it had only just begun.

"I will clean them off," Solomon said.

Grasping each boy by the shoulder, he pulled them over to a very large barrel that was used to catch rainwater. The stone masons had been using it to cool off the stone when they worked on it. Picking up Caius, he promptly dunked the lad into the cold water, pushing his head under briefly, and when Caius came up howling, Solomon lifted him out of the water and set him to his feet. He pointed to the drenched, but now clean, child.

"See?" he said. "He is clean now."

Leonidus, seeing what was coming, tried to run but his grandfather dunked him, too. Soon, Isobeau had two weeping boys on her hands. They were clean but crying because they were now cold and wet. She sighed heavily when what she really wanted to do was laugh. It was unbelievably comical; the children crying while Solomon stood there proudly.

"Do you see now why you should not cover yourself in dust or mud or anything else?" she said to Caius, who was unhappily wiping the tears from his eyes. "Your grandfather will try to drown you."

Caius frowned at his grandfather and moved closer to his mother because he knew she wouldn't try to throw him in cold water. "We will go wait for Papa by the gatehouse," he said, motioning to the still-wailing Leonidus. "Leo, come!"

Little Leonidus followed his older brother, still crying. Isobeau and Solomon watched the boys trot off and Solomon reached down to pick up little Morgana, still standing next to her mother. He cuddled the little girl, who rubbed her hands gleefully all over his bushy beard.

"Ah, my little sweetling," Solomon said, gazing at the dark-haired, blue-eyed girl. "Have I told you lately how much she looks like Rosalie?"

Isobeau grinned, rubbing at her swollen belly. The next child was due next month but she was ready to be done with it. Her back hurt, she had burning in her belly after she ate, and she was at the stage where she was generally uncomfortable.

"She looks just like Atticus," she said as they followed the boys and began their walk to the gatehouse. Her thoughts turned to her husband, gone the past seven weeks. Two of his envoys had arrived early this morning, announcing his arrival that day, and she was understandably anxious. "We've not had any news of what is happening with Edward and Henry as of late, Solomon. Do you think Atticus returning today will be for good? Do you believe he will be home to stay?"

Solomon, the old and wizened soldier, shook his head. "I do not believe so, lass," he said as Morgana continued to run her hands over his beard because it tickled. "These wars have been going on since I was a young man and longer even than that. I am not entirely sure they will ever be finished."

Isobeau didn't like the sound of that. She continued to rub at her belly, frowning, as they made their way towards the gatehouse. They were in close proximity when the call went up from the sentries on the wall, announcing the imminent arrival of Atticus de Wolfe and his army. Solomon shooed Isobeau and Morgana up onto a flight of stairs so they could watch the arrival but not be trampled by the herd of horses that would soon be filling the inner ward.

True enough, a herd of horses and armed men arrived shortly thereafter, bringing clouds of dust and the smell of battle with them. Isobeau kept an eye out for her husband but she also kept an eye on her boys, who were standing on the steps above her, yelling and cheering the sight of the soldiers. They were so excited that she didn't want one of them to fall off in their glee, so she admonished them firmly to stop jumping around, which they mostly did. Caius was always the one to push the limits with his mother and he stopped jumping up and down for a few seconds before resuming. Isobeau frowned and he caught her glare and stopped again. But all of that discipline evaporated when they spied Atticus enter.

Riding a new bright red Belgian charger he had purchased the year before, Atticus thundered into the inner ward wearing full armor, which was unusual for him considering he hated armor. Still, he wore it to please his wife who insisted upon the protection, and he didn't want her to see he'd been riding most of the time without it. Therefore, he pretended to like it, and wore it, as he drew his charger to a halt. Once he did that, the boys flew off the steps and rushed their father.

Atticus was barely off the horse when two wet children came crashing into him. Thrilled to see his boys again, he bent over and picked them up, accepting enthusiastic hugs from them.

"Cai!" he said happily. "Leo! Great Bleeding Jesus, you have both grown a foot since I last saw you. What on earth is your mother feeding you?"

"Anything they will eat," Isobeau said as she walked up on her husband and her sons. She smiled broadly at the man when their eyes met; instantly, love and comfort and joy filled the air between them. "Your sons eat as much as you do."

Atticus laughed softly as he set the boys to their feet. "That is good to know," he said, peering at them strangely. "Why are they all wet?"

"Because they were filthy and your father doused them in the rain barrel," Isobeau chuckled. Atticus came to her and gently took her in his arms. She gazed up into the face she loved so well. "Welcome home, my love. We are glad to have you back."

Atticus studied her beautiful face, the emotion of the moment bringing a lump to his throat. "I have missed you every second of every day," he murmured, bending down to kiss her sweetly. "It was torture without you. How are you feeling? Are you well?"

Isobeau nodded, rubbing at her big belly. "We are both quite well," she said. "The physic says we will have to wait only another week or two to meet our new son, so you have arrived home just in time. I did not want to have this baby without you."

He smiled, putting his big gloved hand on her protruding belly. "I am glad you did not," he said. "What have we decided to name this one?"

"Ares," Solomon said. "You promised I could name this child, Atticus. His name will be Ares."

Atticus grinned at his father, reaching out to touch the man on his hairy face. "So I did," he said. He let go of his wife and reached for his daughter, still in Solomon's arms. "Give me my baby, Papa. I've not seen her in weeks."

Solomon handed over his granddaughter, who was more than happy to go to her father. Atticus kissed the child on the cheek. "I have missed all of you so much," he said, patting Leonidus on the head because the child was demanding his attention. "Shall you take me inside the hall now? I am famished. You must feed your father."

The boys began tugging on him, pulling him towards the great hall. Isobeau and Solomon followed.

"What is the world like these days, Atticus?" Solomon asked. "Where have you been?"

Atticus glanced over his should to make sure his army was being disbanded by Maxim de Russe, who was now his second in command. Much had happened over the past few years; Tertius had returned to Isenhall to serve with his aging father while Kenton had gone to serve with Warwick. Adam Wellesbourne had returned to Wellesbourne Castle, leaving Alec le Bec in charge of defenses for the Earl of Northumberland. The knights of Northumberland were scattered but they were still close, still brothers in bond. Atticus sighed heavily, not knowing where to begin.

"Things are in turmoil," he said. "Warwick has distanced himself from Edward and is now siding with Henry once more. He is at his estates in Yorkshire and Kenton is with him as one of his knights in command. It would seem that Henry may be back upon the throne once again, hopefully for good."

Isobeau slipped her hand into his, listening seriously to the latest news. "And you?" she asked. "How do you fit into this new world?"

Atticus thought on that question for a moment. "I hold the borders," he said quietly. "We saw a few skirmishes over the past few weeks, but Warwick has sent me home to stay for a while. With the Scots siding with Henry, and a good deal of unrest going on in Yorkshire, I have been returned home to hold the borders and support the Scots, and Henry, if needed. Once again, there is a Wolfe of the Border."

Solomon grinned. "You are The Lion, Atticus," he said. "There was only one Wolfe of the Border just as there is only one Lion of the North. Both men are strong and legendary. In any case, we are glad to have you home."

They reached the great hall and Caius and Leonidus charged in, followed by Solomon. Only Atticus and Isobeau hung back, lingering by the open door. Atticus, with his baby daughter still in his arms, turned to his wife.

"I do not know how long I will be able to stay with you, but I hope it will be for a good, long time," he told her quietly. "There is much unrest, sweetling. There is talk of unrest in France and Wales even. I do not know where my new alliance with Warwick will take me, but for now, it has brought me home to my family. There is no place I would rather be."

Isobeau smiled up at him, her hand on his cheek, her fingers in his hair. "You know that wherever you go, your heart is here," she murmured. "*I* am here. I will always be here, waiting for you, no matter where your duties take you."

He smiled faintly, drinking in the sight of the face he loved so well. "Have I told you lately how much I love you?"

"Not lately."

He sobered. "Then hear me now," he whispered. "I cannot remember when I have not loved you. You belong to me and I will love you, and only you, until I die."

Isobeau smiled sweetly, accepting his kiss as he rubbed her belly, feeling the life that they had created together. "As I love you," she murmured. "You are my heart and soul. Without you, I would be lost."

He kissed her again and then was distracted when Morgana wanted to be put down. He put the baby on her feet, watching her toddle over to her brothers and grandfather, over near the feasting table as the three men demanded food and drink. Solomon was encouraging his grandsons to yell quite loudly, praising them when they would bellow. Atticus had to chuckle at his father.

"I have never seen my father so happy," he said, taking his wife's hand and leading her over towards the rest of the family. "I remember when I was young and my mother was alive, how much happiness there was in this house. I never thought I would see such times again. I wish…."

He trailed off and Isobeau looked up at him, seeing his wistful expression as he gazed at his father and children. "What do you wish, my love?" she asked.

He shrugged. "I wish that Titus could have been here to see this," he said. "The joy returned to Wolfe's Lair, and father's happiness. I think it's in moments like this that I miss him most."

Isobeau squeezed his gloved hand. "If he was still here, there would be no children, at least our children," she reminded him softly. "Nay, Atticus; I am under the belief that everything happens for a reason and everything happens as it should. Titus' passing is still a sorrowful thing, and I am still saddened when I think of it, but mayhap he is gone so that our children could be born. Mayhap Cai or Leo or even the child I carry is meant for greatness, mayhap to change the course of history. That is the way I think about it and wherever Titus is, I know he understands that. I like to think that he can see your father now and see how he dunks our boys in the rain barrel or plays tricks on them or makes them yell like knights for food and drink. I also like to think that he can see how happy you and I are and knows that he made the right decision by asking you to marry me those years ago. For certain, it is something we can both thank him for."

Atticus smiled at her, warmed by her words, thinking that she made a good deal of sense, as always. He kissed the tip of her nose.

"That is all true," he said. "But I still wish he was here."

"He is. In everything around you."

Atticus liked that thought. "Your wisdom is something I have come to depend upon," he said, wincing when Caius yelled so loud for food that his voice cracked. He grinned when Isobeau laughed. "As much as my father wants to name this child Ares, I have been thinking on naming him something else."

"What would you prefer?"

"Something that means a great deal to us both."

Two weeks later, after four hours of a very fast and somewhat easy labor, a big, healthy boy was born much to the delight of his parents and grandfather. When his grandfather demanded to name the child Ares, Atticus and Isobeau put up a united front to deny the old man.

Initially upset that his wishes had been denied, that irritation had vanished when he was presented with the new child and the name his parents had chosen to give him.

Solomon wept as he held Titus Warenne de Wolfe, who would go on to do great and noble things.

THE END

ABOUT KATHRYN LE VEQUE

Medieval Just Got Real.

KATHRYN LE VEQUE is a USA TODAY Bestselling author, an Amazon All-Star author, and a #1 bestselling, award-winning, multi-published author in Medieval Historical Romance and Historical Fiction. She has been featured in the NEW YORK TIMES and on USA TODAY's HEA blog along with numerous other publications and blogs.

In September 2014, Kathryn was the 41st MOST READ author on Amazon and now she is finding success on other platforms. She is extremely prolific with over 50 published novels and 37 #1 Hot New Releases in Medieval Historical Romance since May 2012.

THE LION OF THE NORTH has three books that are 'related' to it as part of the de Wolfe pack Series. Those novels are all available on Amazon:

The Wolfe

Serpent

Scorpion

You can find all of Kathryn's library at all major retailers. Please visit Kathryn Le Veque's website for a complete list of books and ordering information.

On Facebook

Kathryn Le Veque on Facebook

facebook.com/kathrynlevequenovels

On Twitter

Kathryn Le Veque on Twitter

@KathrynLeVeque

On Tsu

Kathryn Le Veque on Tsu

www.tsu.co/Kathry_Le_Veque

Made in the USA
Middletown, DE
24 October 2022